# NEVER GIVE YOUR HEART TO A HOOKUP

LAUREN LANDISH

EDITED BY
**VALORIE CLIFTON**

EDITED BY
**STACI ETHERIDGE**

## ALSO BY LAUREN LANDISH

*Big Fat Fake Series*:

My Big Fat Fake Wedding || My Big Fat Fake Engagement || My Big Fat Fake Honeymoon

Standalones:

The French Kiss || One Day Fiance || Drop Dead Gorgeous || The Blind Date || Risky Business

*Truth Or Dare:*

The Dare || The Truth

*Bennett Boys Ranch:*

Buck Wild || Riding Hard || Racing Hearts

The Tannen Boys:

Rough Love || Rough Edge || Rough Country

*Dirty Fairy Tales:*

Beauty and the Billionaire || Not So Prince Charming || Happily Never After

*Pushing Boundaries*:

Dirty Talk || Dirty Laundry || Dirty Deeds || Dirty Secrets

# CHAPTER 1
# SAMANTHA

"SO, I only need to sell fifty dildos to become a Gold Star representative of Bedroom Heaven?" The young blonde girl several seats down from me asks the question with a completely straight face, making it sound like that should be a ridiculously easy thing to do.

Of course, she did say that she's the entertainment chair for her on-campus sorority, so maybe Trixleigh can slam out that many sales in her living room under the guise of a buzzy good night social. I can see it now . . . Trixleigh's Tricks and Treats. Maybe with a 'XXX' substituted in for good measure.

Because of course her name is Trixleigh, which she spelled for us cheerleader-style with a bonus of mentioning she's definitely 'not for kids' like the cereal, ending with a *tee-hee* laugh I'm sure she does every time she introduces herself with the bunny ear fingers she popped to the top of her head.

But while she might not think her question is that out there, my head whips around so fast I look like the possessed chick from *The Exorcist*, only to see Jaxx Reynolds, the dark-haired girl in goth makeup sitting next to me, cover her mouth and giggle, along with several other girls around the room. Jaxx is the one who got me into this.

*This* being a pseudo-business presentation with a healthy dose of sexual innuendo being led by a suburban mom who's currently standing in the middle of her living room wielding a butt plug big enough to make King Kong cringe.

*Please tell me why I'm doing this again?* I ask myself for the umpteenth time. But the truth is, I already know the answer. I need the damn money.

I'm buried under a mountain of student loan debt, and with the interest rates being sky high, I'll be battling with that mountain well into the next couple of decades.

And with only one semester left in my graduate program, I'm looking down the barrel of the day those loan payments are going to come due, right as I'm trying to figure out my post-college plans. But I'm like most people, and at some point in my life, I'd like to be able to afford luxuries like a house or a decent car . . . or cheese on a sandwich.

So you know what they say, desperate times call for desperate measures. Though I never dreamed it'd mean selling big, fat cocks from the trunk of my car.

A nudge in my side breaks me out of my reverie, and I blink to refocus on Jaxx, who has a devious smirk on her face. I wonder how many dildos she's sold. Or maybe she sticks to leather restraints? Of course, with her style, she could sell those as fashion accessories.

I take a closer look at the cuff bracelet she's currently wearing, noting the silver loops that could definitely be used for restraint purposes. It's paired with black fishnet stockings, black shorts, and a black rock band shirt that's been rough-cut at the belly button.

It could be a harsh, off-putting look, but on her, it's enchanting, and the dry humor she stoically spews makes her all the more bewitching. Some might say she's inspired by Wednesday Addams, but the truth is, I think Jenna Ortega might've done a secret character study on Jaxx.

It was Jaxx who got me to grudgingly agree to try out being a sex toy rep for extra cash to help pay the bills. She's already been doing it for months and swears it's easy money, and it does make some sense for me to have sexual aids in my repertoire for my future practice as a licensed therapist focusing on intimate relationships. Some people call it a 'sex therapist', but it's so much more than that.

Then again, Jaxx's Aunt Kara doesn't exactly look like the professional businesswoman I aspire to be considering she's now holding up a dildo that's swirling in a circle while vibrating intensely enough to make the rabbit ears on one side of it flop around wildly.

"That's right, Trixleigh. Fifty units and you'll be Gold, and then the sky's the limit. These babies virtually sell themselves."

Trixleigh squeals and goes back to looking at the catalog in her hands, pausing for an unreasonably long time on a double-ended, rainbow-striped, unicorn-horn-ribbed dildo called The Happiest Ride.

Jaxx whispers, "Got her." She licks a black-painted fingertip and draws a tally mark in the air.

Kara smiles, likely thinking the same thing. To help sell me on the idea of this side gig, Jaxx told me the story of how her aunt had been on the verge of a foreclosure after her hair salon burned down and her insurance refused to pay for the damage, citing a cold technicality that left them not fiscally responsible for helping her recover from the accident.

Desperate and not knowing what to do, Kara had turned to becoming a sales representative for an adult company selling sex toys out of her living room.

Now, after three years of throwing parties for Bedroom Heaven and recruiting women to work under her, she's flourishing. According to Jaxx, her aunt is debt-free, living in a new home, and no longer doing hair because her toy business keeps her so busy.

I have no intentions of becoming the next vibrator mogul, but looking at Kara's home and the stress-free smile on her face, I have to admit, she does seem to be doing well. Financially, and I assume, orgasmically.

"You'll get used to it," Jaxx says, her dark eyebrow arched so high in amusement a truck could pass under it. "What's the saying? Life is like a bag of dicks. You're always gonna get fucked, you just never know how hard. Or in what hole. Or holes, as the case may be." She tilts her head as though considering . . . or counting.

I can only shake my head as I whisper, "That is NOT the saying."

Before Jaxx can respond with another stoic retort, Kara laughs, merrily holding up four more vibrating dildos, two in each hand, which looks even more obscene than it sounds. She addresses Trixleigh, "You got it! The more dicks, the merrier! White dick, black dick, brown dick, purple dick! Big dick, small dick, ribbed dick, vibrating dick!"

As she exclaims, her eyes dance around the room to the other women, reminding me of the scene in *From Dusk 'Till Dawn* where the man outside the whore house screams about how there's every flavor of pussy inside. "Get them all sold! Happy customers are repeat customers. We want them coming, and coming, and coming again."

*Craziness has to run in Jaxx's family.* I laugh to myself, watching as Kara animatedly answers questions from around the room. She's in her late forties, wears her long, platinum blonde hair in beachy waves, and has perfectly applied makeup accented with expertly tattooed brows and lash extensions.

She talks with her hands, clicking her long acrylic nails together to emphasize words and making her rings and bracelets jingle as they move. Her cigarette-slim trousers showcase her ass, and though she has on a simple white T-shirt, I'd guess it's an attempt at appearing approachable because the cotton is quality in that subtle way that speaks to money, and lots of it.

All in all, she looks remarkably . . . normal. Except that she's now seriously discussing the pros and cons of vibrating versus sucking clit massagers.

On second thought, maybe this whole idea isn't so crazy. I've learned in my classes and practice groups how important it is to be unflappable when patients say or do any number of seemingly odd things, so maybe I can learn something from Kara to add to my skills as a therapist.

And get a few stress-relieving orgasms out of the deal myself because I intend on being my own first customer. After all, I can't promote what I don't believe in.

"So, who's our target audience?" I ask for everyone to hear.

Kara turns and smiles, sensing she's got me too. "Everyone. But I want to target college-age customers . . . like you."

"Really? I thought—"

"That our customers would be mostly dick-starved, middle-aged horny housewives like me?" Kara finishes for me with a toothy bleached-white smile.

"Oh, no," I begin to say, shaking my head. "I didn't mean it like that—"

Kara cuts me off and dismisses me with a wave of her hand. "Honestly, honey, no offense taken. First rule of sales—start with what you know. I have an entire leg of my team made up with women who've seen it, done it, and been largely disappointed by it. We've got no shame in our game about getting what we know we like or exploring to figure that out."

She lifts a brow, daring me to have a problem with that. Which I don't . . . at all. I support healthy sexual exploration at all ages. And I've done a lot of learning about what is and isn't healthy sexuality, both from books and my own research.

So when I stay silent, she continues, speaking to the room at large once more, "But it's time for business to grow, and that's where you come in. Younger women need that same empowerment to explore, learn their wants and needs, and satisfy them. And though you're all here, by and large, they don't want to talk to their moms" —Kara flips her hair over her shoulder with a sassy smirk— "or their cool aunt about their sex lives. They want to talk to their girlfriends . . . their peers . . . their friends. They want to talk to you and become your customer."

Jaxx leans over and summarizes, "Fresh blood."

"I just don't know," I murmur to Jaxx as Kara continues to go around the room, easily switching from selling product to selling the opportunity of becoming a Bedroom Heaven representative. "There's not a girl I know who has a problem getting a real dick."

Disgust curls Jaxx's black-painted lips. "Are you serious?

That's even more reason. Guys our age suck, especially frat boys. Have you seen them in action? Three minutes, blow their load, couldn't please a girl if their life depended on it."

She sounds more than a little bit bitter, and I wonder if Jaxx has first-hand knowledge about a particular frat boy on campus. "They don't even wash properly. Have you seen that nurse lady on TikTok talk about how guys come in and when they get up from the exam table, there's a skid mark? Ugh . . . can't even wipe their ass or give themselves a scrub, they certainly can't come near my sensitive—and clean—penis flytrap."

Her vehemence, and rare animation, is surprising. She's right about one thing, though. I've unfortunately had a couple of regrets with guys who thought that going down on me was as impossible as hell freezing over.

I consider those encounters lessons learned, though, the steps that got me to where I am now—comfortable in my own body, aware of what I need, and willing to explore under the right circumstances.

But I know that's rare. More common is a sense of shame where sex is concerned, or women who are people pleasers taking that mindset into the bedroom, or worst of all, women who've been brainwashed into thinking that porn-type, overly dramatic acting is real and what they're supposed to enjoy.

So I guess Jaxx has a point.

For the next half hour, Kara goes down a list of products from the catalog, holding up each one from her display table. I watch with rapt fascination as I see sex toys that I've heard about before and some I haven't, which is actually a pretty rare thing considering my studies.

Some look oversized, or studded, or like torture devices that are designed to hurt, which incidentally, Jaxx loves. Others look more friendly and cute, like little round balls and colorful eggs that vibrate.

The room oohs and ahhs as Kara gives demonstrations of some of the devices, explaining how they work and how they're best used.

I'm having such a good time learning all these new gadgets that before I know it, the business aspect is all but forgotten. Except to Kara, who knows she's got us all right where she wants us.

She reminds us about the rules and expectations of being a Bedroom Heaven representative, finishing with the prizes at stake for being a top seller.

"So if you sell 100 Bedroom Heaven gift boxes, you'll be eligible for a $2,000 bonus," she tells the room so dramatically she might as well be dangling a carrot-shaped dildo over us. Which the company sells, in a cheeky appeal to vegans. Everyone's eyes light up, and girls begin excitedly chattering among each other.

Trixleigh narrows shrewd eyes on the rest of the room, warning, "The girls of Gamma Lambda Kappa are mine. Don't mess with me."

I'd laugh, but 2,000 dollars? That's worth a bit of dirty play and understandable possessiveness of potential customers.

*2,000 dollars?* I think to myself, quickly doing the math in my head. On top of the money I make off each individual sale, that would be quite the haul. The question is, how many dicks can I sell?

Even though I'm pretty outgoing, I still can't see myself going to my college buddies and asking them, "So . . . interested in buying a big vibrating weenie, and maybe combo it up with some strawberry flavored lube for when you're getting the real thing?"

"But there's a caveat for you ladies who are just joining in with us," Kara says, raising a manicured finger, silencing everyone around the room. "We're at the end of the sales quarter, and to qualify for any bonus, you have to sell the minimum amount during the current quarter."

"How much time do we have left?" I ask. Deadlines are important. And motivational.

Kara licks her finger and presses it to her curvy derriere, making a hissing sound. "Put a fire under your booty, ladies. Bedroom Heaven's quarterly party is in two weeks to be eligible!

You need to sell at least 100 gift boxes in two weeks, so get to getting!"

A sense of urgency sweeps through the room, exactly as she intended, and she points to a table where a large stack of folders with embossed logos sit, ready for us.

"Also, for those of you who are new, if you've decided you want to represent Bedroom Heaven, you're gonna need to sign a contract that includes the percentage you'll make from every sale, what you can and can't do as a representative, and an iron-clad NDA agreement. I'd advise you to look over it very carefully. If you need help reading and understanding it, me or my niece, Jaxx, would be happy to help."

"Two weeks," I mutter as the room begins chattering again excitedly, crowding around the contract table. "Guess I won't have a chance at that bonus."

I mean for it to be quiet, just to keep myself from getting my hopes up like the other women already spending the bonus on various things from school tuition to rent.

"Nonsense," Kara says, grabbing a folder off the top for me. "I'll help you look over the contract. There's really nothing to it, just the usual to cover their bases. And as far as making a sales goal, you'll have me to help you, and I can sell ice to a polar bear. Just follow my lead, and you'll be a Gold Star seller in no time." She chucks me in the elbow and winks at me. "Now grab a bag of dicks, and get out there and start making some money."

I think it's the first time I've ever heard the term 'bag of dicks' used in a positive light.

# CHAPTER 2
# SAMANTHA

"CAN I TALK ABOUT SOMETHING?" I ask slowly, not sure I want to do this. I sit back on my yoga mat and look at my study group buddies. Sara, Katie, Natasha, and Daphne are also sitting on mats in the rec room we use for our study sessions.

They're also psychology graduate students, but our future focuses are as different as we are. Katie has plans for family counseling, Natasha for behavioral therapy. Sara specializes in PTSD, and Daphne hopes to be a school therapist. Somehow, our differences have never held us back from practicing a little therapy with each other, though we tend to drift off-topic and rant more than is standard in professional sessions. That's what makes us friends, not just colleagues.

"Of course," Katie answers, centering her full attention on me. Her bright blue eyes soften, and she pushes her blonde halo of curls behind her ears. "What's up, buttercup?" As the words leave her mouth, she winces. The greeting is a verbal habit she's trying to break after a professor told her it sounded flippant, but a lifetime of saying it hasn't made it easy.

"I mean, what's on your mind?"

I smile at her correction and pseudo-neutral tone, which makes her sound like a television version of a therapist. "I have a friend who invited me to a party. Well, not a party, exactly, more like an opportunity. But I'm not sure if it's right for me. It's . . ." I trail off, not sure how to describe Bedroom Heaven.

"Did you get tricked into a cult?" Natasha quips. She laughs at the absurdity, but she's maybe not that far off. At my head tilt of uncertainty, she spins her denim-clad legs around, sitting back on her heels. "Tell us everything. Is it a religious thing? End of the world? Sex club?"

Despite working on my blank face, I must have a tell because Daphne's interest piques. "Sex club? For real? Can I get an invite too?"

I shake my head at the sudden rapt attention all four women give me. Maybe Kara is right and sex is what sells, even if it's just the promise of better sex.

I dive in, explaining about Bedroom Heaven and my worries about its implications, both positive and negative, in my future as an intimacy therapist. "I've looked through the contract with Bedroom Heaven and our code of conduct for the psychology program backward and forward and every way in between. I'm in the clear, but am I crazy for considering this?"

Sara, who's been silent the whole time, finally speaks. "You've done your due diligence, already know what you're going to do, and don't need our permission to do it."

She dips her chin, making sure I heard her loud and clear. Of all of us, she's the most naturally gifted at therapy, but that skill has come at a price. She's been in therapy herself since she was a kid after a traumatic childhood that was only made worse by therapists who didn't know what they were doing. She now wears those scars inside and outside, which is why she wants to specialize in helping people with PTSD.

"Thanks," I tell her, recognizing that she's one hundred percent right.

Katie holds her hand up. "One question . . ." I look her way, and she grins widely, looking much less angelic than usual. "Can I see that catalog? A girl needs a little variety, and my Little Bunny Foo-Foo is on his last hops."

"Little. Bunny. Foo-Foo?" Daphne echoes. She shouldn't judge considering she's walking a thin line of being a Disney adult, wearing various character and park shirts almost daily. In fact, she has on a Thumper T-shirt right now, so it's probably a good thing Katie didn't name her vibrator after Bambi's rabbity friend.

"Me too," Natasha adds. "Not the Foo-Foo part, but the variety. I've sworn off men for a while after my last date."

I dig into my bag, pulling out a couple of the catalogs Jaxx gave me. Katie and Natasha crowd around one, Daphne takes another, and Sara uses her phone to snap the QR code on the front so she can shop privately online.

Natasha continues, "Did I tell you about my date? Rugby player, hot as hell, able to string together more than three words, so I—"

"Took him home," Sara finishes. "You really need higher standards. You deserve more than that."

Not giving a shit, Natasha ignores Sara's advice. "Went with him back to his place," she corrects, as if that makes a difference. "It was going well, too—kisses in the living room, pressed me up against the wall in the hallway, then into his bedroom, where he threw me on the bed. I was ready to get my world rocked!" she says wistfully.

"But no amount of using his ears as handlebars and leading him straight to X marks the spot worked. I swear, he nutted in three minutes, climbed off, and collapsed. I mean, rugby requires some endurance, right?" She rolls her eyes and huffs. "Apparently not. And when I went to the bathroom?" She pantomimes gagging. "It was a hazmat zone. I don't think it'd ever been cleaned, like, ever, which means he was that disgusting too. Can't get clean amid filth. I left while he was snoring, and when I got back to my place, I scrubbed every inch of my body—and I do mean every single inch and orifice—and ghosted him. Not that he texted, anyway."

She sounds annoyed at that last bit, but we all know the truth . . . she's hurt. Sex is intimate by nature. That doesn't mean it needs to be all roses, sweet nothings, and promises of forever. Hell, it can be a rough, filthy, one-night stand and still be intimate. But if it's a disappointing experience, it still hurts on some level.

Which is where handling things yourself comes in.

At least for Natasha, because she's already flagged three different products. "Put me down for these, with whatever STAT shipping I can get."

"Because you've sworn off men," Katie reminds her.

By the time our group pseudo-session ends, all four women have ordered gift boxes, and I feel significantly better about my decision to become a Bedroom Heaven representative.

---

*Two weeks later . . .*

"I cannot believe I've sold almost two hundred dicks," I murmur to myself as I drive down the highway in my rusty, yet trusty, Nissan Sentra. She might not be the most stylish transportation, but she's dependable enough to get me where I need to go, and today, that's to the Grand Hotel for the Bedroom Heaven quarterly party.

Most of my sales have been specific items from the catalog, which ship directly to the customer in discreet packaging. But with Jaxx's help, I'm almost sold out of gift boxes. If I can sell just a few more at the sales portion of the quarterly party, I might still qualify for the bonus.

I send a silent prayer up to whatever sex god is listening that the sales flow as readily as the strawberry flavored lube that Bedroom Heaven is widely known for, because I'll admit that I've got plans for that cash. Exciting things like rent, and maybe a new vibrating treat of my own.

I glance in the rearview mirror at the stash of products in my backseat, considering which one I'd like to try. Definitely not the U-turn, which is girthy enough to concern me, or the Diesel Stroker, which has a thrust mode with thirty speeds and patterns that promises to match or be better than any human male could be from any position, but it costs over two hundred dollars. I've got a small clit vibrator and a bare bones dildo already, so maybe something a bit more exciting that won't break the bank?

*Too bad the real thing isn't an option.*

I haven't dated much recently. Being too focused on school, too distracted by trying to make ends meet, and too selective about partners has left me alone more nights than I'd like to admit. So I'm glad my new gig has the potential to make those lonely nights a lot more 'fun'.

I pull into the lot of the Grand Hotel, driving down a few aisles before I can find a parking spot. There are a lot more cars here than I expected, which makes a spike of nerves shoot through my gut. Sales isn't my best skill, but like Kara said, the promise of dead Franklins is enough to get me pumped for this. "Twelve gift boxes and that bonus is yours, Samantha. You can do this."

I'm not crazy for talking to myself. It's a valid self-pep-talk method that's recommended by many professionals.

Right as I'm about to step out, my phone rings. I'd ignore it, but I want to make sure it's not Jaxx with some last-minute instructions, so I dig it out of my purse.

Mom.

Shit. I have to answer.

"Hey, Mom, I'm running into a . . . uh, meeting. Everything okay?" I spit out quickly. I don't know why I don't tell Mom about my Bedroom Heaven party. She's been accepting of my plans to become an intimacy therapist, but this feels different.

*I'm selling cocks, but don't worry, it's totally for the greater good!*

Yeah, that conversation isn't happening right now.

"And hello to you too, honey," she replies dryly. "I won't keep you, but I wanted to see if you'd help keep an eye on Olivia tonight?"

Olivia is my younger sister. At sixteen, she doesn't need a babysitter. Hell, she is one. But when left to her own devices, she tends to rebel more than she should, especially against Mom's ridiculously strict rules like no drugs, drinking, or sneaking out. Actually, I agree on the first two, but the last is negotiable. Sometimes. But Mom's wildly invasive ideas like 'tell me where you're going and who you're with' send Olivia off the deep end into super-sized, attitude-filled tirades that stress us all out.

"Uhm, I'll be out most of the night," I answer, glancing at the hotel and then the dashboard clock. I really need to get inside.

"That's fine. Just be available if she needs rescue." Under her breath, Mom sarcastically adds, "Or bail money."

"Where are you going?"

"I have a . . . I mean, I've got . . ." I swear, she sounds like a giggly schoolgirl, unsure of what to say, which is nothing like my mother. Susan Redding speaks her mind, whether you want to hear it or not, runs her family like a well-oiled machine, and works her ass off. I'm proud to say that she passed those traits on to me in spades.

Finally, she sighs and admits, "I'm going on a date. An *overnight* one."

"*Mom!*" I shriek in surprise. "With whom?"

My parents divorced years ago, and I've encouraged her to dip her toes into the dating world again. But though the twenty-something pool is full of unwashed, unmotivated frat boys, the over-forty pool is somehow even worse, with men who want to be worshiped by young, impressionable women they can control or who are cheating on their wives, which is what Dad did. Though he did end up marrying his mistress, who's only a few years older than me.

Mom stood by us, though, helping me get to college when Dad said he couldn't afford it because he was buying a new place, and taking care of Olivia even when, filled with hurt and anger, she told Mom that Dad wouldn't have left if she'd tried harder to make him happy. That led to a lot of sisterly conversations where I told her that she needed to grow the hell up and quit blaming Mom for Dad's failures.

"A man I've been seeing for a bit now. His name's Marvin, and he's a day trader. His wife passed away several years ago, and he's been focused on raising his son, who's seventeen now.

NEVER GIVE YOUR HEART TO A HOOKUP 15

He understands some of the difficulties I've had with Olivia, and we just click. He makes me laugh and feel hopeful."

Mom sounds happier than I've heard her in ages, and I have to look up at the headliner of my car and release a slow breath to fight back tears.

"Mom! I'm so happy for you, but do we need to have the sex talk again?" I tease. "It's not all free love like when you were young. Remember, 'Safe, Sane, and Consensual' is the catchphrase now."

She scoffs. "I'm not that old, Samantha. I wasn't even born in the sixties for the free love days. And I'm the one who taught you about condoms, STIs, and what to watch for. Speaking of, are you testing regularly?"

*Errrrk!* I pump the brakes on this whole conversation. "Nope, not discussing my sex life with you. Not now, not ever."

I can almost hear her smile at having redirected our talk away from her own date and tonight's activities. "Okay, but I'm here if you need me."

"Thanks. You too, Mom. And don't worry, I've got Olivia tonight so you can get your freak on with Maaaarvin," I drawl out theatrically. "Though I'm not sure you can moan that name in a sexy way. You might need a nickname for him."

"I've got one, but you'd be surprised how sexy hearing your name from your lover's lips can be, no matter what it is," she says wisely. And mature soon-to-be therapist that I am, I stick my tongue out, gagging silently at the idea of my mother saying the words 'lover's lips'. "I won't keep you, though. I know you said you have a meeting, and I need to head inside. I'm already at Marvin's. He's making us dinner."

"Have fun and behave yourself."

We hang up, and quick as I can, I text Olivia, knowing that calling her won't do any good. She doesn't answer her phone. Ever. But she'll text or SnapChat back.

*Hey, girl! Mom says she's going on a date and asked me to check in on you. For her sanity and your safety (because I will kill you), please behave. Need anything?*

Two seconds later, I get back an eyeroll emoji. I hope that

doesn't mean she's up to no good, but I've got to trust her. Plus, she knows I'm only half-kidding about killing her if she does do something stupid or dangerous.

*Maybe we can hang out tomorrow?*

When she sends back a pancakes emoji, I breathe a sigh of relief. If she's thinking about brunch, she can't be up to anything too bad, right? I heart her emoji and then send Jaxx a short message to let her know I'm here and on my way inside before shoving my phone back into my purse.

I was already late, but now I'm *late*.

I grab the pink bag full of loose products from my backseat, knowing I'll have to make another trip for the gift boxes, and click-clack across the parking lot in my heels as fast as I can.

Inside, the lobby is elegant and grand, apt for the hotel's name. At the front desk, the receptionist is typing furiously on her phone—her personal one, not the hotel's—and doesn't look up at my approach.

"Excuse me?" I wait for her to respond or at least look up from her phone, but when she continues typing, I clear my throat. "Excuse me," I repeat a bit louder. She glances up, one brow arched as if I'm the one being rude. "Could you tell me where the Bedroom Heaven party is?" I ask quietly, not wanting to announce to the bustling lobby of people that I'm here for the sex toy convention.

Her eyes drop back to her phone as she answers, "Third door on the left." She waves a hand in the general direction of a hallway off to the side.

I don't bother saying thank you because she's already scowling at her phone and ignoring me again.

Hustling to the hallway she indicated, my heels sink into the lush carpet as I count doors. I get to the third one, which looks remarkably plain, and pause. I smooth my hands over my hips, straightening the jumpsuit I chose for this shindig. It's a few shades darker than my pink bag, with a deep V neckline and small ruffles at the shoulders that give it a feminine look but wide legs that flow like trousers. I shake my dark curls so they flow down my back and take a steadying breath.

"Here goes, girl. You've got this."

I'm expecting to walk into the sexual wonderland of shoppers, tapas, and cocktails Jaxx told me to expect from a Bedroom Heaven quarterly party. Instead, it's dark and I hear faint applause. "Shit, I'm late," I whisper to myself, thinking I'm missing the intro to kick off the festivities.

I try to make my way through the darkness toward the sliver of light ahead, but I trip over something. A cord, maybe? Whatever it is, I go flying forward and hit solid ground with a hard thud. "Fuck," I hiss, suddenly blinded by a bright light.

Any other time, I might think I've died in some freak *Final Destination* type accident, but my hip hurts too much for me to be dead.

I hear a chorus of gasps, and as I blink away the dark spots in my vision, I realize that I have an audience filled with young men watching my misfortune with rapt attention. Some look horrified, others seem amused, and still others are looking at my askew legs.

I shift, trying to make sure a breast hasn't escaped in my fall, and vaguely wonder where all the women are. I was expecting a penis party, but I figured they'd all be silicone, not flesh and bone.

And then I realize that with my tumble, my bag of goodies has spilled everywhere and I'm surrounded by dildos, vibrators, butt plugs, and cock rings of every size, shape, color, and texture. It's a 'lions, tigers, and bears, oh, my!' type situation of the toy variety, including one dildo that's rolling toward me threateningly, stopping mere inches from my face with the pee hole—which is a convenient lube dispenser—pointing right at me.

I *wish* I were dead.

But as bad as this is, it gets worse as a tall, blond man stomps toward me, each step sounding like a hammer of doom. He's glaring angrily and kicking dicks as he comes closer. "What are you doing?"

He's a few years older than me, wearing a finely tailored blue suit with a gold lion pin on his lapel. Under his withering gaze, my eyes fall and I note the fine leather of his brown lace-up dress shoes.

"Uhm, could I interest you in a . . . novelty?" I mutter, not meaning for him to hear. But given the faint growl emanating from him, he heard every word.

Ah, fuck.

# CHAPTER 3
# CHANCE

TEN MINUTES AGO...

Straightening my blue blazer, I pause for a moment to affix my club pendant to my lapel and clear my throat in preparation for my speech. Once upon a time, I would've been a bag of nerves having to speak in front of a large crowd, but today, I feel as cool as a cucumber.

Might be the shot of brandy I had half an hour ago. But more likely, it's the years of speaking experience under my belt.

I feel pumped and ready while listening to my business partner, Evan White, come to the end of his speech to the slightly bored crowd of college-age young men. It's not Evan's fault they're bored. He's just not who they're here to see.

I am.

"There's not a man in history who hasn't needed a wingman," Evan says, smiling as he looks out into the crowd. He's tall and dark-haired, dressed in a crisp black suit, and his gold lionhead club pin gleams under the spotlight. There's a reason he's the lead-in and I'm the star of our two-man show. His skills are top-notch on paper, tracking our growth, budgets, contracts, and more.

I'm the dreamer with the charisma to bring people in.

"Kobe needed Shaq. Brady needed Gronk. Maverick needed Goose. And I'm in the same boat. Without our next speaker, I wouldn't have gotten where I am today, and the Gentlemen's Club wouldn't be over four hundred members strong and growing by the day. Without question, he is one of the smartest, most thoughtful men I know, an exceptional business partner, and an even greater friend. He's passionate and cares about our shared vision, and most of all, he cares about all of you and your future. For a lot of you, he's been a great counselor and mentor, and he has been equally as such to me. So, without further ado, I hand the stage to the President of the Gentlemen's Club, Chance Harrington."

The applause and whoops that ensue from the crowd fill me with fire as I purposefully walk to the center of the stage where Evan pulls me into a brief 'bro' hug, pounding on my back three times.

"Do your thing," Evan whispers to me in support. I nod firmly once, letting him know I've got this, and he steps from the stage to sit off to the side, ready to watch me work.

Stepping behind the podium and focusing on the crowd, I can see the group almost leaning forward, eager to hear what I have to say. I haven't said a word and they're already eating out of the palm of my hand, so I'd better make this good.

"Thank you for that wonderful introduction, Evan," I start off and then glance back to the audience. "But we all know you get paid to wax poetic about my amazingness and not mention my egregious flaws. Not that I have any."

I wink comedically and pause for the good-natured laughter at my self-deprecating joke. Evan chuckles too, holding a finger to his lips as though telling me to keep quiet about that. We've done this back and forth for a long time, and bouncing off one another this way is second nature at this point.

"Seriously, though, we all come here today with strengths, weaknesses, needs, and desires. Each combination is as unique as the individual. Sitting in this room, looking over your faces, I see some I know and some I don't know . . . yet. But each face is that of someone important. Look to your right, your left, behind you, in front of you." I wait, giving them a second to scan the room and then return their eyes to me. "The men you see around you all have dreams, just like you. Maybe it's to be a doctor or lawyer, mayor or governor, or hell, even the President of the United States. Or maybe it's something closer to your heart." I touch my own chest. "To be a husband, father, leader. An example for future generations to aspire to be like."

I can see it happen across the room. They're invested in what I'm saying, in the moment, and most importantly, in themselves.

"Today, we live in a different world from that of our fathers. Truth is, they lived in a different world from their fathers too. It's a never-ending march of change. Unfortunately, too many in this generation have been led astray.

There are those who would have you believe that young men of today's generation, like you, are victims. That the changing times have progressed us to a place where your very existence is rejected on a daily basis. That there is no hope left for you in society because women have become too powerful, holding all the cards in relationships and sex, as well as in the boardroom and business. That *they, women,* are your enemy."

A murmur works through the room. I can see some disagreeing already, while others seem to be agreeing with the sentiment. Those are the men I need to reach.

"I propose that women aren't the enemy. Instead, the enemy lies within us. Look around the internet, on social media, or even in the darker corners to individuals who exploit and manipulate vulnerable young men. They preach divisive, hateful, toxic messages. You know the buzzwords because some of them have worked their way into our everyday speech. Alpha, Sigma, Beta . . . listening to these people, you'd think we were all part of some giant fraternity fest. But the majority of these hatemongers are in it for profit. Some of them—"

"Like Jake McGibbons!" someone in the crowd shouts, interrupting me and causing laughs and snickers all around the room.

I frown at the name. Jake McGibbons is a popular, so-called men's advocate who gives advice to young men. That's not so bad in itself. In effect, it's what I do too.

And on the surface, some of his 'advice' is legit. Push yourself to be the best you can be. Invest in your future. Exercise.

But it's the toxic foundation of his messaging that's the problem. With his aggressive delivery and superficial presentation, he makes sense to a fragile, insecure young mind who desperately wants control over not only his own life, but to be 'over' others, catering to his followers' desires to be superior.

All hope isn't lost, though.

It's one of the reasons I do what I do, creating and running the Gentlemen's Club as an alternative to people like Jake McGibbons. I want to fight against these dangerous narratives and help young men see their true potential rather than falling for seductive messaging that places the blame solely on others, causing resentment and hatred to fester.

There's another way to success, and I want to help these young men discover it.

"Yes, like Jake McGibbons," I answer. Trying to return to my planned speech, I continue, "Creating a hierarchy within our own ranks defeats us all. Only by being our best selves, and helping our brother be his best self, can we all succeed. That's what the Gentlemen's Club is about."

I let that sink in for a moment, hoping they hear the difference in approach between me and assholes like McGibbons who talk about masculinity like it's something you earn at the gym or by degrading women.

"Not too long ago, I was like many of you—a young man with big dreams, held down by responsibilities. Admittedly, they might not be the same ones many of you face. I was lucky enough to not worry about tuition payments or where my next meal would come from. But my last name carries a weight many of you might recognize or perhaps even feel from your own families. For me, that generational march was more like a militant drumbeat. My grandfather started from nothing, my father grew the family business into a household name, and my older brothers are part of that tradition. It was assumed that I'd step right in line too. Obviously, I didn't."

I hold my hands out, showing that I'm here with them and not at my family's headquarters. That's no small feat, either. When I finished school and told Dad that my plans were different from his, he lost his mind, to put it mildly. There was yelling about expectations, threats of leaving me to fend off the wolves alone, and eventually, disappointment when I held steady. My two older brothers, Cameron and Carter, even got into the argument, pressuring me to join them in the family business. But I couldn't see myself playing third fiddle to them, especially when they're already at war with each other too often.

I wanted no part of it.

"But I didn't know who or what I wanted to become at first," I continue "Other than *not* my dad's carbon copy. So I kept my head down and my nose in a book until it hit me.

"The guys around me had become disillusioned with society and often complained about how things weren't going their way, whether it be grades, women, or job prospects. But these same men stayed up half the night, stumbling into class late, reeking of body odor, old beer, and unwashed T-shirts every Monday morning. And still, they would lay the blame elsewhere. They wanted life handed to them on a silver platter even though they didn't do anything to earn it and were, in fact, actively sabotaging themselves."

There's a bit of uncomfortable shifting from more than a few guys. Being called out isn't easy, but recognizing that your minimal effort begets minimal results is the first step to being better.

"They were their own worst enemy. Using them as an example, I did a bit of self-reflection of my own and came up with a plan. Even wrote it on my bathroom mirror." I hold up a finger for each item to highlight them. "Get off the couch. Get your act together. Sleep. Study. Shower. Brush your teeth. The basics." I point at the audience. "And then the hard work starts. Once those things were routine, I could focus on being a better person, effecting positive change around me, and—"

"Do you really expect us to believe that bullshit?" a deep voice bellows.

I squint through the spotlight, shading my eyes and scanning the crowd until I spot who's spoken.

*Lucas Walker.*

He's a newbie, still considering joining the Gentlemen's Club, and exactly the type of man I want to reach. He's got one foot in the door here but has Jake McGibbons-type rhetoric still whispering in his ear.

Right now, he's standing up, his arms crossed over his chest, glaring at me in challenge. If this were a battle of physicality, he'd win, biceps down. He's built like a defensive end. But it's not.

Contrary to popular belief, men have evolved beyond fist fights and bar brawls for the most part. Or at least I have, and I have no interest in beating reason into Lucas's mind. That doesn't work, anyway.

Meeting his glare head-on, I address the interruption. "What 'bullshit' would that be, Lucas?"

He gestures toward me while half turning to address the room, grinning goofily at his peers as if he's saying what they all think too. "That you got here by doing 'the basics'," he mocks, adding in air quotes as if his tone didn't make that clear already. "You expect us to believe that your family money didn't open every door, get you a fancy as fuck car, and make hot chicks drop to their knees and beg to suck your dick? How stupid do you think we are?"

I groan inwardly as the room erupts into snickers and chatter. It's not the first time I've been accused of keeping a squeaky-clean façade while being an entitled asshole behind closed doors. I think people have come to expect that from people with money. It doesn't help that I'm single, don't publicly date, and have strict boundaries about discussing my private life.

But Lucas is wrong. This isn't an act. I simply have high standards and hold myself to them stringently.

"Lucas, if that's your definition of success, then you should leave now," I say flatly, calling his bluff. "But I don't think it is, nor do I think it should be," I add quickly.

"And as I've said countless times before" —I glance around the room, knowing there are those who'll back me up— "I'm here to help. I don't do this for amusement or some weird sense of hero worship. I believe in you, believe you can be better . . . if you choose to be. If you work to be. And then, you can redefine success for yourself however you'd like to."

*Smooth*, I praise myself. Lucas really thought he was doing something there, but I've matched verbal wits with far better. Hell, I grew up with a family that can flambé your guts with a look, much less a word. I hope Lucas hears me, though, and that I didn't go too far for his fragile ego. A beaten dog eventually bites, and Lucas has been beaten too many times, I suspect.

"But—" Lucas begins to protest, but a gruff voice interrupts him.

"Dude, sit the fuck down and shut up. You asked, he answered, and do you seriously think he hangs out with us for fun? In case you're not sure, the answer's 'fuck no'."

There's a bit of chuckling from around the room at that. "Some of us actually want to do more than flunk out and go home to our parents' basements, so let Chance talk to those of us who came to hear him, not your dumb ass."

I look for the new speaker and spot him several rows down from Lucas. Enzo Delano. We've spoken a few times. He seems like a smart guy who honestly doesn't need much guidance. He's got his head on straight, has a plan, and has a healthy fear of disappointing his mother, whom he loves. But he shared that he needed a sense of community and wanted some decent male role models because his father's been absent most of his life, and that was enough to convince me that he'd make a great Gentleman.

Lucas glares at Enzo, pissed at being called out and sensing a new target. But Enzo's no wilting weakling himself and grew up scrappy enough to back up his own outspokenness.

Enzo firmly points at Lucas's seat, and Lucas's face turns red, but he slowly begins to sink into his seat, seething.

"Exactly, shut the fuck up and let the man finish his damn speech."

*If only Enzo hadn't added the last bit*, I think with a sigh. Unfortunately, Lucas has to get in the last word.

"Fuck you," he mutters loudly. I'm not sure whether that's

directed to Enzo, me, both of us, or the world at large, but when Enzo stands, I can see how fast this is going to go sideways.

Considering our club is filled with a bunch of young, opinionated, hormone-raging men in one place, it's not uncommon for insults to be tossed back and forth, but I don't want it escalating into any fisticuffs.

There's a time for slick words and gentle guidance and a time to handle shit. This is the latter. I shout, "Hey! Both of you, settle down—"

Before I can complete my thought, there's a commotion from the side of the stage that draws the crowd's eyes even more than the impending fight.

Following their gazes, I glance to my left and pause in shock as a curvaceous woman in a pink jumpsuit, carrying a large bag on her shoulder, suddenly appears.

But as quickly as she appears, she goes tumbling through the air, her high heel caught on an amp cord. Helplessly, I watch as she hits the stage with a hollow thud, her bag slipping from her shoulder, her dark hair falling over her face, and her legs ungracefully flying every which direction.

Lucas and Enzo's fight forgotten, there's an audible gasp from the audience as dildos of every color, size, and . . . shape? . . . scatter across the stage. I still hear the woman's pained, "*Fuck.*"

*What. The. Fuck?*

My mind rushes through scenarios of why this could be happening. The only thing that makes sense to me is that this is some kind of prank, and fury rages up from my core.

Knowing I only have seconds to react before things get out of control, I walk over to the woman, scowling at her the whole way. "What are you doing?" I demand menacingly.

I falter for a second as she looks up at me in mortified shock.

She's beautiful. I can see that now that her hair is out of her face, along with a small sprinkling of freckles across her nose. Her lips are painted a soft pink and are a bit pouty, making me wonder if she's used to getting her way, and her brown eyes are rimmed with dark liner and long lashes that are fluttering, not flirtatiously but rather with confusion.

Her cheeks turn red in an instant, and she fumbles for words as her eyes fall to my shoes. But somehow, she finds them, muttering under her breath, "Can I interest you in a . . . novelty?"

"Excuse me?" I say sharply. I'm not actually pissed, I'm just . . . if someone had asked me to list the top one thousand possible responses someone would give to my question in this situation, trying to sell me a sex toy would not have made the list.

"Holy Dicks!" a high-pitched voice shrieks in horror, and suddenly, another woman appears. This one is wearing a skintight black dress, fishnet hose, and thick-soled combat boots. Her raven black hair streams behind her as she comes rushing forward and begins scooping up dildos and other various sex toys by the handful and carelessly stuffing them in the bag in front of the shocked crowd. "There you are! I've been looking all over for you! And look, you've dropped our goodies for today's party all over the place!"

I get the feeling her natural voice is at least a solid octave lower because she sounds like she's doing a *Mrs. Doubtfire* impersonation. In fact, this whole thing almost seems like a low-caliber theatrical stage production written by a child. Except for the dicks, of course.

I would laugh if the situation weren't so utterly ridiculous and a huge disruption to my speech.

I'm too shocked to move and simply stand frozen as I watch the black-haired girl scold the other while quickly gathering the toys with lightning speed. But eventually, my body overrides my outraged mind and I reach down to help the still red-faced brunette to her feet.

"Are you okay?" I ask tightly, remembering the sound of her body hitting the stage hard.

She doesn't get a chance to answer because the black-haired girl waves her also-black nails in apology, ignoring my question and gesturing at her companion. "I'm so sorry! We really apologize for the interruption to . . . uh . . ." She glances at the lion pendant on my lapel and arches a black, thin-lined brow. "Whatever cult meeting this is. But we'll be on our way! Sorry!"

Before I can say anything else, she pulls the brunette along, who casts one last embarrassed glance my way as they run for the hills before I can stop them. As she moves, she reminds me of a sexy bunny, quickly disappearing backstage and leaving us all in bewilderment.

It only takes a moment for the room to unfreeze.

"What the fuck?" someone asks as nervous laughter fills the room.

"Holy shit! No offense, Chance, but I gotta go. If those are their 'goodies for today's party', I want an invite to *that* party instead of this one."

A newcomer I haven't met yet raises his hand and calls out, "Yeah, I think I just redefined success for myself and it looks like that." He's using my own words against me as he strokes the air like he's jacking off.

The room erupts in hoots, hollers, and laughs, and I'm forced to shout to be heard.

"Alright, alright, enough!" I bellow. "That wasn't funny. In fact, I'd better not find out one of you staged that. And if I do find out who, you're fucking gone."

My serious tone and use of choice words, something I rarely use in front of them, gives everyone pause as they realize I'm not joking around.

"Yeah," Evan adds, backing me up as he stands and stares flat faced into the crowd alongside me. "I know you guys like your pranks, but this went too far. Wrong place, wrong time."

The room descends into grumbling as everyone looks at each other, but it doesn't seem like anyone is going to rat on the culprit, and looking at all the faces gathered, a part of me begins to wonder if maybe it wasn't a prank.

Is it possible she stumbled into the wrong room and truly is here for another event?

I shudder to think what that event might be considering what all rolled out on the stage. But a part of me can't help but speculate. I'm not as lewd as the club guys, but even I'll admit that it's not every day a beautiful woman tosses toys at your feet.

As I think about the dick that was pointed right at her pink, pouty lips, I feel heat start to grow under my collar, and I hurriedly push those thoughts away lest I embarrass myself in front of everyone.

I clear my throat. "Let's refocus and move on, guys." Too-wide grins and mischievous eyes meet my instruction, and I know I have to get them back with me. "Look, I know it's *hard* . . . but *come* on . . ." I tease, intentionally emphasizing the words to make them chuckle a bit. When it succeeds, I shake my head and smile too. "I've totally forgotten. Where were we before all that?"

I gesture toward the stage, intentionally avoiding reminding Lucas and Enzo that they were near blows before Dickapalooza happened.

Stephen, a quiet guy who's only been a member for a short time, offers, "The basics."

The two words are enough to get me back on track, and I speak for another thirty minutes about how setting intentions, following through, and being your best self are the steps to success, however you define it.

Somehow, by the end of my speech, I feel like I've reached the majority of the guys. Either I've inspired the ones who are already members or hooked the ones who are considering joining.

But as our group activities start and everyone begins to mingle with a drink in hand and freedom to chitchat, most of them are laughing and joking about the 'Sex Toy Barbie', as I hear them calling her.

Evan walks up to give me a slap on the shoulder, saying, "Great speech, man, but that was some crazy shit."

"Yeah," I answer dully.

"Can't win 'em all," he offers. "But I bet our next orientation is full after word gets out about this. You'll have to really bring it, and I don't mean the dildos."

That's Evan, always thinking about the bottom line.

# CHAPTER 4
# SAMANTHA

I'M a bundle of nerves and embarrassment, breathless and flushed, when Jaxx and I enter Bedroom Heaven's party. Apparently, the distracted receptionist was one door off, and Jaxx tried to catch me in the hallway but I didn't hear her calling me. I guess I'm just glad she rescued me from my rather prick-ly predicament.

This room has a totally different vibe from the serious whatever it was I crashed. It's open and spacious, with ambient lighting glowing in pink, purple, and white hues, creating a fun and flirty atmosphere. Tables with a variety of toys are spread throughout the room, and women of all ages are mingling and shopping with plastic cup cocktails in their hands.

Everything is selfie-ready, including a central display with a massively oversized, veined dildo suction-cupped to the table where people are crowded around, cheesing into their phone's camera. I'm not sure I want a picture of me with a three-foot dick, but whatever floats their boats.

"Holy crap, this is like a mini adult convention!" I whisper, and Jaxx laughs. "What?"

"What do you know about adult conventions?"

"Everything. From Instagram, of course." At her dubious look, I quickly tack on, "And for research."

"I bet." Pausing, she tilts her head and points across the

room. "I think that's our table. Let's set up and drop some dongs!" It takes a few trips to both our cars to unload all of our gear, but once we do, Jaxx instructs me to 'spread 'em' with a wicked grin of her black-painted lips.

Jaxx's good humor helps because after that fuckup of a catastrophe next door, my nervous gut has somehow just gotten worse. The table beside us is filled with women wearing feathery boas around their necks and oversized clown sunglasses on their heads like tiaras, both of which are decorated with dangling penis ornaments that clink together with every movement like a dick symphony.

Their team is also wearing matching pink shirts that proclaim 'Cucumbers belong in salad, ask me for something better' amid a display of various Bedroom Heaven vibes and dildos. They're hooting and hollering, loudly talking about wetting the bed from one particular toy, the Suckasaurus Max.

"I needed a Gatorade, a cigarette, and a wipe down before round two, but you can bet I went back for more," what seems to be the lead saleswoman overshares as she nods enthusiastically. "But if you get the Max, also get the waterproof towel. You'll want it to protect your mattress and so you don't have to strip the whole bed every time. Less laundry means more Max time."

I'm glad they're having fun, making sales, and getting pleasure from the various toys, but their vibe isn't exactly what I'm hoping for. Thankfully, there are plenty of customers who like a more low-key approach to discussing their preferences, and I make several sales amid actual sexual health conversations in which I don't use the phrase 'ram a lotta ding-dong' a single time. Unlike my sales neighbors.

Hours pass, and I lose count of how many toys we sell. All I know is that it's a bunch. Including one quite literal bunch—a connected chain of balls that you insert vaginally and, as your inner muscles flex, they roll around inside, creating a pleasurable sensation. Jaxx sold that one to a forty-something-year-old woman who said they're going to be part of her Tantric sex practice.

Honestly, it's pretty amazing the variety of women, toys, and sex lives all contained in this one room.

At the front of the room, someone taps on a microphone, calling out, "Ladies! Can I get your attention, please!"

I look up, where I see a woman who looks like a porn star turned news anchor. Her platinum blonde hair is voluminous, extension-long, and perfectly curled, her makeup is dramatic, with several shades of glittery eyeshadow and fake lashes, and her professional dress is virtually painted over clearly enhanced breasts and a round peach of an ass that makes me want to hit the gym for some weighted squats. She's beaming, which should seem friendly and welcoming but rather seems like she's barely biting back her desire to tell us all to 'shut the hell up and listen' to her.

"Who's that?" I ask Jaxx.

"Shh, that's April. She's the regional representative," she whispers. "Basically, our big boss."

"Welcome to yet another successful quarterly Bedroom Heaven regional conference!" April squeals, hyping the crowd up.

Cheers fill the room, and I clap along politely with everyone. As it fades, April continues.

"This quarter was yet another record-breaking one for us, with sales growing exponentially, and more and more joining the Bedroom Heaven family."

She keeps going, giving some hype numbers that make Bedroom Heaven seem like the Amazon of sex toys, mixed in with a little rah-rah stuff to keep everyone dreaming big. She's good at it, and I wonder if she was a pageant girl, a cheerleader, or both in her younger days. But though my initial impression was that April is a bit 'look at me', the more she talks, the more genuine she seems. She's hyped because she actually wants BH to do well and wants to share everyone's successes, so they get praise too.

"I don't want to be up here all night when we all know what goodies will actually keep you up all night," April teases saucily, getting laughs, "but I can't leave without giving some well-deserved recognition to our top producers this quarter. So, let's give a round of applause to Gennifer Dennis, Layla Johnson, and Mimi Chen! Way to go, ladies!"

There's applause again, and I join in. I haven't met these women, but apparently, they're moving some dicks.

"Most of all, I'd like to give a big shout out to our top regional producer, and one of the top ten reps in the country . . . Kara Jones! Give it up for Kara, yeah, babe! Whooooooo!"

Everyone cheers as April waves for Kara to come on stage. Kara strides across the room confidently, smiling at everyone as she makes her way to April's side. Next to me, Jaxx almost swoons as she sputters, "Holy shit."

"What is that?" I ask, not sure what I'm looking at. A trophy, maybe? Or a penis-shaped side table?

"The Diamond Dick," Jaxx whispers. "Obviously not a real diamond, it's crystal glass or quartz or something, but it's a huge award. In more ways than one." Her typically deadpan expression is lit up like a Christmas tree, her eyes sparkling and teeth flashing as she claps excitedly for her aunt.

I get it. Kinda. I mean, Kara's running a successful boss babe business, but she's also getting congratulated for . . . selling dick. Fake dick, but still. I guess I just never thought my career path would have a Diamond Dick on it.

As Kara accepts the large 'trophy', Jaxx leans over. "Have you been keeping track of your sales?"

I glance at the table, which is still full of display products. "I was, but we got so busy that I kinda lost count."

Jaxx arches a thin brow and purses her lips. "I think you're gonna be more than satisfied," she taunts, "because that last sale you made?" I nod, remembering the woman who bought a gift box, lube, and a cock ring. "That was your twelfth one. You earned the bonus."

"What?" I gasp, looking under the table for the stack of boxes but finding none. "Are you serious?"

"We both did. Dolla, dolla bills, bitch." She feigns making it rain money while spinning in a circle.

Okay, maybe a Diamond Dick wouldn't be so bad. I mean, I

wouldn't have to display it on the shelf in my therapy office, but I'd be quite happy to earn that baby. Especially given the fact that if I just earned two thousand dollars in two weeks, how much did Kara make?

"Dayum!" I grin as excitement and relief wash through me. So much so that I've almost forgotten falling on my face and spilling a bag of dicks in front of a room full of guys. But definitely not forgetting the blond sex god's glare or the gentle but firm way he helped me up. I've got some fantasy plans for that and the Velvetream Rabbit I decided to treat myself with. I can't sell it without trying it, after all.

---

We don't make it far after the quarterly party wraps up. Jaxx informs me that we're celebrating our success with drinks and steers me toward the bar in the hotel's basement. I definitely don't argue with that plan, but when she pushes the 'B' on the elevator, I worry the bar will be a smoky cigar lounge or something.

Thankfully, it's nothing like that. It's classy and upscale, just like the hotel, with a long, gleaming wooden bar along one wall, booths with tall dividers that lend privacy, and a piano player subtly tickling the ivories in the corner.

"That was amazing," Jaxx sighs as she falls into a booth. "So many *satisfied* customers."

I laugh at her obvious double meaning. "It does make me a little sad for them, though. I mean, yeah, a toy can be fun, something to spice up the humdrum maybe, but there's something to be said for communicating your needs with your partner too. If he doesn't know where a clit is, show him. Let him watch you and learn how you want to be touched. Don't just say 'oh, well' and handle things yourself after he's rolled over."

Jaxx rolls her eyes. "You're going therapist on me. We're celebrating toy triumphs tonight, not solving the flaws in the sexual patriarchy."

Before I can argue, a waitress stops by. I order a frozen

margarita, and Jaxx asks for a whiskey with an orange garnish. "Don't start without me, but I've got to piss. Be right back."

I giggle a little as she slips back out of the booth. Her crude language and zero fucks given attitude are somehow charming coming from her.

A moment later, the waitress returns with our drinks plus a plate of tiny sourdough bread toasts, hummus, and olives. "Oh, we didn't—" I start to tell the waitress, but she cuts me off.

"Your friend ordered it on her way to the restroom. Said she's hungry enough to, uhm . . . eat hairy ass?" She seems more than a bit confused by Jaxx and basically runs away while the plate is still clattering to the tabletop.

I take a sip of my margarita, closing my eyes to savor it. I probably should've ordered a water before the waitress scampered off because I'm realizing that I'm thirsty after the day's work. And hungry. I don't want to end up on my ass drunk.

I dig into the toast and hummus too, not waiting on Jaxx despite her instruction to do so. I'm three toasts in when a throat clears beside me. "Oh!" I exclaim, shocked at the man standing there and the dribble of hummus that's escaping my bottom lip. I swipe at my mouth with a finger, slipping it into my mouth to lick it clean.

I'm stunned into silence by his sudden appearance, not to mention his blond, blue-eyed, well-dressed, magnetic presence. Even if I hadn't seen him front and center on stage, everything about him says Head Mother Fucker In Charge.

"Surprised to see you're still here after that stunt earlier," he says. His voice is deep, smooth, and edged with anger.

"Stunt?" I echo. "More like the most embarrassing moment of my life."

I don't extend the invitation, but still, he annoyingly slips into the booth across from me, making himself at home with one arm stretched out along the seatback and the other resting casually on the tabletop. If I were a gambling woman, I'd bet he's manspreading beneath the table, claiming space in that annoyingly, presumptive male way. Like, we get it, you've got big balls, but if they need that much breathing room, you should probably see a doctor about that.

I'm also sure the top-tier glare he's flashing has melted many a man, but I'm made of sturdier stuff than most, so I narrow my eyes and glare right back. "And whatever that cult meeting was, I'm not interested. Especially given the whole 'virgin sacrificial vibe' you were putting off."

His lips twitch as though he's fighting a smile. "Doubt you'd qualify, given your bag of goodies and the 'party plans' your friend mentioned."

"Interested? We're known for our toys for females, but we have a male-focused line with cock rings, butt plugs, pocket pussies, and prostate massagers."

I'm well aware that I'm taunting him, and it feels like a dangerous thing to do, but the way the muscle in his jaw jumps when I say cock rings is too entertaining to step back from. "I'd be happy to get you a catalog and go over options with you."

"What the hell are you talking about?" he grits out from between clenched teeth. I'm pretty sure that he's speaking so quietly because he doesn't want anyone to hear me, though.

"I'm a Bedroom Heaven consultant, specializing in intimate toys, erotic novelties, and adult products," I explain. "No judgment here, just want to help people have fulfilling, healthy, satisfying sex lives." I add a saleswoman smile to the proclamation, enjoying watching him play catch up.

"You sell . . . sex toys? Like the ones in your bag that spilled all over the stage?" he clarifies, sounding slightly less scandalized now that I'm not throwing around words like 'cock' and 'pussy' where someone else in the bar might hear.

"Yep, *those* and lots more. Today was our quarterly party, which was one door away from your *thing*." I wave a hand in his general direction, still not sure what I walked into earlier. "You can blame the receptionist for that debacle if you're still mad. But what the hell was that?"

Before he can answer, Jaxx stomps up to the table. "Hell no, Mr. President of the Young Dickster's Guild. Leave my girl alone."

I can't help but smile at her automatic defense of me. Jaxx is the type who has your back, no matter what.

"It's okay. I was just offering Mr. . . . ?" I pause, realizing I didn't get the Sex God in a Suit's name.

"Chance. Just Chance."

I lift a brow and smirk a bit at his reticence to even share his name. Fine, two can play that game. "Sam. Just Sam," I reply to him before telling Jaxx, "I was offering 'just Chance' here a little lookie-loo at our catalog. I think the Naughty Neighbor is about his speed."

My suggested product is a realistic fleshlight that's as Plain Jane as they come, no nibs or ribbing inside, small labia that look porn-star-esque perfect, and no vibration. It's barely one tiny step up from using your palm.

Jaxx's black lips spread, flashing her white teeth, as she taps her sharply pointed nail to her chin and gives Chance an appraising look, which includes leaning back to check him out head to toe under the table.

"Naughty Neighbor? *Bo-ring*. But yeah, he looks too stiff for anything really fun. Can you imagine *him* with an Ass-Gasm or Black Hole Explorer?"

Not caring about any bar audience, she tenses up her whole body, like she's trying to get away from Mr. Invisible butt-fucking her, and makes a weird dolphin-sounding noise. "Eee, eee, eee!"

"Hey!" Chance blurts out, seeming offended at her impression of him, but when Jaxx and I both glance at him knowingly, he relents. "I don't know what I'm arguing about. I don't even know what those are. Nor do I think I want to," he admits.

Jaxx licks her finger and draws a tally mark in the air. "Point for Chance who recognizes that he's probably never taken one in his life," she declares. Planting her palms on the table, she tells me, "I gotta run. Kara needs help getting the Diamond Dick in her car. Are you good here or you wanna come with?"

She jerks her head toward the door of the bar, offering me an out. I should go with her. I have no reason to sit here with Chance. Jaxx could probably use my help, and I really need to take these heels off. But I was enjoying the banter with Chance before Jaxx walked back up, and I still don't know what that meeting was.

I'm curious, and though I know that's exactly what killed the cat, I find myself saying, "I'm good. Think I'll sip my margarita, eat a few toasts, and see if I can sell one more item today." I offer Chance a flirty smile that he returns, along with a chuckle at my boldness.

"Misbehave, you two," Jaxx instructs us, pointing a finger at me and then Chance. She grabs her whiskey, tosses it back in one swallow, sucks the orange, and slams the glass back to the table.

As Jaxx struts out of the bar, Chance whispers, "I think she meant 'behave', right?"

I purse my lips, fighting back the laugh that wants to escape at his sweet summer child innocence. "Oh, no, she said exactly what she meant."

The waitress makes another appearance, seeming more comfortable now that Jaxx is gone. "Can I get you a drink, sir?" she asks Chance.

"Club soda and lime, please." He lifts his chin in my direction questioningly.

"Water, please."

Now that it's the two of us, I'm not sure what to say, so I stuff a hummus-covered toast in my mouth, chewing delicately. The waitress drops off our drinks in record time, and we're alone again.

"You asked what you walked in on earlier," he reminds me. "It's sort of a motivational speaking meets Big Brothers mentorship-type deal. I help boys be better men so they're prepared for the life they want."

Letting that sink in, I quip in disbelief, "So, no virginal sacrifices?"

He laughs, the sound deep and rumbly. And I'm not surprised when butterflies start dancing in my belly.

# CHAPTER 5
# CHANCE

WHEN I SAW Sam sitting alone in the hotel bar, I told myself to keep walking. She's obviously nothing but trouble—barging into our club meeting, interrupting my speech, and disappearing without an apology. Despite consciously deciding that, my feet turned toward her of their own volition, drawn to her beauty as much as the opportunity to demand an explanation.

What I didn't expect to discover was that she's brilliant, funny, irreverent, and sexy. I'm not sure what's going to come out of her mouth, no matter how mundane the question, which is surprisingly intriguing. Especially given my penchant for planned, orderly, somewhat generic interactions.

But Sam is almost the exact opposite of my 'usual'.

I tell her about mentoring young men, and her response is that it must seem about as effective as swimming upstream. I share that the club meeting today went haywire after her appearance, and she grins and says, "You're welcome for adding some razzle dazzle to your boring club meeting," while giving me some sassy jazz hands.

I cringe as I tell her, "You know, the guys were calling you *Sex Toy Barbie*," but she shrugs.

"I've been called a lot worse by a whole lot better."

Somehow, hours pass, and we're still talking about this and that and nothing at all. I want to hear more of the outrageousness that passes over her full, pink lips as if it's completely reasonable, and I want to give it back to her, making her eyes sparkle when I say something she likes.

"That's when I told her she should go for the jugular. Cut him off, handle things herself, and if he's lucky, *maybe* he'll get to watch. But no touching her until he earns it." She grins evilly as she tells me about her recommendations for a customer from her quarterly party.

"Harsh," I say dryly. She shrugs and tilts her head carelessly, not offended at my judgment. "You're proud of yourself, aren't you?"

Sam preens, sweeping her hair over her shoulder, and I can't help but follow the dark curls down to where they brush over her full breasts. The neckline of her pink jumpsuit is tasteful, but I find myself watching closely as she moves, hoping it will dip down slightly. "Of course. If he's not willing to put out any energy, why should she put out at all?"

"Does that truly solve anything, though?" I don't know why I'm challenging her. I actually believe she's right and that a partnership requires effort from both parties.

"I'm not going to fix her marriage in a hotel ballroom party surrounded by light-up, vibrating, bedazzled dicks that'll probably make her fragile-egoed husband feel like he's been replaced by a bigger, better version of the literal only thing he's got to offer, because fuck knows he's not offering anything else. Not support, companionship, or even help, though I hate that word in that context because he's not 'helping' her manage their relationship in any way other than the one that gets him off."

The pause as she inhales a deep breath is marked with a change in her tone to one much more serious. Sad, even, or maybe resigned. "She's not looking for therapy. She's looking for orgasms that'll make her able to face another day covered with peanut butter residue from the lunch she made yesterday, a release that doesn't require her being touched by another human who wants something from her, and pleasure that doesn't come at the cost of being seen as selfish."

Her eyes fall to the table, her dark lashes fluttering over the pink rising in her cheeks. I don't think, don't consider the consequences or care about what's right or wrong.

Instinctively, I reach out to cover her fidgeting hands with my own, gently tracing along the length of each one with my fingertip. "Hey, are you okay?"

The straight set of her back collapses as she sags in on herself. "Yeah, sorry. It's not your fault some men are bastards. Just hard to hear story after story, damn near copies of the last, all while there's white, glittering rhinestones sprinkled around like bukkake confetti."

I choke on my own spit. "I'm sorry, *what?*"

What she said seems to have sunk in because she laughs a little at her own description. "I know. There were actually three-foot tall penises with rhinestone cum shots." Her brows rise, like 'can you believe that?'

"Don't think I've ever heard that word combination before."

Her dark mood is lifting, but neither of us moves our hands back. Now that I'm touching her, the sparks between us are palpable. I can feel my body leaning toward hers, my stomach pressing against the table, trying to get closer and cursing the two feet of wood between us.

"Sounds like falling onto the stage and spilling dildos was the easy part of your day. Who'd have thought a penis party would be the hard part?" My lip curls in a sexy smirk at the double entendre, mostly because it's not my usual M.O.

Hell, flirting isn't my usual style. I so rarely allow myself to be distracted from my single-minded focus on The Gentlemen's Club and my goals.

Her laugh is brighter, almost tinkling this time, and she pins me with a teasing light in her eyes. "I see what you did there. You think you're clever?"

I grin. "I know I am. I'm also good-looking, intelligent, generous, ambitious, and kind. Notice, I didn't say humble because I think it's important to know your good and bad qualities and be honest about them. Especially with yourself."

She nods agreeably, though her smile says she's not sure about my laying it out there so boldly. "Good and bad, you say?

Alright . . . I'm smart, a great friend, and a fantastic lover. I'm also addicted to reality TV, have to work to filter my mouth, and I'm a pushover when it comes to my mom and sister."

I blink, having only heard one thing she shared. *A fantastic lover.*

Beneath the table, my cock is rock hard and begging for attention. And not from my hand again. This need is not about answering an urge so I can maintain clear-headedness. It's about the woman across from me. This desire is for Sam specifically, with her wild hair and wilder mouth. I want to taste the things she says, do the things she wants, and experience her fully.

It's not like me. I don't make split-second decisions without considering every angle, consequence, and possible result. But maybe, just this once . . .

I don't think and rethink and then think once more for good measure. I act.

"Would you like to continue this conversation upstairs?" I ask carefully, well aware that while she might say yes, odds are equally good that she'll torch me where I sit. But fortune favors the bold, and I'm extremely fortunate.

Her eyes dip to my lips and then scan my face in an instant. I await her decision, trying not to scoop her up and make a run for the elevator. That wouldn't be proper, after all.

"You promise there's no sacrificial cult thing? And that you're not going to steal my kidneys?"

Before I answer, she's already rising. I quickly follow her move, tossing a twenty to the table and then taking Sam's hand once more. I'd like to say we make our way discretely to the elevator, but the truth is, we're nearly running for it, and as the doors close, trapping us in the small confines, it's Sam who makes the first move.

She wraps my tie around her hand and pulls me into her space, planting her back to the elevator wall so that I press against her. There's only a few inches difference between us with her in her heels, and with her face tilted up to mine, I cup her jaw with one strong hand. I move in slowly, giving her an opportunity to stop me, but she meets me in the middle. Her lips are sweet and soft, molding to mine as I delicately claim her mouth, exploring and learning her.

Sam kisses me back, more aggressively than I'm used to, but I like it. A lot. I shift my hips, my hard-on rubbing across her pelvis, and she groans into our shared breath. Her head falls back, and I trace kisses along her jaw, down to her neck.

"Please promise me you know what to do with that thing. If I have to pull out a toy, I might as well just go home and do this on my own because I know what I like and I've got an inventory's worth to choose from." The threat is real, but given the continued rough groans she's making as I touch her, she doesn't want to do that.

She wants me.

And I want her.

"I know what I'm doing." The arrogant vow is made with gentle kisses to her mouth—the right, then left, then fully centered as I let my tongue dive past her lips to write the promise deep.

"Thank fuck!" she sighs as she runs her fingers into my hair and kisses me back.

When the elevator dings and the doors open, we don't break apart. Not until a voice says, "Getting off?"

I feel Sam's smile before I see it, but when I open my eyes, it's just as bright and mischievous as I thought it'd be. "I'm trying to, but you're cock-blocking me here. And I *want* what he's packing."

The woman huffs in distaste as Sam pulls me past her. Habits are hard to break, though, and I murmur, "Sorry, excuse us." The apology is not accepted, and the woman gets on the elevator looking as though we left a splattering of sex in the space just by being in there. "This way," I tell Sam, guiding her to my room.

I make quick work of the electronic lock and hold the door open, waiting for her to decide again. Sam doesn't seem impressed as she enters the room, which is oversized and decorated in what a designer would probably call 'modern luxury'.

The king-size bed has more pillows than any two people might need, the white sheets are that perfect combination of crisp and soft, and the headboard is tufted ivory velvet. Behind the floor-to-ceiling drapery is a view of the hotel's garden, which can be perfectly appreciated from the chaise lounge chair, and the desk holds a large ginger-jar style lamp along with my laptop, which sits where I left it earlier when I wrapped up work to go downstairs for the club meeting.

None of that matters to Sam, or to me right now.

I yank at my tie, blindly pulling the knot free, but become instantly distracted when I see Sam reaching beneath her hair to the nape of her neck. "Let me," I offer.

She spins. "There's a small button here, and then a zipper on the side," she answers helpfully. The button is easily conquered, but I take my time with the zipper, letting the backs of my fingers brush over her skin and the silk of her bra. Sam dips her shoulders, letting the top fall to her waist as she turns back to face me.

The pink fabric is puddled above her hips, exposing the cleavage that's been teasing and tempting me all night. I dance my fingers over her mounds, touching her gently and enjoying the responding gooseflesh that rises in the wake of my touch.

"I want to worship every inch of you. Feel, taste, enjoy your skin until you're ready for me."

There's a sassy comeback poised on her tongue, but instead of waiting for it, I kiss her hard enough that whatever she was going to say disintegrates between us, along with her jumpsuit as it falls to the floor and she steps out of it without breaking our connection.

Until she pulls back, taking my hand in hers to guide me to the chaise. I finally get a full look at her. She's stunning in her matching bra and panties, which are a nude color a few shades darker than her tanned skin.

"Gorgeous," I whisper. Her smile says 'I know' as she lies back. Her hair fans around her in a dark halo against the navy fabric of the chair.

Leaning over her, I lay a line of hot, wet kisses over the exposed flesh of her shoulders and down her collarbones, getting a hint of her perfume as I get closer to her breasts. I plant my knee between her thighs, and her hips buck as she rubs herself on my leg. It's one of the sexiest things I've ever seen. And felt, because I can feel the heat from her core, the slickness spilling from her to create a wet spot on the silk of her panties.

"I want to see you," I confess. She responds instantly, expertly undoing her bra and dropping it to the floor and then slipping her hands into the sides of her panties to wiggle them down. I help her, rolling them down her legs, which she lifts into the air. I press a kiss to her ankle . . . her calf . . . the inside of her knee.

Working my way up, I let my eyes trace over her center. She's gorgeous there too—bare and pink, with shiny juices coating her skin. I repeat the kisses up her other leg, wanting to appreciate her every inch.

"Can I taste you?" I ask as my fingers drift higher and higher. In response she relaxes, letting her legs fall open to give me full access. I groan as I sink to the chaise between her legs, giving myself room to work. More kisses lead me to just above her clit. I use my thumbs to spread her wide, and as I meet her eyes, I lay a long lick to the sensitive nub. She spasms already, not coming but overwhelmed at even the gentle sensation. Still, she grabs at my head, pulling me in for more, which I gladly deliver. I test and tease, learning what she responds favorably to, and then slip a finger inside her, curling it to pet along her front wall.

"*Yes*," she moans, "right there . . . and lick me fast."

Loving how bold she is, I thrust in again, keeping my fingertip where she wants it as I flutter my tongue over her clit. "Oh, oh, oh!" Her keening cries get higher-pitched and louder, and I can feel the tension throughout her body as she rides the edge. And then she shudders violently and groans, "Chance . . ."

I keep going, giving her as much pleasure as I can, wanting her to be satisfied. I feel like she needs this almost as much as I do. Especially after the highs and lows of her day.

"You," she says clearly. "I want you inside me."

She doesn't have to tell me twice because I'm on the verge of coming in my slacks as it is. Making fast work of the buttons, I pull my shirt off and then do the same speed trick with my belt and slacks. Over my boxer briefs, I give myself a firm stroke, hoping to stave off a too-quick release. I want to enjoy this . . . enjoy Sam wrapped around my dick.

"Condom's in my purse," she offers, pointing to her bag. I raise one brow, remembering what else is in her bag. She smiles, amused. "Different bag."

I grab her purse, letting her dig inside. Partly because I don't trust that there's not a single dildo inside and I don't want to give it a hand job and partly because I know better than to invade a woman's bag. That's a crime punishable by death.

While she finds it, I push my underwear down to give my dick a few more slow, tight strokes. The skin on skin of my hand is all-too-familiar, and I want more. I want her.

"Got it!" she exclaims, holding up a foil packet. "You want to put it on or want me to do it?"

I reach for the condom. "I've got it because if you touch me, I'm gonna explode."

She grins and watches as I unroll the latex over my length and line up at her entrance, holding steady and not breaching her yet. "Sam?"

She nods, her white teeth digging into her bottom lip and her dark eyes pleading silently. I push forward, slowly filling her inch by inch as she envelops me. Pulling me down, she takes my weight as I press her to the chaise. She's pinned beneath me, impaled on me.

Neither of us says a word, but we simultaneously begin bucking, chasing our pleasure. Our eyes lock for a moment, but then Sam's roll back and I can't focus beyond the sensations coursing through my body. I thrust fast, hard, deep, and occasionally, I stay there to grind against her.

Too soon, I'm walking a razor's edge and I know my release is imminent and won't be staved off for much longer. I find a rhythm we both like and stay steady, letting it build between us.

I interweave our fingers, holding them above Sam's head, and she lifts her chin, jutting it out almost in challenge. Daring me to come or seeing if I can fight it off, I'm not sure which. But I win, coming suddenly with a force that starts deep in my belly. I can feel jet after jet of cum filling the condom and have an errant thought that I wish I were bare inside her, filling her with my cum. I jerk once more and then collapse, panting heavily.

---

### Samantha

Chance snuggles up on the chaise with me, our arms and legs a tangle and heads perched side by side on the chair's pillow as we recover. That was . . . wow. He's different from how I thought he'd be. I guess I thought he'd be bossy, domineering, and out for his own. Probably a shitty assumption on my part, but the whole big man on campus vibe of Chance leading the club meeting today is stuck in my mind.

But instead, he was attentive, listened to me, and definitely focused on my satisfaction. I don't know when I've felt more cherished and appreciated, at least physically.

"Wow," I mutter, and Chance smiles victoriously. Half drowsy and blissed out, I say philosophically, "Did you know sex is so much more than most people think? It's a whole spectrum of activities, styles, and things that bring people pleasure."

Chance's smile falls by degrees to be replaced by a frown. One brow lifted in question, he carefully asks, "Are you saying that wasn't pleasurable? Because you were making sounds to the contrary."

Shit, I've hurt his feelings unintentionally because that's not what I meant at all. "That was amazing," I rush to reassure him. "I meant that people like all sorts of things. Kinks, fetishes, sweet and gentle, humiliating and brutal, and everywhere in between."

"Is this your roundabout way of telling me you have a foot fetish?" he says dryly, but I can see the light in his blue eyes as he realizes I'm not talking shit about his bedroom skills.

"No," I answer, laughing. "Though that's a common one. I guess I meant more that you're a very thorough lover. I don't think there's a spot on my body that you didn't kiss, touch, fill. It was . . . unexpected. Like a whole girlfriend experience."

"Girlfriend?" he echoes vacantly.

I meant it to be a compliment, but given the horror stricken look on his face, he definitely didn't take it as one. "Don't freak out on me, Chance. I'm not moving into your house or changing my relationship status to hearts and flowers around your name. I'm simply wondering if that's your style . . . your thing. Or do you sometimes explore, experiment, and try new things? Because that was a newer thing for me." I trail off, making it obvious that I'm baby stepping toward something.

He looks at me carefully for a solid minute before responding. "I don't want a butt plug."

I snort-laugh at the one line he's drawing because that should be the least of his worries with what's in my goodie bag. "Okay, but how about for round two we try something that'll make your inner boy scout blush? No pressure, no judgment, just fuck me rough, hard, and dirty. I bet you don't get the chance to do that very often, or ever, but I think I can handle you at your filthiest."

"Round two?"

I nod. "Yeah, unless you need more time to recover." I cuddle into his chest to give him a few minutes, but he's got other plans in mind.

"Get on your knees," he orders.

My whole body jerks, perking up in interest at the change in his tone. I move, sinking to the floor beside the chaise with my ass resting on my heels and looking at him expectantly, fire already relighting inside me.

He sits up on the chaise, one leg on either side of me. His eyes search mine, and I watch as he takes a rough swallow, his Adam's apple bobbing in his throat. I can tell this is already a different vibe for him, but he's interested for sure. "I want you to promise you'll tell me if it's too much."

I can't help but smile at the seriousness with which he's taking this. It's sexy that he wants to be bossy but wants to respect me too. A perfect balance . . . *if* he's actually filthy.

"I promise, and I'll also tell you if I can take more."

His lips quirk, but he dips his head, accepting my vow. He

leans back on the chaise, one leg stretched out long and the other foot on the floor, spreading his legs wide. I drink him in with my eyes—tanned skin with a dusting of blond hair over his strong, lean muscles, his cock already thick and leaking, and his blue eyes full of fire.

"Suck me, Sam. Swallow me with that sassy mouth of yours." He runs a thumb roughly over my bottom lip and grips himself, angling his cock toward my mouth. "And then I'll fuck you rough, hard, and dirty," he repeats, letting me know he heard exactly what I asked for.

Eagerly, I lean forward to lick a long line from his balls to the tip, savoring the salty fluid that's already leaking. "Mmm," I moan. "Hold my hair."

I don't wait for him to gather my curls in his fist. I dive right in, taking him in deep in one move. When his fingers tighten in my hair in response, I get a little thrill. Control is a sexy thing. He thinks he's controlling me by telling me what to do and guiding my head, but the truth is, I've got all the power, literally in command of the pleasure I give or don't give.

I take him into my mouth over and over, drool coating him and running down my chin, but I can feel him holding back. Tension is threaded through his muscles, and when I glance up his body, I can see the outline of his six-pack. Gasping for breath, I pant, "Fuck my mouth. I want you to. You want to. I can see it, feel it. Do it. Fuck. My. Mouth."

"God damn it," he growls right before he unleashes the punishing restraint he had on himself.

He slams into my throat, shuddering as he holds himself there for a split second before repeating the move. He finds a fast, deep, rough pace that brings the prick of tears to my eyes, and I fight to keep suction around his thickness. I love it and moan around him to tell him so.

I feel him grow even harder in my mouth, and with a roar, he jerks me off him. "No, not till I get back in that cunt."

Holy. Hell. The Boy Scout is a raging naughty boy in disguise. He might be my dream come true—sweet and filthy.

He grabs at my bag, digging for another condom himself this

time. "Get up there," he directs, pointing at the chaise with a lift of his chin.

I don't have any smart words this time. I do as I'm told, as quickly as I can, lying back on the chaise with my legs open wide. I slide my fingers over my clit, spreading my slickness over my entire pussy. I'm on the edge already, just from how sexy sucking him off was.

Sheathed, he approaches the foot of the chaise, his eyes pinned to what my hand is doing. "See anything you want?" I offer.

In response, he grabs behind my knees and jerks me down the chaise so far that my ass is hanging off, but he holds me tight, not letting me drop an inch. He guides my legs up onto his shoulders, which puts me in a slightly upside-down position with my weight resting on my upper back, but it gets my pussy at just the right level for his cock to slide into me easily. A cry of ecstasy escapes as Chance grips my ass, his fingertips digging sharply into the tender flesh to hold me in place securely.

He slams into me, pounding deep as he pulls me onto him, fucking me while making me fuck him back. "Touch yourself again."

I know I'm a sloppy, wet mess already, but I reach two fingers toward his mouth. He dips down, sucking them to coat them with his spit, and I use his saliva to rub over my clit. Long swipes quickly become blurringly fast, short strokes, and the combination of Chance fucking me and the focus on my clit is too much, putting me on edge in an instant. "More," I beg, not even sure what I want more of. All of it? Him?

Chance licks his lips, and I pause, letting him drip more spit onto my clit, greedily using it for my pleasure. He growls, his eyes watching my movements hungrily as his hips piston fast and hard. "Come, Sam. I want to feel this pretty pussy come on me."

I fly apart, shattering into a million pieces and gushing fluids over our connection. Somewhere in the blackness of my own ecstasy, I feel Chance jerking as he explodes inside me. "Fuck," he grunts.

Once the sparkles leave my vision, I look up at Chance as he helps me lower my legs. I must look wild—panting, sweaty, and smiling crazily—because he asks, "You okay?" Even when he's rough, he's caring.

I nod, stretching luxuriously. "Mmm, more than okay. You?"

He flashes a grin, but there's a shadow of doubt in his eyes as he scans me. "Hey, I'm good. That was amazing. Just like round one, only different."

He sighs, clearly content but at the same time in his thoughts. "Yeah, different. I guess I never thought I'd like—"

He trails off, looking like he's doing some soul searching.

"No judgment, just trying new things," I assure him. "Doesn't mean it's your thing, but at least you tried. I think you could use a shower and some room service. Yeah?"

Aftercare can take many forms, but at its core, it's to prolong the intimacy between partners after sex and provide a sense of connection, and it should go both ways. I start to get up, and Chance takes my hand, helping me to my feet. Standing before him, I lift to kiss him gently and press my hand to his chest, over his heart, which is thudding rapidly.

"What if it *is* my thing?" he whispers, sounding like his entire self-view just went haywire.

I smile as I run a finger along his jaw, feeling the slight beginnings of a five o'clock shadow. "Naughty Boy Scout? I think that might be my new kink," I tease.

# CHAPTER 6
# SAMANTHA

"DO I seriously have to go with you? For real? You could drop me off at home, ya know?" Olivia says flatly. Her annoyed tone drives me insane, but if I mention it, she'll simply quit speaking at all, so I grip the steering wheel tighter and force a smile.

"Home is in the opposite direction, and a little time in the sunshine will do you some good," I reply, trying to sound positive. "Don't worry, you can stare at your phone at the park as easily as you can in your room."

She huffs out a tortured sigh, and without looking, I can sense her eye roll. "Whatever," she mutters to the window.

*Great job, Samantha. Sarcasm's exactly what Olivia needs.*

The chastisement of myself doesn't help. I know better and do better with practice therapy sessions, but with my own sister, I fall into sibling bitch-fest habits from our younger days.

"Look, I'm sorry," I add, trying to course correct. "But Luna asked if I could meet her and Gracie at the park. I swear it'll be fast." I hope I can keep that promise, but Luna didn't say what she needed, only that she needed me.

Luna Harrington is my bestest friend in the whole world. She's the odd to my normal, the sweet to my salty, and the ride or die to my I'll kill for you. She's also a fantastic aunt to Gracie, her husband's brother's daughter, and that's no easy feat because Gracie is a lot of bold, unfiltered energy packed into a tiny eight-year-old body.

"Luna? You didn't say we were chilling with her. Should'a led with that." Though Olivia's mood brightens considerably, I'm left wondering how my own sister hates my existence and thinks I'm annoying but somehow finds my artist-slash-weirdo bestie to be cool and worth her time.

It doesn't take a psychology degree to figure out that I'm a little jealous, but if Olivia sees a good role model in Luna, I'm glad for that.

We find a parking spot and walk down the path, through the tree line, and into the green opening that's a reprieve from the city's hustle and bustle. Pointing to a shaded area on the far side of the park, I say, "There they are."

As if they've been watching for us, Gracie is suddenly running toward us, screeching at the top of her lungs, "Saaaa-man-thaaaa! You're heeere!" Nipping at her heels is a brown, fluffy dog named Peanut Butter but who is more commonly called Nutbuster because he has a bad habit of running head-first, center mass, into his chosen target. But Luna's brother-in-law, Kyle, never seems to teach his dog any manners. Though the dog's questionable behavior might not be *all* Kyle's fault, because I've met Nutbuster several times, and my professional diagnosis is that he doesn't have two brain cells to rub together.

"Hi, honey," I greet the blonde, ponytailed little girl, opening my arms for the incoming tackle hug. She smells like sweat and sunshine, and vaguely like mangos, so I know they've been here long enough to have already eaten a popsicle from the vendor who sells them from his cooler-accented bicycle as he rides around the park. When I let Gracie go, I shield my crotch from Nutbuster. "And you too, Mister PB," I add with scratches to the dog's head. "Good boy."

"C'mon! Aunt Luna's been waiting on you foreverrr," she tells me, her voice loud enough that half the park can probably hear her as she drags me toward Luna. "Hi, Olivia," Gracie throws over her shoulder when she remembers her manners.

"Hi to you too, kid," Olivia answers dryly. I give her a look of apology, but you can't really blame Gracie for being excited. The park is one of her favorite places, and I'm one of her favorite people. Of course, I think Gracie meets a new favorite person just about every day. She's overly friendly, scarily mature, and it's always a hoot to hear what comes out of her mouth.

Luna's perched on a small blanket in the grass with a half-painted canvas leaning up against the tree in front of her. She holds a finger up as we approach, her other hand gently layering acrylic paint to the canvas. It's a still-life of the park, but realism isn't Luna's style so in her version, the trees are a vibrant fuchsia, the grass is highlighter yellow, and the turquoise pathway is dotted with black and white figures.

Used to her hyperfocus, Gracie and I giggle as we mimic Luna's one-finger communication, doing it to each other over and over with increasing degrees of pseudo-annoyance and rapidly spreading grins, but Olivia is watching Luna with rapt attention.

"Is that supposed to be Peanut Butter?" Olivia asks a couple of minutes later. "The fur texture is perfect." Having heard his name, the dog hops up, standing tall to put his paws on Olivia's belly and pant for attention, which she gives happily.

Luna smiles as she pauses. "Thanks! It is this little fella." She makes a kissy sound toward the dog. "Hey, guys," she says, finally greeting us.

I lower to the blanket, sitting next to Luna, and Olivia follows. Gracie couldn't sit still if she wanted to and resumes bouncing, Nutbuster doing the same, probably thinking he's supposed to copy her.

"Hey, girl, that looks awesome. Personal, professional, or commission?" I ask.

Luna is an artist of varying specialties. We met when she did tours at the art museum, but since, she's taken over as a manager for a large, private collection, so she's got the classics on lock. She also does digital art for her wildly successful original graphic novel series, *Alphena*. But I think there's a part of her that likes smearing paint on canvas just as much.

"Personal," she answers. "Hey, Olivia! How's life?"

It's a generic question, but Olivia takes the opportunity to piss on me. "Annoying. I've got this one" —she throws a thumb my way— "hauling me around like I'm her latest fashion accessory, Mom pawning me off so she can get her freak on with her latest boytoy, and—"

I don't let her finish. She can talk shit about me all she wants, but Mom? Hell, no. "Olivia, Mom has dated exactly one man since Dad left, and she deserves to be happy. And yeah, to get her freak on."

"What's that mean? Gechur freak on?" Gracie echoes, and I freeze, realizing belatedly that I shouldn't have said that in front of her considering she echoes everything, even if she only hears it once in passing. But her follow-up little girl giggles are wild and loud. "Psyche! I know that means s-e-x. So does screwing, banging, and fu—"

"No!" Luna shouts, lunging for Gracie and covering her mouth with a paint-smeared hand. "That's an adult word."

"Uncle Kyle says it," Gracie answers behind Luna's hand, adding a shrug of 'who cares' for good measure.

"He's an adult," Luna argues as she moves her hand away. "Well, mostly."

Kyle is Nutbuster's dad and the youngest brother of the Harrington family. He's also the black sheep for reasons I don't understand. Luna says he doesn't play well with others, mostly his father, who has lots of expectations of what being a Harrington entails. Ones that Kyle essentially said 'fuck you' to and rode off into the sunset. He didn't even come to Carter and Luna's wedding, though it was last-minute and a bit of a farce, but still . . . he should've come.

Trying to get us back to the point, I remind Olivia, "Have you even met Marvin yet? Or are you just pissed that Mom's dating?" She doesn't answer other than to roll her eyes and scoff haughtily, but I can translate her teen-speak. "That's what I thought. Could you maybe pull your head out of your own ass, realize that the world doesn't revolve around you, and be happy for Mom that she's found someone she wants to spend time with?"

"Whatever," she snarls, jumping up from the blanket. "C'mon, kid. Let's go somewhere that focusing on ourselves isn't seen as self-centered by narcissists who're blind to their own shortcomings."

With that, Olivia leads Gracie and Peanut Butter away toward the playground equipment.

"Why did I waste my sixth, seventh, and eighth birthday wishes hoping for a sibling?" I sigh as I flop to the blanket. "I should've wished for a Barbie dream house or a cat."

Luna grimaces sympathetically. "Trouble in paradise?"

She knows that my home life wasn't a vacation, but Mom did the best she could. I just wish Olivia could see that. "I can't with her. I don't think I was ever that . . . *ugh*," I finish with a growl. But a moment later, I'm asking, "Is she right? Am I doing the whole 'pot-kettle-black' thing, telling her she's acting like the world revolves around her and simultaneously acting like I think it revolves around me?"

I truly want Luna's opinion, but I'm already doing some self-analysis too. Luna's quiet for a moment, and if it were anyone else, I'd be worried they didn't want to risk hurting my feelings with an ugly truth.

But Luna's more likely doing a thorough character, behavior, and intention analysis. "Nope, you're not self-centered." My relief is short-lived, though, because she adds, "But I don't think Olivia is either. She's worried about her mom dating for the first time after an ugly divorce where she got a surprising, up-close, and personal look at what douche canoes men can be from the one man who's supposed to be her rock. Maybe she's not jealous of your mom's time but is trying to protect her . . . awkwardly."

Huh. I hadn't thought of it from that angle, though I definitely should've because it actually makes a lot of sense. Olivia blamed Mom after the divorce and had a lot of anger, but maybe she's finally realizing that Dad carried way more than half the responsibility for imploding their marriage. That's enough to make her mad all over again, and probably a bit jaded where men are concerned, right as Mom's taking a chance on another one.

I turn my head, examining the fluffy clouds in the blue sky as I mull that over. "Okay, Dr. Harrington, what about this?"

I tell her a brief version of my day—and night—yesterday, from rushing into the hotel, falling on stage amid a flurry of dicks, running into the hot speaker in the hotel bar, and going upstairs for the best sex I've ever had.

"You what?" Luna screeches incredulously, her eyes so wide, I can see the whites all the way around the blue centers. I think her reaction to my best-sex-ever comment is a bit dramatic, but she adds, "Flat on your face, dicks everywhere, spotlight on you, yourself, and you, and Jaxx had to rescue you?"

Oh, she's reacting to my sex toy debacle. Oddly enough, that seems like a long time ago after the double round of sex with Chance.

"Yep," I tell her, "And as bad as it sounds, it was one billion percent worse to live it. The only things that made it better were the orgasms and earning my two-thousand-dollar bonus." I drop that bombshell on purpose, a little humble brag among friends who typically celebrate each other's wins, but she's focused on something else.

"You're not usually into the hookup scene. He must've really charmed the jumpsuit off'a you." She helped me pick out the pink jumpsuit for the meeting and knows it's not exactly a shove it up and shove a dick inside type of outfit. Not that I've done that . . . in a while.

"He did," I confess. "Didn't hurt that he was a blond, blue-eyed sex god, either." A blissed-out smile takes my face as I remember Chance laid back on the chaise, waiting for me to suck him down.

"I've got one of those at home and know how persuasive they can be. Carter can hakuna ma-tata's anytime." Luna's description of her husband as a blond, blue-eyed sex god jars me more than her bastardization of a Disney movie saying because she watches more kid movies than anyone I know and doesn't have kids of her own.

But come to think of it, Chance did vaguely resemble Carter, in that 'Hamptons in the summer on a private yacht' way.

"You gonna see him again?"

I probably should've said something to Chance before leaving this morning, but he seemed too good to be true, and in my hazy mind, I hadn't wanted the awkward moment of 'I'll call you' when we both knew he wouldn't, so I'd quietly snuck out, leaving nothing more than a lipstick kiss on his shoulder, where it stuck out of the sheets as he slept. Something told me that it'd both irk and amuse him to wake up and find a long-wearing mark staining his skin.

"Nah, one and done. I snuck out for my walk of shame, not that I'm ashamed of a thing after that awesome night. But we'd never work anyway, and I've got to focus on school and making bank. The good news is that I'm giving notice at the store. Bedroom Heaven is way more money, in my area of expertise, and flexible for classes. And they don't treat you like you're as disposable as the straws."

"Save the turtles!" we intone together, a silly habit we picked up anytime someone mentions straws.

Then Luna's brows lift almost to her hairline. "Are you sure? Huge congrats on the bonus." She smiles as she acknowledges my boast. "But it takes a lot of hustle to sell that much all the time. What if you can't do that again?"

I nod, reasonably sure of my decision. Jaxx was right. Sex sells, and orgasms sell even more. And worst-case scenario, I can get another job in the blink of an eye if everything goes to hell. Being a college area, there are always jobs available at retail stores, restaurants, and coffee shops. It's not ideal, but it's supported me well enough the last few years.

"Speaking of, could I interest you in our new Velvetream Rabbit?"

"What? No!" Luna protests . . . too much.

"Babe, I know you're not that innocent anymore. You and Carter get up to some probably illegal, definitely immoral, and totally unholy things, and you can't tell me otherwise." I'm mostly teasing because Luna was a virgin before she met Carter, but she's definitely made up for lost time with her new husband.

Luna laughs, covering her mouth with her paint-splattered

hand as though she's a little embarrassed by my assessment. "Nope, maybe, and you're *daaaamn* right. But I don't think we need to add anything buzzy to the rotation."

"Buzzy, non-buzzy, sucking, thrusting, numbing, sensitizing . . . we've got it all. Direct and indirect stim, Bluetooth, remote controlled, and more." I add a little bit of a snake oil salesman vibe to my list of possible contenders, but Luna's not having it.

"Thanks, but no thanks. Carter's enough for me."

Shaking my head, I give it one more go. "It's not about his not being enough. It's more about adding some spice, some va-va-va-voom, some surprise."

"Mm-hmm," she murmurs disbelievingly, but she's saved from my next round of sales tactics by Olivia screeching.

"You fucker!"

I look over and nearly panic because I think she's talking to Gracie like that. But thankfully, that assumption is quickly assuaged because though she's looking down at the girl, she's talking to Peanut Butter, whom Gracie is lying over protectively as if Olivia is going to attack him instead of vice versa. Peanut Butter doesn't seem concerned with the yelling and is licking Gracie's face like this is a new game.

I jump up and rush over, Luna right behind me. "What's wrong?"

Olivia is wiping away at her jeans and kicks off her tennis shoe as she tells me, "I was sitting here, minding my own business—"

Gracie interrupts and corrects her, "Texting on your phone to Mercedes, whining about how bitchy Samantha is. Which she is *not*." Gracie throws her hands on her hips and glares at Olivia in my defense.

Luna whispers to the girl, "Don't say bitchy around your dad either."

Olivia grits her teeth and hammers on, "Minding my own business, and that monster peed on my new 550s." Her shoes are chunky, white, grass-cutting, Dad-style and currently covered in yellow tinted liquid. "Can we go now?"

Without waiting for an answer, she starts stomping across the park toward the car, her whole body going up and down, getting taller and shorter with each step depending on whether it's her bare foot or shoed foot.

"Guess I'm leaving," I tell Luna. "Sorry, Gracie. Maybe next time we can swing?"

"Okay," she says unhappily. "Olivia's mad at Nutbuster, huh?"

"Yeah, but I think she's mad at a whole lot more than that," Luna says wisely. To me, she adds, "Hey, Carter's taking me ice skating at the mall tonight. Wanna come? Zack'll be there for a minute. He's got some prospect property for Carter to look at."

Zack is Luna's brother, her husband's business partner, and she hopes, my soon-to-be-boyfriend. But Zack and I are polite acquaintances with Luna in common, nothing more.

"I don't know—"

"I'll send you the details. And you can probably sell a product or two to Carter and Zack. If nothing else, they'll buy your whole stock to get you to stop talking about it," she teases, knowing that I'll show up if there's a chance I could get another sale.

"Fine, see ya later!" I shout back, nearly running to catch up with Olivia.

The drive home is completely silent. Olivia's anger is heavy. Her lips are pressed into a straight line, and she's pointedly looking out the window in an effort to avoid me entirely.

When I pull into the driveway, I try to apologize. "Olivia, I'm sorry about your—"

She cuts me off. "You owe me new shoes if these don't clean up. They'd better be *pristine*." And with that declaration, she slams my car door and hobbles to the house.

Seeing that Mom's home now, I turn off the car and head inside too. I don't knock or anything like that. Mom told me when I moved out that this will always be my home and to treat it as such. Admittedly, knocking on my own front door would be strange, so I'm glad she made her feelings about it abundantly clear.

"Mom?"

"In here," she calls from her bedroom.

I stand in the doorway for a moment, taking her in. Mom is beautiful in a quiet, understated way. Her dark hair flips and flops around her chin in a messy bob, her freckles have been joined by some wrinkles over the years, and her face is bare of makeup besides mascara and tinted Chapstick. Her outfit is comprised of out-of-style, dark-wash skinny jeans, Birkenstock sandals, and a high-neck T-shirt. Nothing about Mom is loud or attention grabbing other than her kind heart.

And the beaming smile with a stranglehold on her face right now.

"Looks like your date was a success," I venture.

Somehow, her grin grows even wider. "It was. Marvin made us dinner. He's a grill master of sorts. Has a smoker, a Traeger, a Blackstone, and maybe some other thing? I can't remember, all I know is that I've never had chicken that juicy and delicious. And then we watched the sunset and the stars come out."

She stops there, and I prompt, "And then? I don't need details, but did you have a good, very good, or very, very good night? Fair warning, if it was less than stellar, you deserve better."

She giggles in that way I swear I've never heard from her before and then emphatically holds two thumbs up.

"Enough said," I tell her with an answering smile of my own.

I'm happy for her and hate to burst her bubble at all, but I think she needs to know about Olivia's reaction to the overnight date. "Olivia was okay at brunch today, but Luna said something that made me think. Do you think maybe she's worried about your dating because she doesn't want you to get hurt? I mean, Dad's an ass and did a real number on us all. Maybe Olivia's finally realized that and is worried that'll happen again?"

Mom sits heavily on the edge of the bed, her eyes falling to her hands in her lap. "I don't know. I've tried talking to her about it so many times, but she shuts me out every time. Or blows me off, laughing like it's no big deal when I know it is."

"Keep trying," I advise her. "She might not act like it, but she hears you. And seeing you make your happiness a priority is a good example for her. As long as this Marvin guy treats you right and you keep smiling like you were when I came in here, she'll come around. Eventually."

I cross my fingers, holding them up for Mom to see, and she laughs a little. "Honey, I've got my fingers, toes, knees, and eyes crossed that this goes well. I'm not made for this dating stuff anymore. One of my friends dated a guy, then he disappeared on her. Ghosted, I think she called it?" she says, looking to me for confirmation that she's using the word correctly. "And then, months later, she's moved on, hasn't given him a thought, and he messages her out of the blue. She said it was 'zombie-ing' or something?" I nod, agreeing that's what it's called and that it's awful. "But you'll never guess what he messaged! It was a picture of his penis and the letters DTF. Can you believe that?" She didn't even know what it meant, and I certainly didn't, so she Googled it." She makes a face of scandalized confusion. "Like did he really think she was gonna be that desperate?"

"Sadly, yeah. He probably did," I reply. "And unsolicited dick pics are ridiculously common."

Mom's confusion morphs into anger. "Have you gotten one? From whom? I'll kick his behind."

I laugh at her indignation on my behalf. "More than one, Mom. Ridiculously common," I repeat. "I used to engage—send back dick pics from the internet, tell them they should get that checked out, or send ratings like 2/10 or the fingers one-inch apart emoji."

I hold my hand up, demonstrating. "But now, I just block and move on. I don't have time to fix that kinda twisted thinking for guys who don't think they're doing anything wrong. And my mental health assistance costs money. I'm not giving it away for free," I joke, both of us aware that all my counseling sessions are strictly for practice and with other psychology students, not actual, paying clients. Yet.

"That's my girl. Using your noggin," she tells me proudly. "And stay away from boys like that. Anyway, I'll see if I can get

Olivia to talk to me or listen to me. Or hell, be in the same room without my mere presence annoying her."

I smile grimly. "She'll come around, Mom. Eventually . . . maybe . . . hopefully."

The decreasing likelihood is merciless but accurate considering Olivia is just as stubborn as Mom and I are.

# CHAPTER 7
# CHANCE

"WE SHOULD COORDINATE OUR TIES BETTER," Evan says as he checks himself in the test feed. We're ten minutes to go-time, and by this point, things are routine. We have a near-pro setup—good lighting, excellent microphones, and two high-quality cameras feeding into our laptops. All we have to do is plug and play.

We started our podcast a couple of years ago. It's a bit of a 'which came first, the chicken or the egg' type deal with us, only the chicken is the podcast and the egg is the Gentlemen's Club. We dreamed them up together, a way to mentor a select few right in our own backyards and simultaneously help a wider audience. They've grown individually in fits and spurts, sometimes one requiring more of our attention than the other, but we do our best to grow in an intentionally-diversified, well-rounded way.

"What do you mean?" I ask as I tweak the ring light that's on my left. It moves an inch over, eliminating a shadow that was stretching across my cheek. Good. I glance down at my red tie and shrug. "I can change if you think it matters."

"If you have a Duke blue one like mine . . ." Evan comments, but trails off as he fidgets with his laptop.

He's likely already forgotten his suggestion, but I get up and go to my office to grab another tie anyway. Of course I have a navy blue one, or close enough. I pull it around my neck and quickly do my favorite double Windsor knot before going back out to take my seat. "Better?" I ask, holding my hands wide so he can see my coordinating tie.

"Perfect," Evan says, his eyes never leaving his screen. "Son of a bitch!" he hisses suddenly.

"What?" In my chair, across the table, I can't see what Evan's upset about, but his eyes are flicking left and right as he reads something.

"Fucking trolls." He hits a button on the keyboard harder than necessary. "Nothing to worry about. Let's do this."

"You sure?" I ask. He's obviously upset. I'm guessing it's over a fan letter if he's talking about trolls. We get positive ones that hype us up and provide inspiration for future show topics, but along with those come a fair share of negative ones too. People calling us names, saying we're full of shit, and that we're coattail riders of real men like Jake McGibbons. We do our best to let those slide off our backs, but sometimes, it's hard.

Evan must've gotten one of those.

In response, he hits a button and the opening theme to our podcast plays, and the little light above my camera turns white, showing that I'm on the primary feed.

"Good evening, everybody, and welcome to another episode of *Two Men And A Mic*. Here we offer nothing but advice, encouragement, and the simple truth. I'm Chance Harrington, and with me, as always, is my best friend, Evan White."

An hour flies by with Evan and me bantering back and forth, and before I know it, Evan is doing our sign-off and turning off the live feed.

The stillness when the show ends is always a bit jarring. It's like the lack of talking is so loud, almost roaring in my ears, and my whole body feels on-edge like I could take on the world.

"Great show, man," I tell Evan.

He leans back in his chair, hands behind his head with his elbows spread wide, and grins. "Yeah, I'm pretty good like that," he agrees.

I chuckle at his teasing brag as I grab my phone. We have a

hard and fast rule that we keep phones silent and out of sight while we're on-air, so I'm not surprised that I have a bunch of notifications. But the texts from my brother, Carter, do surprise me.

*You available tonight? Got something to show you, but Luna and I are taking Gracie ice skating. Swing by the rink around 7?*

There are two more with the same basic message. Guess he didn't bother to tune in to the live show today, not that he ever does. Or the on-demand versions later. I don't think Carter's ever listened to one of my podcasts, or if he has, he's never mentioned it. And he would, if only to tell me what I could've done better.

Carter's my older brother, not quite the golden child of the family since that would be Cameron. But Carter's definitely the silver child, and though I'm third in line of our siblings, I'm not the bronze. That honor falls to my sister, Kayla. Then tied for no medals, there's Kyle, the black sheep, Cole, the vanisher, and me, the dismissed.

*Yeah. See you at 7.*

I send the reply, not expecting anything further. Whatever Carter wants, he's probably already made the assumption that I'll be there. He's used to people jumping whenever he says to, even if I'm not one of those people. But he threw out the bait he knows I can't refuse—my niece, Gracie, and Carter's wife, Luna. Our whole family protectively rallies around Gracie at all times, ever since Cameron lost his wife, but it's admittedly a bit like playing hot potato because she's with a different family member nearly every day. And Luna has my brother wrapped around her pinky finger, which is hilarious to watch because I never would've put the two of them together, but they make an odd but cute couple.

---

Walking through the front doors, I'm immediately hit with a blast of cold air. The Westlake Warriors aren't the best youth ice hockey program in the state, but they've got a nice facility with a bright, clean entrance area that's separated from the ice by thick Plexiglass, and cream-colored tile is on the floor before you get to the skates area.

Glancing over, the ice is busy, but not so crowded that you can't move, except along the boards in a packed oval. In fact . . .

"Hey!" a familiar voice calls out. "Uncle Chance!"

A smile breaks out on my face, and whatever Carter's got planned fades away as my niece comes clumping across the rubber matted area of the lobby, barely staying upright in her ice skates. I meet her more than halfway to gather her up into my arms. "Ooof, you're getting big, baby girl!" I say as I shake her around until she giggles. "How'd you get so tall when I just saw you a couple of days ago? You must've grown three inches at least!"

"It's my skates, silly!" Gracie says, grinning.

I feign complete surprise and confusion and grab her leg, holding it up to stare at her ice skate as though I've never seen such a marvelous invention. "This? They make you taller?"

Shaking her head, she laughs hard. "No, they make me skate like an ice princess," she explains with a tilt of her head, looking at me like I'm completely stupid.

"Ah, mm-hmm. I see," I say in my best mad scientist impression.

"You're my favorite uncle," she whispers.

"Heard that, young lady," Carter says behind me.

Gracie's eyes go wide. "Oopsie! I meant you're all my favorite uncles, and I'm your favorite girl, right?" She might as well be batting her lashes at Carter, but the best part is that if he doesn't agree, she'll flip the script to threatening to take out his kneecaps. Gracie's learning from the best of the best and is skilled at knowing when to charm, when to threaten, and when to cut your losses.

"I think she should be a lawyer," I note to Carter, who nods agreeably.

"Or a politician," he adds out of the side of his mouth where only I can hear him. "Gracie, can you go check on Luna for me? She's not the best skater and could probably use a little cheerleader hype from my favoritest ever girl."

Gracie beams, proud at the assignment and the title Carter bestows, and clomps off to do his bidding.

"Well played," I praise.

Carter glares at me, one brow lifted in a 'shut the fuck up' move. "Come on, Zack's here too."

Carter directs us to a table where Zack, his best friend and sometimes business partner, is peering at a stack of printouts. His glasses have slid down his nose, but he's too focused to push them up, instead running his hands through his hair. I wonder if he realizes how much he looks like his sister right now, who has episodes where she falls into her graphic novel world and seems almost crazed with the alternative reality.

"Hey, man!" I say, not sure if he'll hear me. But he looks up easily and smiles.

"Good to see ya. Check this out, guys." Zack turns one of the papers around to show us a real estate listing. "This is gonna be my next deal."

A quick glance tells me that it's a commercial property. I'm familiar with the area because it's not too far away from the Gentlemen's Club headquarters. "Staying in the area?"

Zack is a professional real estate investor and developer, and he actually found the building we renovated into the club. Instead of investing himself, he charged us a small finder's fee. Evan and I made the buy, and now we have our dream set-up. I'm not surprised Zack found another prospect nearby, considering the neighborhood is going through a major rejuvenation.

"Yeah, wanted to see if you might have any insight on the seller or property?" he asks me. "Because it looks like a quick flip. In and out in a month or two, tops," he tells Carter. I guess this one is a joint venture for them.

"Sorry, never even driven by it, so I don't have any top-secret insider hints to help you make a deal," I say. "But make sure you sell to someone who'll be a good neighbor," I warn.

Truth is, I'm not worried about any potential purchaser being good for us, I'm more concerned they'll be understanding of our business model and not call the police on the 'herds of young men gallivanting around the streets' as our members have been called.

"Will do," he promises.

They keep talking about the property, and slowly, my attention wanders to the ice full of skaters. I see Luna making her way around the oval, her arms outreached for balance, and I can't help but smile at the unsure way she's wobbling.

My smile melts a moment later, though, when I see Gracie skating smoothly and holding hands with a dark-haired, beautiful woman in painted-on jeans, an ivory V-neck T-shirt, and a stack of gold necklaces against the bare skin of her chest.

Skin I've touched. Skin I've tasted.

"What the fuck?" I murmur, the unusual curse word falling off my tongue easily and garnering Carter and Zack's instant attention.

"What?" Carter asks, his eyes following my gaze and likely thinking he'll see Gracie doing something outlandish he'll have to apologize for.

"The woman . . . Sam . . . what's she doing with Gracie? What's she doing here?" I'm stammering, a blend of confusion, worry, fear, and shock swirling in my gut.

What's going on? How is Sam with Gracie? Did she follow me, stalk me, or something even more sinister? I've received some awful hate mail but never been a target like this . . . where a woman shows up with my family after a hook-up. Or what if she was a set-up all along?

I'm up and dodging the crowd on my way to save Gracie in the blink of an eye. I step onto the ice in my shoes, fighting to stay steady and keeping my attention locked on my niece.

"Gracie!" I shout across the ice. She looks up, beaming with happiness and then laughing a little at me on the ice without skates. "Come here, now." My voice is sharp, garnering the interest of other skaters.

I hold my hands out, encouraging her to my side, but see her squeeze Sam's hand instead. For her part, Sam seems shocked to see me—her eyes wide, and her mouth open in an O—or at least she's a good actress. She pulls Gracie tighter to her side, almost protectively. But what's she protecting her from? Certainly not me.

She's the threat.

# CHAPTER 8
# SAMANTHA

I STARE in shock at the men standing at the edge of the ice. One is Carter, Luna's husband. Another, Zack, Luna's brother. And the third?

Chance. From last night.

He looks furious and terrified all at once, like he might shove me to the ice, grab Gracie, and make a misguided run for it across the slippery ice because he's actually *on* the ice without skates.

What is he doing here? And why is he with Carter and Zack? And most importantly, how the hell does he know Gracie's name? Because she might not be my actual niece, but I'll fight to the death before I let somebody kidnap her, even if she is a monster sometimes.

"What's going on?" I ask sharply as I skate closer, keeping a tight hand on Gracie, whose confidence is better than her ability.

Chance is wearing dark blue jeans, a black button-down shirt opened at the neck, and dress boots. I'm guessing this is his version of casual because this outfit doesn't include a tie. His hair is slicked back, his blue eyes are flashing, and his jaw is clenched tight.

"Come here," he repeats, and my body automatically responds to the order.

"Not *you*," Chance says, his narrowed eyes not missing my reaction. "Gracie, come here."

Luna skates up to my side, and Carter walks onto the ice, demanding, "What's wrong?"

"Get your hands off her," Chance orders, reaching for Gracie. He pulls her away from me, sliding her behind his back, effectively putting himself between Gracie and me.

"Hey!" I yell sharply. "What the hell, Chance?"

"You know him?" Luna asks me. "And you know her?" she asks Chance.

"We met yesterday," he tells her flatly, though his eyes never leave mine.

"Wait. You're the . . ." Luna gasps, turning toward Sam. *Sex god*, she mouths, putting two and two together instantly. "Oh, my God! Sam, do you know who he is?"

"Chance?" I answer uncertainly, feeling like that's somehow the wrong answer.

"Yeah, Chance *Harrington*. My brother-in-law."

The world stops spinning, time stands still, and if it wasn't for my knees being solidly locked, I'd probably fall to the ice.

"No, he's not," I argue, hoping this is some joke. I did not sleep with Carter's brother, especially considering how very little sleeping we did.

"Guys, let's take this over here to discuss without an audience," Carter suggests. "Grace, can you skate with Zack for a minute?"

Zack blinks, glancing down at his non-skate covered feet, but then seeing Carter's grim expression, he nods and says, "Sure thing, man. C'mon, Gracie girl."

Once they walk-skate off, with Zack holding Gracie's hands so she can show off some new trick skills, Carter looks from me to Chance. He's a little slower at putting it together, but realization is dawning on his face too. Chance speaks first. "What are you doing here?"

Offended, I inform him, "I was invited by my best friend." Then I throw out an accusation of my own. "You didn't tell me your last name. And especially not that it's *Harrington*. I never would've . . ." I trail off, not saying what we did, but saying it all the same. Not that anyone needed confirmation when it's this obvious.

"I don't make it a habit to give out my whole resume . . . name, address, net worth, and social security number. Especially to women who run out in the morning."

Fire flashing between us, chests rising and falling with accusations and words unspoken, I'm confused as hell. It seems like Chance is too.

"Did you know? Is this some sort of stunt?" he asks quietly, and I can sense that this is his true concern.

"I had no idea who you are," I say as I shake my head wildly. "Falling on stage amid a sea of penises in front of a room full of people wasn't on my bingo card. Neither was going to your hotel room," I confess quietly. "Luna, I'm gonna go," I tell her, and then, as fast as I can, I skate off toward the far side of the rink where the lockers are.

I left Chance this morning, and now I'm leaving him again. *Chance Harrington*, I think, filling in his last name and trying to match it up with everything Luna's told me about the man. There's not a lot—businessman, started his own company, mentors young men, and is a good soldier type with rules, responsibilities, and expectations at the forefront of his mind at all times.

Except last night, that wasn't who he was at all. He was flirty and sexy, gentle and then rough, worshiping my body one minute and then pushing me to my limits the next.

Chance has taken the circular route that doesn't involve ice and meets me in the locker area. "Sam . . . Samantha?" he corrects himself. "If you'd said your full name, I might've realized, but Luna never calls you Sam. At least not to me. I didn't . . ." He shakes his head regretfully. "Can we talk?"

"About what? You're a Harrington. I sell sex toys. There's nothing to discuss," I summarize neatly.

"Except there is," he counters. "Like how soft your skin is, how I woke up wanting to drink you down this morning, and how after one night, you're all I've been thinking about." His words heat my body, but then the embers are dashed out when he adds, "What kind of witchcraft is that?"

I snort, trying to stay amused. "If you think that's witchcraft, you should spend some time with a coven because a hookup has nothing to do with it. I didn't sneak you a love potion, didn't bewitch you with my pussy or anything like that. I'm not playing some twisted game. More like the Sisters of Fate are fucking with me. I'm sure as shit not trying to trap you. I didn't even know who you were."

He's quiet for a moment, his blue eyes searching my dark ones, and then he sighs. "You left. Why?"

It's my turn to be pensive. "I didn't want to do the 'I'll call you' thing when I didn't think you would. I left so you wouldn't have a chance to string me along."

He's staring at me like I grew a second head out of my shoulder. Finally, he lets out a long, slow breath, then holds his hand out. "Let's start over. Hi, I'm Chance Harrington."

I look at his outstretched hand for a moment, not sure this a good idea, but with Luna, Carter, and Zack watching from afar, making more of a scene doesn't seem like a good plan either. So I shake his hand gently. "Hi, I'm Samantha Redding, but you can call me Sam if you want."

"Nice to meet you, Samantha." He says my full name with a little extra emphasis on it, daring me to correct him. "Would you like to go ice skating with me?" His face is completely straight, but I can see the joke teasing at his lips. We're at an ice rink and just had a big blow-up, so of course it seems like the only logical question.

Except it's not. At all.

This whole thing might've been a big mix-up, no real fault on either of our parts. But I still feel betrayed. It doesn't make sense, but his holding out on something as basic as his name feels like a big omission. Though it didn't occur to me to think that until I found out what his last name is.

And I'm no better, sneaking out the way I did. He should be running for the hills.

But he's heading for the desk where they rent skates, even

though I didn't agree. Visually, I measure the width of his shoulders, the taper to his waist, the long legs that I know are muscled and covered with blond hair. But what I'm really looking at is the man inside the sexy body, trying to figure him out.

Chance makes quick work of putting skates on, stands sure-footed, and holds his elbow out to escort me to the ice's edge.

"What are you doing?" I ask blankly. "This" —I move my hand between us— "doesn't make sense. Last night was great, but we both know what it was. It's okay to walk away."

"And if I don't want to?" he counters.

I don't have an answer to that. Instead, I find myself taking his elbow and letting him lead me onto the ice.

The din of the people around us is the only sound as we make a slow loop around the rink. I'm still trying to figure out how I ended up here.

Not literally, as in the ice rink. But with Chance Harrington.

I gave Luna so much shit when she got with Carter, but him? I threatened to feed Carter to a herd of pigs if he hurt her. Probably not the healthiest reaction I could've had, but I have issues with men after my dad's shenanigans, and ones with money? Even less trustworthy, in my experience.

I'm giving Chance a way out—no hard feelings, no harm, no foul. Why isn't he taking it?

"I'm remembering all the things Luna's said about you now," Chance says after a bit. "But I'd like to hear it from you. You're a student, right?"

"Yeah, I don't only sell dicks," I say dryly, assuming he's trying to make me into something I'm not. I'm not ashamed of my Bedroom Heaven sales gig, but it's not something most people have a positive reaction to. I've definitely learned that over the last couple of weeks, and given that Chance is probably replaying my stage fall and subsequent talk about sex toys, it's a logical leap. "Don't get too excited, though. I'm a psychology grad student, focusing on intimacy and relationship counseling. In other words, I'm gonna be a sex therapist."

I don't need a psychology degree to know I'm trying to scare him off. Testing him and pushing buttons to get a reaction like my very own, small-scale, single-subject science experiment.

"You'll be good at that," he replies evenly, not taking the bait. "What drew you to that specialty?"

I glare at him, mad that he's showing actual interest in me. Frustrated, I grit out, "Because when you choose someone to be your partner, you're giving them power over your heart, your head, your life, while also taking responsibility for theirs too. In little ways and in big ones. It becomes you, me, and we, so choosing wisely and making that relationship the best it can be is important. Intimacy, which isn't always about sex, is a cornerstone of that foundation for happiness." My answer is delivered as though we're fighting even though Chance hasn't said anything to the contrary yet.

"That makes sense," he says.

The too-simple response to something I'm so passionate about is another nail in Chance's coffin until he adds, "What if your partnership isn't built on 'you, me, and we' in that way, though? That's too idealistic, don't you think? For example, what about a marriage of convenience or companionship rather than for love, or for money and power? Not everyone is lucky enough to find some utopic, blissful, love-of-their-life connection."

Chance looks at me, skating smoothly as he gives a thoughtful, well-constructed argument. I, however, stumble. Both my feet and my brain, not having expected an intelligent, thought-provoking response. Especially one in which he effectively calls me a hopeless romantic, something I've never been accused of being.

I catch myself, finding my mental balance as Chance grabs me, his grip strong as he helps me reset physically. Both skates beneath me, I agree with him. "That can work, as long as both people have their eyes fully open about what their relationship is and isn't. Unfortunately, that's rare. More often, one person is giving their all, digging into their soul to support a person who's not invested at all, or only shallowly."

"Sounds like someone you know," Chance says wisely. He

hasn't let go of my hand since I almost fell, but it doesn't feel like he's unsure of my skating abilities but rather, just wants to touch me. It feels . . . good . . . warm and buzzy from where our skin touches, and my mind is a spinning tornado too, trying to make sense of every word he says.

I sigh and nod. "My dad. He cheated, left, and Mom had to pick up the pieces . . . of their relationship, of her own broken heart, of my and my sister's anger, of our whole life. It shouldn't be like that. For anyone."

"I'm sorry."

Two little words, but they patch a little rip in my soul that's been torn for a long time. Especially when Chance stops us and wraps his arms around me, hugging me tightly. Skaters pass by us on both sides, but I ignore them, sinking into him. It shouldn't matter—they're meaningless words from a near stranger—but they do.

Too soon, I pull back, swiping at my eyes though there are no tears, only the echoes of ones I've cried in the past. "It's okay. His loss, because Mom is doing great now, even dating again."

"You too. You're doing great too," Chance adds.

A skater breaks in between us, and I look down. "Uncle Chance! Skate with me! I love this song!" Gracie demands loudly. Not waiting for an answer, she grabs his hand and drags him off as the lights become a discotheque swirl of colors over the white ice.

He's grinning at Gracie, another one of the minions she has wrapped around her finger, but he glances up at me with a warm smile too. Realizing that Chance is way more complex than I gave him credit for, I smile back. I kinda hate that I misjudged him so harshly, especially when I hate it when people do that to me all the time. But he's made of sturdier stuff and is forcing me to give him a chance.

I'm glad.

I tune in to the music, realizing it's classic *Hip Hop Harry, Who's Next?* and the other skaters are chanting 'go, go, go Harry'. But instead of spotlighting someone in the middle of the rink, it seems like every skater is getting faster and faster, swooshing by me in an infinite race to nowhere.

I'm doing my best, but mostly, I'm watching Chance and Gracie. They're adorable, and when Chance swoops her up into his arms to skate as though they're dancing, I'm charmed beyond belief. He's skilled, obviously better at skating than most of the others on the ice, and when he moves them to the center, far away from everyone else, and spins with Gracie in his arms, happy laughter escapes from her in big belly laughs.

Suddenly, Carter is there alongside them, taking Gracie's other hand, and they have a niece sandwich, with her skating between both her uncles in the center of the rink.

It becomes a competition, each uncle showing off a move for Gracie as the remix goes on and on. From nearby, I hear Luna squeal with delight as she breaks out her phone and takes footage of the two uncles battling each other for their niece's heart.

I don't blame her. It's like an uncle show-off challenge and it's the cutest thing I've ever seen.

Chance, along with being a good skater, is actually a really good dancer, too. He does some lawnmower-starter and sprinkler moves, but on him, they look charming.

And then there's the bootie shaking, which is done with a silly smirk, showing he's not taking himself too seriously, but his ass doesn't get the memo and looks downright smackable as I skate past to stand beside Luna, who's still videoing.

But the hottest thing he does is the footwork. He's obviously played hockey or something because he's near-tap dancing on the ice, feet crossing over each other and blades gliding forward and back. I can only imagine what he could do in true hockey skates.

"Think they're going to measure each other's hockey sticks?" Luna questions with a grin.

"They already have. They're brothers. They've had each other figured out since they were kids—the buttons to push, the weak spots to exploit, and the strong points to use when convenient."

And then with a grin and eye roll, I add, "And yeah, they probably literally measured too. It's a guy thing, I hear."

Luna and I laugh at our own jokes.

I'm mid-laugh when a blast of pain shoots through my leg and I'm suddenly flying through the air. "What the—" My own outburst is cut off when I land ass-first on the cold ice with an *oof*! "*Shit!*" I hiss.

"Oh, my God!" Luna cries, dropping down beside me.

In the next instant, Chance slides up to me on his knees. "Samantha! Are you okay?"

"Yeah? I think so," I answer, but when I move my leg, sharp pain shoots through my knee and I cry out. "What happened?"

Luna explains, "A kid was going really fast and clipped you as he passed."

Chance is tenderly probing at my knee with sure fingers. "I don't think it's bad. Maybe sprained or twisted?"

I straighten my knee, noting that it feels weird and a little painful, but nothing I can't handle. "Help me up?"

Chance on one side and Luna on the other, they get me vertical on the slippery ice. I slowly and carefully put weight onto my foot, but my skate wobbles, which hurts my knee more.

"Nope, not doing that," Chance murmurs right before he scoops me into his arms princess-style and easily skates across the rink with me. "Coming through," he warns. Thankfully, people give us a wide berth, especially given that the blades of my skates are floating through the air at kid-height.

In the lobby area, Chance sets me on a bench and kneels in front of me to remove my skates and then his own. Seeing him kneeling before me would normally be sexy, but right now, I'm too focused on my knee and making sure that his pulling off the skate doesn't irritate it because it really hurts.

Luna, Carter, Zack, and Gracie surround us, and while Luna fusses about taking me to an urgent care, it's Gracie who makes me feel better.

"That kid was flying and plowed right through you! Like *ka-blammo!*" she says, offended on my behalf. "Want me to take him out for you? I can make it look like an accident."

"Grace!" Carter scolds. "That's not funny."

But I give Gracie a chin nod of appreciation. "Nah, I'm good. Or I will be. I'm made of tougher stuff than this." I wave my hand at my leg dismissively even though it hurts like a sonofabitch.

"So, urgent care or ambulance?" Luna asks me.

Shaking my head, I say, "Neither. I just want to go home."

"You heard her. We're out," Chance says as if there's any other option. He stands, scooping me into his arms once more. I hang on, my face nearly buried in his neck, where his spicy, woodsy cologne fills my nose.

We get a standing O as Chance stomps across the area with me in his arms. This could definitely be more discreet, but I'm also not complaining. Except . . . "Why are they clapping?"

"Sports thing. Applaud for the injured player as they leave the ice. Not into sports?" he questions.

"Nope."

He carries me outside into the still-blistering hot evening, and I scrunch my face from the sudden heat after the cold ice.

Chance approaches a sporty, matte-black, two-door Lexus, something fancy and sporty but not ridiculously so, and swings the passenger door open while balancing me in his arms. He crouches down to set me inside and buckle the seatbelt.

"I could get used to this," I tease. "A little bump and suddenly, I'm royalty."

Chance's brow furrows. "You should be treated this way all the time, Samantha."

Shocked at his matter-of-factness about something that definitely doesn't happen, I stare at him open-mouthed. Oblivious, he stands, closing the door carefully to make sure he doesn't slam a door handle into my knee and running around to the driver's side. Once buckled in himself, he drives off into the night.

But he doesn't ask for my address. Instead, he confidently drives me somewhere else . . . straight to his place.

# CHAPTER 9
# SAMANTHA

MY KNEE HURTS, but I think I owe that speed demon of a kid a hearty thank you because his skate-by assault got me here.

To Chance's condo.

When he scooped me up to take me home, the expression on Luna's face stood out to me. It was a combination of *you go, girl* and *be careful*!

The ride is mostly a blur as I try to figure out why Chance is so devotedly steadfast to taking care of me when last night was supposed to be a one-and-done. He seems overly upset at the minor injury, too—his jaw set in stone, his hands gripping the steering wheel, and if I so much as move, his eyes jump to my face, reading it for any sign of a worsening condition. If that kid had been an adult, I'm not sure what he would've done.

"I'm okay," I reassure him.

"I know."

If he knows I'm fine, he's sure not acting like it. He whips into a space in a private garage, throws the car into park, and is around to my side of the car in a blink. He picks me up again, and instead of arguing that I can probably walk on my own, I go with it, deciding to see where this leads.

I told Chance to try new things, so maybe I should take my own advice. Though it's a little tragic that being respected and treated well is a novel experience. But I'm not going to look a gift horse in the mouth.

He carries me to the elevator and says, "Reach in my back pocket. Key card's in my wallet."

I do as instructed, holding a blue card up to the scanner and pressing the button for the fifth floor when he tells me. When the doors open again, it's directly into Chance's condo, so I guess he has the whole floor.

I don't get much of an opportunity to look around as he strides to the couch and sets me down on the buttery soft, warm brown leather. All I can see are the floor to ceiling windows along the far wall, which likely look out over the city, though they're covered by linen curtains right now.

Chance props my knee up with a pillow, but for an unknown reason, it's not to his liking, and he takes the pillow back out, fluffs it, and then slips it beneath my knee again.

I can't help but smile at his nursing skills. "You're good at this."

It's a statement of fact, but he shares as though I asked a question. "Me and my brothers were basically live-action WrestleMania when we were kids, except it was all real, not choreographed fakery. And more often than not, we wanted to hurt each other for some imagined wrong or slight. Stupid kids always wanting to be king of the mountain," he finishes with a look of humor in his eyes. A moment later, it evaporates. "How're you feeling?"

"Think I'll have to cancel my morning run tomorrow," I deadpan. His eyes jump to mine, the worry plain to see. "Kidding," I promise. "Occasional yoga? Yes. But I don't run unless it's to catch the alcohol truck on campus."

"The what?" He looks concerned I might've hit my head, given the gibberish I'm talking. But it's a real thing.

"Think ice cream truck, but for stressed-out college students. Randy drives through the quad, playing early 2000s hip-hop, and people run out from every direction—from housing, classes, the cafeteria, and more—to get in line for a beer or White Claw.

When the weather's nice, he sells alcohol-infused Otter pops too. That's about the only thing I run for, and it's not often."

I'm laughing at my own laziness by the end of my explanation, knowing that I haven't run since . . . I don't even remember when.

"Alcohol truck?" Chance echoes, shaking his head. "What'll they come up with next? Is that even legal?"

"Don't know. Personally, I'm hoping for brownies on demand. You can get cookies all hours of the night, but brownies? Gotta make your own, and I don't have the time or patience for that."

He chuckles and steps back. "Let me get some ice."

When he disappears around a corner into what must be the kitchen or a bar area, I take the opportunity to look around. Everything is neutral, mostly charcoal gray, ivory, and brown. There are very few knick-knacks or things with any real personality, other than the shelves along one wall, which are filled with books that have been meticulously sorted by color and size. I wonder if he's read them all or if they're strictly décor?

"What do you think?" Chance asks, coming back with a Ziploc baggie of ice in his hands.

"It's pretty much what I expected," I confess. "Clean, non-offensive, luxury . . . clean," I repeat.

"I don't have kids and Grace never comes here, so it's easy to keep it clean." Something in the way he says it makes me realize that he takes care of his space himself. There's not a maid coming to pick up his dirty socks, and that's sexy in an oddly mature way.

I decide to test him about the books. Pointing at the wall, I ask, "Which is your favorite?"

He tilts his head, considering the entirety of each shelf. "Probably *The Hitchhiker's Guide to the Galaxy*."

I'm surprised, not only that he's read them all, which tells me something important about Chance—he's not only interested in appearances—but that his favorite is so lighthearted. I thought for sure it'd be something self-improvement based and super-serious like *How to Make Your First Million by Sixteen* or *Charm Your Way to A Cult Following*.

"I think my current most-read is the DSM-5. I'm basically memorizing it at this point," I joke. As he lays the ice over my knee, I say, "Thanks. You know I could've gone to urgent care."

"Or you could let me take care of you," he argues. His charming logic is faultless, so I lean back on the couch and let him gently probe around the ice bag at the edges of my knee, which is probably swelling beneath my jeans.

"You need to take these off so we can see how bad it is," he suggests, a dark thread of desire woven into his husky tone. If he thinks he's being subtle, he's dead wrong because I can read him like one of his books. He wants me.

I lick my lips, the space between us warming quickly. "Chance, you know what'll happen."

The warning falls on deaf ears as he reaches to undo my jeans. I'm not worried about me, but rather, him. He had mixed feelings after what we did, or at least how we did it, and I don't want to be something he regrets later. But he's a big boy, and given the surety of his fingers, I help him take my jeans off, being extra-careful over my knee.

He sits on the couch, pulling the pillow into his lap and laying my leg over it once more so he has an up close and personal view.

My kneecap is pink from the cold ice, but the surrounding skin is already bruising a slight purple color and it's a bit puffy. "Shit, Samantha," he rumbles as his fingers brush over the discolored skin. "You want me to run you a bath? You could sit and relax, see if that helps?"

I shake my head. "Not now," I say softly. "Maybe later."

He continues testing around my knee, his touch delicate but still building heat throughout my body. His pinkie finger dances up on my inner thigh, and I stifle a moan as my other knee falls open to give him space to move higher.

This is no longer about my injured knee. Not even zero percent about it. This is all about hunger.

My nipples are pearled up, their bra prison causing an ache as they demand to be let free. My panties are wet between my thighs, and I wonder if Chance can see that from his vantage point.

In a desperate attempt to slow this down and give him time to think, I force conversation. "The club meeting. I remember Luna saying you mentor young men. Was that what you were doing?" The staccato breathiness makes it obvious I'm fighting for control . . . of my own wild desires.

Chance doesn't slow his soft exploration of my thigh as he answers. "Mm-hmm. Our new club facility opened not too long ago, and hyping the guys up to keep coming, keep improving, keep growing is important. There's too many messages to the contrary, so it's a war I wage every day . . . for them."

Even with his attention locked on my inner thigh, he's brilliant. "Who are you fighting?" I ask huskily, running my foot along his thigh right up to the bulge filling his jeans.

"Toxic masculinity pseudo-gurus like Jake McGibbons, social media, news, religion, friends, and family. Even women because they get convoluted messages too. It's a big clusterfuck . . ." he says before his voice trails off and he focuses on the delights in front of him again. "Fuck, Samantha."

He's trying so hard to fight the good fight, to be a good man. Every day, and right in this moment. But those curses falling off his tongue tell me he's losing the battle and being overtaken by his dark, dirty desires.

Good thing that's exactly what I want.

I pull my T-shirt over my head, revealing the long cami I have on beneath. He groans, sounding like a wild animal in pain as he clenches his fists, trying not to touch me. "I don't want to hurt you." A breath later, he adds, "Your knee."

We both know that's not what he's talking about at all. Oh, he doesn't want to injure me further, but he's not thinking about a little bruise that'll be fine tomorrow. This goes deeper than that.

"My knee's fine, and I know what I'm getting into, Chance *Harrington*. I'm okay with another hook-up. Are you?"

I'm not above playing dirty to get my way, so as I ask the

question, I yank the neckline of my cami down, letting my breasts rest on top of it like a boobalicious balcony shelf. I tease my own stiff nipples, seeking some relief for the need coursing through me.

Chance reaches up, his fingers joining mine for a moment before he brushes me out of the way and squeezes my breasts roughly. I don't know why he's punishing me, or if it's himself he's punishing, but I don't mind. I like it . . . a lot. The delightful pain sends sparks through my body, straight to my core, and I feel myself growing even wetter.

"It's different now and you know it, Samantha. A semi-anonymous fuck in a hotel room is one thing. You're part of my family's circle. I know you. Not just what makes you come hard, but where your heart lies." Though he's talking about my heart, he's massaging my breasts—plucking and pinching my nipples, cupping their fullness, and kneading them sharply.

He's right. We do know each other better now, but that doesn't mean this has to have strings attached. We can still be two people who have amazing sex and then go on with the very busy lives we're passionate about.

"Please, I need it. I need you to fuck me," I beg unashamedly.

If you'd asked me if I would have sex with a Harrington, I would've laughed my ass off and said you were out of your mind. But Chance is nothing like I thought he'd be. He's kinder, sweeter, and smarter than I expected from a man born with a silver spoon up his ass, but also dirtier, sexier, and more generous with his time and attention to my body.

I do need to come. But equally as much, I need Chance to do it with me.

"Dammit."

He's up and off the couch in a blink, ripping his clothes off. "Turn over and lie flat. I don't want to hurt your knee."

More carelessly than I should, I pull my cami over my head and rip my panties off, then flip onto my belly, feeling the soft fabric of the couch tease at my nipples. With Chance behind me where I can't see him, the anticipation builds, especially when I hear the tell-tale crinkle of a condom wrapper. I'm probably leaving a puddle on his expensive couch, but instead of being mortified, I'm amused at the idea of marking his impeccably clean space.

When Chance's finger runs down my spine, I arch into his touch, lifting my ass as he swoops down my crack and into the wetness between my thighs. "I'm soaked for you," I say, even though I know he can feel it.

His finger slips inside me easily, and he leans over me to whisper in my ear. "I want you to lie there and do nothing. Just take me. Can you do that?"

I nod eagerly.

Chance throws a leg over me, his knees on the couch on either side of me as he hovers, nearly sitting on the backs of my thighs. He takes hold of my ass, gripping full handfuls of flesh and squeezing them harshly, almost pinching me. It's delightfully sharp, and I cry out, arching to give him even more access to my butt and even lower.

He shifts, and I feel his head at my entrance for a quick moment before he thrusts forward, filling me from behind with his big, hard cock. Chance grunts a primal, guttural sound as I welcome him into my body, stretching around him.

Moving his hands to my shoulders, he uses the leverage to stroke into me again with sure, deep thrusts that massage the front wall of my pussy, right where I'm most sensitive. "Good girl," he praises me, and wetness floods between us.

If anyone else dared to call me a girl, I'd bitchily correct them that I'm a full-grown woman who should be respected as such. But apparently, I have a praise kink where Chance is concerned, and his rumbly voice saying 'good girl' gets me to the edge near instantly.

"Ohmagawd, Chance. Fuck my cunt hard. Whatever you want . . . please . . ." I'm mumbling so much that I don't know if he can even understand me, especially with my face half-smushed into a couch pillow, but I hope he gets the point.

An arm wraps around my chest, lifting me slightly, and I glance back to see Chance looking wild-eyed and crazed. Prim, proper, well-mannered Chance has left the building, and in his place is Caveman Chance.

And fuck, do I like him.

There's a saying about men liking a lady in the streets and a freak in the sheets. I think the same holds true for me. Chance is a gentleman in public and a monster in private. I have a tiny seed of pride that I helped him find that part of himself.

"You want me to treat you . . . like a slut?" he asks gruffly. The word's not natural to him, but I see the way he licks his lips after, like he's tasting it, testing it to see how delicious it is.

I nod like a bobble-head. "Claim me, possess me, take me. Fuck my cunt with your big cock like I'm your slut."

It's more dirty talk than I've done before too, but it's turning me inside out as much as it is Chance. I'll examine why that is later, but right now, I want to see what Chance is going to do, feel what my body can handle, and explore new territory with him.

He shoves my chest back to the couch, gathering my arms behind my lower back to pin my wrists in one hand. I hear him spit on my ass and then feel his thumb swiping through it. "Gonna fuck this pussy with my thumb in your ass, Samantha. If you don't want that, you'd better tell me right the fuck now."

His thumb dips between my cheeks, swirling over my rosebud, and instead of stopping him, I say, "Do it."

His thumb pops through my tight knot easily. I'm so aroused, I think he could shove his cock inside my ass and I'd take it with no problem, so his thumb is nothing. Except when he starts riding me hard and fast, his dick slamming into me so deep that it scoots me up the couch, and with his thumb pumping in and out, it's everything.

I hang on as long as I can, wanting this edging to go on forever.

"You gonna come for me?" Chance pants, the words forced out in favor of breathing.

I nod senselessly, lost to the pleasure he's piling on my body as I'm forced to lie here and take it, unable to move my legs, my hips, my arms. But he's not using me like a fuck toy. No, he's giving as much as he's taking.

"Do it," he says, repeating the permission I gave him only moments ago.

It's all I need to fly apart. The room, the couch, even Chance disappear as I fall into a black void of ecstasy. Somewhere through the roaring in my ears, I hear Chance tell me, "Use that cunt to squeeze me like a good girl." And I do, wanting to please him, wanting make him feel as good as I feel.

"Fuck!" he grits out, spasming as he fills me over and over. I know he's wearing a condom, but the fantasy of him painting my pussy with his cum is filthy and sexy, and another, smaller aftershock orgasm rocks through me at the thought.

Sometime later—maybe a minute, maybe an hour, I have no idea—I come back to awareness. I'm fully flopped on the couch, one arm dangling toward the floor, the other balled up beneath my chest, with my legs relaxed. Chance is panting hard, his forehead pressed between my shoulder blades as he tries to catch his breath.

"Holy shit, Samantha," he mutters after he forces deep, shuddering breaths through his powerful chest.

Face still pressed to a couch pillow, I smile. "I don't think I'm Samantha anymore. Just Chance's cum slut . . . that's it . . . because . . . Wow."

A tiny laugh shakes me, and Chance pushes deep inside me. Though he's soft after that back-blowing orgasm, I don't want him out of me yet, either.

I sense his smile. "Should I remind you of that later when your sanity returns?"

He's hilarious. Because that's not who I am, and anyone who suggested as much would enter the find-out phase of the fuck-around-and-find-out process. But right now, it's the truth. I just want to lie here and luxuriate in what we've done.

"Only if you want me to remind you that you commanded me to use my cunt to squeeze your cock like a good girl," I tease as I look over my shoulder to catch his reaction.

Dirty talk is a strange thing. In the middle of sex, it's the hottest thing ever and crazy things will make you have a damn-near instant orgasm. But seconds later, when the haze clears, it sounds like a cringe-worthy PornHub script written by high school boys.

Chance laughs a little before more seriously asking, "You okay? Your knee? Your . . . the rest of you?"

I couldn't even tell you if I have knees right now, but I answer, "Yeah, I'm okay. You?"

He shifts on top of me, holding his weight up on his knees. "Other than needing a shower and food, I'm awesome." He pops my right ass cheek with a playful swat that sounds worse than it feels. "Come on, let's get cleaned up and then I'll make us some dinner."

Orgasms and dinner? I'm not going to argue with that. Ever.

# CHAPTER 10
# CHANCE

"I THINK your bathroom is fancier than any spa or gym one I've ever been in," Samantha says, noting the walls and floor covered in swirled marble slabs, the light wood vanity, and the huge shower enclosure with more heads than a car wash. "Not that there's been many, mostly just the gym at school and the spa I treated myself to when I finished undergrad."

"It works," I reply modestly. I take pride in my home, and I enjoy luxury, but my needs are also relatively simple. I'd be fine with a locker room shower as long as it was lukewarm. Thankfully, I don't have to be, though.

Because I wouldn't want Samantha in some jockstrap infested locker room. She deserves the best, which is why I'm washing every inch of her body, making sure the scented body wash lather gets absolutely everywhere.

"I could get used to this," she moans as I work shampoo through her hair.

"Warning or threat?" I ask with a smile she can't see because her eyes are closed in bliss.

"Both?" she answers, cracking one eye and peering at me cautiously.

I bet her eagle eyes don't miss much. But unlike last time, I'm not having second thoughts about what we did or how we did it. This time, I feel . . . great.

Maybe it's because of Samantha's positive reaction? Or maybe it's because I can't be too upset at anything that makes me come that powerfully?

"How about omelets for dinner? I make a mean spinach and feta version."

Samantha bats her lashes flirtatiously. "You cook too? How has nobody snatched you up?"

"Maybe I didn't want to get snatched," I counter. "Really, it's that the club has been my focus, priority, and obsession, so I haven't spent much time fighting off women."

That's not the whole truth, which has a lot more to do with my being an asshole teenager, a fuckwit college kid, and an adult with standards so ridiculously high that most women don't pass my first consideration.

Until Samantha.

Who doesn't meet any of my checklist, mostly because she took it, wadded it up, and lit it on fire. Metaphorically speaking. Though she'd probably do it literally if she knew there was such a list.

She tilts her head back to let the water rinse through her hair, and I press up against her, helping to sluice the suds out. "Tell me more about it? The club."

I gather my thoughts, wanting to give her more than the elevator speech I give most people, especially since she already knows the basics. "I was in college, surrounded by guys who were half-ass stumbling through every day, assuming they were going to be big shots after graduation, but they wanted to be treated like they already were." I chuckle, remembering one of the guys whose Daddy was a rich CEO-type and how he'd lead with that as if he had something to do with it. He'd literally introduce himself as Max Winston, of *the* Winston Warehouses. It'd worked okay for him until he pulled that shit on an actual prince who was at school on a diplomatic student visa and answered with, 'Prince Pietro, of *the* crown'. Max deflated pretty quickly at that, and no one would let him live it down, laughing and mocking him anytime he tried that shit again, especially if it was to get a girl.

"Competition for a place in the hierarchy is weird at that age. When I graduated, Evan and I talked a lot about how to have a positive impact. We came up with the club and the podcast and have been working our asses off ever since. He's the realist, the planner, and I'm the dreamer, the connector. We balance each other so that we can give guys a place to become their best selves. A little guidance, a lot of positive peer experiences, and a sprinkling of learning opportunities disguised as fun."

"Still sounds a bit like a cult, ya gotta admit," she teases, and I can't help but laugh.

"And you're still saying it wrong . . . *club*, not *cult*," I over-enunciate dramatically. "We have basketball courts, so it can't be a cult."

Snorting at my declaration, she disbelievingly clarifies, "That's the defining factor?"

Turning the water off and handing her a towel, I feign certainty and reassure her, "It is. You can trust me. I'm one of the leaders, so I wouldn't lie about an important distinction like that."

"Wanna know a life hack?" she asks, grinning so widely that I know this is a joke, not something serious. I nod, and as she dries off, she continues, "If someone tells you that you can trust them, nine out of ten times, you can't."

I press my lips together, fighting an answering grin of my own because, to be honest, I think she's right. But she's not done dropping a dose of her brand of wisdom on me, and I can't wait to hear the rest.

"If they say they're a good guy? *Ehnt!* Red flag. Nice guy? Totally gonna stalk you. Smart? Probably hasn't read a book since elementary school. Rich? Maxed credit cards and a credit score under five hundred. Tough? Total pussy who calls his Mommy when he has a cold. Honest? He lies so much, he doesn't even know what the truth is anymore."

She shrugs at the harsh judgments like they're no big deal, but I just learned a hell of a lot about Samantha Redding and what it takes to get through her walls. She might be half-joking, but that means she's also half-serious and those things are what she really thinks.

"So what I'm hearing is that I should tell you that I'm needy, messy, broke, jobless, stupid, and . . ." I pause, acting like I'm searching my memory, and then finish, "an asshole to have a chance with you?"

Her grin is bittersweet, and I wonder what stories she has in her past. "Unfortunately, once upon a time, yeah. Exactly that. Skinny jean wearing, tatted up bad boy, especially if you've got a bit of a stoner vibe? Step right up!" Lighter, she adds, "But I'm in my 'manifesting myself' phase, so I'm not even looking for someone right now."

It's like she's reminding me that this is just sex. Nothing more, nothing less. But that irritates me on a deep level I'm not willing to examine right now, because if we're nothing more than a hook-up, then why does the idea of some 'stoner guy' in her past make me want to hunt him down?

I'm not the casual sex type, usually. I've had a handful of relationships over the years, all of which ended when the woman, who swore she was fine with the amount of time I dedicate to my work, became significantly less fine with it. But I've had some relationships that were based on sexual compatibility too. Women I've dated solely because we scratched each other's itches and didn't want or need more than that.

I could see Samantha and me falling into that category, especially given she's discovering itches I didn't even know I had.

"Do you use your own products?" I blurt as I hand her one of my T-shirts to put on and grab a pair of boxers for myself. The question is a bit out of nowhere, more to do with the tract my thinking was on, not our conversation, but Samantha smirks evilly, rolling with it.

"Why? You afraid you didn't do a good job? Or you wanna watch?"

She looks fucking fantastic in my shirt, long legs sticking out, bare breasts pressed to the thin fabric, and I know her pussy is bare underneath too. Somehow, I find the strength to lead her past my bed and into the kitchen, immediately pulling ingredients out of the fridge for the promised omelet as she sits at the island.

"Watch. Participate. Whatever," I answer, going back to my question. "I'm curious."

"Pervert," she accuses, pointing at me with a damning finger, but her eyebrow is quirked up teasingly. "I like it."

"Sales 101, know your product inside and out. Especially given you have a product you can have first-hand knowledge about. It seems like that'd be helpful."

"Great, so what I'm hearing is you're volunteering to be my testing assistant and occasional test subject for the male-oriented devices." She acts like she's writing it down in an invisible notebook. "I'll have my people call your people. By the way, I don't have people. I'm it, a one-woman show."

And what a show she is.

A few minutes later, after some quick chopping, swirling, whisking, and flipping, I set two omelets down, and she gasps. "This looks delicious! Definitely better than what I was gonna have tonight."

"Which was?"

"Whatever frozen dinner is on the top of the stack. Microwave four minutes, and voila, dinner is served." I cringe, thinking that sounds awful, but she bumps my shoulder for the obvious judgment. "It's protein and veggies in a convenient package, thank you. Not all of us have fridges recently stocked with fresh spinach. Some of us have that week-old bag that's already turned to brown sludge and glares at us in disappointment every time we open the door to grab a two-a.m. desperation cheese stick."

I make a mental note to add cheese sticks to my grocery list. Just in case.

I've only eaten a few bites when I hear a strange noise coming from the living room. "Excuse me," I say, setting my fork down to go investigate. I find my phone going nuts on the coffee table with an alert from the club's alarm system.

"Dammit," I grumble, frustrated at the interruption but also worried about the alarm. It's new, one of our recent renovation updates. So odds are, this is a false alarm. But I have to check it out. "I gotta go to the club. Sorry. But I can drop you at home on the way?"

Samantha's eyes narrow, and she hops up from the stool, forgetting about her hurt knee. She hisses, shifting her weight to her good leg, and I automatically reach for her to keep her from hitting the floor.

"You good?"

"Hell no, I'm great because I'm going with you to see what this place is all about." She's wiggling her knee back and forth and seems to be doing better already because she reaches over the couch for her jeans. "Unless its 'no girls allowed'? Which, to be clear, is *so* late-1900s and not acceptable today."

I flash an apologetic smile. "We actually don't allow female members, but it's after hours, so I guess you can come with me." I act like she's twisting my arm and I'm doing her a favor, but I'm not ready to end this . . . date? Or whatever this is.

I'm breaking the Gentlemen's Club's number-six rule, which is no female members or visitors, but considering I wrote the rules, I can also choose when to break them.

"That's what I thought. Wise choice, Mr. Harrington," she declares with a triumphant smirk.

"You're a bad influence."

She pats my bare chest a little too hard as she says, "You have no idea, but you like it. Let's go."

―――

The drive to the club is quick and mostly spent on the phone, reassuring the alarm system security company that I don't want them to roll police just yet. I'm gambling that it's a false alarm because there's a hefty service fee for the police coming out. I'd like to avoid that if I can. I might have money, but I'm not in the habit of throwing it away for no reason.

Pulling up to the freshly-painted, renovated space, I'm half scanning the white brick for graffiti, black framed windows for cracks, and double front doors for any sign of entry, and also watching Samantha's reaction to what she sees. This building, the club, is akin to holding my baby up for inspection, and if she says one critical thing, there'll be no going back.

But she's looking it over with concern too, like she cares about the club because she knows it's important to me.

I don't see anything worrisome, though, and everything seems to be in order. I park in the empty lot, right by the door. "Wait here. Let me check it out first."

I should've known better than to tell Samantha to do anything, at least outside of a sexual encounter, because she laughs. "Yeah, right, Batman."

She opens her door, and I'm stunned in place for a split second before I jump out too. But by the time I get around, Samantha is prepped with a stun gun in her hand. "Let's go, Batman."

"Where the hell did you get that?" I hiss, trying to keep my voice down in case there is someone inside. It's not like there's anywhere she could've stashed it that I haven't seen.

With her empty hand, she gestures at herself and enlightens me like I'm an idiot. "Female, student, on campus at all hours, where guys think a dark parking garage is a good time to hit me up. I'm not stupid, I'm gonna do what I can to keep myself safe, so I keep this in my purse. It's legal, and I'm trained."

She's answering all my questions before I answer them, but the idea that campus isn't safe enough for Samantha to walk from class to her car without confrontation makes me angry as hell. That's something I'll have to address later, with her and with the club guys who are students. Maybe they can do a Gentleman escort on demand or something for students who don't feel safe walking around campus?

I table that idea because for now, I have to focus on the club. "Alright, Wonder Woman. Let's do this."

I unlock the front door and open it carefully, keeping Samantha behind me as I peer inside. She does at least allow that and doesn't go charging in, stun gun snapping and crackling in front of her with a warrior's whoop of attack. I would've bet that'd be her style.

Not seeing anything suspicious, I put the code into the panel by the door, shutting off the silent alarm. In my pocket, my phone vibrates, noting the activity.

"This is the part where you offer me a tour," Samantha whispers. I cut my eyes her way and find her grinning like this is some sort of crazy, fun adventure.

Which it's not. This is dangerous, or potentially dangerous, at least.

So why do I feel myself smiling back at her?

Slowly and methodically, I lead Samantha around the clubhouse like we're an investigative team of two. The front desk is undisturbed. The weight room is cleaned up, with everything in its place, and Samantha picks up a ten-pound dumbbell to do a couple of bicep curls. I glare at her, and she sets it back down, precisely in place, with a sheepish look, though I don't think she's sorry in the slightest. The class area is clear, the locker room is empty, and even the bathroom is surgical-level disinfected.

I'm beginning to consider an electrical surge or some sort of wiring issue with the alarm when a sudden crash makes that idea poof into the ether.

"What was that?" Samantha whispers as she grabs my shirt, twisting it in her hand and holding the stun gun out at an invisible enemy.

I look at her wryly, one brow raised. "How should I know? I'm right here with you," I answer pointedly.

Not liking that, she lets me go, straightens her back, and starts toward where the sound came from. I stick my arm out, stopping her. "Hell no. Get behind me."

It's not some chauvinistic initiative or doubt in her skills with the weapon she's holding in front of her at the ready. It's that this building and what it stands for are my responsibility. If there's a threat, it's to me and mine.

Following where the sound came from, I can hear the

quietest crinkle of plastic packaging. "The vending machine area," I whisper.

We tip-toe to the doorway of the dead-end area where we have a bank of snack machines. I hold my hand up, stopping Samantha. "On three," I mouth, and she nods. "One, two, three!"

I leap into the doorway, fists up to fight. "Freeze!"

Samantha jumps out with me, by my side even in a bad situation. "Hiii-yah!"

But there's not an intruder looking to rob the club. Or at least not in the way I worried.

It's a raccoon who lazily turns his eye masked face toward us, looking annoyed at our interruption.

"Aaaaaah!" Samantha screeches, virtually teleporting into one of the dining chairs at the couple of tables we have set up for people to eat their snacks. Crouching there, she points at the raccoon to make sure I'm seeing him. As if I could miss him.

He's roly-poly fat, obviously well-fed, and laid back against one of the vending machines with a bag's worth of M&Ms scattered around him. The lure of the candy is probably why he doesn't so much as flinch at our loud appearance. She's acting like he's going to rabidly attack her, while he's looking at us like ''Sup?' and ready to offer me a blue M&M.

I can't help but laugh at her overreaction to the cute critter.

"It's okay," I reassure Samantha, holding calming hands out to her rather than the animal. "He's more scared of us than we are of him."

"Agree to disagree!" she shouts.

As if teasing her, the raccoon plucks a green M&M from the floor, looks at it, and then nibbles it from his black, too-human hand. He's not scared at all. He's chilling as if this is his place and we stocked his pantry, then interrupted his solo snack party.

Deciding the raccoon is the least of my worries right now, I reach a hand to Samantha. "Come on down." Awkwardly, she takes my hand and steps uncertainly to the floor, but her eyes are locked on the critter as if he's going to fly up from his M&M

stash to attack her with grabby paws and snapping teeth. "You're fine."

Once her feet hit the floor, she ducks behind me, her face pressed to my shoulder. I can't help but grin at her dramatics. This woman is badassness personified, but she's terrified of a raccoon who can't be bothered to run when approached by humans?

"Hey there, Rico," I purr soothingly, giving the raccoon an impromptu name. "How'd you get in here?" Construction and remodeling have been done for months now. Has Rico been trapped in here this whole time, or is he coming and going in some way we haven't discovered? If he has a secret door, it'd have to be a pretty big one to fit his belly.

"More importantly, how do you get him out?" Samantha asks.

I pull out my phone to look up pest control companies that do all-nighter calls and dial the first one I find. After waking up a grumpy, grumbling man, I explain the situation and he tells me he'll be here asap. I have no doubt that his trip will involve a pit stop for coffee and it'll be a while before we see him.

We settle in to wait, sitting in chairs, though Samantha chooses one furthest away from Rico and pulls her legs up into the chair. Trying to seem cooler with the whole situation than she obviously is, she teases, "Even your intruders are male. Guess I should be flattered that I'm the only woman allowed entry." She points over to Rico, who's got his back legs spread to the sky, making his furry belly and balls glaringly obvious.

"There's a joke in there about manspreading, but you're right. You're the proof that I don't always follow the rules," I offer. "Not sure I'm going to shout that from the rooftops, though. There's something to be said for thoughtfully breaking a rule when you keep most of them at all times. A calculated risk." After a moment, I add, "The guys here? Some of them break rules regularly, like it's the only way they know to live. The mere existence of a rule chafes them. They're the ones I try to reach, to show how rules can be good for them."

"Yet here we are, breaking all the rules," Samantha says with a satisfied smirk. "You gonna show me your office after we get Rico evicted? And your big . . . hard . . . *desk?*" She laughs, proud that she's got me on a short hook because I was not thinking about my desk and we both know it.

Fuck, I think I might be breaking a few more rules before the night is through.

# CHAPTER 11
# SAMANTHA

RULE NUMBER *ONE* OF HOOKUPS: Don't text him. It shows you're potentially clingy, which I'm not.

However, I'm having a hard time sticking to that rule because it's been a few days since Chance dropped me to my car after our Rico the Raccoon adventure. I've been hovering over my phone to see if he would message me and talked myself out of at least three different possible conversation starters I could text him.

*Knee's feeling much better. Should I expect a Dr. bill for the 'house call'?*

*You up?*

Another idea is a GIF I found of a raccoon wearing a party hat and confetti . . . a surprise Rico, if you will.

Of course, none of those are going to work. One makes it sound like I'm paying for dick, two is desperate, and three is stupid. All potential red flags.

I could just be honest—*10/10 dick, would ride again!*

But I'm pretty sure that'd have Chance blocking my number, not to mention making any run-ins with Luna and Carter a bit awkward. I've talked to Luna every day, telling her everything because that's what besties do, and she was blowing up my phone by eight a.m. after Chance swept me out of the ice rink, wanting immediate answers. And a good story.

She was shocked when she connected my story about the

hotel sex god with her brother-in-law, but when I told her about him blowing out my back again, she nearly crawled through the phone to shake me in excitement. For me, it confirmed that he's as straight-laced as she's always said he is, and this thing between us is a boundary-pushing adventure. For us both.

And could happen again . . . if he'd text me. Or call. Or send out a fucking smoke signal. I'd be there with nipple clamps on, ready to go.

"I'm pouring out my guts here, bitch, and you're off in la-la land like I'm boring you to death," a voice says, breaking into my reverie.

I'm lost, imagining ways I might get Chance back inside me, beneath me, or on top of me, but when I blink and focus, I find four pairs of eyes peering at me. Three look curious, but one is furious.

"Sorry, Natasha. You were saying that your date went well?" I'm echoing the bare bones of what she's been ranting about for the last ten minutes because I honestly quit listening when she started repeating the same concerns over and over in a loop despite any advice to the contrary.

She huffs, "Not *well*. Immaculate. Perfection. Dream-like." She iterates every word with a wave of her hands, like she's doing magic in midair to bring them to life.

"But you don't trust it because you've been hurt," Sara adds, filling in for what I didn't say. She's got the trauma response on lockdown and knows it when she sees it, though we all see it in how Natasha's behaving. Truthfully, even she sees it in herself, but that doesn't mean she's ready to deal with it yet.

"Right! How can I? I mean, Josh is perfect, which nobody is, so I keep searching for the red flag, testing him at every turn. But he's all patient with me and shit, talking through my worries when I haven't even told him what they are." She looks downright offended at his caring response. "He even liked the Powerman 5K I got from Samantha and wasn't intimidated by it at all. Sat right there and sexily jacked off with one hand and flicked my bean while I took care of business with the vibe. Who does that?" She throws her hands wide, looking at us expectantly.

"You got that one?" Daphne gasps, grinning in carnal camaraderie. "I did too! Did you know it's waterproof? I tried it in the tub and almost drowned. *Glub, glub, glub.*" She makes a sound like her last breath is escaping from under the water and then grins. "Could've died, still would've been worth it."

"Even better with a friend," Natasha proclaims, stuck on Josh.

I did catch that she met him on campus when she was grabbing coffee in the central quad area. He's an employee, not a student, already well established in the computer science administration, and he's sexy, smart, and kind, according to Natasha. And thankfully, great in bed, because Natasha near immediately broke her proclamation swearing off men when she met him. Another selfish sex incident or ghosting like with her rugby player probably would've sent her to the nunnery. Instead, she's staring down a lifetime of happiness with a great guy and freaking out about it.

I tell Natasha, "You deserve good. You deserve a man who listens to what you say, hears what you don't, and responds accordingly to both. You deserve a partner who shows up for you, celebrates you—win or lose—and wants what's best for you. Maybe Josh is all that, or maybe he's not, but don't go in carrying baggage like a pack mule climbing Mt. Everest, letting your past taint your present or your future."

She glances up with glossy tears in the corner of her eyes. "Thanks, Sam. I'm just scared because I think he might be the one, but what if I'm not ready for my one yet?"

"Then you get ready. But also, don't be a greedy bitch," Katie adds. "You want him to do all that stuff Samantha said, you can't keep one foot out the door. You gotta give too."

"Who you calling a greedy bitch?" Natasha questions, her brows climbing her forehead and her tone turning sour. But she's kidding and a moment later, she's laughing with Katie. "Got it . . . no pack mule-ing and no greedy bitching. Be ready."

"Back to the Powerman 5K," Sara says, leaning forward to

meet my eyes. "How's business going? You feeling good about joining Jaxx with all this?" She's good, remembering my concerns and following up on any changing thoughts.

I consider carefully, but to be honest, the money makes it an easy answer. "Yeah, I hit my party goal and got my bonus. I really needed that, but I kinda hit up everyone I know to do it, so I've only sold around ten units since then. But I'm cohosting a party with Jaxx tomorrow in the community rec center, so that'll be big for sales, hopefully." Then I remember, "Oh! There's a new product if you want to look at the site. The Velvetream Rabbit." I pause as all three women scramble for their phones and start clicking into the Bedroom Heaven website. "If you want to order one, let me know and I'll do a special delivery to you after tomorrow's event."

"Put me down for one," Daphne says so quickly that I'm not even sure she's gotten to the preview page yet. I guess she enjoyed the Powerman 5K so much that she's expanding her horizons.

———

A party is a party is a party, I tell myself. But this community rec center set-up is approximately two percent like our deal at the Bedroom Heaven quarterly party.

"Are you sure we're going to get any traffic here?" I ask Jaxx.

She doesn't look up from the banner she's fidgeting with as she answers, "For the tenth time, yes. This place is full of orgasm-starved people at lunch time. Today, they're going to get a little extra pizzazz with their study sesh."

I hope she's right, but whether she's right or wrong, this party's happening, so I need to do my part.

I lay out our sample products on the table, along with the pink name placards, then organize the bins so that we can fill orders easily. We've even got an area to wrap purchases up with silver foil tissue paper and matte black bags to make it look special. Because everyone deserves a little gift for themselves!

But beyond our table, the rec center looks about as festive as a library. There are a bunch of empty round tables, a high bar along one wall with privacy dividers, and some tall plants beside a water feature that's probably supposed to be soothing but makes me need to pee every time I see it. Add in some industrial carpet, fluorescent lighting, and a guy who keeps hushing people for simply existing, and we've got party central. Or at least it is according to Jaxx.

"Yeah, that one'll get you there, guaranteed," Jaxx promises a girl a bit later. "It's heavy duty, though, so don't get addicted or you'll never be satisfied with a plain old, boring dick." She winks, and the girl grins back, handing over her credit card happily.

"Not a problem. Don't want or need one of those. Ever," she retorts.

Thankfully, Jaxx was right and I should've trusted her more because we've been swamped with customers. Sure, some have been looky-loos, but that's still a win because we've been pimping the QR code for the catalog like crazy, and some of those people will likely place orders later from the privacy of their own homes. But even if they don't, the ones who've been interested have been buying.

Jaxx is definitely a flashier salesperson, touting horsepower and pulse modes, but I'm holding my own, talking to customers about their specific needs. We agreed to go fifty-fifty on the profits and sales credits for the party, and I think my share is already up to a few hundred dollars. I can't believe this, both how much money I'm making and how many people I'm helping.

But it's not all party-fun-times.

There's a table of guys who've been eyeing us for the last half hour. They're not bothering us, exactly, but the attention and laughter from them aren't making our sales any smoother, and we've definitely had less traffic since they took up residence. Nobody wants an audience staring them down while they choose a toy.

Which is why I'm leery when one approaches. The last thing I need is to deal with some fuckboi.

"Hey, uh . . . do you have any . . . like, uh . . . butt plugs? My buddy over there needs one. A real big one. Maybe one with like, uh . . . a tail attached?" He chuckles, sounding like Beavis, or maybe it's Butthead? Stupid, either way. "Yeah, cuz he's my . . . bitch. Like my dawg, ya know."

He looks back at his crew, who're grinning maniacally, probably having dared him to do this as some sort of testosterone-fueled challenge, and they all start barking loudly.

*Woof—woof—woof!*
*Awhooooo!*

Completely prepared and straight-faced, Jaxx whips out one of our rarely sold products. I didn't even know we had a sample of it. "Actually, yes. We have the Furry Friends Fucker, or Triple F, if you'd rather." She flips it around in her hand, showing the flared end to the gobsmacked guy. "See? This particular plug has a twist-to-attach mechanism so you can buy any of our tail accessories and switch them out with your mood. Dog today, cat tomorrow, or if you're really feeling spicy, we have a dragon one that's scaled for your partner's pleasure."

Having reached her limit of letting this guy think he's actually doing something, she gives him a pointed and withering look up and down and finishes with a scathing, "Though I don't think *you* could handle that."

I'm pretty sure the guy's brain is short-circuiting or something because his mouth is opening and closing like a water-starved fish. He doesn't know if he should be offended by Jaxx's assessment that he can't handle a dragon tail or thankful that she doesn't think he's some sort of furry because in his little mind, that's strange.

Not having the mental strength to come up with anything better, he swats Jaxx's hand away. "Shut up, slut," he snarls angrily.

It definitely doesn't help that Jaxx laughs loudly as he stomps back to his friends with his metaphorical tail between his legs.

"You can use the QR code to order secretly so your bros don't know," she calls out after him.

"Jaxx!" I hiss, pulling her back. "Don't get us kicked outta here."

"He's the one who should get kicked out. I'm not kink shaming. I showed him what he asked for. He's the one who thought asking for a butt plug was gonna be some big woo-hoo deal." Jaxx brushes off her shoulders. "And I for damn sure will not let some douche nozzles shame me, or our customers, because their minds are littler than their dicks."

She's right, but the scene has still scared off most of our customers, though we now have a wider audience watching the show.

"I didn't know we had that," I say, pointing at the plug still in her hand.

"Yeah, it's not a best seller," Jaxx admits, "but you know what they say, there's something for everyone."

She's putting the goodies into a bin beneath the table when a male voice says, "I changed my mind. I wanna get that thing."

I flick my eyes up to find the same guy standing at our table, but in the next instant, it registers that he's got his whole crew with him. One blink and they've all grabbed various products from our table, nearly clearing it of samples.

"Dude, what kinda whore can fit this monster in her cooch?"

"What are these antennae things?"

"Catch!"

The guys are holding up vibrators and dildos with their gross commentary, tossing them to each other keep-away style and laughing raucously. One goes sailing across the room, slapping into a window with a thud.

"Hey! Asshole! What the fuck?" Jaxx screams. She makes a dive for one of the guys, trying to get back the pink dildo he's wielding like a sword.

He dodges and laughingly shouts, *"En guarde!"*

Another bro-type holds his vibrator up like a sword, and they start smacking them together. There's a joke about crossing swords and repressed urges in there, but I can't laugh right now. Not when our product samples are going everywhere.

*It's raining dicks!* plays through my head to the tune of *It's Raining Men* as another flies by.

"Give that back!" I shout at another guy who's waving a double-ended toy over his head like a spinning helicopter blade.

He flashes a too bright, Crest-commercial smile my way, having entirely too much fun with this. "Make me."

He holds the toy straight up into the air, using his height against me and smirking down at me victoriously.

But I'm not some stupid nitwit that'll jump to reach something, making my breasts bounce for this asshole's enjoyment. Nope, instead I lift my knee up sharply, feigning that I'm going to forcefully introduce his nuts to my kneecap. He jerks reflexively, curling in to protect himself from the assault. But I was never going to actually do it. I just wanted him to bend down so I could reach the toy.

I rip it from his hand, and one end smacks across his cheek. Shock and anger flash in his eyes, but the shouts of his buddies draw his attention away from me.

"Let's go!" one of them yells, and they all take off like it's a coordinated withdrawal. What the fuck, this isn't Lululemon!

Jaxx isn't done, though, because they're stealing our merchandise, running away with it held high in the air like phallic trophies. She gives chase, taking the direct route and stomping up onto a chair, table, and then another chair to get down on the other side, her boots clomping loudly with each step.

"Give those back! If you want to fuck yourself in the ass, you gotta buy one like everyone else, Chad!" she screams after them.

We both try our best, but the guys get away with our products.

"What the fuck was that?" Jaxx snaps at no one in particular.

"Assholes, that's what," I answer angrily.

We make our way back to the table, which is in shambles. I pick up tissue paper, trying to stack it into some semblance of order to distract myself from the stupidity that just took place.

"Son of a bitch!" Jaxx hisses.

"What?"

"They took stuff from the supply bins too. Look." I follow

where she's pointing and see the totes that we stashed under the table have been opened and rummaged through.

"No! How much?"

Jaxx purchased all the merchandise in those bins, and we have to sell it to make a profit. If it's stolen, we lose the money. It just poofs into thin air, leaving us in the red.

"I'll have to do an inventory, compare what I bought with what we sold, but . . ." She looks up at me, and even with her heavily made-up eyes, I can see pure fear in them. "I think it's a lot. A thousand at least, maybe more?"

My stomach flip flops in my gut. I just got the bonus money, paid some bills, and banked a little, and now this? All because some Chad-bros thought they'd be funny.

"We need to call campus security," I say, and Jaxx nods.

---

"So let me get this straight," the campus security officer says slowly. He's tall, rail thin, and too baby-faced for me to comfortably talk about sex toys with. He looks like he's not even old enough to have graduated college himself yet, let alone be security at one.

Although, that also might have to do with the fact that he's grinning like this is some sort of joke as he manhandles what's left on the table of our merchandise. "Some guys grabbed your winkie-dinkies and bolted for the door?"

A snort comes from nearby, and Jaxx and I simultaneously turn a glare on the officer's partner, a big, burly man who's Officer Friendly's exact opposite, with ruddy red cheeks who looks like he's two steps from the grave. At our matching glares, he schools his face into an empathetic frown and clears his throat, standing at what I'm guessing is his version of attention —rocking back on his heels and placing his hands on his impressive paunch.

We expected them to laugh at the incident at first. I mean, I get it . . . stolen dildos isn't exactly the most common report. I figured they'd get their jollies off and then actually help. But that's not what's happening at all.

Officers Pork and Beans can't get over their juvenile reactions long enough to actually do their jobs, and we're losing our patience.

"Yes!" we both snap in unison, turning our eyes back to the taller officer.

"That's exactly what we're saying," Jaxx snarls. "Which you would've heard if you weren't so busy laughing like a juvenile boy who heard the word vagina for the first time."

The tall officer narrows his eyes, not happy at the insult. "And just what exactly are you doing with that many of these, uh, *products*?" Rather than seeming like an attempt at professionalism, his tone makes our party goods seem even dirtier.

"Does that matter?" Jaxx snaps. "Who gives a crap why? It was our property and it was stolen. It doesn't matter if we're selling them, giving them away, or doing dick drawing classes with them. Mine!" She slams her palm to her chest and then does running fingers through the air. "Someone took." She finishes her dramatic and caveman-esque interpretation of the last fifteen minutes by drawing a finger down her cheek to indicate that she's sad about this whole thing.

"Actually, it could matter," the older officer says. "Y'all get approval to be selling this stuff on campus? I don't reckon administration would be too keen about all this . . . devilment." There's a threat woven into his assessment that I don't like.

"Are you kidding me?" I demand. "Everyone on campus is over eighteen. We're not doing anything wrong."

"Isn't there a law against having so many of these?" the tall officer asks, though it sounds like he knows the answer. But he's escalating—first, suggesting campus admin would have a problem, and now, the police.

"Nah, that's only in Texas," his partner says. "Can't have more than six there. Too bad that's not the case here, even though six still seems like too many if you ask me." He trails off, looking at the spread on the table like he wishes the restrictive law were in place here.

"If you're not going to do a damn thing, you can go," Jaxx tells them. Her arms are crossed over her chest in anger, but she manages to wave at them, telling them to shoo.

Indignant, they whirl on their booted heels and laughingly make their way off, bitching about us the whole way.

"I think Mr. Too Many Dicks, Can't Concentrate took a picture of the QR code on his way out," I tell Jaxx.

Even in her frustration, she's a salesperson. "I hope he's married, and his wife orders the biggest, fattest cock we've got, makes him watch while she uses it, and comes for the first time in her life. Because you know she never does with him."

The smallest hint of a smile washes across her black-painted lips at the satisfaction in her imaginary story.

"Seriously, though, what are we going to do?" I ask.

Jaxx takes a shaky breath in and forces a grim smile. "Sell our asses off. It's going to take a few weeks of our profit margin to offset this loss."

Shit. Just when things were looking up, the Sisters of Fate knock me down a notch. A big one.

I swear, if I die and meet those twisted bitches, we're gonna have a little chat about interference.

# CHAPTER 12
# CHANCE

"WANT TO HIT THE BASKETBALL COURT?"

"Maybe in an hour or two. I've got some homework to knock out first."

I overhear the comments from two of the guys as they come into the club and it fills me with pride. The club's booming with activity, and there aren't too many 'quiet' hours where we don't have members about. Whether they're coming after class, after work, before work, or whatever, the guys like coming here—to decompress, work out, network, or find someone to chat about life with.

But whatever their needs, The Gentlemen's Club has become that place, a grown up "boys club" that mixes self-improvement, mental health, and community. I never knew that combining all of those could be a successful business model, but I'm glad we took the risk because we're changing lives.

Unfortunately, it's not always copacetic.

A lot of the guys are still searching for their own identity, and clashing heads with other members is inevitable as they fight for rank. We've had to break up a few arguments before they descended into full-on brawls, but we expected that. Unfortunately, it's how guys assert themselves—like the tussles I had with my brothers as a kid, and then later, on whatever ball field we were conquering.

Overall, though, things are going smoothly. With the guys and with Rico, who's been rehomed to a far-away sanctuary where he can have all the healthy, raccoon-appropriate food he wants, AKA not massive amounts of chocolate candy.

Hopefully, there's even a few lady raccoons for him to meet.

"Hey, Lucas, you ready?" I ask as I enter the counseling area and find him sitting on the couch, picking at his cuticles.

One on one mentorships are one of the most personally satisfying things we offer, giving guys a chance to talk with Evan or me on a more personal level.

"I guess," he mumbles.

Not exactly a rip-roaring beginning to our session, especially considering he's the one who requested it. But getting these guys to open up is hard sometimes. Most of them have been brought up with a 'boys don't cry' mentality and don't want to show weakness, especially to another man. But it's my job to make them feel safe enough to share so that they're able to grow.

"Been hitting the bag?" As I sit down opposite him in a leather armchair, I point at his hands, where his knuckles have fresh redness on top of healing bruises.

Lucas nods, examining his hands. "The heavy bag in the gym's a little firmer than I'm used to."

"There are bag gloves you can use." I watch his reaction carefully, noting the slight downtilt of his lips. "But you already knew that and chose to bare knuckle it. How come?"

"I wanted to feel . . ." Lucas says, his voice fading. When I wave him on, he continues. "I wanted to feel *something*."

"By hurting yourself?"

"By being tougher than some fucking bag!" Lucas snaps, his eyes shooting fire directly at me as if I'm the one who made him feel weak. I've done no such thing, but I'm a target that he trusts to not back down from his worst. "Real men don't wear some pussy pads on their hands when they fight."

Humming thoughtfully, I counter, "I'm betting there's a few who'd disagree with you. Ali wore gloves. Conor McGregor wears gloves. They're real men, whatever that means. So what's this really about, Lucas?"

"What do you mean?"

"I mean," I reply, sitting forward, "what's making you worry about your tough guy quotient?"

It could be any number of things because guys worry about their toughness for a lot of reasons—being challenged, feeling out of control, facing something difficult, or even as a way to prove themselves.

Lucas opens his mouth, then closes it, not ready to share his thoughts yet. Facing a problem head on is something Lucas has avoided at all costs in the past. When he was struggling in school, his first response was to hit the weights harder than the books, and though he increased his bench press PR by thirty pounds, he failed a class he needed for his major. When his family was hurting financially, he complained about how his scholarship funds weren't enough to live on instead of getting a job to help support his younger siblings.

He always tends to run opposite of his problems when they arise.

But he's been working on it . . . and finally, he sighs. "Nora."

I lean back, taking the pressure off and giving him space now that he's talking. "Nora. What happened with her?"

Nora is a girl he's been interested in for a while, and we've talked about her a few times. But the way he says her name this time tells me that things are different now.

"Look, man, I tried to do what you said," Lucas says, frustrated and obviously hurt. "I tried talking to her, being respectful. I even fucking listened as she droned on and on and on about Taylor Swift's new album, like I give a shit. And then, when I asked her out, you know what she said?"

I already know what she said, given his outburst, so I stay silent and raise my brows, encouraging him to go on.

"Blake Christian," Lucas spits. "She told me she's dating the star defensive end for the football team. The dude who's fucked his way through half the chicks on campus but keeps getting chances with the next one because they all think they'll be the one to magically change him like *poof*." He snaps his fingers.

"Or they just like him?" I suggest, and Lucas's eyes pop wide open in anger. But I keep going, pushing the idea to prove a point. "Or they want a fuckboy, or he's actually a nice guy?"

Lucas scowls at me, snarling, "What the hell are you talking about?"

"The point is, you don't know why Nora wants to go out with Blake, but she must have her reasons. Reasons she doesn't have to share with you or anyone else. However . . ." I hold my hands up, telling him to let me finish. "Did she lead you on? Or was there nothing between you two yet?"

I know the answer because he's been talking about her for a while, but he hasn't 'sealed the deal', as he called it last week.

"Well, I was texting her 'good morning, beautiful' and good night texts. Telling her how great she is, talking about all the boring stuff she's into, and when she was studying, I took her pizza from her favorite place and sat with her for dinner, kinda like a date. And I saw her out with friends one night, so I bought them a round of drinks, which was expensive as fuck, and we danced." He huffs, letting his head fall back on the couch to stare at the ceiling. "All the shit you told me to do."

"Okay, and what was her response to all that? Did she text you back, talk with you, seem happy to see you?"

I'm tip-toeing a bit with Lucas because truthfully, he's not a nice guy. He just thinks he is, and that's what I'm working to help him realize. His attention is transactional in his head, even if he hasn't identified that he connects actions with emotions that way yet.

On a deep level he's not aware of, he thinks 'I was nice' and 'I bought you drinks' translates to 'you'll date me' and 'you'll want to have sex with me'.

"I don't know, man. She was fucking happy to let me buy her drinks, that's for sure. I bet Blake's not doing shit like that for her. But I'm sure she's sucking his dick like a hungry whore."

"Whoa, slow down!" I protest. "I know you're upset, but—"

But Lucas is in full-on rant mode, his emotions and dark

thoughts having festered inside his brain like a toxic pimple. And now he's squeezing it out . . . all over the room. I guess it's better than doing it someplace else, like in front of Nora. "That's why this is all bullshit." He gestures to the room at large, and at first, I'm not sure what he means. But he keeps spitting out ugliness. "Nice guys like me finish last. Bitches really just want the top percentage of guys who are hot, tall, and have big dicks. It doesn't matter how they treat them. The shittier the better, and they swallow it down. That's why all this simp stuff you're preaching is a fucking scam."

"Enough," I say sternly, taking the gloves off to stop his downward spiral. Coldly, I give him the hard truth, still not entirely sure he's ready for it but knowing he needs to hear it. "You went in expecting Nora to fall at your feet because you bought her a drink? If it's that simple to you, hire a sex worker. At least then she'll know going in that you think the barest of human kindness and ten dollars entitles you to a blow job. As for Nora, did you really like her? Want to get to know her? Or only fuck her?"

"Does it matter?" he retorts with an eye roll that lets me know he didn't hear a single thing I said.

"Yes, it matters!" I bark, losing my cool a bit. "Why are you here if you think I'm a scam?"

Lucas sits, sullenly silent for a moment. "Because I have friends in this club and they believe in you. But it's hard. It's hard when every girl I meet ends up being a fucking whore who wants to be railed by a football star or trained by the whole team."

I sit forward in my chair, pinning him with my eyes so he hears this loud and clear. "Lucas, I'm not teaching you to act a certain way or to use niceness as a means to an end," I chastise him. "It's got to be who you *are*. You have to actually care about other people, including the women you want to date. It's not about *what* you're doing, it's about *why* you're doing it. Right now, you're not a nice guy." I pause, letting that sink in before throwing an even harder truth. "You're an insecure asshole with a superiority complex, but you can do better, be better."

"Whatever," he huffs, crossing his arms over his chest.

I half expected him to jump up to throw hands. But the fact that he took that sitting tells me that he already knows I'm right, he just doesn't like it. So I temper my tone a bit to be more encouraging because ultimately, I don't want to tear him down. I want to build him up.

"You care about your friends enough to be here? That shows you're a good friend. Use that as a jump-point for how to think about others and to communicate your needs. If your buddy wanted pizza and you wanted a burger, you'd say so. Yeah?" I ask, and he nods. "It's the same with romantic relationships. If you want a fuck buddy, find a woman who wants that too and tell her upfront. If you want a deeper romantic partner, you have to be desirable as a partner first."

"Yeah, I'll get right on that," Lucas says sarcastically, standing up and stomping out of the room.

"Well, that went well," I say to the empty room as I sit back, scribbling a few notes to myself on what to keep my eye on with Lucas and what to talk to Evan about.

Lucas could be a problem. And his session casts a dark pall over my mood.

A lot of these guys come here, listen to the podcast, and benefit from both. But when they're outside our cultivated environment, they hear, see, and live the opposite. Lucas's demeanor and anger are disturbing, and it makes me wonder, am I pitching my message the right way? Or am I pissing into the wind and pretending that the wetness is rain? Am I really making a difference here?

While I ponder, I hear a ruckus out in the club. Getting up to go investigate, I send up a silent prayer that Rico didn't have a secret raccoon girlfriend hiding out that's pissed at her missing man or a gaggle of baby Ricos.

"Toro, toro, toro!" someone shouts.

I have no idea what I walked into, but there's a small group of guys wielding various dildos and vibrators as the other guys cheer them on like warriors returning from battle. And the 'toro' seems to be directed at Anthony, who has a twisted, silver glitter dildo suction cupped to his forehead. He's acting like a raging bull, running penis-horn first into a towel another guy is holding up like a matador's cape.

"What the hell?" I mutter to myself, a small grin blooming.

It's ridiculous, it's stupid, and a bit wild, but the guys acting crazy isn't that unusual. They need to let off steam sometimes. And they definitely seem to be having a good time considering Anthony's running at various guys now and they're jumping over him bullfighter style.

"*Ole!*" a new guy shouts with a flourish of his hands and a stomp of his feet.

"Check it out! They were all 'oh, no, give 'em back' and the goth girl chased us over the table on the way out."

"Yeah, and Sex Toy Barbie was shouting—"

"Fucking bitch almost racked me to get one back."

Wait, what? Their commentary is still processing, but what does register is 'Sex Toy Barbie'.

That's Samantha. That's what they called her after the bag of dicks stage incident.

My good mood evaporates in a blink. "What the hell is going on here?" I bellow. I cross the room, standing in the middle of the group to break it up. "I want answers. *Now.*"

Anthony grins widely and shakes his head to make his penis-horn wiggle triumphantly. "Got her back for you, Chance. Sex Toy Barbie won't embarrass you ever again."

I can feel anger building in my gut, hot and sour, but I force myself to stay steady. "Explain," I demand coldly. I need to know what these knuckleheads have done because I know that I need to talk to Samantha. Whatever they did, in some ways, it's my fault. And I need to deal with it ASAP.

Anthony's smile falls by a few degrees, but as he speaks, his pride is still obvious. "We were hanging in the community rec room and saw the two girls from the meeting selling this shit with no shame, right there in front of everyone. We took care of it."

He makes it sound like they did a mob hit right in the middle of campus. "What do you mean you took care of it?" Keeping my voice even is getting tougher and tougher.

"We confiscated some merch, made enough of a scene that they're definitely not gonna get invited back, and avenged you a bit," Anthony summarizes with a chuckle.

He holds a hand up, and another guy jumps in to offer a high-five like anything he just said is a good thing. "Fucking right," he says. "Good work, Anthony."

I scan the crowd around us, shocked at their eager eyes and approving grins. There are a few who look uncertain, but overall, the guys think I'm going to whole-heartedly approve of what Anthony's done.

"Seriously? You thought I'd be happy that you gave those women a hard time and took their merchandise?" I bite out. "Have you learned nothing from being a member here?"

"Wha—" Anthony mutters, his smile all but gone.

Louder, I tell the gathered guys, "I talked to that woman after the meeting. She was horrified, so embarrassed at what happened, all because she walked in the wrong door. Something that could happen to any of us." Gritting my teeth, I glance around the group, seeing if they're hearing me. "And do you know why she had the sex toys? Because she's a businesswoman, a successful one, I might add. Nothing to be joked about there, is it?"

I meet the eyes of every guy surrounding me except one. Anthony's head has fallen, his horn pointing to the floor as he stares blankly like a scolded child.

"What's going on?" Evan asks, coming up and pushing his way through the guys to the center next to me. It's been a long time since it's been me and him against the world, but it's good to know that he's still got my back.

I exhale heavily. "Was thinking as I came in this morning that I'm damn proud of the good work we do here. Heard guys supporting each other, saw the community of good men building relationships, and know the growth some members have made since joining." Even the good things I'm saying sound accusatory because I'm that furious. "But I just got a really bitter wake-up call that, when given half a chance, some of them will bully women, steal from them, and then celebrate like they did something to be proud of. I'm just damn fucking disappointed and angry as hell."

I push my way through the circle, shoulder bumping a couple of guys to get face to face with Anthony. "That's probably gonna leave a big fucking hickey on your forehead. I want you to think about what you did to those women every day when you have to explain the penis-horn stunt you pulled."

There's a snicker of giggles, but for the most part, the guys try to swallow down their laughs, especially when Anthony pulls the suction cup from his head with a loud *pop!*

There's most definitely a four-inch round red and purple bruise front and center on his forehead. Serves him right.

I rip the glitter dildo from his hand as I stride away, back to my office, and behind me, I hear Anthony say, "Sorry, Chance. I thought . . . it was just a joke."

*A joke?*

I want to roar at him. I want to punch him. I want to annihilate him. All things I teach my guys to reason their way through, but I think for the first time, I'm realizing how truly hard that is.

I slam the door to my office, the sharp sound reverberating through the space and pace back and forth across the area in front of my desk where I threw the toy. I swear it's staring at me, one-eyed mocking everything I thought I'd accomplished at the club. I've made a handful of laps when there's a knock on the door as it opens. Evan pokes his head in.

"Dude, what the fuck? You okay?"

I jerk my head, and he comes in, closing the door behind him. Still pacing, I let loose. "Can you believe that shit? Anthony said Samantha almost kneed him. That means he was using his body, his size against her, to intimidate her. One step away from *assaulting* her. And he . . . no, *they* thought it was funny. What the hell is that?" I throw an arm, pointing back at where I left Anthony.

Evan's quiet for a long minute, maybe two, just staring at me without an answer, and I think he's processing what Anthony did. Finally, he says, "How long?"

Confused, I echo, "How long what?"

"Don't be a dumbass. I know you better than you know yourself, Chance. How long've you been seeing bag o'dicks girl?" he asks wryly.

"Don't call her that! Samantha. Her name's Samantha," I correct. And then with a sigh, I admit, "Since that night. Turns out she's best friends with Carter's wife. She's a psychology grad student and sells the sex toys."

"It's serious?"

I lick my lips, knowing he's not gonna like this. "No. Casual."

Evan laughs mirthlessly, looking at the ceiling for celestial assistance. "You've built your reputation on being against fuckboy culture, but you're fucking a girl who threw dicks at your feet? Did I get that right?"

"Don't be crude," I growl, but it's a hollow chastisement. "We went in with clear communication. We're both too busy for a relationship, but if we can meet some of each other's needs, why not?"

"*Why not?* Are you serious?" he asks, turning his glare to me. When I don't wither beneath the weight of his gaze, he shakes his head resolutely. "She's already got you hooked and you don't even know it. Reagan pulled the same shit on me."

Reagan is his fiancée. She's a data analyst for a mutual fund company, spending her days staring at charts and graphs and her nights staring at Evan. And while he's saying Reagan hooked him, the truth is, he fell for her hard and fast. Not because she made him but because she's that amazing. Evan chased her, wooing her at every turn, and had to win her over.

"It's not like that with me and Samantha," I argue.

He chuckles, holding his palms up. "If you say so. But if Anthony pulled that stunt with someone else, you'd be pissed as hell, but you'd talk him through it analytically so he'd see why it's wrong and brainstorm how to make the proper amends. Instead, you went scorched Earth on him a la Daddy Harrington."

It's a low blow. Saying I'm acting like my father when he knows I don't have the best relationship with him, mostly because I ventured out on my own with Evan to start the Gentlemen's Club instead of joining the family business like Carter and Cameron.

"I need to see if she's okay," I admit. "I'm gonna cut out early."

I'm already three quick steps to the door when he says, "Good."

Confused, I glance over my shoulder, and he stares at me in exasperation. "Good because that means it's not casual. You just haven't figured that out yet."

"Shut up, asshole." I laugh. Right before I leave, I remember, "Hey, watch Lucas for me. He had a tough mentoring session, and I was pretty rough on him. But he's gotta pull his head out of his ass before he goes blind from the long-term darkness."

Evan does a stupid two-finger salute. "Got it. Go check on your Sex Toy Barbie." He's grinning, and later, I'll tell him to never call Samantha that again. But right now, I want to go.

As I head through the game area and the lobby, silence drops down over the guys when they see me. I know they're wondering about my reaction earlier, but I stand by it.

One hundred percent.

# CHAPTER 13
## CHANCE

OBLIVION COFFEE IS NOT a place I would ever go on my own. It's dark, gothic, with skulls here and moon phase art there, and metalcore music playing. Thankfully, the music's not too loud and I can at least order a drink.

If the barista behind the counter would actually take my order.

"Bruh, are you lost or something?" He chuckles as he looks me over.

Admittedly, I don't look like anyone here. I'm wearing the leftovers of my daily suit—navy slacks, blue button-up shirt with the sleeves rolled up, brown loafers, and a Patek Phileppe on my wrist.

On the other hand, the barista has black, jagged-cut hair and smeared eye makeup that crosses the bridge of his nose, where a silver barbell rests. His T-shirt has a Lucifer-esque image and is layered with a leather harness vest, his black jeans are more shredded than ripped, and when he walked over, I saw that at least five inches of his impressive height are from the platforms on his boots. His name tag reads 'Syd' and has a middle finger sticker.

In Oblivion Coffee, I'm the odd man out.

I lean in, answering just between the two of us and hopefully creating some sense of fellowship so he doesn't sacrifice me right here on the counter to the Coffee Gods. "No, meeting a friend. She said here, and to be honest, I'd go wherever she asked me to."

"Bet. What're you drinking today?" he asks flatly.

Alright, calling that a win because at least he's willing to take my order. "Large black." I'm keeping it simple, though a twisted part of me wants to order something sugar-laden and whipped cream-topped to see if the barista's head would explode. "Need a name?"

"Nah," Syd says, clearly amused that he might have trouble finding me when my drink's ready. "Gotchu."

With that declaration, he spins on his booted foot and stomps away as I tap my card to the machine to pay, praying that my black coffee won't be as bitter as Syd seems.

Sitting down, I drum my fingers on the cold metal of the table and watch the door, impatiently waiting for Samantha. I need to make sure she's okay after the stunt Anthony pulled.

*And after you basically ghosted her after the Rico Rollout.*

*That's not true. She said casual, and we're both busy. I didn't want to be pushy.*

Arguing with myself isn't getting me anywhere, and when the door opens and Samantha walks in, my mind goes completely blank in an instant.

She's stunning in a summery white dress with red polka-dots that she's paired with high-top yellow Nikes, gold necklaces that lay over her cleavage, and a straw bag with woven sunflowers.

I'm embarrassed that my first thoughts are filthy—bending her over a table, flipping the full skirt of her dress up, and taking her. I can imagine the silky feel of her skin, the sweet taste of her pussy, and the spark in her eyes as she falls apart around me still in her tennis shoes.

I mentally slap myself.

*Is she okay? That's what's important. Her knee, Anthony's behavior, us.*

As she walks my way, her hips swish back and forth, hypnotizing me. But her smile isn't for me, it's for Syd as she waves at him.

"Hey, Samantha, usual?" he asks. He doesn't smile back, but there's a light in his eyes and an energy in his voice that certainly wasn't there when he helped me.

She nods, then sets her sights on me, and I stand to pull her chair out. "You look gorgeous," I say by way of greeting.

"Thank you." She sits primly, smiling at me. "I was surprised to hear from you. Is this some sort of 'don't call too soon or she'll think you actually give a shit' deal?" Blunt. Bold. Confident as fuck.

I like it.

"Not at all. I was trying to respect your wishes for casualness, but truth be told, you've been on my mind a lot. Forgiven?"

"There wasn't an apology in there." I open my mouth to speak, happy to apologize if that's what she wants, but she holds up her hand. "Nor do you need to. Just trying to see where you're at. So, what's up? You said this was an emergency."

The easy acceptance of my explanation is a surprise. I guess I expected her to give me a harder time even though she said she was fine with no strings attached. Her unpredictability delights me at every turn.

"Straight to it, but first . . . how's your knee?"

Her brows lift. "It's fine. Was sore for a day or two, but all good now."

"I'm glad." I pause, knowing the next part won't be so easy. "We had an incident at the club today. One that involved you."

"Me?"

Before I can explain, Syd appears tableside. "Samantha, a cinnamon roll and espresso. Suit, coffee."

"Oh my gawd, thanks, Syd. This looks sooo good," Samantha purrs as she swipes a finger through a drizzle of icing on the plate and sucks the sweetness from her finger.

Both Syd and I watch her unintentionally sexy move with a hunger of our own. I clear my throat, and he cuts his eyes my way before returning his gaze to Samantha. "Let me know if you need to sneak out the back." With that, he goes back to the counter.

Samantha giggles at Syd's offer but is quickly distracted by the cinnamon roll in front of her. Digging in with a fork, she moans as the pastry hits her tongue. "Jaxx introduced me to this place and this monstrosity of amazingness. It's one of my favorites. Here, try it."

She cuts another bite and holds the fork out to feed me. It's oddly intimate, especially considering all the other things we've done to and with each other, but I lean forward and take the offered bite.

She's looking at me expectantly, so I tell her exactly what I'm thinking. "Delicious."

I'm not only talking about the pastry, which is light, fluffy, and filled with layers of ooey-gooey, buttery goodness. It also has more cinnamon flavor than I expected, which keeps it from being too sweet, but all that aside, I'm talking about her.

Samantha takes another bite for herself, grinning at my flirting. "You said there was an incident involving me?" she reminds me as she digs in with abandon, keeping every bit for herself now.

I'm honestly distracted by the gusto with which she eats the cinnamon roll. It's sexy how much she enjoys it, her moans and smacks musical, her lips wrapping around the fork to get every drop of white icing.

"Uh, yeah. One of the guys was . . ." How do I explain what the hell Anthony was doing? "Imitating a bull, wearing a suction-cup dildo on his forehead," I say quietly.

Samantha chokes a little but coughs to clear her throat. Looking at me in confusion, she repeats, "Dildo bull?" When I nod, she follows up with, "Were the other guys riding him?"

I laugh at the image that brings to mind. "No, picture more like Spanish bullfighting. But the toy, I think it was yours. Did something happen at a party today?"

I want to hear her side of what happened because while I'm already furious at Anthony's version, I'm afraid her truth will be even worse.

Her eyes narrow instantly as she glares at me. "Yes. What did you hear?"

I lean back, folding my hands on my knee to try and maintain some self control and calm of the situation. "Just that a group of guys hassled you pretty badly?" She nods slowly, and I continue, "I wanted to make sure you're okay."

"More like furious," she corrects. "Those assholes stole our merchandise after doing some immature impersonation of *After School Special* bullies, leaving a mess of our products all over the whole room and making Jaxx and me look bad."

Her response to Anthony's behavior is absolutely warranted and completely justified. I kinda wish she had made contact with his balls to teach him a lesson.

"They're club members," I admit, holding my head high though I'm ashamed of their behavior and how it reflects on our entire community. One I'm trying to build based on integrity, leadership, and self-awareness. They failed spectacularly in that, but I won't shrink away from taking some ownership of my guys' behavior. If I allow myself to be proud when they succeed, I have to feel equally responsible when they do something incredibly stupid.

Gesturing with the fork and nearly slinging cinnamon roll bits around, she snaps, "Are you serious?"

"Unfortunately, yes, and I'm so sorry for what they've done. I had no idea about any of it, but apparently, they thought they were 'avenging' the club after the interruption at the hotel."

"Not exactly an eye for an eye, was it?" Her voice is hard, accusing me as if I'm the one who did this to her. "I accidentally fell into your stupid club meeting and embarrassed the fuck out of myself. Those douche canoes thought they were better than me, better than any of the women. Calling us sluts and whores, making jokes about half the fucking population like they're prize stallions. Trust me, they're not."

She's ranting as much as I was earlier, the words pouring forth coated in acid. I understand her anger, but something in what she says stops me short.

Quietly, I remind her, "I called you that too."

Should I apologize? She's lumping me in with Anthony and his group's actions, so it feels like I should.

She rolls her eyes harshly before glaring at me. "That's

completely different. And if you don't see that, we've got bigger issues than some immature bros who need a life lesson shoved up their ass, dry and without prep."

Ouch. That'd be one rough lesson.

Actually . . . wait . . .

"You're right about our being different. But I don't want to hurt you—physically, mentally, or emotionally, and I think I've been quite clear that you bring out something in me that I didn't know was there, so I want our communication to be fully open, always." She nods, agreeing with me. "I want to talk about Anthony some more, though."

She huffs but makes a 'go on' gesture, rolling her hand.

"I'm still not sure what the consequences will be for him at the club, but there will have to be some. He claimed he was acting for us, on my behalf, but he most definitely was not, and I can't have the other guys thinking anything about what he did is acceptable. But I think you're right. He needs a life lesson about women."

An evil idea is taking shape in my mind. I do everything for the club, basically live, breathe, and bankroll it because I believe in what we do and the positive impact we're trying to have. But what if we could do more?

"I don't know what's on your mind, but I'm not fucking him and leaving him swinging-dick-naked in the campus quad, and for plausible deniability's sake, I'm also not going to ditch his dead body at a pig farm for destruction of evidence." She takes both options off the table with equal casualness that sets me back.

"What? You're not fucking him. Ever." I dig a fingertip into the tabletop as if I have any say-so in what she does or doesn't do. But the very idea of Samantha with someone else, anyone else, makes me jealous as hell. Something I have no right to be, but I'm honest enough with myself to admit the feeling is there, and strong. "Why would you think I'd want that?"

She grins and notes, "Not too worried about the pig farm, though?" When I don't smile back, too stuck on fucking her over the table in some caveman attempt to claim her, she laughs lightly. "Calm down, Chance. You had this diabolical look on your face, and Jaxx and I already came up with fifty different ways to fuck this guy over if we could find out who he was. And now I know."

"Anthony Cordram." I give her his name without hesitation, confident that he deserves any punishment she decides to mete out. "But I have an idea for your consideration."

"I'm listening." She takes another bite of cinnamon roll but does seem open to hearing my idea.

Of course, she's probably hoping it'll involve stringing Anthony up by his dick to a flagpole, but I'm hoping she'll think this is better. At least in the long run.

"Come to the club and do a class for the members. We already talk about dating, relationships, sex, and all that, but it's me and Evan giving our perspective of what's right, successful, and best. It's a male lens, no matter what we say. But what if it was from you? You're brilliant, can hold your own against any pushback, have a psychology background, and specialize in improved sex lives. You're perfect! Like a paid guest speaker for our own TED talk. What do you think?"

Her brows have been scrunching down little by little while I made my proposal, but I really hope she'll do this. I think it'd be perfect.

"And Anthony and his crew?" she asks.

"Your star students because fuck knows, they need it. They'll sit there, listen, and learn or they can get the hell out of the club. We need people open to growing and doing better. If they refuse, I'm not investing more of my time in them," I say dismissively.

We've never kicked anyone out of the club before, but if I have to do it for Samantha, I will. In a heartbeat.

"Let me think about it," she answers, and I can see her mind already whirling with ideas, doubts, excitement, and nerves.

I hope she agrees to do this. For the guys. Though having her around definitely benefits me too.

---

"So, wrapping things up today, yes, you need to wrap it every time. You are equally responsible for birth control with your partner, and if you don't want to be a baby daddy, it's on you to prevent that from happening. If you don't do your due diligence or statistics don't work in your favor . . . *ahem*, cough, cough—I'm talking to you, two-percenters—then you own the consequences as well. Choose wisely—your partner, your contraceptive, and your child if the situation arises." Evan pauses, letting that sink in, and then finishes, "I'm Evan White—"

"And I'm Chance Harrington," I pick up, "saying thank you for joining us for another episode of *Two Men And A Mic*."

The outro music plays, and Evan taps his keyboard, closing the feed. "And we're . . . out," he says, sitting back in his chair. "I'll run the feed through the optimizer to level out the sound feed, and it'll be up by midnight."

"Cool."

Evan looks over, curious. "You good? You've been weird tonight. Not down, just . . . your energy was off. Did the check-in with Sex Toy Barbie not go well?"

"I've been wondering . . . hypothetically," I reply, knowing I'm bullshitting my friend. "How would you feel about bringing a woman in to talk with the guys about some of their issues? To offer a different point of view and give insight on things we can't."

I don't have to say Samantha's name. We both know exactly who I'm talking about.

"Honestly?" Evan asks, and I nod even though his jaw's gone stone tight and I know what he's thinking. "It's a bad idea. Chance, the reason they open up with us is because the club is a safe space. You bring a female in here? They'll shut right the fuck up, and it'll turn into a dick-measuring competition instead of brothers having each other's backs."

"But some aren't listening now as is, and if she's not interested, they'll have to learn to behave. That's like Basics 101 on how to be a good guy. Hell, a good human who respects others."

"The guys who don't listen to us aren't gonna listen to a woman. That's their issue. They're their own worst enemy, but *we've* always pulled them out of the shithole of their own making and taught them ways to do better," Evan argues. But seeing my face, he sighs. "It's not hypothetical, is it?"

"Look, she can appeal to them in a way we can't," I offer.

"I see where you're going, and you're not wrong, but they could also spend the whole time posturing and acting like they don't need help," Evan points out. "I don't like it."

"She can handle them, and I'll be here if she needs backup for anyone." We both know I'm talking about Anthony, but there are other guys who could really use an opportunity to see a woman who's bright, well-spoken, and strong.

Especially one who takes an interest in helping them learn.

"You already did the deal, didn't you?" Evan asks, genuinely hurt. When I dip my chin affirmatively, he adds, "This is our thing. We run this ship together, and you should've come to me first."

He's right. I'd be pissed as hell if he did something like this, and he's never let Reagan affect the plans we have for the club. But I also really think I'm making the best choice here. For the club, the guys, and even for Evan and me. "I'm sorry. I should've discussed it with you first."

No frivolities or justifications, just the truth. That's the way it should be done. But I'm also not stepping the decision back, so I don't offer any leeway.

He pushes his chair back and stands up, sighing. "You made this deal without me, so if this blows up, it's on you. But given that you already slept with her, there's a complicating factor here. That's got to stop if she's an employee, or even a contractor, and you need to keep that history under wraps. Any hint of nepotism will be damning to both of us. And your sleeping with an employee would look even worse. The last thing we need is to hand ammunition to the trolls on a silver platter. You'd be Jake McGibbons 2.0 overnight."

I nod. "Understood."

# CHAPTER 14
# SAMANTHA

THE KNOCK on my door is loud and demanding. "Come in!" I shout from the kitchen, already guessing who it is. "It's open!"

"That's it? That's all you've got for your best friend in the world? The one who is so concerned about you that she's literally *early* to our work sesh?" Luna asks, barging in.

She's schlepping an oversized bag that's covered with pins from anime conventions, wearing a tank top and sweats that've been chopped off at the knees, her blonde hair is hair piled up in a messy bun, and her black framed glasses are halfway down her nose. She honestly looks like a bit of a dumpster fire, but that's pretty much her MO on a work day. You'd never guess that she's large, in charge, and wildly successful in her own right, nor that she's married to a man who basically shits dollar signs.

Luna drops her bag on my couch and then sits down on the floor with her legs crisscrossed, making herself at home.

I can't fight the laughter her entrance triggers. If there's one thing Luna never is, it's on time. Ever. She'll start her day with the best of intentions and then get lost in a world of her own making somewhere along the way and stop to scribble out plot notes or draw a scene for her graphic novel, *Alphena*. At that point, schedules become suggestions, and 'seven o'clock' becomes 'sometime around sunset'.

"Concerned? That's what you're rolling with?" I echo. "And

you're not early, but you are *only* fifteen minutes late, so that probably qualifies for you."

"Whatever," she quips dismissively. "Spill the good stuff. Catch me up on the 'Chance is a sex god' storyline." She throws her hands high in the air and sing-songs the teasing reminder of the description I gave of Chance before pushing her glasses up her nose so she can hear better.

Yeah, that makes sense when it comes to Luna.

I set a bowl of popcorn and my huge, insulated tumbler on the coffee table, then curl up in my favorite chair. "Shouldn't we work first? Our forty-five/fifteen deal only works when we do the work part first."

Luna and I have been doing these sprint sessions together for years at this point. I study, she draws, and then we take breaks to stay fresh, but we always start with work. Always.

"Rules, schmules. Spill it or I'm going to start talking about art." When I don't immediately give in to her threat, she starts, "Michelangelo's famous David sculpture notably represents the biblical subject pre-battle with Goliath, a distinct difference—"

"Okay, okay . . . stop!" I shout, covering my ears with my hands and closing my eyes to tune her out. "You know I hate it when you go all tour guide on me."

I feel a nudge on my knee and crack one eye. Luna's glare is amplified by her glasses, and I can see the one raised brow above her frames. Most importantly, her mouth isn't moving, which means she's not talking about art anymore. Thank fuck!

She's a great tour guide, I'll give her that, but I have zero interest in her favorite subject. Which is kinda ironic because back when we met, she was a virgin and I was planning my career as a sex and relationship therapist. Opposites attract isn't only about romance, but friendship too.

As I lower my hands, Luna's in her rarely-seen boss-babe mode, forcefully telling me, "You wanted this sprint, and I don't think it's because you need to study. You don't have a test for weeks."

"How do you know that?" I ask, my brows furrowed in surprise at her utter certainty of my schedule.

"I know everything. Including that you *want* to talk, so quit stalling." Luna's right, about all of it, but I'm also really proud of her personal growth to call me on my own shit. She used to be painfully shy and the barest side-eyed glance would make her self-conscious for days, but now? She's a beast. A quiet, sweet one, but a power house nonetheless, writing her own ticket for her work, but also her time and attention.

So I get to it. Because when the nicest person you know tells you that you're wimping out, she's likely being overly gentle and you're actually being a full-out fucking coward. And I am not one of those.

"I had a really shitty day a couple of days ago. Jaxx and I were doing a party, and it was going so *good*. We were selling hand over cocks" —I mime jacking off a dick— "right up until some assholes with legs decided to play whack-a-dick with our merchandise. They stole some too, running out with our toys like dine-and-dashers bailing on a hundred-dollar tab."

She interrupts to ask, "Do you need some funding to replace those? Loan or gift, I've got you, girl."

I smile softly at her generous offer. We used to be equally broke—for real, one brick of Ramen noodle split into three meals for the day, pick a bill to pay and pray for the rest kind of broke. Now, she's so bankrolled that she doesn't even call it money anymore. It's funding, because she works in the seven-figure arena at a minimum for deals. But she's still my best friend who'd do anything for me. Including paying for my stolen fake phalluses.

"Thank you, but Jaxx and I have a plan to get outta the red." The immediate worry evaporates from her eyes, and I continue with my update. "But there's some good luck in the bad circumstances because Chance called me. Finally." At Luna's questioning look, I explain, "The thieving assholes were his guys, and it pissed him off *big* time. He raked one of the guys up one side and down the other so badly he needed Neosporin for the burn, and then he called me to meet so he could apologize."

"That's nice." Luna's working hard to give nothing away, but I know her too well and can see that she's foaming at the mouth to say what she thinks about Chance's reaction. But I'm sticking to the point of today's sprint session, which admittedly isn't only work for me.

"He feels like some of the guys aren't getting the messages he's sending and that maybe hearing it from the source is a way to beat it into their heads. This one . . ." I tap my head. "Not this one," I circle over my crotch region. "So enter Samantha, the Man Educator."

"The what?" Luna asks, laughing like she's sure she misheard.

I laugh too, because I said exactly what she thinks I did.

This idea, even though Chance explained it at length and we talked about possible topics, is crazy. I'm a student, not some hotshot psychologist. But Chance swears that's what'll make the guys listen to me. In some ways, I am them—same general age, working hard at school, planning for my future—all things Chance says his guys are going through too.

"Right? I'll have to come up with a different name—maybe the Womansplainer? You know like mansplaining, but womansplaining." Not liking that either, I wave my hands through the air, wiping that option away. "But Chance wants to hire me to do classes at his club."

Luna shakes her head, rattling her thoughts loose. "Chance . . . wants you . . . in his boys-only club . . . to talk about sex?" she says in broken bits as she puts it together.

"Well, gender, relationships . . . and yeah, lots of sex," I admit as she stares at me disbelievingly. "That's why I wanted to do a sprint. I need to work on the outline for my first class."

"I'm stuck on him not only letting you, but wanting you, in his dicks-required club. To talk to the guys, of course, because we've already established that he wants you here, there, and everywhere." She smiles evilly, and for a moment I can see her ballsy alter-ego in her expression. "This is a major improvement for him, Samantha. I don't know if you understand how much of an uptight, good soldier he usually is. He's got rules for his rules. I'm surprised he didn't have you sign a retroactive NDA once you knew who he was."

She thinks she's right, I can see it in her eyes. But she doesn't know Chance the way I do. "Except he's not like that. At least, not with me."

She nods, but it feels a bit patronizing. "Of course, sure. Uh, what are you going to do for your first session?" she asks, trying to step it back because I sound a bit annoyed at her assessment of Chance. Not that I have any reason to be, but I'm offended on his behalf.

"I'm going in bold and obscene. I think they'll respond to a strong, informative, be better in bed in one hour deal. And if I'm promising orgasms, who's gonna tell me to shut up and get out?"

Luna laughs so hard she falls over into the coffee table and uses it to stay semi-upright. "Uh, probably Chance and Evan, but I wouldn't expect anything else from you. To be clear, you mean conversational orgasms, not actual ones, right?" When I twist my lips sarcastically, she switches gears. "Does Chance know your topic *du jour* is going to be 'Be a Great Fucker, Not a Fuck Up' yet?"

I blink at her brilliance. Holding up one finger, I scribble that down on my tablet screen as a possible title. Once I've got that and a few other ideas noted, I shrug. "He knows my specialties and what I'm bringing to the table. He can be okay with it, or I can bounce."

I'm not going to hold back from giving the guys what they need, even if it's a kick in the ass. Literally. And Chance didn't give me any restrictions or guidelines, just said to help them be good men. That's his mission in five words, basically, and I can support that. As long as I can tell them how to lick a clit as part of that education.

Luna seems unsure, and I eat a couple of handfuls of popcorn as I wait for her to get her thoughts together. "Be careful, Samantha. That's all. Chance puts on a good front—confident, strong, proud. But I've seen him with Carter and the rest of the brothers. It's not always pretty. He was the first one to walk away from Charles, which took some big brass ones, but he paid a price. For a while, I think he was looked at as a traitor to the family."

That is new information to me.

I've heard about Luna's in-laws, Charles and Miranda, and all of Carter's siblings, including Chance. But they're all scattered around town, doing their own things. Cameron is the only one following in Daddy Harrington's footsteps at the family business now. Carter's doing private estate management for the same woman Luna manages the art collection for. Cole seems to dip in and out randomly, and the going theories are that he's a spy, an escort, or both. But that's a joke, not serious suspicion. Kyle is the black sheep of the family, doing whatever he wants, which seems to be flipping his middle finger at anything his father holds dear. And Kayla is her mother's right-hand woman.

"Good soldier family man is the traitor?" I echo, confused as hell because nothing about Chance is worthy of that title.

"Not now," Luna rushes to clarify, "but in the early days, when he was struggling over his idealistic dream of making the world a better place? Yeah, that's not really Charles's love language. And the club, however unusual it might be to us, is Chance's baby. Just . . . don't mess it up for him, 'kay?"

She makes it sound like I'm going in with blow-up dolls as balloon décor for an informational session on making a woman scream in ecstasy with first-hand demonstrations. Which I'm not doing . . . the blow-up dolls or the demos. Well, not first-hand ones at least, but a frame-by-frame dissection of skill in a pre-selected video is still an option. I think.

"I won't," I promise, holding out my pinkie finger. She wraps hers around mine, and we lift and lower them three times, silently vowing to hold the pinkie promise in the utmost esteem. "You ready to get to work?" I ask her, and she nods absently. I've already lost her to Alphena and whatever ideas she's cooking up in that mind of hers.

"Hey, Alexa, set an alarm for forty-five minutes."

*"Alarm set for three-oh-two p.m."*

"Let's go, girl. On your mark, get set, git it!" I tell Luna as Alexa starts our timer. Luna gave me a lot to think about, but first, I have to do an outline for this class. If I get up there and stutter and stammer with no real gameplan, they are going to eat me alive. And not in a good cunnilingus sort of way, but rather, an uncomfortable, awkward session of Q-and-As that'll put my practice therapy rounds to shame.

I can hear them now . . .

*"What's your O-face look like?"*

*"How can I get a girl to deepthroat me without puking all over my dick?"*

*"If she's really tight, can she break my penis?"*

Plus basically every awful definition from Urban Dictionary that has to do with sex. Donkey show? Dirty Sanchez? Superman?

And I do not want that. So I get to work, side by side, with Luna drawing her superhero alter-ego on her tablet and me typing on my laptop to create a class that'll be informative, helpful, and not involve me saying filthy things to a room full of guys who'd rather fuck with me than fuck me but would be happy to go either way.

# CHAPTER 15
# SAMANTHA

WALKING into the Clubhouse for class, I can't help the butterflies in my stomach. Being the only woman here makes me feel like I stand out, in a target acquired sort of way. This must be what Daniel felt like when he was thrown into the lion's den. Get it . . . the mascot is a lion?

Even the tiny inner joke with myself doesn't ease my nerves, and I repeat my mental checklist once more, knowing that nothing's changed since I did it the last ten times.

I'm dressed conservatively, in a blue pantsuit, with my hair pulled up into a bun that's not messy, but not librarian tight, either. Everything's covered and no fantasy spank bank material there. My makeup? Light and again, toned down. No cum-swatter lashes or suck-me red lipstick.

It's ridiculous that these things are even necessary, but I want to look like I'm here for business and to preemptively not give any of these man-children the wrong idea.

And then maybe I can learn something from this class time too.

These men are going to grow into my future clients, their partners sitting at their side wondering why he's stuck on face down-ass up as the only acceptable sexual position. But if I can reach them now, I can help change that future so that there's a better outcome for all.

Or at least that's my hope. And my job.

The entrance to the Clubhouse is welcoming, or it would be if my stomach wasn't flip-flopping like crazy.

*Oh, shit! Is there even a women's restroom here? I didn't see one when Chance and I did our alarm-check, so maybe there's not one?*

The idea stops me in my tracks, right outside the double doors, though I shift from one heeled foot to the other, considering my options. Logic and reason remind me a moment later that it's required by code, so I'm probably okay there. Not that I want to pee in a building full of guys, anyway. The fear of being that vulnerable means I probably couldn't relax my bladder enough, anyway.

I shake my head to rattle the random thoughts loose and focus on my mission. Opening the door, I'm hit with a faint blast of cool air and a clean, woodsy scent. It thankfully doesn't smell like sweaty balls and unshowered assholes.

Chance is waiting for me, perched on the lightly stained oak reception desk with his legs stretched out in front of him, crossed at the ankles, and his arms laced over his chest. He's dressed in a stunning suit, a three-piece blue one that makes his eyes pop, with a burnt orange patterned tie that makes him look powerful but fashionable.

"Thought you were gonna bail," he teases straight-faced, and I realize that he could see me freaking out on the other side of the front doors.

"Nope, was hoping I don't piss myself when a roomful of bros see lil ole me in their midst." I say it lightly, like I'm joking back, but it's more truthful than I'd care to admit.

Concern fills his face instantly as he pushes off the desk to come closer. "Samantha, you're safe here. I promise."

I nod diplomatically even though I don't fully believe him. He truly thinks I'm safe, but he's never walked into a space feeling anything less than powerful and in charge of his own destiny. I'm days away from being harassed in public for simply doing business. And the guy who did it is going to be in my class.

"Welcome to The Gentlemen's Club," Chance says formally, taking my hand. Though the handshake is professional, his eyes smolder, reminding me that we're already much closer than polite handshakes. "This is my partner, Evan White."

Another man steps forward. His dark hair is side-swept loosely, his herringbone patterned suit surprisingly untraditional, and his smile charmingly inviting. But his gaze is shrewd, measuring me head to toe as well as the inches between Chance and me.

"Nice to meet you," he says, extending his hand.

Shaking his hand, I taunt, "Two big brains between you and you still couldn't come up with a name that doesn't sound like a strip club?"

Chance laughs outright at the comment. Evan's lip twitches, but he doesn't so much as crack a smile. "Would you like an *official* tour?"

The acerbic tone of his offer lets me know that Chance told him about my coming here already. Rule six has already been smashed to smithereens, and I'm coming in to kick the remnants away. And Evan isn't a fan—of me or my presence in his second home.

Deciding his tip-toe through the landmine approach isn't going to get us anywhere fast, I go full-frontal, center-mass assault. "Look, I get what you're trying to do here. Men's clubs aren't inherently awful, as long as you're not excluding women from opportunities, which doesn't sound like what you're doing. I support your trying to help young men become kind, successful, emotionally aware men who'll enter relationships, professional and personal, with their eyes wide open. I'm here to help with that, if you want it. If not, I'll go."

Evan's eyes have widened incrementally as I speak, his eyebrows climbing at the same time. Out of the side of his mouth, he grumbles to Chance, "Fine, you're right. She's perfect."

Chance smacks Evan on the back in a bro-like move. "Told you. Now, tour?"

We start down the hallway, and I can feel the eyes on me and the whispers from the few boys already here. As we pass the weight room, I chuckle. "I feel like Wendy among the Lost Boys."

"Thankfully, we've got no Tinker Bell to sabotage you," Chance says. "And up here is one of our multipurpose rooms. We do counseling sessions here, but also, the guys can reserve it for their own usage, like if they've got homework they need complete silence for or if a couple of the guys are getting together. There's a few subgroups here—a Dungeons and Dragons group, a band, and a bunch of investment guys."

I look inside because though I saw this area when we walked the space before, that was with a fear-filled focus that somebody was going to jump out at every turn. Seeing it in the daylight, as my new workplace, is an entirely different vibe. "Nice," I compliment, and Evan nods approvingly. I'm winning him over by degrees. "Better than the study pods on campus for sure."

"We have a dedicated counseling room too," Evan says. "If things go well and you're comfortable, maybe you could do some one-on-one talks with the guys? You could choose what space you prefer."

I smile at him thankfully. "I'd like that." After a beat, I add, "But let's see how today goes."

"It's going to be great," Chance proclaims as if he can make it so by simply stating it into existence. "Anthony should already be setting up the room for you."

"Part of his penance?" I assume, and when Chance flinches, I know I'm correct. "Does his parole also include getting me a Sprite? I'm afraid I'll lose my voice talking for a whole hour, and the bubbles would probably be good for my nervous belly."

"I'll get you one," Evan assures me.

Up ahead, I see an older man, his belly slightly stretching out the front of his gray polo shirt above his black pants and leather belt.

"This is Jim Delaney, our head of security," Chance says, waving the man over. "Jim, our new part-time mentor, Samantha Redding."

"Hmph, head of security? I'm the head, body, and legs of it. A one-man show, if ya will," Jim says, his voice gruff and low, but he's smiling welcomingly. "G'ta-meet-cha." His words all run together as he extends his hand, but I get that he's happy to meet me and smile back as we shake. "But I'mma hopin' you got some thick skin to deal with these boys and a maybe a wooden spoon to beat 'em upside the head. If not, you call Ol' Jim and I'll sort 'em for ya. Already off to a bad start today."

"What happened?" I ask, worry blooming and a fresh round of bubbles gurgling in my stomach.

Jim grumbles. "Oh, nothing too serious, just boys being dumbasses. If someone would'a shown these pups the power of belts to asses back when they actually were pups, it wouldn't even be a problem. I might not'a be able to do it ma'self these days—laws and all—but I can show 'em that they ain't all that, no matter what their daddies tell 'em."

I can't help but giggle at the idea of Ol' Jim fighting Anthony to teach him a lesson for his behavior. Violence might not be right, but Ol' Jim might have a point that if Anthony ever had someone more powerful than him put him in his place, he might not be such a bullying ass.

But Jim's not done. "In my day, we had real men. Not a bunch of boys who can't change a tire on their electric car without complaining about getting a blister on their pinky fingers -" He holds up a gnarled hand, pinkie extended and wiggling, "or a lil dirt on their uncreased tenny shoes." He huffs, rolling his eyes. I can't help but look down at his well-worn, but painstakingly polished, black leather shoes. They're honest to God work shoes, not Doc Martens or anything like that . . . but they look like they've seen a thousand miles and could go a thousand more.

Jim Delaney is a man of another generation, and I'm a bit surprised that Chance and Evan hired him. He seems so diametrically old-school compared to everything they're preaching.

"Jim, you could certainly teach them a few things," Chance offers, sounding like this a repeat conversation. "Maybe we can put you down for a Saturday car maintenance class?"

Jim grumbles, "Nah, I ain't teaching these young'uns that shit. Waste of my damn time, they'll end up paying someone to do it anyways. Even though they could do it themselves if'n they gave half-a-shit."

"Mm-hmm." Chance doesn't agree or disagree, and I'd bet my left ovary that he's never changed a tire in his life. "Well, if you change your mind, let me know. But we've got to finish the tour and get Samantha set up."

"Yeah, yeah. Like I said, welcome," Jim says, waving us off like he's dismissing us from his presence rather than the other way around.

We get to the end of the hallway, where Chance opens the door with a flourish. "And here's where the magic happens," he says proudly.

Inside is a media setup with tables, chairs, and a whole lot of electronics. Judging by the microphones, I say, "This is where you do the podcast?"

"Yes," Chance answers. "Have you listened?"

I cringe. "Not yet. I was a little nervous about what I'd hear," I admit and then reluctantly add, "Men's podcasts aren't exactly known for being female listener friendly."

Chance looks hurt, which wasn't my intention, and I have to fight myself from taking his hand to apologize.

"That's okay. You can tune into the next one." Evan's acceptance of my lack of engagement with the podcast is much easier won, but I make myself a mental note to go back and listen to several episodes to see what they're like. It should be quick. I've become an expert at listening to videos at 1.25 speed in order to study more in less time.

Because if I'm working with them now, and if I'm associating with The Gentlemen's Club, I should know what Chance and Evan are putting out there, not only what they say and think they are. After all, there are plenty of toxic assholes with a microphone who think they're God's second coming, but they're actually the devil in the barest of disguises.

We leave the podcast room and go down the hall, around a couple of corners, Chance speaking the whole time. "There's one last room, where we have our group meetings," he says. "This is where we've arranged for your class today."

"I'm okay with that," I reply, and Evan snickers. "What?"

"You say that now," Evan says as he opens the door for me. "Let's see how you feel in an hour."

Inside, the meeting room is large and open, probably used frequently for its flexibility. The floor is hardwood that looks original to the older building, with wear and tear obvious under a gleaming fresh coat of polyurethane. Along one wall are high stacks of chairs, and at the front there's a podium standing ominously alone.

There are roughly thirty guys seated in rows, most of them slightly younger than me, I'd guess.

"Gentlemen," Chance says as he comfortably takes the podium, and I can see the displeasure in his eyes at the casual appearance of a few of the guys who are in sweats, socks with slides, or are sprawled out in their chairs like we interrupted their naptime. On the front row, I can see that one of them is Anthony Cordram, looking annoyed and angry that he's here. "Let me introduce Samantha Redding. She's graciously agreed to hold a class for us today, highlighting things from the female perspective. Normally, I wouldn't feel the need to remind you of this, but given recent circumstances, remember your manners when you speak to her. She's Miss Redding, understood?"

"Yeah," one of the boys says. "*Miss* Redding."

There's approximately zero respect or manners on my name in his mouth, and I have to choose how to deal with that. Right now. Because it'll set the tone for the whole class.

"Thank you," I reply stiffly and equally disdainfully, stepping forward until I'm right in front of him and staring directly into his eyes. "And you are?"

"Lucas Walker," he says, reluctantly sticking out a hand when Evan glowers at him. We shake, and I go around the room, meeting more of the boys.

I give back the same energy I get from each one intentionally. Some, more warmly. Some, flat-out bitchy. When one guy leaves his foot out in the aisle, purposefully in my way, I low step over him to slide my sharp heel over his shin, knowing it won't hurt him, but it'll make my point clear. It works, and every other guy moves his legs quickly, some even sitting up straight as I approach.

By the time I've walked the room, I'm in charge, though there are several who aren't happy about it. Chance waves me forward, and I join him at the podium. "Gentlemen, I wanted to let Miss Redding tell you herself what she'll be doing here. So please, Miss Redding?"

He's intentionally repeating my name, drumming it into the guys' heads. And maybe later, there'll be something sexy about him calling me that . . . while on his knees worshiping at my vaginal altar. But right now, it's showtime.

Swallowing my nervousness, I take a deep breath as Chance leaves me alone at the podium. But I'm not sinking, I'm rising to the occasion like a rocket-fueled dick on a birthday. Pulling my laptop from my bag, I sync it to the screen behind me and up pops my presentation, complete with slides.

"Okay, boring stuff . . . I'm Samantha Redding, a graduate student at the university, finishing my degree to become a psychologist specializing in relationships. Specifically, intimate relationships." I click a button, moving from my introduction slide. "Less boring stuff . . . Mr. Harrington asked me here to help you with issues relating to sex, gender, and relationships."

"That gonna involve demos with your toys, Barbie?" Anthony mumbles. It's quiet, under his breath, but he makes sure it's loud enough for me to hear.

"Anthony!" Chance shouts from the sideline, ready to jump in, and by the looks of it, jump Anthony to teach him a lesson. The guys around Anthony go from giggling quietly to zipped up silent in an instant at Chance's rebuff, but Anthony looks proud of himself.

I hold up a hand, staying Chance's defense. I don't need him to handle this for me.

"I'd be happy to show you how some of the toys work to improve your sex life and make your partner happier. Or . . ." I drop my voice, stage whispering conspiratorially, "I can help you decide on a fleshlight for your personal use yourself since I'm pretty sure a pocket pussy's all the action you're getting. And it's Miss Redding, Mr. Cordram."

"Oooh . . ."

"Slick burn, Miss R!"

"Fuck, she got you good! Like she knows you ain't got no game, A!"

Approval for my management style abounds, but Chance and Evan seem uncertain. And Anthony looks embarrassed, so I pull the attention away from him, hoping he learned a lesson about trying to goad me in class.

"On that note, I thought today's topic needed to be bold. You don't want to hear me talk about how you should ask girls on dates, what to say in your DMs, and how to get out of the 'friend zone'—which doesn't actually exist." I throw out the declaration, knowing it'll get their attention, and am rewarded with several 'what?' and 'huh?' responses throughout the group. "Though, if this goes well, I will cover all those topics and more in future classes. But today, I thought, what do you need to know right now, today, to be better that I have the knowledge, experience, and education to teach you?"

I click to the next slide and read aloud, "Be a Great Fucker, Not a Fuck-Up." There's a gasp of shock across the room, but I smile mildly as if I've said nothing unusual. "My sister-in-law came up with the title, though I don't think she actually thought I'd use it." I pretend to be contemplative because I knew the instant Luna said that what I was going to cover for this class to get the guys on the hook so I can do more emotional intelligence type classes in the future. If I go in talking feelings, they'll check out. Go in promising orgasms, they'll come back for more every time.

"What do you guys think? I'm planning a no sugar-coated, step-by-step lesson on how to be the best lay your partner's ever had. Because newsflash, women like sex too. And fun fact number one, if you're out there in these streets with women sounding like a porn soundtrack and you're feeling like a rockstar, I can guarantee you, she's faking and you're shit in the sack. Anyone interested yet?"

Every single guy is sitting up, leaning forward with rapt attention. I glance at Chance and Evan who look horrified, their mouths open. When I flash a wink to Chance, he swallows thickly and slowly grins. He backhands Evan's chest, and though I can't hear what he says, it seems like he's reassuring Evan that this'll be fine.

I hope he's right.

# CHAPTER 16
# CHANCE

STANDING on the edge of the room next to Evan, I have to say I'm impressed by Samantha's presence. She was noticeably nervous at first, but her backbone is stronger than the tornado of testosterone in this room. And now that she's actively talking and teaching, she's got the entire room in the palm of her hand.

She's doing what so many good public speakers do almost unconsciously. Whether they're politicians, motivational speakers, or church ministers, they psychoanalyze the room on the fly.

And because of that, the watchful eye I had at first on the guys to make sure nobody got out of hand has turned toward Samantha. The guys, who will bow up to me and Evan almost daily, who can barely get through a day without some form of dick wagging . . . are like little lovesick puppies with her.

It's almost unbelievable.

And though I'm embarrassed to admit it, I've learned some things from her too. So as she clicks to a slide about erogenous zones, I'm all ears.

"Name three," she demands, pointing to Lucas.

"Clit, nipples, cervix," he answers easily.

Samantha golf claps and smiles approvingly. "You get bonus points for appropriate names and that you named female ones first, not dick, right ball, left ball." The guys laugh along with her. "And yes, the clitoris—which remember, is located at the top of the vulva" she says, reminding them of her anatomy slide from earlier, "the nipples, and the cervix. Though that last one is a your-mileage-may-vary experience. Some women love for you to bang it like a drum, while others are going to punt you across the room if you bump it too hard. So, what do we do?" she prompts.

"Ask what they like—before, during, and after," Stephen answers, quoting Samantha's advice. He's been listening closely, respectfully taking notes and even taking pictures of some of Samantha's slides for later reference. I'm glad to see him coming out of his shell a little bit, even speaking up, given his usually quiet nature.

"Exactly," Samantha praises, and Stephen beams back at her. "Can you name three more?" she asks him.

Pink flushes his cheeks, but he complies. "Uhm, ears, mouth, and neck?"

"Yes!" She pumps her fist like he won the national spelling bee with a seven-syllable trick word. "More. Who else?"

The guys are calling out body parts like it's an auction.

"Hands and feet!"

"Back of knees!"

"Head. Stomach!"

"Good, good. Those are true for everyone. Now, what about male specific?" she asks.

"Dick, right ball, left ball," Anthony answers wryly, quoting her earlier statement and showing that he's at least paying attention.

She nods at him. "Anywhere else?"

He swallows but reluctantly adds, "Asshole, prostate."

"Yes!" Samantha shouts, sounding nearly orgasmic herself. Or at least it would sound orgasmic if I hadn't actually heard her sounds personally.

Anthony grins and asks her, "Like those, do you?"

Smiling, Samantha answers, "The point is that people like them. Don't go tab A, slot B, and assume it'll be good. There's an entire body in front of you—both yours and your partner's—so play around. Lick, touch, kiss, bite, suck it all over. It's the only way to figure out where you and your partner enjoy attention." She clicks the slide to one showing the entire human body with arrows up and down the figure to note erogenous zones, and two pull-outs to the side showing male and female anatomy points of interest. "Take notes—write it down, take a picture, or whatever. You'll thank me later."

She steps aside, giving the guys a moment, and I'm surprised to see even the ones who've been a little reluctant to participate grab their phones to snap a quick picture for reference.

"Good. Now let's discuss oral sex—cunnilingus and fellatio," she says, glancing at her watch. "And then we'll move on to actual intercourse, including vaginal and anal."

I swear to fuck, I'm going to come in my slacks if she keeps talking like this. It's all professional and educational, but I'm not the only man shifting around.

An hour later, I've basically taken to standing with my hands over my crotch and thinking about multiplication tables beyond one thousand to keep my dick from noticeably twitching. Every time Samantha says penetration, I want to throw her to the ground and penetrate her—mouth, pussy, and ass. Whatever she wants, wherever she'll take me.

"Remember, there's this whole mystique about anal sex, but it's really not that big of a deal. It's an orifice, just like any others, and we all have one, so there's no need for it to be this magical thing. If you or your partner like it, giving or receiving, that's fine and understandable. There are loads of nerve endings, and for men, the prostate's there, so stimulation is naturally pleasurable. But if you or your partner don't like it at all or only like it one direction—you or them receiving, that's fine too."

She pauses, letting it sink in that while they might automatically think of fucking someone's ass, maybe some of the guys might enjoy being pegged. I've never done that myself, but given everything else I'm exploring with Samantha, and the way we both liked my thumb in her ass, maybe we need to add a little backdoor play for me too? I've never thought about it, and definitely never seriously considered it, but now? I'm not gonna say

I don't like it until I try it, but my asshole involuntarily constricts in disagreement.

"But if you're consensually exploring, remember to go sloooooow," Samantha drawls out, "and use lubrication because it's a non-lubricating orifice, unlike a mouth or vagina. And not your jack-off lotion," she adds sharply. "Your hands can handle that. An anus cannot."

Guys nod like they're making plans for tonight, and Samantha smiles.

"Okay, I think we have about five minutes left. Questions?"

Almost every hand in the room goes up.

"Oh! Might have to make these quickies," she jokes, laughing.

"Damn," Evan whispers as Samantha answers the guys' thankfully appropriate questions. "She's awesome. Maybe you were right . . . we could have done this sooner."

"You're admitting I was right and you were wrong?" I whisper back, and Evan rolls his eyes. "I was just lucky, man."

"Even so, see if she'll do a whole series of classes covering sex, relationships, dating, or whatever. Maybe have her send us the topics for each one ahead of time, though?" He raises his brows, a reminder of his original response to Samantha's outrageous topic and title for today's class. "We can put them on the club calendar for reservations because I'm betting that after word gets out about today, she's gonna have a full roster."

"Will do," I agree.

Evan dips his chin. "Think I'm gonna cut out early today. My schedule's clear, and Reagan's working from home. Think I'll see if she has time for a quick interruption." He clears his throat pointedly.

I'm definitely not the only one affected by Samantha's class today. "Quick? Did you learn nothing?" I tease quietly. "Slow, explore, enjoy," I echo from Samantha's lesson.

"Shit. I'll be lucky if I make it to Reagan and don't shoot a load from the vibration of my car on the way there."

I laugh, knowing that his car's virtually vibration-free, with a smooth as silk ride.

Samantha wraps up, and the guys all applaud for her. I approach the podium once more, hoping that I'm not walking too awkwardly because of my hard-on. "Thank you, Miss Redding. I think that was rather eye-opening for many of us." To the guys, I say, "I hope you learned a lot and appreciate the knowledge you've been gifted. Use it to improve your uhm . . ." I hesitate, unsure how to professionally and appropriately describe what Samantha's shared information can do. But taking a lesson from her, I go for blunt. "Your sex life and your current or future partner's sex life."

"Thanks, guys," Samantha adds. "It was great meeting you. I'll hang out for a few minutes if I didn't get to your question or you have something you'd rather ask privately."

It's a kind offer, but selfishly, I wish she hadn't made it because that means it'll be even longer before I can relieve this pressure in my dick. Not that I can do that here, and unlike Evan, I have sessions this afternoon and can't sneak away for some afternoon delight.

The room starts to clear out, but Samantha stays at the front, though she does sit down in one of the chairs. I start to sit beside her, but she waves me off. "I've got this, and some of them might not want to ask personal questions in front of you. You're scary."

She winks, letting me know that she's kidding and doesn't mean I'm some terrifying monster, but rather that these guys might be nervous to ask embarrassing things in front of their mentor depending on the intimacy of their question.

"As long as they're appropriate. You give the signal and I'll be at your side," I remind her.

"Okay, here's the signal," she informs me, but then she makes a loud bird noise that gets everyone's attention. "*Ca-caw, ca-caw!*" At my shocked face, she laughs.

I can't help but laugh too, adding, "Maybe just give me the 'help me' eyes?"

She demonstrates with a glance that's somewhere between puppy dog eyes and a 'what the fuck' stare. "Like that?"

"Yeah, that'll do," I tell her, grinning as I step away to chat with some of the guys who're hanging around. But I keep my eye on Samantha as various guys sit down to talk with her.

Some are quick, like Anthony, who I pray is apologizing for his previous behavior. Others are with her for a while, like Stephen. I'm glad to see him opening up to someone, and given his usual nerves around women, I'm extra thrilled to see him talking comfortably with Samantha.

But finally, it's just the two of us.

"How'd I do?" she asks, but her smile says loud and clear that she knows she rocked it.

"I had high expectations, and you smashed through every one of them in the first five minutes." It's high praise and not something I hand out lightly.

"Knew it!" she cheers, her fists in the air with invisible pompoms and her smile growing even wider. But then she pats my tie with her palm. "You were worried for nothing."

I catch her hand, holding it to my chest and cursing the layers of fabric between our skin, wishing I could feel her touch. "I wasn't worried for you. I knew you'd be able to deal with anything, but I was worried the guys couldn't handle you. I'm glad I was wrong and they did me proud, eventually."

Her smile melts into something more intimate, and the space between us charges.

"You care about them so much. They know that, even the ones who fight you. They have good reasons not to trust you're for real or that you actually give a shit and aren't going to bail on them. But you keep showing up for them, and eventually, you'll earn their trust and change their lives."

She gets it. So many people don't, but she does.

"Go out with me," I say. It's not a question, but not an order either. A prayer? A wish?

And doesn't only break my self-prescribed rules, it breaks a promise I made to Evan—that I'd stay away from her if she's working here. I don't like doing that. It goes against everything I'm about, but at the same time, I can't stay away from her.

Samantha's brows furrow together. "Like a date? Or back to your place?"

"A date, though I'll admit I'm rock-hard and wanting to bury myself inside you after hearing you talk like that for the last hour." She lets me guide her hand to my cock, and though I mean to keep one eye on the open door to check for anyone walking by, my eyes flutter closed at her barest touch.

She squeezes me, giving me one good stroke through my slacks, and thankfully, no one interrupts us.

"I don't know if a date is what you really want, Chance. In public, sitting and chatting, getting to know each other better like this thing between us is going somewhere." She's purring, making that sound like the sexiest thing ever. Huskier and sharper, she says, "No, I'm pretty sure you want a quick, dirty fuck to make this ache in your balls go away."

Her hand dips lower, cupping my balls and rolling them gently. I have to stifle the groan she's pulling from me. Getting too close to the point of no return, I jerk away from her and take a deep, jagged breath to steady myself.

"Can't I want both?"

"You're learning," she tells me, the light in her big brown eyes bright and excited. "How about this? I'm busy tonight, but tomorrow, you can pick me up at eight. On one condition." Her lips quirk, and I know I'm going to hate her condition.

"What's that?"

"Keep that for me," she says, pointing between us at my raging cock. "No jacking off, no coming, nothing . . . until tomorrow night with me."

I do groan at that, low and gruff in my throat, before admitting, "Tomorrow? I don't know if I can."

That truly sounds so far away.

"Then no date. Your call. If you don't show up, I'll know you were too weak to wait." She licks her lips like she wouldn't be too disappointed to know I was so aroused by her that I couldn't handle a twenty-four-hour delay.

But I've written and read enough contracts to know a loophole when I see one. "How will you know? I could jack off the second I walk into my office, still show up for our date, and you'd be none the wiser."

She tilts her head, pressing her lips together thoughtfully. "But you'd know. And that's not the kind of man you are. Plus, do you really think I wouldn't be able to tell?"

Logic tells me that she wouldn't know if I'd come once, twice, ten times, or not at all. There'd be no way of being sure unless I was wearing cum in my hair like gel in some sort of *Something About Mary* scene. But the clever look in her eyes makes me pause. Though it makes no sense, I truly believe she'd know on sight if I jacked off before seeing her.

"Deal," I agree, glancing at my watch and doing some quick math. "Twenty-nine hours, twelve minutes, and thirty-five seconds. I can do that."

She laughs. "Not that you're counting."

I shake my head. "Of course not. On another note that's perhaps a bit distracting." I jokingly look at my watch, bouncing my head with every passing second before looking back at her with a devil's grin. "Evan agreed that we should host you for a whole series of classes if you're up for it. What do you think?"

Her eyes nearly bug out of their sockets, and her smile flashes big and happy. "Are you serious? That'd be awesome!" A heartbeat later, she confirms, "At the same pay rate for each, right?"

I agreed to pay Samantha an appropriate appearance rate for doing the one class today. We've done that before for guests of various specialties that we've hosted. But if she's going to be on-staff for an entire series, technically, it should be a slightly lower rate per class and one lump-sum payment for the series.

But she brings something no one else does.

"Yes, same fee for each class," I say, knowing Evan won't exactly be happy, but he'll understand after what he witnessed today. "We'll also need to discuss an hourly rate if you decide to do the counseling sessions Evan mentioned, beyond the quick after-class talks."

"Dolla bills, dolla bills, watch it falling for me, love the way it feels . . ." she sings, doing some sort of arm-swinging, hand-flapping dance.

I chuckle in surprise at the impromptu performance. "What was *that*?"

"Money dance, Lisa from Blackpink," she explains without explaining anything. I shrug, still confused, and she laughs. "Just make sure the checks clear and we're good."

"That I can do," I promise. My phone dings in my pocket with a calendar reminder. "Sorry, I have a counseling session soon. With Stephen, the guy you were talking to last."

She looks thoughtful. "He seemed sweet. A little unsure, inexperienced, and jumpier around women than a cat in a dog pound, but sweet. Help him with his confidence and he'll be a force for good."

It's not a professional recommendation, but it's pretty spot-on for what I've learned about Stephen. And she got that in a five-minute chat, whereas I've barely gotten more than that in weeks of private sessions. He's eager to please, and talkative in our sessions, but I don't feel like he's really opened up yet. To me or the club.

"Did he say anything useful to you?"

She wags her finger at me. "Uh-uh, private conversations. Your guys need to know they can talk to me about things, you about other things, and Evan about others. Or all of us about the same thing to poll for advice if they want. But confidentiality is important."

She's right, though Evan and I do share insights about the guys, strictly as a way to best help them. But Samantha has a professional confidentiality viewpoint, and I can understand that, given her degree work.

"Okay, fair point," I concede. Regretfully, I add, "I have to go. Want me to walk you to the front?"

"Nah, I know my way. And it'll do the guys good to see me here. If anyone starts something, I'll handle it or call Jim to bring his belt," she jokes, acting like she's whipping an invisible target with her hand.

Though the idea of her needing backup makes my blood run hot, I know that's not likely and reluctantly let her go.

"Thanks, Mr. Harrington," she says, stepping toward the

door. It's perfectly polite and her smile is nothing more than friendly, but her eyes? Those dark orbs are full of mischief, and that mixed with the 'Mr. Harrington' does something to me.

I groan, my hips bucking involuntarily. It suddenly occurs to me that our deal is completely one-sided.

"Uhm, Miss Redding? Our agreement? Perhaps we need to make a few amendments," I suggest, my eyes boring into hers.

She grins devilishly, knowing exactly what I'm talking about. And it's not the class arrangement. "Nope, a deal's a deal."

And with that, she waggles her fingers at me in a triumphant wave and struts off down the hall.

That minx. She knew what she was doing. But I'm not angry. I'm impressed.

I won't let her know that tomorrow night, though. No, I'll punish her appropriately for crafting such a one-sided arrangement when she knew all the blood was in my dick and not my brain.

Though I wonder if that means she'll be touching herself tonight? Thinking of me as her fingers brush over her clit? Or crying out my name as she fucks herself with a vibrating dildo from her collection?

"Shiiit," I hiss to the empty room. I glance at my watch again. "Twenty-nine hours, one minute, and three seconds. You can do this, Harrington."

On my way to Stephen's counseling session, I pull up my email app on my phone to do a quick scan. There are the usual spam ones, a few fan letters that Evan will handle, but the last one's subject line stops me short.

*ROAR!*

I click on the email and scan it, my eyes rolling harder with every word.

*An army of sheep won't stop the lion from taking what he wants.*

They've taken creative liberty with the whole wolf/sheep idiom, replacing it with lion in recognition of the Gentlemen's Club mascot, and I'm not exactly sure what they're trying to say. Are we the sheep? Am I the lion? Are they?

Sighing, I close the email and tuck my phone away. I was

feeling good after the class today, but I guess it's always one step forward, two steps back. There's going to be haters for the good Evan and I are trying to do, no matter what.

That doesn't mean we stop. Nope, we go harder, dream bigger, and help more guys.

The more we rattle them, the more progress we must be making.

And today, we made huge strides thanks to Samantha.

# CHAPTER 17
# SAMANTHA

RULE NUMBER *Two of hook ups: Don't go on an actual date with your hook up . . . who's now your boss.*

Clearly, my rules are getting amended on the fly as I get ready for a date with Chance. And this is definitely an official date. Though I'm worried I'm going to climb into his lap and ride his dick like a pogo stick within two minutes of his picking me up.

I might've told him to hold off, but in solidarity, I was a 'good girl' too, and I'm on edge in a major way.

But we're going on this date first.

If—and that's a big if—I can decide what to wear, which I need to do quickly because it's seven thirty, and I'm still standing naked in front of my closet.

What does someone like me wear on a first *official* date with someone like Chance Harrington?

I hold up a pair of almost sheer bikini panties that I bought myself as a joke last Christmas. Screen printed on the thin nylon is an arrow, with the caption *LICK HERE* right above it. They're part of a set. The other one has a similar arrow, just on the backside with the instructions *STICK HERE*.

I consider both pairs, laughing to myself about their cliché naughtiness, and then go with the lick option. I slip them on with a smile, knowing that Chance will be shocked with their silliness.

Or maybe just be inspired to follow suggestions.

But what else do I wear?

I go through my entire closet twice before deciding on a pink strapless dress that clings to my body by sheer force of will and subtle amounts of elastic in all the right places to make sure I don't fall out.

I'm tempted to pair it with sandals, and if this were a daytime date I would, but this is nighttime, so I find my sexiest silver heels that make my legs look dynamite, even if I'd be the first victim of the zombie apocalypse if I had to run in them.

Dress and heels on, I look in the mirror at the full effect. My hair is pulled up loosely, a few face-framing layers intentionally escaping, and my makeup is light pink, giving me a sort of sun-kissed look. The outfit is flattering and sexy without being in your face. I feel . . . pretty. And not a minute too soon because Chance knocks on my door.

Surprisingly, I'm almost shy opening up for him. This is real on an entirely different level. "Hi." When he doesn't answer, standing outside my door in a black suit and looking like the world's sexiest secret agent, I stammer a little, fidgeting with my hair and smoothing my dress. "What is it?"

"You look . . . gorgeous," he says, visibly swallowing. "In all the world tonight, there must be millions of men taking millions of women out on dates. Yet I'm certain none are as lucky as I am right now."

"Poetic," I comment dryly. "Did you practice that or read it in a book?" I'm judging him harshly, but guys don't really talk like that, not seriously. It's either a line or sarcasm.

"Actually," Chance says, not offended by my response, "I have read poetry. I think a gentleman should be acquainted with at least a little bit of poetry. And not just dirty limericks, either. You truly are breathtaking, Samantha."

"Oh. Uhm, thank you," I say, more accepting this time to the compliment without all the fancy-schmanciness around it. "You wanna come in?"

"For a minute, but we have reservations." He steps into my apartment, but only by a few feet.

"We do?" I ask.

Chance nods, looking around as he says bluntly, "Was afraid if I didn't, I would push in as soon you open the door and bend you over the nearest surface. A reservation seemed like a way to stop myself."

"An appointment is all it takes to stop you from fucking me?" I challenge with a sly grin. Now that I know what he's doing, I'm flirting hard, almost as if I want to push him too far to see what he'll do. Sex is a familiar and comfortable zone. A date is not.

"Samantha," he warns, his voice deep and rough. "Show me your apartment and then let's go out. I want to take you on a date."

That stops the bratty response I had at the ready on the tip of my tongue. "You do?" When he simply stares at me, I give in and gesture around me, still not exactly sure how it got to this point. Chance and I are on an actual date. It's madness. "The ten-second tour. Not in your view is my bedroom, which is slightly bigger than your average broom closet, and my bathroom, which is slightly bigger than an airplane's. That's pretty much it."

It's ridiculous in comparison to his place, and we both know it, but he smiles. "It's lovely. Like its resident." He cocks an arm. "Shall we?"

Snagging my purse, I take his elbow and lock my door as we leave. "So, what poetry have you read?"

"The masters," Chance says breezily. "Homer, Dante, Shakespeare, Byron, Yeats, Tennyson, Jagger, Dre . . ."

"Wait . . . Jagger . . . Dre?" I ask, and Chance grins at my catch. "Rock and rap music?"

"Songs are poetry put to music," Chance points out. "The poetry of our times, a way for those who are looking for a voice to find theirs."

"That's actually very astute," I say in agreement. I'm not surprised by Chance's appreciation of music, but I guess I expected his tastes to run somewhere other than old-school rap. Maybe someone with a John Mayer *Body is a Wonderland* type of vibe would seem more his speed.

After a short drive, Chance pulls up in front of Macrosine. "Health food? I guess I shouldn't be surprised given your reputation as a health nut. Thine body is a temple," I tease.

"Macrobiotic, organic, and the head chef used to have a Michelin star. You'll love it," Chance assures me, getting out and handing the keys to the valet. Offering me his arm again, he leads me into the restaurant, where we're quickly seated at a prime table, the host almost deferential as he hands us our menus and nearly disappears into thin air.

I can't help it, I laugh. "Wow."

"What?" Chance asks, then smirks when I wave my hands around like 'all this'. "Yeah . . . I know."

He looks around, like he's never so much as bothered to do so, but I'm scanning the whole restaurant gobsmacked. It's all white and light wood, with plants here and there. The chair I'm sitting in is linen-covered, the table is set with wood-handled silverware, and the water and wine goblets look handblown with tiny little bubbles in the glass. It's understated but luxurious, and definitely expensive as fuck. I bet I can't even afford an appetizer here.

I glance at the menu, and the first item I see is a dandelion salad that costs more than I spend in a week at the grocery store.

*Isn't a dandelion a weed? They're charging grocery prices for annoying grass people yank from their yards?*

A woman appears at the tableside, silently and discreetly filling the water goblets, and before I can say thanks, I swear she bows her chin and skedaddles away.

*Toto, I'm not in Kansas anymore!*

Turning back to Chance, I find that he's completely unbothered, having not even noticed her, much less acknowledged her. "Have you literally spent your entire life having people trip over themselves to make sure your every whim is catered to?" I ask disapprovingly. "I mean, I think if you'd said you wanted your ass kissed, someone'd pull out fresh Chapstick for it."

Admittedly, I have a bit of a chip on my shoulder on this topic. I've worked enough coffee shops through the years to have experienced my fair share of people who want to be treated like royalty despite a Halloween costume being the closest to a queen they've ever been. Mistreating others or demanding top-tier service because you feel entitled to do so, for absolutely no reason, is a sign of a shit human as far as I'm concerned. I'm past the days of smiling through gritted teeth so I don't get fired and most certainly won't be sitting here on a date with someone so arrogant as to think I'll be impressed by this.

"Thankfully, I haven't had people dote on me that way, or at least I don't now, by my choice," Chance says evenly, not rising to my challenging tone. "But I wanted to take you someplace nice and delicious. This is one of my favorites. And yeah, unfortunately, they probably would do that. It's ridiculous." Chance huffs, apparently annoyed with the status quo I assumed he'd appreciate and expect.

"Oh. You don't like that?" I ask, confused.

He chuckles and looks around but leans in to whisper between the two of us. "Hell no. It's awkward and uncomfortable. I've even used fake names before so they wouldn't pull the 'Harrington' act out for me. But from experience, I know getting caught using a fake name is even worse. They go double pandering, while at the same time trying to poke around to see what it is I *must* be hiding. So I'm just . . . me. I'd like to say I'm a 'regular person', but that's not really true. Not with the upbringing I had, but I can't change it. Some people would say it's disrespectful to try and act otherwise." He lifts a shoulder, shrugging dismissively as he leans back in his chair and returns his attention to the menu.

"Would you change it?" I'm not ready to let this topic go. It feels important, like a start or no-start to something beyond sex for us. Actually, if Chance has more of a prince mentality than I thought, I don't know that I could sleep with him again either, no matter how good the sex is. It'd change the way I feel about our dynamic if he thinks people exist to serve him.

He thinks for a minute but smiles. "Nope."

I'm point oh two seconds away from tossing my napkin to the table and sashaying my happy self right out of this fancy joint, making the last sight he sees of me be my ass leaving him.

But Chance goes on. "Instead of changing me, I change others, giving them the opportunities that being privileged since birth, through no effort of my own, has brought. In a foundational way, that's why the Gentlemen's Club is important. It's a Sisyphean task sometimes, but getting the guys to a point where they can walk into any room—whether filled with CEOs and presidents or janitors and beggars—and feel confident and be successful, that's the goal."

The irritation I'd been working up deflates with every word, and I realize that I'm the one being bitchy. Chance has done nothing but be polite and let people do their jobs. I'm the one judging him, assuming he thinks they're somehow beneath him. But he doesn't feel that way at all.

I take a sip of water, considering that, and do a bit of self-analyzing that's not particularly comfortable or complimentary.

*Maybe it's that I feel out of place in his world? I've never been to a restaurant like this, or on a date with a man like Chance, so maybe I'm the one feeling a little inadequate and chafing at that?*

"I'm sorry. I misjudged you," I confess, knowing that he read my irritation and ugly assumptions in my questions and tone. He smiles warmly, seeming completely unoffended by my bitchiness. Hoping it'll break the awkwardness, I point out, "Not exactly everybody goes around throwing Greek mythology into regular conversation, though, do they?"

He blushes, and his eyes fall to the table, making him look more adorably boyish than he should.

"Growing up, I always had my nose in books," Chance says. "Being seven years younger than Cam and three younger than Carter, I had this sort of middle ground thing going for a long time. And they were big, gregarious personalities. I was quieter, even a little nerdy—though if you tell anyone I admitted that, I'll deny it vehemently."

"You? Nerdy?" I echo doubtfully.

His grin is self-deprecating, and I struggle to see any shred of nerdiness in the confident, well-spoken, sexy man across from me.

"Maybe intellectual is the better description? Always reading, planning, dreaming. But Carter usually went for calling me a nerd when he swiped my books and hid them from me."

I think about what I know about my bestie's husband. "Yeah, I can totally see him doing that. He's a good guy . . . now. Luna did some major rehab on him, but I can see him being an ass when you were younger. Or maybe like, last year?" I smile with the jab at his brother, whom I do like now that he's with my friend.

"Last week, more like it," Chance corrects, but it's good-natured shit-talking about his brother, not actually insulting.

A waitress comes by to take our order, and though Chance makes recommendations on what he's tried and enjoyed previously, he's happy for me to order whatever I'd like.

I start with a tofu square that's been seasoned with what looks like everything-but-the-bagel seasoning and wisps of grass. "Enjoy," the waitress says, professionally remaining completely straight-faced even as I tilt the plate to see if there's more food hiding under the tiny chunk of tofu.

"If the entrée is this small, I'm gonna need to run through McDonald's on the way home, 'kay?" I tell Chance.

He laughs and asks, "You've got McDonald's money?"

Shocked—both at the joke and that he knows the reference—I balk. "You did not just ask me that!" But I'm laughing too.

"One of the club guys always says that," Chance says, not surprisingly. "Told me that he knew he was going to be okay the first time he ordered a combo meal without checking his bank account balance."

"Been there," I agree as I take a small nibble of the tofu appetizer, mostly because that's all it is—a nibble. But it's tasty. "Mmm, the sauce is good, a little dark tasting?"

Food critic, I'm not. But it's the best I can do because the blackish drizzle does taste . . . dark.

"It's the truffles," Chance agrees, taking a bite of his appetizer, which is something with beet juice jelly cubes over heirloom tomatoes and watermelon, with white chunks of feta cheese. "What about you, do you have family?"

It's a reminder that we know a lot about each other—what

we like, what makes us come, and what our usual bedroom activities are like. But Chance doesn't really know much about me. Or at least not as much as I do about him, even though that's largely through Luna's lens.

I would like to change that, see if there's something more than sexual gasoline and fire between us.

Thoughtfully, I reveal, "Mom and sister, Olivia. She's sixteen and giving my mom hell, but she's a good kid. Mostly . . . sometimes." I chuckle at the too-accurate correction. "My mom's amazing, though, especially now that she's getting her groove back, Stella-style."

"Good for her. What about your dad?" Chance asks carefully.

"He's in the area, but he left us as I was starting college. Married his mistress who's basically my age. I haven't seen him in a long time." I know my voice has gone flat. I can hear it myself as I basically quote facts about my father as though I have no personal ties to him. I might as well be giving a general description—six foot-one, hundred and eighty pounds, likes steak, hates his family.

"I'm sorry," Chance says, taking my hand. His thumb slips back and forth over the delicate skin between my thumb and index finger soothingly. "He doesn't know what he's missing."

I try to brush it off. "I turned my give-a-shitter off where he's concerned. But it did help me figure out that I wanted to go into psychology. Mom sent me and Olivia to therapy during the divorce, and I could feel how it helped me reframe some of my thinking, so that became the jumping point. Then, the whole idea of how something like sex—so simple, yet so complicated, something everyone does, and almost nobody does well—drew me in. Intimacy and relationship counseling became my focus."

Chance mulls that over, then asks, "Are you hoping to repair other people's relationships since you weren't at a place to help your parents?"

Shell-shocked, my mouth drops open and I sputter, "No. That is *not* what I'm doing. At all."

I don't like the allegation, but luckily for Chance, the waitress returns with our salad course. "Thank you," I tell her quickly before she can jet away.

The slight break gives me an opportunity to calm down. It's not the first time I've heard that. Hell, even Sara has told me that. But I don't like that Chance could see it so easily. Am I that transparent?

"I just want to help people be happy. In themselves, in their relationships, and in their sex lives," I amend. "And yeah, I saw my parents in happier times, but I also saw them unhappy. And though my dad's in love with his wife now, it started with an affair. With sex."

It's as much as I can give. Maybe as much as I can admit to myself.

Chance senses that and shifts our conversation. We finish the course with lighter topics, getting to know each other with any deep, dark, past trauma left in the rearview mirror. It's easy first date stuff, likes (corndogs), dislikes (ripped jeans), loves (hot baths) and guttural hatreds (Pop Smoke).

And it's fun. Chance is funnier than I expect him to be, and not at all caught up in his own amazingness. If anything, I think there's more of the nerdy boy in there than he'd care to admit.

"The fish is locally caught," he tells me as the waitress brings our main entrees. "They pride themselves on using fresh, line caught, sustainable fish."

"I wouldn't know the difference if it was caught this morning, frozen a year ago, or Captain Gorton's fish sticks on a fancy plate," I quip, looking at the lightly battered filet in front of me. It's accompanied by some green seaweed looking stuff and little boba-looking ball things that I'm pretty sure are caviar.

I take a bite, expecting heaven. But it's . . . salty. Like licking a margarita glass rim salty. And I don't like it. But I don't want to be rude, to Chance or the Michelin chef, so I swallow it nearly whole and smile. "Mmm," I hum as I grab for my wine glass.

I take a too-big glug and then redirect Chance, pointing at his plate, "How's yours?" He ordered mushroom Wellington, some sort of vegetarian take on the beef version that has mushrooms, squash, kale, and farro. That dinner option lost me at mushroom

—gross, little, dirty forest fungi—and I don't know what faro is and didn't want to ask and embarrass myself.

"It's delicious! Would you like a bite?" he offers.

I pick at my fish and smile. "No, thank you. Saving room for dessert."

I move more of the food around on my plate than eat it, but I do manage to get a few bites of the fish down, without the seaweed and caviar, followed by big drinks of wine to drown the taste.

It's too bad I don't have tartar sauce or some ketchup for the fish filet. It might be slightly more palatable then. But something tells me asking for that would be akin to standing on the table and ripping my clothes off—completely inappropriate.

Thankfully, dessert is delicious, a black bean brownie topped with crème brûlée, and I dig into that with abandon as Chance explains that the dairy ingredients are ethically sourced, the sugar is fair trade, and the black beans are organic.

All I care is that they're tastily filling up the hole in my belly because the tiny tofu square, weed salad, and three bites of fish I forced down aren't gonna cut it for the evening I have planned.

Because there's another hole I need filled too.

# CHAPTER 18
# CHANCE

AS WE PULL AWAY from *Macrosine*, I rack my brain because there's at least one more stop we need to make. I just need to figure out the closest location without alerting Samantha.

"Where are we going?" she asks, her head lolled over to the side so she can stare out the window at the night.

I smile to myself in anticipation, knowing my answer is going to wind her up. "It's a surprise."

Her head rolls toward me. "What?"

I risk a glance her way and find her eyes boring into me. I smirk, enjoying her fire so much that I want it to grow even hotter. "Be patient. It'll be worth it," I promise smoothly.

"Let me guess, it involves your dick," she snaps sassily.

I turn right, into the parking lot, and watch closely as the yellow light of the golden arches gleams over her face.

"Are you serious?" she shouts, her mood changing in a blink. "All right! Big Macs on me, bay-bee!"

She sounds like an exuberant child and has nearly thrown herself to the floorboard to grab her purse. Digging in it, she's dancing in her seat while she looks for money.

"I've got it."

"Nuh-uh, this was my idea, so my treat. How'd you know I'd even want this crap after such a fancy dinner?"

Pulling into the drive-thru line, I laugh. "The only thing

you liked out of that whole meal was the crème brûlée. Everything else, especially the entree, wasn't to your liking, though you fought valiantly to make it appear as though it was delicious."

Her mouth drops open into an O. "How . . . what . . . it was good," she lies.

I lift a brow, smirking at her knowingly because not only is she an awful liar, but she also barely picked at her dinner. I didn't call her on it because she seemed so intent on making it seem like she was enjoying it, so I scarfed mine down as quickly as possible, knowing that my plan to stop and get her McDonald's was already in play after she mentioned it.

She sighs and acquiesces. "Fine, the fish was disgusting, the seaweed and caviar were like biting into the actual ocean, the salad tasted like the dirt in my grandpa's backyard where the dog pissed, and the tofu was okay, but I'd need like a whole block of it to consider it dinner, and that's only with the truffle syrup. You happy now?"

My laugh is loud and comes from my belly. I don't think I've ever heard a more honest dinner review. "We could've ordered something else or left. Why didn't you say something?"

"Because you're Chance Harrington and I'm Samantha Redding," she says.

"That makes *no* sense."

"Can I take your order?" a disembodied voice says.

Samantha leans over me, her hand on my thigh for support, to yell into the speaker. "Yeah, can I get two Big Mac meals, with fries and Cokes, please? And is your ice cream machine working?"

"Let me check."

Confused, I whisper in her ear, "Why wouldn't it be working?"

She side eyes me and laughs. "That says more about your growing up a rich boy than anything else has. Their machines never work. If it does, it's basically like winning the lottery."

A moment later, the voice comes back on the speaker. "Ma'am, the machine's off for the night."

Samantha silently says 'I told you so' with her eyes, grinning a bit that she was right. "No worries. Just the meals, then."

She sits back in her seat, and not missing a beat, continues our conversation as if we weren't interrupted. "It makes perfect sense. The same way you wanted to take me out to a nice dinner, I wanted to be the type of woman you could take to that kind of place. But I'm not. I want spaghetti, pancakes, steak, potatoes, and yeah, an occasional Big Mac."

"Maybe we can throw in a salad every once in a while," I suggest. "You need veggies too."

"Rich boy rabbit food? Need I remind you that you actually ate beet jelly tonight? And liked it!" she teases, sticking her tongue out in disgust. But then she smiles brightly and decrees, "I could do that. If I pick the veggies."

"Maybe our next date can be to the grocery store? And then we can cook dinner together."

She straightens, looking at me with an odd expression, and I realize that I just assumed we'd be going out again. But we are, aren't we? I certainly want that. Doesn't she?

Her eyes softer and her smile gentle, she says in a quiet voice, "I'd like that."

We get our food from the drive-thru window, and though I consider paying myself, knowing the differences in our bank accounts, I let Samantha pay because it seems important to her. "Where to?" I ask.

"What else did you have planned?" She's digging in the bag, and her hand reappears with two fries that she munches on happily. The next grab, she holds two fries out for me. It feels intimate for her to feed me, and I slowly lean over to eat them from her fingers.

I cough. "The seaweed and caviar was too salty for you, but those aren't?"

She laughs at me, already eating another bundle of fries. I think she only eats them two-by-two. "Don't like them? Too bad, so sad for you, and more for me," she taunts with a mouthful. "Let's go to the club. I have an idea."

Her idea sounds like it's going to break a whole lot more

rules, but I press the gas pedal anyway as I rush to the club, excited to see what she's got stirring in that dirty, sexy, beautiful mind of hers.

---

Making our way into the club, I turn the alarm off and let Samantha lead me through the building. She grabs two big towels from the locker room shelves and then walks out the back door to the yard where the guys play basketball. It's not regulation size—real estate is too expensive for that—but it's close enough that the guys enjoy games out here, and we did a pretty extensive renovation to make it top-notch.

We're alone, the magic of the stars and dark sky above us and the quiet of the night surrounding us.

"Are we playing a pick-up game?" I ask, gesturing toward a net.

Samantha laughs and kicks out a leg. "Not in these heels."

She keeps walking to the far side of the yard where there's an area of foam-cushioned artificial turf. The guys use it for soccer drills and CrossFit style workouts, but in the moonlight, it looks like a beautiful patch of grass. Samantha flicks her hands to spread out both towels, side by side, and then holds them out wide. "Ta-daaa! It's a picnic!" she explains.

She eases to the towel and takes off her heels. Legs outstretched and leaning back on her hands, she looks up to where I'm still standing like an idiot, looming over her. "You joining me or not? Just know, I'm getting that burger either way." She reaches one arm up with a grabby hand toward the bag I'm holding.

"Oh. Here you go," I tell her, handing it over. I kick my shoes off and lower myself to the towels beside her, not staying on my own but getting right in the middle to be closer to her.

She hands me one of the burgers, already unwrapped to show the top half, and smiles as she clinks hers and mine together like champagne glasses. "To new things. I ate literal ocean and dirt for you. Now, it's your turn to eat processed semi-food for me. I expect you to be just as polite as I was about it, too," she warns with a twinkle in her eye.

I feign preemptive disgust, thinking it can't be that bad but acting like she's feeding me the most horrifying thing on the planet, even going so far as holding my nose. I take a bite and chew.

It takes like . . . plastic? Or food-flavored plastic?

I wrinkle my nose and frown hard. "That's downright gross," I proclaim. Meanwhile, Samantha is chowing down like it's the most delicious thing she's ever had.

"The tiny, baby onions? They dehydrate them to ship and then rehydrate them in big buckets of water. *Locally rehydrated*," she tells me with a smart-ass grin, and I realize she's teasing me about my whole speech about *Macrosine's* supply chain.

"Not sure that's the same pedigree to brag about," I joke back deadpan, and she laughs.

She eats, and I rewrap my burger, knowing I'm not going to force down another bite. I must be staring out over the basketball court because Samantha asks me, "Do you play?"

"No, not really," I answer, shaking my head. "We had a hoop at home, but Cameron and Carter played more than I did. I tried, mostly as a way to connect with them, but it didn't work out that well." I shrug at the memories flooding back.

Cameron and Carter playing keep-away with the ball.

Carter bouncing the ball off my head.

Playing two-on-two with them as a team and me and Cole as the opponents, as if that was remotely fair with our age differences.

"I have a decent three-pointer, that's about it," I confess. "Mostly because if I could get the ball away from them outside, I was less likely to get fouled."

"Sounds like you and your brothers were always competing?" she asks, shooting a three-pointer of her own as she tosses the wadded-up burger wrapper into the bag.

I huff sardonically. "Some of us. Others basically never gave a shit, like Cole and Kyle. I wish I knew how they did it."

"Luna told me . . ." She pauses as if unsure she should share what her friend divulged. Hesitantly, she continues, "That you were kinda the odd man out for a while when you turned your back on the family business. Maybe Cole and Kyle learned from your example to not give a shit?"

It's a sweet, kind angle, though it's a bit of a twisted point of view.

"I don't know. They always did their own thing, so I won't take any credit or blame for their actions. Kyle was hell on wheels from when he was a toddler. My earliest memories of him are of Mom running after him, shouting 'no' on the daily." I smile, able to picture it perfectly in my mind. "And Cole? He was family, but not at the same time. I think by the time Mom had Cole and Kayla, Dad was already checked out of hands-on parenting. Kayla got attention because she was a girl, but Cole? I think he felt like an afterthought."

"Do you talk to them?"

"Kayla, for sure. She's the most reasonable of all of us, knows how to use the family name when it suits her—to open doors or shut people down—but also has a solid head on her shoulders in her own right. She stays on the fringes, working with Dad, but at a healthy distance where he can't control her. Hell, I don't think he even knows what she does. But people assume she's there for nepotistic reasons, underestimating her . . . until she ramrods right over them with a smile. Professionally speaking, of course."

Samantha grins. "I think I'd like your sister."

I nod. "I think she'd like you too."

"Have they seen what you've created here?" Samantha asks me earnestly. "Do they understand how amazing you are?"

I don't open up with people this way, certainly not someone who I know is skilled at digging deeper than most. But with Samantha, it feels natural and safe.

"Not really. Carter stopped by when I bought the place because Zack found it," I tell her, and I'm surprised at the hurt in my voice. I didn't even know that existed. "The rest of them don't care . . . well, Kayla would, but . . ." I trail off, and together, we say . . .

"Rule six."

Laughing, Samantha sings, "Breaking the law, breaking the law . . . unh, unh." At my confused look, she smiles sadly. "It's an old rock song my dad used to like. I heard him say it so many times—for things that weren't even bad, just like ice cream Mom didn't know about—that it comes out automatically."

"You said you haven't seen him in a long time, but do you talk to him?" I ask, a near quote of her earlier question about my siblings.

She's quiet for a long time, lying back to stare at the sky above us. So long that I wonder if she's forgotten the question, but I wait patiently for her to decide whether I'm worthy of her truth.

I've already figured out that she doesn't have any easy roads to her heart. Her body, she gives thoughtfully, when it suits her. But her soul, absolutely not. She holds that in a death-grip, buried beneath her sass and smiles, and she watches analytically as she reveals tiny tidbits. Any flinch and she'll bolt, writing me off with an easy flourish.

"I can't," she says quietly after a while. "Or won't? I haven't forgiven him, I know that much. Mom says he didn't leave me and Olivia, he left her, but that's not true. She's trying to make us feel better and take the hurt on her already overly burdened shoulders. I'm angry that he cheated, that he broke the trust we all had in him and our family." She makes a humming noise that says she's thinking. "Ugh, but at the same time, he deserves to be happy too. He fell in love, accidentally he says, but who knows?"

She blinks several times, her lashes fluttering, and I don't think she's looking at the stars anymore but into her heart. "I'm not ready. Don't know if I ever will be. And that's okay because I'm allowed to take however long I need to sort through my feelings."

She's giving herself therapy. I can hear it in the change of her voice, though she's speaking so softly that I'm not even sure I'm meant to hear.

"Sounds reasonable," I agree as I lie down beside her to stare up at the stars too.

She gave a lot of herself just now, and I don't want to push too hard, even if I'd like to hear it all.

We're both quiet for several minutes, watching the stars shine above us. I can't remember the last time I stopped this way—my mind, my body, my planning. Just stopped and existed.

Actually, that's not true.

It was with Samantha. It's only been with her that I've been able to exist in the present and not live for the future.

I reach over and take her hand, interlacing our fingers. With my other hand, I point to a grouping of stars. "Big Dipper."

"Easy one. Orion's Belt," Samantha counters.

"Little Dipper?" I indicate another bunch.

"Aww, I wouldn't call your widdle-dipper little."

The baby talk about my dick is somehow cute, not insulting. Especially when she sits up abruptly and straddles me, her knees on either side of my hips and her palms flat on my stomach. With her dress riding up her thighs, I grip the soft skin there, moving up and down from her knees to higher, almost to her core. She rolls her hips, and I'm instantly rock-hard, every hour spent aroused since her talk hitting me full-force at once.

I groan, telling her, "I waited like you told me to."

She falls forward over me, putting our faces inches apart. "I know."

I see her smile, and then her lips are on mine. I let her lead, her tongue dipping past my lips to taste me, our tongues swirling and entwining with each other. With her hips shifting over my cock, hands gripping my chest, and tongue thrust deep into my mouth, I reach the edge fast.

But I want more. I want her.

I flip our positions, gently and quickly lowering her back to the towel and centering myself between her spread thighs.

"Can't wait?" she taunts as she drags her hands up my sides and reaches between us to my belt.

I grab her hands, one then the other, to pin them above her head. Looking directly into her eyes, I vow, "I can wait long enough to make you come first."

She bites her lip, baiting me. "I have a surprise for you too. Take my dress off."

I don't have to be told twice. I push back onto my knees, and Samantha helps me lower her dress to reveal her full tits. I drop to suck one, but she writhes. "Nuh-uh. Lower."

I push her dress up so it's bunched around her waist and in the moonlight, I squint at her panties. They're pale—pink or peach, maybe? And there's something on the front. "Does that say something?" I ask.

"Get closer and check," she orders.

I sit back on my heels, spreading my knees wide so her legs lay over them, opening her core to me. Bending down, I inhale her sweet, musky arousal, and from this up-close perspective, I can see that her panties read LICK ME!

I chuckle aloud. "Cute, but you don't need your panties to speak for you. You have no problem telling me exactly what you want."

"*Touché!*" With that, Samantha pulls them aside to reveal her puffy, bare lips. "Then do it."

Smiling, I touch my lips to . . . her right inner thigh, kissing and licking and nuzzling. And then her left, getting closer to where she wants me but not giving her what she wants yet. If we had time, I'd start at her fingertips and worship her entire body again, but neither of us has that degree of control after waiting.

*Next time*, I vow to myself.

Especially when I see that Samantha is taking matters into her own hands and rubbing her clit lazily while I pay attention to her delicious thighs. I groan, "That's mine."

Holding her finger out, she says, "Then take it."

I suck her finger into my mouth, savoring the juices. Once clean, I move to her clit, and she shifts, settling in to let me work. Happily, I do—drinking her down with licks and sucks and sliding two fingers into her slippery pussy to fuck her. It only takes seconds before she's got her hands in my hair, holding on for dear life as her hips rise to get even closer to my torturous tongue.

"Yes . . . yes . . . yes . . ." Samantha cries into the night.

I look up her body, her breasts shaking as she quivers and her head thrown back. She's on the edge, and I want her orgasm. She deserves it, especially after opening herself for me by sharing thoughts and feelings she typically keeps locked down. I want her to know that she can trust me with it all—the physical and the emotional. I double my efforts, and she spasms, shattering beneath me and spilling her juices over my hand.

"Goddamn, Samantha," I groan, stunned at her utter beauty when she completely lets go. But I'm at my limit. Past it, perhaps. I pull my fingers from her, licking them sloppily, and when I sit up to rip my shirt open and undo my belt, I tell her, "Touch yourself. Keep it going. I wanna feel you coming when you're wrapped around my cock."

Her fingers return to her pussy, dipping inside to gather cream and then smearing it over her clit. "Like this?" she asks, smirking. She knows exactly what she's doing to me and is enjoying the hell out of it.

I get my pants and underwear pushed over my ass and take my cock in hand.

"Want me to suck you?" Samantha purrs, and I have to squeeze the head sharply so I don't come instantly.

I shake my head. "Can't."

She seems to understand that it's not that I don't want her mouth but that I'm about to come right now after waiting so long. "Then fuck me. I want your big cock inside me, Chance. I need it."

She's holding her panties out of the way, her pussy right there, and I don't think, I fall over her, one hand on either side of her head as I slam inside her, bottoming out deep on the first stroke.

Samantha cries out at the invasion, and I grunt hard. "Too much?" I manage to grit out, praying she doesn't say yes because I want her like this—powerful, hard, raw.

"Moooore," she moans instead, and my soul ignites inside me.

I give her what we both want, thrusting into her roughly, my balls slapping against her ass. I feel her gripping me all over, her nails leaving marks on my chest, my arms, my waist as she tries to find somewhere to hold onto as I pound her into the soft turf beneath us.

She's unlocked a beast inside me I didn't know existed, and that side of me relishes the freedom of unleashing my primal lust on her. The power of the night, the woman under me, her breasts shaking with each savage thrust, her mouth open as she begs for more, harder, deeper. It's freedom.

It's power.

I grab her throat, holding her tight as I pound her mercilessly. "Tell me you love it. That you want me to fuck you on the ground like a dirty slut."

"I . . . I love it," she rasps around my fingers. "I love your cock."

"Who *owns* this pussy?"

"You do."

I growl, pumping harder. I squeeze her throat tighter, and she moans, grabbing my wrist when I'm on the edge of going too tight. For half a second, I go past that line before letting up, and we lock eyes. But then hers roll back and flutter shut.

She's spasming, her pussy clenching again and again around me, and I can see she wants to come.

"Look at me," I command, forcing my hips to still but staying deep inside her.

Her hips buck, trying to fuck herself on me, and I move my hands to her breasts, pinching her nipples sharply. She hisses but holds my hands there as she arches into them for more. She fights to open her eyes and focus like I told her to, and when she does, I can see that her eyes are begging for it, but I grit my teeth and ask her, "Are you being greedy? Wanting to come again when I haven't come once?"

She nods, biting her lip at the scolding.

"You'll come when I'm good and ready for you to or maybe not at all," I growl.

She whimpers, and I feel completely in control. Right up until she drops her hands between us and grabs the base of my cock with one finger, making a tight ring around me and squeezing. It hurts, but it's a good pain. Her other hand goes back to her clit, rubbing over it roughly.

"Or you stay right there—don't move, don't come, and don't you dare fucking spill your seed in me—while I come all around you. Be a good boy, Chance. Let me use your dick to get off. It's so much better than any of my toys, ya know?"

She's lost in pleasure, almost mumbling as she taunts me, and I don't know where to look. Her using me for her pleasure is so fucking sexy, and if I watch her touch herself, I'm going to come. I know it, I can feel it right behind the tightness of her makeshift cock ring. But her face is contorted in pleasure too, and it's so fucking sexy that she's got this filthy, creative mind.

"Samantha," I warn, so close to falling apart. Whatever mirage of control I had is gone. But she squeezes hard, painfully so, and the edge slips away. At first, I mourn it desperately, but then I realize she's giving us more time, and I enjoy the feeling of her around me for a little longer.

"Don't," she snarls, and then she shatters.

I'm sweating at the restraint it takes to feel her every quiver, flutter, and wave and not be able to come myself, gritting my teeth so hard my jaw is going to hurt later and watching the most beautiful sight I've ever had the gift of witnessing.

I feel the convulsions slow and yank myself out of her, rising to my knees and then standing over her. "Get up here, now."

I hold my cock out for her, but as she moves, I grip her face in my other hand, holding her mouth open. I savagely kiss her and then spit in her mouth. "Swallow it all, like a good little whore. Everything I give you."

Her eyes go bright with excitement, and she rearranges herself so that she's sitting on her shins, her mouth at cock-level. She tries to lick me from root to tip, but the time for play is long past. I weave my hands into her hair on one side and hold her still, feeding her my cock inch by inch until her nose is pressed to the short hairs on my body. I keep her there, teasing at the entrance to her throat to see if she's ready for that.

When I release her, she gasps, and I see that there's a shine of tears in her eyes, but she's grinning in delight. "Fuck my mouth. I love it."

I cup her cheeks in my hands, holding her still the same way she did me as I thrust my cock into her mouth deep and hard, burying myself into her throat and growling as I feel her muscles contract as she tries to handle it. Pulling back, I do it again and again, force fucking her mouth until I feel the tears running down her pretty cheeks and her lips swell from the force of my hips. My balls slap off her chin, but instead of trying to pull back, Samantha moans in lust.

I can't see her hands, but a moment later, I feel that she's wet one finger with her own cum because she reaches beneath me and touches her fingertip to my asshole. I nearly jump out of my own skin, but Samantha hollows her cheeks at the same time and it's too much. I can't pull away from the pleasure, not even because of the fear.

"Do it . . ." I grit out, still only fifty-four percent sure. But she hasn't steered me wrong yet, and exploring is what it's all about with Samantha. I want to experience it all . . . with her.

It's weird and uncomfortable, so I pound into her face harder, punishing her. But then suddenly, there's an ease. I feel . . . full? And when she crooks her finger and electricity shoots through me, up my spine and into my balls, I come nearly instantly.

"Holy fuck, Samantha," I hiss, my voice deep and raspy as my head falls back. I don't see the stars, though. My eyes are clenched tight as I ride a razor edge of ecstasy. Forcing my focus back down because I don't want to miss this, I ask, "You want it? Want my cum in your mouth?"

She whimpers her assent as she crooks her finger again, and I pull back out of her throat just as I start to cum, three thick spurts filling her mouth before I pull out to cover her tits in the rest of my ejaculate. The sounds I make are more animal than man, primal and raw, and as Samantha gasps, her mouth pearly with my seed, an animal voice inside me roars to life too . . . *mine.*

Gasping for air, I collapse back to the towel, gathering Samantha at my side after we both clean up a little. I stroke her hair, looking up at the stars as my brain tries to reset, to form words again, and the beast retreats to its cave inside me, sated for now.

"Can't believe we just did that," I finally whisper. "*All* of that."

Samantha nods, cuddling against me. "The final frontier, where nothing has ever gone before." She wiggles her index finger in the air. "Till now."

I can't help but laugh and look down at her. "Did you just quote *Star Trek*?"

She shrugs, grinning. "With a little artistic liberty."

She surprises me at every turn, intoxicating and addicting me with her body, her mind, and her spirit. This is more than anything I've ever experienced before. The closest I can compare it to is being high.

The world doesn't feel the same, and I can't go back to how I was before. It's like I've been blind, and not only can I see now, but I can see in searing colors and high-definition sharpness, contrasts that never existed before.

All because of Samantha.

And yet, the thought terrifies me because I feel like I'm on the edge of losing control. I'll do anything to feel this again and again. *Anything.*

# CHAPTER 19
# SAMANTHA

THE LAST TWO weeks have flown by in a wild whirlwind of sex—classes at the club, selling dildos, and actual sex.

Jaxx and I have been peddling toys hand over fist. We're basically like the toy store with the last Tickle *My* Elmo on Christmas Eve and people are nearly cat-fighting to get one for themselves. I swear it's like they don't realize they have ten fingers that can do all sorts of things.

But it's working out for me. With our last party, I netted more than an entire paycheck from the coffee shop I used to work at, and the breathing room in my budget is a major relief.

Sex with Chance has been all over the place—literally. My place, his place, at the club, and in his car. But also, all over metaphorically. We've had long, slow hours of luxuriating in each other's bodies, quickies with our clothes haphazardly shoved out of the way, and some fun sessions with every toy I've got. Those seem to start silly and playful and turn delightfully torturous, so maybe my customers have it right.

But it hasn't all been sex with Chance. We've talked and laughed a lot too.

Like Chance suggested, we did make it to the grocery store, which was a hilarious date. Accustomed to his delivery service, Chance had no idea where anything was or what it cost. Meanwhile, I went straight for the croutons made with day-old bread and generic brands. But together, we got enough ingredients to make a delicious candlelight dinner that did admittedly end up with a tapered candle in places I've never put a candle before.

Another day, he showed up with Peanut Butter on a leash and nearly begged me to go on a walk with them, saying the dog kept headbutting him 'in a rather sensitive area.' But the sweet animal sat and shook hands with me, happy to trot along around the park at my side, and Chance deemed me a dog whisperer in addition to my man whisperer title.

Last but not least, I've had two more successful classes at the club, and hopefully, today's goes equally well. The guys are mostly attentive, willing to learn, and only give me shit off and on, not constantly. I'm calling that a win, especially when my mentor sessions have been tougher. A couple of the guys came in to chat, but they mostly seemed to want me to talk dirty to them or shock me with their own crudeness. But I've had more good than bad, so that added success on top of the classes makes me feel ten-foot-tall and bulletproof at the club.

"Good morning, Jim," I tell him with a smile as I walk through the double doors. My heels click on the floor, but his are completely silent as he rises to greet me. I'd love to think he's happy to see me, but he's not reaching for my hand. He wants what's in it. I snatch the bag back out of his reach. "Ah, uh-uh! You know the deal."

This has become our routine on days I come to the club, and I enjoy the banter with him. I think he does too, though if I'm not careful, he'll talk my ear off with an unfiltered stream of consciousness and I'll still be standing here at the front desk when my class is supposed to finish.

"You're as bad as these shit-for-brains boys." He gestures behind him where there's a group of five guys who, in opposition to Jim's declaration, seem to be studying. "They been noses down in that book for at least two hours. You know what can be accomplished in that time? Hell, I've solved whole cases in less time than they take to write some paper about shit that don't matter a lick."

Jim is a retired police officer, I've learned, and he's lived a history book's worth of experiences.

I tilt my head to add a lil' sumpthin-sumpthin to my mock glare. He huffs, annoyed. "Fine, but you're not nearly the sweet thang I thought you was." He levels his gaze at me, but I don't shrink. Acting like some small talk is hard as hell, he says, "Fine, g'morning, Miss Redding. Lovely day, ain't it? Now can I have my dadgum cinnamon roll?"

His thieving fingers steal the bag from my hand, and I tease, "See? That wasn't so bad, was it?"

"Pain in my ass is whatchu are," Jim grumbles, but it's a hollow gesture. "And when my wife figures out that I'm packing on the pounds because you're feeding me cinnamon rolls, I'mma give her your name and let you handle the row you sowed."

It's an empty threat. Jim's wife is sweet, kind, and hung the moon with strands of her silver hair according to him, so my bet is she wouldn't hurt a fly, much less me, over some sugary bread.

He sits down behind the desk and pulls out the box from Oblivion Café. He opens it, grinning like it's the gold, glowing light inside the briefcase in *Pulp Fiction*. I swear he's hearing angels sing. "Enjoy," I say, not sure he'll register that I've spoken now that he's in a cinnamon roll coma.

*Forget sex toys, just feed this man cinnamon rolls.*

I'm almost past him when Jim calls out, "Hey, Samantha!" I pause, glancing back questioningly. "Thanks so much, honey. These things give an old man a good reason to get outta bed in the mornin'. But I cain't go in that café with all that racket." He sticks his pinkie in his ear and wiggles it roughly. "And that fella in there sets off my internal metal detectors just with what's in his face."

I laugh. "Happy to get you a snack because then it means I get one too."

I didn't get a roll this morning, but my iced coffee has enough cinnamon and caramel syrup in it to count as a dessert. The hope is that the caffeine and sugar will get me through today's class topic because it's gonna be a bitch and I'm already exhausted just thinking about it.

In the meeting room, I find Chance leaning on a table, his legs outstretched and crossed at the ankles, looking casually sexy without even trying. He's staring at his phone with his concentration face on, his brows knit together, his jaw set, and his thumb flicking over the screen as he scrolls. His gray suit is cut to perfection, and the green tie gives him a look of freshness rather the stuffiness he fights against.

"Mr. Harrington," I say formally as if we didn't have phone sex less than twelve hours ago. He's the reason I need the liquid pick-me-up because we stayed up afterward, talking until we were both falling asleep.

His head jerks up, and his entire demeanor changes, relaxing as he smiles the charming grin that drives me crazy. "Miss Redding, I was hoping to see you before class."

This is the dance we do here at the club, walking the line of professional and flirty. I never thought the dichotomy between how we act at a place where we have expectations to fulfill and how we act behind closed doors would be so sexy, but it is. It's almost like role playing all day with him as the good guy boss, me as the naughty but nice teacher, and then later, we're our true selves, only more intense, recklessly enjoying each other with abandon.

"Were you wanting to join today?" I ask, setting my laptop up and syncing to the screen.

I've rearranged the room from the rows of chairs into a large circle so it's more welcoming and less structured, but the slides are a good way to keep classes focused so I get through the whole lesson in the time allotted.

"I wish," he says, one brow quirked in a not-so-professional way as his eyes scan me from head to toe, not missing a detail, "but we have a podcast to record today. I was looking over Evan's notes." He holds his phone up before dropping it into his pocket. "I did notice the topic of today's class . . ."

He trails off, so I fill in for him, "Sex appeal and desirability.

Don't worry, it's not about big dicks. Or at least not *all* about them."

His jaw drops open. I swear he's still shocked every time I talk about sex in normal conversation like it's a no-big-deal part of life. Later, he'll tell me to swallow his cock like a good slut and talk about how good he wants to make my pussy feel, but saying the word 'dick' aloud in public? Totally taboo!

I laugh and push his mouth closed, lifting his dropped chin with one finger. "It's about what's deemed sexy and how it changes through time and can be different for each person. I'm expecting it to be a button-pushing one. The time-tested question . . . which is better, tits or ass?" I hold my hands out, balance testing the options thoughtfully.

His phone makes a noise in his pocket and he inhales heavily. "I've got to run. Evan wants to test the new set-up in the recording room."

It feels odd to simply walk away from each other. No kiss, no hug, no touching. Chance walks past me toward the door, but pauses. "Talk to you later."

I grin evilly, knowing exactly what I'm doing when I say, "Yes sir, Mr. Harrington."

He groans deep and quiet in his chest. "You're killing me."

"You like it," I tease, winking at him salaciously.

He shoots me a stormy look, vowing that I'm going to pay for that before walking out to do the podcast.

*Though he might have to make a stop in his office to handle things first,* I think with a self-satisfied smirk.

They must've passed in the hallway because Stephen enters one second later. "Hi, Miss Redding." He adds an awkward wave to the greeting and sits down on the other side of the circle from me. "How're you doing?"

"Hi, Stephen!" I greet him, genuinely glad to see him. He's got so much potential and is doing better with every class. "Welcome!"

Stephen nods, and I greet all the guys as warmly, waiting as they fist-bump and high-five each other before sitting down for class.

"Today, we're going to talk about what's sexy—"

"You are," Lucas interjects, and several guys chuckle.

I cut my eyes his way, calling him on his shit. "Is that supposed to be a compliment?"

He licks his lips lasciviously. "Yeah, you know, just letting you know that I appreciate you."

"But that's not appreciating me. It doesn't flatter me, acknowledge my value, or show even a bare-boned understanding of what it's like to be a woman in today's world. You worry about getting rejected when you shoot your shot," I chastise him, flatly and professionally. "Meanwhile, women worry about getting assaulted. Hell, do you know that I can't even pee here? I won't take the risk of being that vulnerable in a building full of men. It's not an even playing field, and nobody asked for your opinion on my body, so keep it to yourself and mind your own business, m'kay?"

Lucas's eyes have gone wider and wider with embarrassment, but then they narrow as he glares at me angrily. "Dayum, I was just trying to compliment you. No need to get all bitchy about it."

"You should apologize," Stephen says. His voice is stronger, more commanding than I've ever heard from him, and inside, I do a tiny cheer for his confidence growth.

"Thanks, Stephen. But rather than an apology, Lucas . . . I want you to think about what I've said and *evolve*." Suitably chastised, he nods, and I continue with the lesson. "Let's discuss—like adults—what's sexy and how our experiences shape our preferences."

I click to the title slide, forcing lightness into my voice. "I Like Big Butts And I Don't Know Why," I say as I get started.

We go through it all, both female and male traits that are typically considered attractive—big butts, little butts, big breasts, little breasts, smile, hair, height, muscles, dad bods, beards, clean-shaven, big dicks, long dicks, and thick dicks. Because of course they want to talk about dicks as much as possible to see if I'll blush, which for the record—I don't.

I think by the end of it, they're getting it—it's *all* sexy.

"And those ideals of what's sexy to you specifically are shaped by everything around you—advertisements, social media, society at large, or even something as simple as a big-titty Goth girl being nice to you one time and now that's your dream girl," I half-joke. "So be mindful about what you're inputting into your mind as sexy."

Soon, we run out of time, and the guys stand, ready to carry on with whatever else is on their calendar for the day. Lucas gets my attention and sends me a chin lift of acknowledgement on his way out the door. It's not an apology, exactly, but he's saying he'll think about what I said. It's enough for now.

Surprisingly, it's Anthony who comes over to me.

"Miss R, wanted to say sorry again. We were being stupid that day, goofing off, and I didn't think for a second that we might've scared the fuck out of you and your friend." He runs his fingers through his hair anxiously, and I can still see the faintest suction cup outline on his forehead, even this many weeks later.

"Thank you. I truly appreciate that," I tell him.

When he leaves, I realize Stephen is still here, stacking chairs along the far wall.

"Let me help with that," I say with a warm smile. "Thank you, Stephen . . . for the chairs and for calling Lucas out. It makes a difference when your peers do it instead of me."

He snorts derisively. "He's not my peer. He's a cretin looking to get laid."

A small laugh escapes at his vehemence, but Stephen doesn't crack a smile, much less laugh. I glance back at the door the guys walked out of and wonder if Stephen's right.

"I liked your perspective on attractiveness increasing as you get to know someone—"

Whatever Stephen was going to say is cut off by Jim coming in. "Hey, Samantha, come check this out. The boys are chattering 'bout your classes on the podcast. You probably wanna hear this."

"Oh!" I exclaim. "Thanks, Jim!" I'm halfway to the door when I remember that Stephen was saying something. I turn back, but he's finishing up with the chairs and his back is to me. "See ya next class, Stephen?"

He throws a wave my way with a small smile. "Sure. Bye, Miss Redding."

I take off down the hall, my heels clicking over the tile to the media room where Evan usually edits the podcasts. The one they're recording right now is playing on the computer.

I sit down in the chair and watch the colored lines going up and down to indicate the sounds of Chance and Evan talking.

"Okay, I'll admit it . . . you were right," Evan says. "Adding a female perspective has made a big difference in the club. But I still say rule six has its place."

"Blah, blah, blah, all I'm hearing is . . . I'm right," Chance teases back. "You heard it here first. Evan's going to listen to me from now on. My opinion is the best because I'm right!"

I can almost see Chance throwing his arms up in victory as he exaggerates wildly with what Evan actually said, and I laugh to myself, trying to stay quiet so I don't interrupt their recording.

"That is not what I said," Evan sputters, though I'm pretty sure it's part of their banter. "But I'd like to put it out to our audience . . . how would you feel about a guest star for the show that's a woman so that we get a more varied viewpoint? Let us know in the comments."

Is he talking about me joining in on the podcast too? I kick my feet and spin in the chair, silently squealing at the idea.

*Not only would it help the Club,* I think, *but what a way to launch my professional bona fides! Samantha Redding, world-famous sex therapist! Move over, Dr. Ruth!*

# CHAPTER 20
## CHANCE

"DON'T MOVE. I'll be right back," I tell Samantha. Hopping up from my bed where she's spread out like a starfish in a post-bliss haze, I smack her ass and laughingly promise, "Snacks and hydration, STAT!"

She laughs too, calling out weakly, "Gatorade, please!" A moment later, her head flops back to the pillow.

Naked, I stride to the kitchen and dig around in the fridge. I grab a cheese stick for Samantha from the stash I now stock. Two Gatorades, and then I pop an egg-white-veggie muffin into my mouth for some protein.

I've got it all balanced in my hands when I hear the elevator ding.

*Shit! Who could that be?*

Only a couple of people have my building code. Not many need that type of access to me, and none of them need to see naked.

The doors open, and I lunge for a pillow to hide my dick, letting the cheese stick and drinks fly. "No!" I shout, and my muffin falls from my mouth to the floor.

Not giving two fucks about what she might be walking in on, Kayla struts from the elevator and into my living room like it's her own. "Sent on a mission from on high, so your objection is vetoed. And it's nothing I haven't seen before."

Kayla looks like she's come straight from the office in a professional blouse and skirt paired with high heels that make her model tall. Her blonde hair is gathered at the nape of her neck, and behind the glasses she typically wears to block the blue light on the computer, I know her eyes miss nothing. Whatever she's here for, her secondary assignment is clearly information-gathering.

I press the pillow a bit tighter, making sure nothing private is visible, and sigh heavily. I want to scream, but the fastest way to get her out of here is to let her complete her mission. "What do you want, Kayla? Who sent you?"

"Mom, of course," she says with an eye roll as she sets her purse on an end table. I'm pretty sure she gives the surface a swipe test for dust too. As if she'd find any here. "Aunt Viv's coming to town for her birthday, so we're all being punished with a family dinner."

I don't give a shit about Aunt Viv. She's my dad's sister and completely insufferable. When people started calling entitled, bossy, I'm-better-than-you type women, we'd privately joked that they should've called them Vivians because the caricature fits her one hundred percent. She's never met a person she'd consider her equal, never thought about someone else before herself, and drones on endlessly about how her son is basically the Second Coming.

None of which is remotely true.

Hating her is one of the few things my siblings agree on.

"Not me—" I start to say, but I'm interrupted by a sweet voice saying filthy things my sister most definitely does not need to hear.

"Chance, if you don't hurry up and fuck me again, I'm going for round two with the Unicorn Horn . . . and without you." Samantha appears in my bedroom doorway, wearing my thankfully-mostly-buttoned dress shirt from today and a bratty grin. She looks sexy as hell in my shirt, and when she shifts from bare foot to bare foot, I realize that she still has the butt plug we were playing with in her ass. Unbidden, my cock stirs behind the pillow, which I cannot have, so I force myself to think about

Viv's last appearance in town, during which she told us that we're 'disappointments to the Harrington name'.

That does it, redirecting blood from my dick to my whole body in a whoosh of anger, and my cock deflates. A little.

I look pointedly toward the living room, and Samantha follows my gaze.

"Oh, shit!" she exclaims when she sees Kayla. She tries to back up into the bedroom, but I clear my throat.

Samantha's eyes jump to mine, and ever so subtly, I shake my head, telling her she's not going anywhere. I want her to stand there, my cum dripping from her pussy, a plug in her ass, and my name still on her lips as she tries to hold a polite conversation. She's turned me into such a ridiculous monster, but I wouldn't change it. Not now, when I know the rewards that'll come from it later.

Sassily, she plants her feet. Challenge accepted.

Secretly, I can't wait to see who pays for this later . . . me or her?

"Good to see you again, Kayla," Samantha says with an easy smile.

"Uh, you too. Samantha, right? Luna's friend? I think we met at the wedding?" Kayla's looking around for clues like she's Steve with a handy-dandy notebook, but what she's walked in on is abundantly clear. When her eyes jump to mine, peering deep, I can almost hear her in my head asking, "Are you for real, man?"

I don't date. I don't bring women home. My family knows me for one thing, my single-minded focus on the club. Yet, here's proof that something completely different is happening. With my sister-in-law's best friend. There are so many things wrong in that thought, Kayla probably doesn't know where to start with giving me shit.

"Yeah," Samantha answers and then holds up her hands. "Guilty on all charges."

The dress shirt lifts, exposing higher on her thighs and dangerously close to even more, and jealously, I don't want Samantha flashing her pussy to anyone but me. "Kayla, could you say what you came to say and kindly get the hell out?" I say, taking the reins of this awkward moment.

But I've played my hand, and Kayla knows it. Her eyes glint, and I can tell she's considering doing the exact opposite. That's how Kayla rolls, chafing against what anyone tells her and doing whatever she wants.

"I can go . . ." Samantha offers, more to let us speak privately than to hide away.

But Kayla's three steps ahead already, and though she does what I asked, it's with one of those Kayla-special twists. "Oh, it's fine, Samantha. I was telling Chance that Aunt Viv's coming to dinner this weekend. All hands on deck and expected to be there, with no excuses accepted," she says staccato, like a family dinner is a military function. "Oh!" Kayla blurts as though she just had this completely new, novel idea right this instant, which she most certainly did not. "Samantha, you should come to dinner too. Luna will be there."

"I don't think—" I start to decline on Samantha's behalf, not wanting her to be subjected to the horror show that is my family, especially Aunt Viv. But when I look at her, Samantha's smile has all but crumbled, and I realize she thinks I don't want her there for selfish reasons. She has no reason to consider that I'm saving her, not hiding her. "I mean, yeah, of course. We'll be there."

Kayla watches the drama play out between Samantha and me with rapt interest, but after a moment of calculation, she snaps out of it. "Guess I'd better get going. My work here is done," she says breezily.

———

"I don't have to go. It's no big deal," Samantha states again, her voice utterly and eerily calm.

That makes the fifth opportunity she's given me to not take her tonight, and I refuse, the same way I have the other four times.

"I've never been less sure, but not of you." I sigh, squeezing the steering wheel as we drive down the highway. "In a way, I'm ashamed of my family, and I'm taking you up-close for a front-row seat of the Harringtons at their worst. The big deal, as you called it, is that you're going to see me differently after this."

She drops her voice, whispering sarcastically, "Hey, Chance, I already thought you were a rich-boy asshole." When I laugh a little, she smiles triumphantly and continues in her usual voice. "You've proven to be more than that, so their treating you some sort of way isn't going to make me suddenly figure out that you're a big shot. The good news is, I don't care. Tonight, I'm here to support you, not infiltrate 'The Family'."

She makes it sound like we're royals, and I guess to some people, we might as well be. There have been plenty of women who have approached my brothers and me, hungry for a meal ticket to wealth.

Ironically, Samantha isn't interested in easy money but instead wants to earn her own, and the only thing I can hold over her is the sex, which while amazing, is only a small part of what I enjoy about her. Our time together has become much more meaningful than that, but I'm careful to not let on because, money or not, dick or not, I think she'd bail on me in a second if she thought I had real feelings for her.

"Thanks for that," I say as I slip my hand onto her thigh and squeeze gently, purposefully making the moment physical. "Did I tell you that you look beautiful tonight?"

She does—in a red dress that's modern, knee-length, and skims over her curves in a tasteful way that still gets me revved up because I know what's beneath the structured fabric.

Dinner at my family home isn't exactly a typical Saturday night, so I'd offered to shop with her. Honestly, I wanted to see her trying on dresses, twirling happily and smiling in them, and buy the dress for her since it's my fault she needed it in the first place. But I'd understood when she said she and Luna would go shopping together.

"You did mention it a time or two. And I told you that you look like a politician trying to garner votes in a contentious district," she teases, looking me up and down.

We both know I look great, but admittedly, I'm dressed for war because it feels like that's what I'm walking into. Black suit, white shirt, and a red paisley power tie that unexpectedly coordinates with Samantha's dress. It's much more traditional than my typical suits, but this dinner warrants it.

"More like combative," I correct. "Me versus the rest of my family."

"But you've never gone in with me at your back. I've whipped Carter into shape, gotten you speaking in tongues, and I think Kayla and I are kindred spirits. Like this," she says, crossing her fingers. "As for the rest of 'em? I'll tell 'em to fuck off ten different ways before the salad course if I have to and suggest a toy or two with which to do it."

I have no doubt that she would. Or might still.

"I think this has a distinct possibility of being the best family dinner ever," I predict, "though I'd still rather do almost anything but this tonight."

Exiting the highway, I drive through the backroads toward home. I'm taking the long way, trying to delay the inevitable, but it's having the opposite effect from what I'd hoped. Instead of the overhang of trees and deserted road helping me calm and centering my mind before battle, I'm getting more and more stressed with every passing mile as I play out potential scenarios and how I might respond.

"Are you trying to leave fingerprints on my leg? I'm not against a handprint here or a hickey there, but visible ones at the Harrington estate? What will *they* say?" she declares, sounding mock outraged as she places a hand to her chest to grab invisible pearls.

I laugh, thankful for the lightness she brings. "I needed that." I squeeze her thigh once more and then relax my grip.

"I know what you need," she suddenly says.

When I cut my eyes her way, her mischievous smile both excites and worries me. I lift my brows in question.

"You need to relax, and the best way to do that is . . ." Before I figure out what she's up to, she's twisting in her seat and leaning over the console. "Watch the road."

"Samantha," I argue, "we can't." I'm still not sure what she's planning, but it can't be anything safe or reasonable in that position.

"*We're* not. I am. You're driving, so eyes forward, Mr. Harrington." Her deft fingers have made quick work of my zipper, and with a bit of adjusting, she frees my growing cock and takes it into her hand, giving me a few loose strokes.

I glance down and find her already looking at me, testing to see whether I'll obey her order. This is dangerous, ridiculously so, but she's so irresistible and there's no one else on the road in front of or behind me. There's a part of me that loves the idea of doing this on the way to a proper dinner too, like it's a rebellion against what I *should* do.

Sensing my indecision, she leans over further and kisses the tip of my cock. "Fuck," I hiss, cursing my seatbelt for keeping me from burying myself into her throat in one stroke. She knows she's got me.

Her tongue devilishly traces the rim before she takes more in and out of her mouth. She can't swallow all of me, the angle isn't right for that, but it's enough to get me on edge quickly. With each suck, I press the gas a little, creeping up in speed as I lose myself in the moment.

The world doesn't exist. The law and rules have faded away. Only the thrill of her mouth drawing me higher as we go faster matters. She can sense it, hearing the engine roar as she speeds up, and her tongue . . .

I give in to her, surrendering to the ecstasy and mind-blowing pleasure, lost in the moment as she uses her hand, her mouth, and her tongue to draw me to an explosive brink. Surprisingly, being restricted by the seatbelt and the requirement to focus on the road, and therefore having to submit to Samantha's mercy, is a major turn-on I never would've guessed I'd respond to, but fuck if I'm not already on edge.

"Get ready," I growl as I feel my climax coming. "Don't you dare spill a drop. Swallow it all like my good cum slut, m'kay?"

She moans her agreement, and the vibration does it.

I grip the steering wheel tight and push the gas a bit harder as I explode, the world almost dissolving in a rush of white light as I fill her eager mouth. And true to her bewitching nature, she drains every single drop from me, not missing a single bit.

Sitting back in her seat as I slow back down, Samantha hums and wipes at her lips in a ladylike move that belies the decidedly unladylike thing she just did. "Delicious."

"You're amazing," I sigh as I fumble with resetting my clothes one-handedly.

Satisfied with herself, she smirks. "Feeling better now?"

I chuckle under my breath. "You know I am, and though I'd love to make you put a foot on the dash and watch you work magic on yourself too, I've been doing loops on the backroads to give us more time, and we're late."

Touching up her lipstick, Samantha cuts her eyes my way. "I want more than a quickie, and later, after we rock this dinner party, you can thank me properly. On your knees."

"With pleasure," I agree easily, more than eager to do that.

Before her, I never would've done something like this. I mean, I've never gotten so much as a seatbelt ticket and am more Boy Scout than Bad Boy. Doing wild things in the privacy of our homes, or even at the club behind locked doors, is one thing.

Doing them while driving down the road is another completely.

I'm so far from my professed morals and values that I don't even know what to call myself. If the guys at the club knew what I'm doing with Samantha, they would accuse me of being a hypocrite. But I don't feel like a hypocrite. I feel like the world's finally making sense, and the chaos I constantly try to organize has instead become a beautiful, blurry watercolor.

I feel more in control of myself as we pull up to the estate, my remote control giving me unfettered access through the heavy iron gate. As we drive in, I notice the cars filling the parking area . . . minus Kyle's motorcycle, of course, because there's nothing that sets him off more than a mandatory appearance requirement. He's probably left the city, if not the state, for the night.

"The whole gang's here," I note as I park. Looking over, I take Samantha's hand. "You ready?"

"Is that a trick question?" she replies. "No one could be ready for this. It's like asking if I'm prepared for a zombie apocalypse, but the zombies are all raccoons, and I'm armed with a whisk and a prayer. And you know how much I love raccoons."

"A what?" I laugh, still not sure exactly what she just said. But she's right, dinner at the Harrington estate with my whole family, plus Aunt Viv, is nearly apocalyptic, and no amount of planning or strategizing is enough.

# CHAPTER 21
# SAMANTHA

THIS IS A BIG FUCKING DEAL.

Chance has been anxious about this dinner since Kayla made her surprise appearance, and I've done everything I can to help him chill, to no avail. I'm not sure if it's the aunt thing, or his dad, or me?

Now that we're here, I'm freaking out a bit . . . on the inside. Outside, I look around at the impressive Harrington estate as though it's a typical suburban home, despite the artificially perfect green lawn, the scale of the front porch, and the museum-worthy statue in the center of the driveway.

Yep, nothing to see here . . . just a little-dicked Greek god standing amid spitting water streams.

Outside, I try to make it seem like that's what I'm thinking. Inside's a whole different story.

*I do not belong here, for so many reasons.*

Chance takes my hand as we approach the front door but stops short, staring at a large, deep red Lincoln Navigator with a custom license plate that says *CHUCK*. Sighing deeply, he mumbles, "Shit. I should've known."

"What's wrong?"

"Kayla said Aunt Viv was coming. I knew that meant her annoying son would be here, but I didn't know my grandparents were coming."

"I feel like I'm supposed to know why that's bad, but I don't." I'm looking at the SUV like these unwanted grandparents might hop out and attack us, whether physically with smacking hugs, emotionally with backhanded compliments, or gastronomically with expired Werther's candies from the bottom of her purse.

Chance drops his voice, and speaking quickly, he tells me, "Grandpa was a bit of an old-fashioned chauvinist with his kids. Only cared about having a son and started off with four daughters. When he finally had Dad, he put everything into him. Time, resources, education . . . the company. My aunts were hurt, in particular, Viv. And she brings it up. A lot. Grandpa learned . . . too late."

Still processing, I say, "Sounds like your dad didn't learn much from that example, huh? He didn't treat you and your siblings much better."

Chance blinks, his brows furrowing like this is new information, but surely, he's put that together before. It's so obvious. You parent the way you were parented unless you make a conscious effort to do something else. Hopefully, something that breaks the cycle.

Before we can dig deeper into the idea of generational trauma, the front door opens. Chance doesn't introduce me to the man who answers, who acts as if he's as invisible as the air around us as he steps out of sight behind the door, reminding me of the staff at the fancy restaurant. No wonder Chance didn't give their behavior a second's notice, it's the same at home. Instead Chance leads me deeper into the house as the heavy door slams shut behind me. I suddenly feel trapped in an extremely gilded cage.

This is ridiculous—house staff, a foyer the size of my entire apartment, and a family line where inheriting an entire company is the norm.

I whisper to Chance, "I can't imagine growing up like this."

Chance glances around, and though he's been honest and recognizes his privilege, he seems to not see anything unusual in his childhood home. "To me, this is normal. Never knew anything different. Just home, sweet home."

"Remind me to smack you later for that," I tease. The way he grew up isn't his fault, it's just a fact of life, but that doesn't mean I can't give him a little good-natured hell for it. Especially when it breaks the tension.

"Whatever it's for, it's deserved," Kayla interjects as she comes from a side doorway, only hearing the last bit of my conversation with Chance and instantly on my side.

She looks stunning—blonde hair, blue eyes, perfect, lightly tanned skin, and wearing a dress that I suspect is custom. If she wasn't so damned sweet, I'd hate her out of jealousy, but she's kind as can be. Bitch . . . she's giving me girl crush vibes, hard.

And I respect her brains . . . a lot.

"Agreed," I tell Kayla as she leans in to press our cheeks together.

As she pulls away, she flashes a knowing grin. "I can greet you properly this time since you both have clothes on."

Grinning right back, I answer with a little faux casual shrug of my shoulders. "Would've been more awkward than you even know if you'd tried it last time."

Her eyes flare, and she looks intrigued, but she doesn't ask questions. "Everyone's already in the dining room. Aunt Viv's fashionably late." Flat and monotone, she adds, "Shocker."

Together, we walk into the dining room. I'm eternally grateful to have Chance on one side and Kayla on the other because when all eyes focus on me, I swear my knees knock.

*Every* set of eyes. There's an old man, an old woman, who I assume are Chance's grandfather and grandmother, and next to the old man is Charles Harrington. He's a lion of a man, broad-chested and just starting to go silver-maned. Handsomeness runs in the Harrington family genes, that's for sure.

"Samantha?" Mrs. Harrington says, her eyes wide and jumping from Chance to Kayla to Luna before returning to me. "What a lovely surprise!" she says, her manners kicking in.

I haven't seen her since Luna and Carter's *last* wedding—long story—but she stands to greet me warmly. "Hello, Mrs. Harrington," I reply as she wraps me in a polite, friendly hug. "It's nice to see you again."

"Hush that formal nonsense. You know you can call me Miranda." She swishes her hand with the order, as if she has no idea why anyone would behave uppity and on their best behavior around her. "I didn't realize you were coming tonight. Let me get you a chair by Luna."

She turns to Cole, who's sitting next to Luna, instantly shuffling chairs in her mind.

"Uhm, Mom," Chance says, "Samantha's here . . . with me."

I thought everyone was looking at me before, now they're *looking* at me. I can almost feel them taking my measure in an entirely new way.

"Let the games begin!" Kayla announces in a low, amused voice, heading to what must be her seat.

"You can still sit by me," Luna rushes to say, nearly begging me to not freak out the way she said she did the first time she came to a Harrington dinner.

At the same time, Carter's giving Chance a hard time, chuckling as he offers, "Thought surprise dates at family dinners were my thing."

"*Was* your thing," Luna corrects. "We all know the next surprise date you have will be your last."

Everyone laughs, and Carter shrugs, knowing she's right. I'm proud of her. My bestie's come a long way in speaking her mind, and her marriage is happier for it.

"Can someone please tell me what the hell's going on?" the older man says, obviously accustomed to being the man in power in every room he steps into. "Young lady, I'm Charles Harrington, Senior, and you are . . .?" he trails off, prompting for me to fill in an answer.

"Grandpa Chuck, this is Samantha Redding," Chance says. "My date."

Talk about a just-the-facts, bare-boned answer, but given what Chance quickly told me of his grandfather and the vibe he gives off, I'm not surprised. Until . . .

Senior leans over to Junior, and not bothering to lower his

voice at all, asks, "Do we like her or is she a gold digger after my grandson? She looks a little cheap."

"Chuck!" the old woman at his side admonishes with a backhand to his bicep. "You can't go around saying stuff like that where people can hear you. It's impolite."

I notice she doesn't tell him that he can't say it, only that it shouldn't be in public.

"Beth, I can say whatever I want. It's one of the privileges of being me," he argues back.

I get the feeling this is their norm—he says something outrageous, she calls him on it, he dismisses her, and lather, rinse, repeat like cheap shampoo.

With Chuck and Beth involved, it's like everyone is holding their breath, even Chance, as it's decided whether or not I'll be accepted at the dinner table.

Fuck that.

"I can't speak for whether Mr. Harrington likes me, but I can assure you, I'm not a gold digger. I would rather Chance be broke as a joke than have to deal with your crusty judgment." Though I can only see to the top of the table, I look him up and down, as if he's the one who should be worried, and then hold his gaze unflinchingly.

A moment of utter silence and stillness stretches. I can tell that no one speaks to old Chuckie like that, but I'm not going to bow down to him because he's richer than Bezos. I'm impressed by people because they're kind and care for others, are smart and generous, and things like that. Everything about Chuck might as well scream he's more about money than character.

Finally, he grumbles, "You'll have to sign a pre-nup."

It's not approval, but it's taken as such, everyone releasing their held breath.

"Not getting married, so not a problem," I quip back, taking the win because Chance is squeezing my hand and my goal in being here is to support him.

And maybe cause a little shake-up to this whole situation where he feels like he's not enough for his parents. Well, his dad.

Because that's pure bullshit.

Cole hops up easily now, making room for me and Chance next to Luna, and flashes me an impressed smile. He whispers something to Chance, and though I don't hear it clearly, it kinda sounds like 'cojones', but I can't be sure.

He makes his way to Kayla, sitting next to her.

Though all the Harringtons have that California beach beauty look, Cole and Kayla are copy/paste fraternal twin versions of one another—down to the same natural highlights in their hair and the observant spark in their eyes. Cole's wearing black slacks and a bright blue shirt, but though he's dressed the part, there's something a little rougher about him than the other brothers. I can't put my finger on it, but he seems a little more physical than cerebral like Carter and Chance, like he'd be more likely to pick you up in a farmer's carry than get into a verbal debate over thread count minimums for sheets.

I sit down as Chance pulls out my chair, and beneath the table, Luna pats my thigh in support, but then she pinches me, so maybe a bit warningly too.

Miranda sits back down at Charles's side, and I realize that he's said nothing. I kinda took away his opportunity with my little speech. Politely, I say, "Good to see you again, Mr. Harrington."

His eyes narrow, and he picks up the small glass of brown liquid in front of him. He lifts it the tiniest bit in some sort of salute and then sips, still not saying a word.

Yeah, I probably pissed him all the way off, but he's not my concern. Chance is.

And maybe I want to show Chance that his family isn't *all that*, so he doesn't need to be scared of angering them or, more likely, disappointing them. They're humans, flaws and all, too.

Echoing his father's lead, Cameron takes a drink from his glass, but rather than a sip, he tosses both fingers back in one go. I don't know Cameron other than through Grace's stories, and to hear her tell it, he's always busy with work, but he calls her 'beautiful like her mother'. I'm not sure what happened to her mom, only that she passed away when Grace was little, and I wonder if Cameron is still dealing with his feelings about that.

I'd love to give him a recommendation for a grief counselor who could help, but he's probably seen one already or isn't ready to face that loss yet. And professionally, it's not really my place. Still, my heart breaks for him a little. Nobody deserves that kind of pain.

"Is Gracie here?" I ask Cameron.

He shrugs but still answers, "She's with a sitter. She'll be here soon."

"I saw her at the park the other day. She's growing up so fast! I think she and my sister had fun with Peanut Butter," I say, trying to make conversation with him.

"Yeah."

*Okay*, so either he's not a conversationalist or he doesn't want to talk with me.

"I didn't know you have a sister," Miranda interjects, covering for Cameron.

I nod affirmatively. "Yeah, Olivia's sixteen, with all the accompanying drama. My mom's basically going for sainthood with that one." I smile lightly as if teen girls and drama are an absolute given.

Miranda winks at Kayla. "Well, I wouldn't know. My daughter was, and is, an absolute angel." Everyone here knows that Kayla is no such thing. Chance describes his sister as 'a bomb in pretty packaging', and I imagine that's a developed trait to make Charles proud of her considering she's not one of his favored sons.

"How'd you two meet?" Beth asks. "Did I catch that you and Luna are friends?"

I look to Chance, letting him take this one. He can share as much or as little as he wants about us, though I don't expect him to say we're hooking up and I'm only here because Kayla invited me.

"They are," Chance starts, "but somehow, I'd never met Samantha through Luna since I missed the 'wedding'." He says it with air quotes because technically, it was Luna and Carter's vow renewal that he missed. Their wedding was teeny-tiny and drama-filled. "But Samantha and I ran into each other one day at a, uh . . . *conference*, and we hit it off."

I grin, trying to swallow the giggle at our dicks-out meeting being called a conference, and oh, did we 'hit it off' in a spectacular show of fireworks and orgasms. Chance places a heavy hand on my thigh, reading my mind.

"She's helping at the Gentlemen's Club now too, offering classes for our members. I think Evan and I have her talked into being a guest on our podcast as well." He sounds proud—of himself, his business, and me.

"Oh, that's lovely. What sort of classes?"

Beth's seemingly innocuous follow-up leads right into dangerous territory, and I can feel Chance's stress as he tries to figure out the best way to describe what I'm bringing to the club table.

But I've done this before. My scope of practice is always a shock for people, and I've learned that blunt professionalism is best to dissuade any lewd jokes or tactless commentary.

Taking over, I say, "I'm finishing my graduate studies in psychology, with a focus on intimate relationships. I'm helping the club members reshape expectations born of decades of indoctrination to find more intentional mental space, which will allow them to be good partners in their romantic relationships."

Beth blinks and then looks at Chuck. "Did you catch that?" He doesn't move his head in the slightest, which I take to be a no. Turning back to me, Beth says, "Tell it to me like I'm stupid."

She's no such thing. If anything, I'd bet she's the most emotionally intelligent person at this table, having grown up in a time of 'sit still and look pretty' but somehow managing to become a powerhouse in her own home. Oh, Chuck's the boss, but I suspect it's because Beth lets him be. Or think that he is. She's a wily one.

So I do what she asks and break it down to essentials. "I'm a sex therapist, focusing on mental wellness and physical satisfaction."

"Oh," she says, her eyes blank. "Oh!" she suddenly exclaims, having realized what I said.

Winking at her, I quip, "Exactly."

I leave out the Bedroom Heaven gig, deciding I've already pushed dinner conversation far enough.

But Charles sputters, "You do *what* now? At my son's club? Oh, I don't think so. Chance."

Charles looks to Chance as though his disagreement will have instant sway, like Chance will jump away from me in horror and hiss, "Back away, demon spawn. And stay away from my club."

Just because his daddy said so.

Of course, that's not going to happen.

Chance lets go of my hand beneath the table to pointedly lay his arm on the back of my chair, visibly claiming me to his father. With a deadly smile on his face, Chance tells his father, "The change in our members since Samantha began classes is measurable. She's worked wonders on my mental health too, helping find my . . . what'd you call it?"

When he looks at me expectantly, there are so many things I want to say, prostate being at the top of the list because I know it'll go over like a fart in church. But going easy, I ad-lib, "Your give-a-shitter?"

His eyes sparkle with humor, enjoying this. "Right, she's helped me find my give-a-shitter and reprioritize what's important to me. Namely, any type of family approval."

If I could jump up in my chair and cheer for Chance, I would. Hell, I want to climb up on the table, knock the place settings and China out of my way, punt a candlestick, point a finger at Charles, and shout, *"Stick that up your ass! And maybe if you did stick something up there every once in a while, you wouldn't be such a coldhearted jerk to your kids!"*

But I don't. One, it wouldn't be right to rejoice in Charles being put in his place, especially when he's not going to learn anything from it. And two, because it's not about Charles. It's about Chance. So I simply lean into him encouragingly.

I'm so proud of him. Standing up to a parent who's been

doing you wrong is hard. He's gone through rebellion, trying to prove himself, working to earn favor, and now, to finally not needing any of it from Charles because he's proud of himself.

"She might be a miracle worker," Cole whispers to Kayla, who nods like 'I know!'

Charles looks from Chance to the people surrounding his position at the head of the table, feeling the tides turn against him, and I'm afraid he's going to say something hurtful. If it's to me, I can take it. If it's to Chance, Luna might have to hold me back or use some of her *funding* to bail me out of jail. But it's Miranda who answers, "As long as you're happy, honey. That's all we care about."

Miranda places her hand over Charles's and with the barest touch calls him off, telling him to shut up and leave her babies alone.

Beth and Miranda both have some powerful mojo.

"I am," Chance tells his mother, but his eyes are locked on Charles in a battle of wills.

Slowly, conversation starts up again, everyone choosing wisely to avoid the club, Chance, and me as topics.

We're mid-chatter when the doors to the dining room once again open and a woman enters. She's tall, blonde, and statuesque in a fitted dress that shows she's still got a top-notch figure at her age, which I'd estimate to be in her late fifties? Though her face looks a little tight, so maybe sixties?

"Not waiting on the guest of honor?" she accuses, and though she smiles, it looks faker than the orange glow from dollar-store self-tanner.

This must be Aunt Vivian.

At her side is a younger man, whose elbow she's holding. He's over six feet tall, blond, and muscled in that gym way that says he never actually physically works. But on another level, he looks like he could be another Harrington brother.

Behind them, a young woman with strangely high cheekbones and large, otherworldly eyes stands in a simple, but expensive looking, black dress. She's beautiful too, though not in the California wine country commercial way the rest of the Harringtons are.

Chance whispers into my ear, "Cousin Devin and his girlfriend, Bridgette."

Okay, makes sense. The blond guy is a Harrington, just not a brother.

But why is Vivian on Devin's elbow instead of Bridgette? Does she need help of some sort? Chance didn't mention that. Or maybe it's that Vivian is the 'ranking official' in their family so she gets the escort, leaving Bridgette the odd woman out?

That's probably it. And *blech*.

"Of course we are!" Beth tells Vivian, not putting up with her accusation of bad hosting for a minute. She's clearly used to this sort of nonsense. "But when you're late, you can't expect everyone to sit around twiddling their thumbs, waiting for their evening to start until you deign to make an appearance."

Vivian's lips lift, though I wouldn't call it a smile, and nothing else on her face moves a bit. Yup, her face has seen its fair share of scalpels and Botox.

She scans the table, not for attendees for this dinner party but for placement. Seeing the only empty chairs are on the side of the table, she sniffs faintly, as if that's some sort of rebuff.

On the other hand, Devin seems proud and carries himself in a way to be bigger than he is, coming in gregariously as if we're all here to see him. As he passes by Cole, he slaps him on the back heartily like they're best pals, but it's a bit too hard, and I can see Cole bite back words.

With Cameron, though, he doesn't take the chance, mainly because Cameron gives him a look that would freeze the alcohol in his refilled glass. Cameron's wintry smile says very clearly *touch me and you lose your fucking hand*.

Devin bypasses Cameron, ignores Kayla, which is a dick move, and sits down with his girlfriend. Once everyone's seated, Devin between Viv and Bridgette, she speaks up again. "Thank you so much for coming—"

Vivian's making it sound like she's the host, and I'm more than a little pleased when her big introduction speech—one I'm sure she worked on before tonight—is interrupted by Gracie running in.

"Daddy!" she shouts, "Look what I got!"

She's holding up her hand, fingers spread wide, to show off a pink bauble ring on her index finger.

To his credit, Cameron's lips lift into the first true smile I've seen on him and his shoulders drop by inches as his daughter climbs into his lap and gets right up in his face. "That's beautiful, Gracie. Almost as beautiful as you." He taps her nose, and she smiles happily in response to his compliment. "Do you want to have dinner with us or hang in the living room?"

The awareness that this type of fancy dinner party is probably boring to a kid is a pleasant surprise. I guess I thought Cameron would be all 'sit down and be quiet, the grown-ups are talking' with Grace, but he seems downright wrapped around his daughter's finger.

"Can I have dinosaur nuggies in here?" she asks, dropping her chin and batting her lashes.

"Of course, you can," Miranda answers for Cameron.

"Ooh, can I have one too?" Luna asks, joking with the little girl.

"Yum, me too!" I say, playing along. Hell, dino nuggies sound better than that crap Macrosine tried to pawn off on Chance and me. And given the fanciness of the Harrington home, I'm afraid I might need a McDonald's stop on the way home again

But my comment triggers all hell to break loose as Grace realizes I'm here. "SAMANTHA!" Grace shouts at one hundred and twenty decibels before immediately diving *under* the table to get to me faster.

We all lean back, looking down to see Gracie crawling across the rug right toward me. "Hey, uh, Grace . . . you could'a just walked around the table, you know?" I say, grinning as she pops up beside me and wraps her arms around my neck tightly.

"Too slow and you need to see my ring," she states as though the shortcut makes perfect sense now that she's explained her reasoning.

She holds it up for my inspection, and I hum thoughtfully. "Pink diamond? Very pretty."

"Pink sapphire," she corrects even though the ring is obviously costume and not a real stone. Even the metal of the ring itself shines a bit too brightly, clearly cheap plating on an even cheaper base metal.

"I thought sapphires were blue," Luna says.

Knowing more about everything than most adults, Gracie educates her. "Sapphires can be lots of colors, depending on the minerals where they grow."

We nod along with her, not sure if she's telling the truth or making shit up on the fly. It doesn't matter either way. No one will call her on it.

"As I was saying—" Vivian says, trying again to get to her welcome speech.

This time, the swinging door to the kitchen opens and two staff walk out with plates of food in their hands.

Guess this dinner party is finally getting started . . . officially.

# CHAPTER 22
# CHANCE

I'M READY TO LEAVE.

We're barely into our salad course and I'm fighting to stay in my seat when all I want to do is stand, take Samantha's hand, and walk right out the front door.

But I don't.

I don't care as much about rules and expectations as I once did, but leaving mid-dinner would be rude. And secretly, I kinda want Samantha to see what she's getting herself into. Because I intend for her to be at my side for every family dinner from here on out, especially after she smoothly put my grandfather in his place, charmed my grandmother, and had my back when I stood up to my father.

If only Aunt Vivian weren't here, or would shut the hell up, it'd be perfect.

She's going around the table, asking for the update on my siblings with a sneering, condescending frown on her face. She's looking for bits of information, nuggets she can turn not into gold, but shade she can throw back at us.

I swear, Cameron could say that he's being considered for the Nobel Peace Prize and she'd bitch about how it's a political nightmare not nearly worth the gold it's minted from. As it is, apparently, he's still 'riding on daddy's coattails', according to her.

"What about you, Cole?" Aunt Viv asks, zeroing in on her next 'victim'. "I've lost track a little bit. What is it you're doing?" Rather than sounding like a forgetful older woman, she manages to make it sound like what Cole's doing is so utterly forgettable that she didn't bother to remember.

"I've got a couple of irons in the fire," Cole answers evasively.

Still, I wish he would answer because I think we're all curious about him. He keeps everything secretive, and I honestly can't tell you what my brother does, which is ridiculous. For all I know, he could be a day trader or a hitman, and I think he gets off on withholding that information from us. I don't think Kayla even knows, and if anyone's run a background check on their own family, it's Kayla.

"So, blacksmithing?" Aunt Vivian retorts coolly, using Cole's answer against him. "Charming. Your coattails are rather broad, Charles."

She offers an icy glare to Dad, measuring his reaction to her trust fund comment, but Dad simply stares back at her, blank-faced and uncaring. He's dealt with harsher critics than his whiny older sister, and apparently doesn't feel the need to explain to her that none of us have trust funds. College, yes. Trust, no.

"I'm riding on Dad's coattails too, Aunt Viv," Kayla volunteers, holding a hand up and grinning. "Blue Lake Asset Group has been so good to me, welcoming me with open arms, giving me a home away from home where I can work hard and succeed," she says wistfully, almost sounding like a pageant girl, which she isn't.

*If she mentions world peace, puppies, or Rihanna, I'm going to lose it and laugh out loud.*

To the uninitiated, it'd seem like Kayla's making light of her work, but we know exactly what she's doing—rubbing Aunt Viv's nose in the fact that while she was never allowed to be a part of the family company, other women are. Grandpa Chuck might've been a staunch misogynist in his day, but that can be overcome . . . by the right woman, someone made of sturdier stuff than Vivian could ever dream of.

Hell, Aunt Vivian's own mother did it and was a prime role model for her, if she'd bothered to open her eyes and look.

"Hmmph, I was just curious what you all have been up to because Devin's been doing some amazing things recently. Haven't you, Devin?"

She starts on a series of 'fishing tales' that, if they were even ten percent true, would make Devin the richest, handsomest, most popular man on the planet, as well as Mr. Universe, the champion of the Super Bowl, and possibly the next Pope and/or President if he wants.

Through our soup course, she talks about his business acumen. Through our entrees, it's his physical prowess. And into a sorbet palate cleanse, it's how lucky Bridgette is to have a man like Devin at her side.

I'm used to Aunt Vivian and her anything-but-humble brags, but it's still a bit much, even for me. Looking around the table, I can see that Carter and Luna have tuned out and are having a silent conversation with their eyes, Cole looks ready to pummel Devin unprovoked, and Cameron is playing 'sticks' with Gracie, a finger tapping game that usually keeps her distracted and entertained. Mom and Dad have on the polite, bland faces I've seen hundreds of times at fundraisers and events over the years, and I know that Mom is singing in her head, going through her mental library of pop classics. Grandpa and Grandma are the only ones listening, but the boasts are about their grandchild so it seems warranted.

*"And my Devvy-poo, my wittel baby goes potty all by himself now,"* I whisper in Samantha's ear as Viv talks about some sort of clean water initiative Devin's 'working with', which we all know is code for 'sends money to and schmoozed at a cocktail party for'.

I try not to burst out laughing, but a snort still leaves my throat, and for the first time, Aunt Viv deigns to pay attention to me. It's funny, but I've actually appreciated her hysterical gloating because it's literally taken all attention off me and Samantha. After tonight, no one will remember that I showed up with a surprise date who said outrageous things to Grandpa Chuck. All we'll remember is Aunt Vivian droning on and on about Devin.

"I'm sorry, I didn't mean to interrupt," I apologize automatically.

Placated, Aunt Viv starts again when suddenly, there's a thunderous *ROAR* from outside.

*She can't catch a break!* I think to myself, laughing at the continued interruptions she's been 'victim' to.

All attention turns to the windows behind the head of the table as a bright light stabs through the darkness and the distinctive sound of a ridiculously loud, barely muffled motorcycle comes through from outside.

"*Uncle Kyle!*" Gracie yells as a motorcycle comes tearing onto the side lawn of the estate. The motion-activated lights kick on to show us the driver planting the front wheel and cranking a hard donut, sending chunks of grass flying in a large circle before he parks.

*Gardener's gonna be pissed at that one.*

A minute later, Kyle comes striding through the French doors that Grace unlocked for him, like it's totally normal to show up for a family dinner through the side door in dirty jeans, a slightly ripped T-shirt, a leather jacket, and boots.

"'Hey, folks," Kyle says in way of greeting, pausing by the yet to be sliced birthday cake to zigzag-slide a finger through the icing on top, making sure to contaminate as much as possible. Slipping the large glob of icing into his mouth, he sucks at his finger before sighing, "Mmm, damn, Grandma. How do you do it? Always killing it with the food. It's the only reason I came tonight."

He winks Grandma's way, his blue eyes similar to the rest of the family's but his darkly stubbled cheeks and dark hair making him an obvious outlier.

Grandpa glares, and Grandma chuckles at his wayward antics as though they're charming. "You know that's my secret, Kyle-baby."

Dad isn't amused, though. "I thought you weren't coming?"

"Wasn't going to," Kyle says with a shrug as he picks up Gracie one-handed and slings her on his hip like a baby, though her legs dangle down well below his knees. "Even when Mom tried telling me I had to. But Grandma asked me to stop by, and you know I can't tell her no. Just running a little late. Stacey's mom says sorry."

I was half believing him until that last bit. Kyle clearly meant to show up, but only in a way that'd make the biggest splash. He lives to piss off Dad, and bonus points if it embarrasses him too.

I've always considered it childish, still do mostly, but I can see how Dad's expectations of all of us have shaped our behaviors toward him, if not toward the family as a whole. Dad never gave Kyle attention, so naturally, Kyle did more and more outrageous things in an attempt to get some, negative or positive. But at some point, Kyle needs to quit fucking around and be his own man despite Dad.

"This is what he does to make Dad mad if he's asked to do something he doesn't want to," I quietly explain to Samantha. "Should've seen Christmas." When she looks at me questioningly, I cover my mouth with my hand and whisper dramatically, "Oh, I've seen some shit between the two of them. Your professors could do an entire series on how messed up they are. The horror . . . the horror."

Samantha smirks at my quote. "*Apocalypse Now*? Really?"

"You know, Kyle, it's my birthday, and that was quite *rude*," Aunt Viv says primly before I can reply. "I was just telling everyone about Devin's—" She gestures to her son, trying to get attention back to her golden child.

"Latest and greatest? I'll bet," Kyle interjects with an audible eye roll even though his blue eyes stay locked on his latest target —Devin. Smirking and throwing his voice high and animated like he's talking to a toddler, Kyle says, "Yeah, lil buddy, how's your fantasy football league going? Do you think you're gonna win the Superbowl? Goooo Devinators!"

"Wha— why, I never!" Aunt Viv exclaims.

"Kyle!" Dad shouts, losing his cool. "Sit down and behave or I'll have to ask you to leave."

He's attempting to draw a line in the sand, but Kyle's always happy to stomp right over those so I don't know why Dad tries. As much as Kyle needs to get his shit together, Dad needs to quit trying to shove Kyle into a box that he's never been remotely close to fitting into.

Kyle smiles widely at Dad, malicious compliance in his eyes. "Sure thing." He struts over to Grace's chair and plops down roughly. If Gracie wasn't in his lap, he'd probably throw his boots up on the table to needle Dad even more. "What're we talking about?"

"Hmph, well, as I was saying before I was so rudely interrupted, Devin has something important—"

"Oh, shit, you really were still harping on him? I thought I'd timed it to miss all that. Pity," Kyle says, interrupting once more. Reaching out, he snags a dino nugget from Gracie's plate. "Open up, Graciesaurus."

"Next time, I'll text you when the coast's clear," Cole offers straight-faced. Kyle plops the nugget in Gracie's mouth and holds up a fist. Though they're far away at the table, Cole holds one up too, and they air-fist bump.

A staff member sets a plate of pork roast in front of Kyle, and he picks up Grace's unused fork. "Good food, good meat, good God, let's eat." He stabs the biggest slice of roast and lifts it like a leg of lamb, taking a huge bite out of it while letting the rest stay on the tines. He sits back, chewing thoughtfully, and for some reason, we all watch in silence.

I don't know how he does it. I think mostly he just shocks everyone to the point they don't argue with whatever stupid stunt he's pulling. He's like a walking, talking, living car crash you can't turn away from.

Glancing around the table, he pauses on Samantha, and I can feel my hackles rising. He can be the Black Sheep of the family if he chooses, but he's not going to fuck with Samantha.

Pointing at her with his meat-laden fork, he says, "I know you." It's a statement, but his eyes are questioning, trying to place her.

Gracie answers before anyone else. "Uncle Kyle, that's

NEVER GIVE YOUR HEART TO A HOOKUP 219

Samantha. Luna's friend. Well, now I think she's Uncle Chance's friend too." The last part is whispered in the vicinity of Kyle's ear, but Grace has zero concept of volume control so we all hear it.

Kyle's eyes pop to me and then back to Samantha, trying to fit the puzzle pieces together.

"You're with *him*?" Kyle asks Samantha.

"Yes, but don't worry, as I've already explained to everyone else . . . I'm not a gold digger. I'm only in it for the dick," Samantha says evenly, as if saying it's a beautiful night outside.

I should've known not to worry about her. If anyone can deal with Kyle, it'd be her.

"What?" Aunt Vivian sputters.

"Oh, yeah, you weren't here for that part. Sorry." Samantha smiles, serene as can be, as she apologizes to Vivian, who's still sputtering at the crude comment.

Kayla, apparently trying to smooth things over, leans over and whispers something in Kyle's ear. From the look on her face, I'm guessing she's trying to play peacemaker, but who knows?

Suddenly, Devin stands up, pushing his chair back to give himself room between his mother and girlfriend. "To get things back on a positive note, I'd like to say something. I know Mom doesn't ask for much, but I thought this was the best birthday gift I could give her. And the most fitting."

Devin gets down on one knee and, as several gasps fill the room, reaches into his jacket pocket to pull out a ring.

I have a moment of complete confusion. Ring plus down on his knee should equal a proposal. But Devin said this is a gift for his mom.

*Oh, fuck, is he proposing to his mother?!*

*Ewwwwwwww. I think I just threw up in my mouth a little.*

I mean we've always joked that Aunt Viv and Devin are oddly close, but I thought it was more in a babying sort of way, not an Oedipus complex way.

Thankfully—is that really the minimum to be grateful for— he turns to Bridgette.

"Baby, you make me so happy and I can't wait for you to be part of our family. Will you marry me?"

Before Bridgette answers, Aunt Viv has her hands on Devin's shoulders, leaning in beside him and grinning maniacally. "Yes! Say yes, and join us!"

Us? Is she talking about in matrimony or in a Stepford Wife, resistance-is-futile way? Because given Vivian's wild eyes, I'm not sure.

Bridgette, who I've only met a couple of times but seems remarkably *normal* to be tied up with Devin, nods happily, only having eyes for him. She reaches for Devin, wrapping her arms around his neck for a hug, but she virtually has to rip him from Vivian's grasp.

Bridgette starts to sob into their hug, mumbling something that sounds like, "I told you I wanted you to propose when it was just the two of us."

But Aunt Vivian wails dramatically, drowning out anything Bridgette might be saying and drawing the attention back to where it belongs—on her. Always and only, on her.

"My baby's getting married! I know just the place and season —Mykonos in September! It'll be so stunning. Oh, and we'll have to get an appointment at Jacob's, of course. He's simply the best at bespoke suits. And the food? We'll have to decide on which chef to hire."

Aunt Vivian's loud rambling tells me that she probably has a notebook already prepped and ready for Devin's nuptials.

Everyone else's reactions are more appropriate—clapping and cheers and congratulations coming from around the table.

As Bridgette and Devin separate and he slips the ring onto her finger, they seem truly happy. Except for the harpy that's flitting about, bothering them.

"Let me see! I told Devin to get you a princess cut ring so we'd match." Aunt Vivian holds up her own hand, flashing her huge engagement-wedding-anniversary ring combo. When she sees Bridgette's ring, whose solitaire diamond is visible from here, she squeals, "Oh, it's so *cute*! Great job, Devin!"

With that, she pulls her son into a huge, tight hug, exclaiming, "That's the best birthday gift you could've gotten me. Thank you!"

Bridgette is sitting there, shell-shocked and completely excluded from what should be a couple's moment.

Grandpa Chuck is watching with raised brows but says nothing, Grandma Beth is smiling sweetly, and my whole family is biting their tongues to keep from laughing out loud at Vivian's theatrics. Not that she'd care what any of us think, exactly, but she is putting on this show for us, I think. Otherwise, why would Devin do the whole proposal thing at his mother's birthday dinner, especially if Bridgette asked him for something different?

*She asked him to.*

Samantha leans into me and whispers in my ear, "Forget your Dad and Kyle. I want to do an entire case study on Vivian and Devin." As she leans back, we lock eyes and I can see the professional horror in hers. "Wow!" she mouths animatedly.

She's absolutely right.

Realizing she's lost our attention, Aunt Vivian snaps, both her literal fingers and her tone at Samantha, "I'm sorry, I've forgotten your name. What was it again? Sarah? No worries, point is . . . you'll have your day too. If you learn how to speak without the obscenities." She crinkles her nose in delayed distaste at Samantha's earlier use of the word dick. "But today is about Devin. Pay attention to what matters."

Aunt Vivian's being intentionally obstinate, trying to put Samantha firmly beneath her and still offended by her comment that she's with me for sex, not money.

If I allowed myself to think about Aunt Vivian and sex in one sentence for more than a second, I'd probably come to the conclusion that, like everything else in her life, Vivian uses sex as a tool to get what she wants. She's never considered that it might be something done for simple pleasure between two people without an ulterior motive.

And that's enough of that thought stream, because again . . . Aunt Viv and sex.

*Blech*, and pass the brain bleach!

But Aunt Vivian's never gone head-to-head with someone like Samantha, and I'm equal parts terrified and excited about what's about to happen because while Vivian thinks she's had the final word, Samantha's pulling her thoughts together, prepping for maximum impact and effectiveness.

I think I hear Kayla whisper, "Watch this."

To Kyle? To Cole? Who knows? But I suspect Kayla recognizes a sister-in-kind, and sees that Samantha is well-spoken, strong, and about to lay down a verbal beating the likes of which Aunt Vivian can't even fathom.

"It's Samantha, not that you asked before launching into a fifty-five-minute diatribe. I must say, I'm impressed with your breath control, though I doubt you put it to good use." She shakes her head in mock sadness, and I nearly choke from trying not to laugh at what she's implying. "And some of us are looking for more in life than a ring and our Daddy's love. But exaggerating about your son, singing his praises in such a romanticized manner, and putting yourself in the middle of what should be *their* moment is, to put it bluntly . . . *professionally concerning*."

"Chance!" Dad hisses, telling me to get my date under control . . . now, or pay the price.

I lean forward, meeting Dad's eyes boldly. "Well, Samantha is a professional. She'd know. Besides, we've all said it. It's weird and gross."

Dad tilts his head, silently reminding me that we're not supposed to repeat private gossip in public, or even in front of family when it's about other family members.

"What? You're talking about me? About my Devin?" Aunt Vivian wails, sounding horribly wounded. "Daddy!" She pouts, turning her attention to Grandpa Chuck, and though she screws her face up, there's not a tear in sight.

If she could stomp her foot like a toddler, I think she would. As it is, sitting at the table, she throws her napkin to her plate in a vague threat of leaving.

"Hell, if you're starting the waterworks this early, you should've had your little birthday *par-tay* at Chuck E. Cheese. They're used to dealing with tantrum-throwing kids," Kyle suggests. "Probably used to hissy fits from adults too. Could'a just thrown you in the ball pit or something."

"I *LOVE* ball pits!" Grace adds helpfully.

"Vivian, I wasn't the best father, and it's one of my few regrets in life, but you've got to admit, this was a bit much," Grandpa says carefully, taking control of the room. Holding hands with Grandma Beth, I get the feeling this is a conversation they've had many times over the years.

"Me? You're blaming this on *me*?" Aunt Vivian screeches, standing up abruptly. "Of course you are. It's always my fault. I'm not good enough, not smart enough, not male enough for you," she spits out. "Thank God, Charlie Junior came along so you'd have at least one kid to love." She sends an angry glare her brother's way before returning her vitriol to her father. "I thought maybe you'd have it in your old, shriveled raisin of a heart to at least love your grandson too since he's the only thing that matters to you—a son."

"You don't want me to love him. You want me to bankroll him, and by default you, but I haven't given a single cent to any of Charles's kids, or your sisters'," Grandpa says evenly, "and it wouldn't be fair to give Devin any."

"Fair? Fair? *Faaaiiir!*" she bellows, but she's run out of steam. Having spewed the venom she's been holding for most of her life and been called on her true game, she huffs, "Come on, Devin. We're leaving."

Devin hops up, accustomed to following Mommy's orders. Bridgette is a little slower from lack of practice, but she rises too. As they follow Aunt Vivian out of the room, Samantha gets up quickly and rushes over to stop Bridgette.

"This might not be my place to say, but if you need someone to talk to, call me at Chance's club. And for the love of all things holy matrimony, you have to watch *I Love a Momma's Boy* on TV. Girl, you're living it in high-definition and don't even recognize how deep you're in. Every alarm is ringing, but you're not saving yourself. Please, I've got one word for you . . . *RUN.*"

Having realized that Bridgette wasn't trotting along after

him, Devin pops his head back into the dining room. "*Come on, she's gonna leave us if we don't get out there.*"

It's obvious where his loyalties lie, and Bridgette looks torn for a split second but then follows Devin.

Samantha sighs to herself, "Did what I could." When she turns around, her eyes jump all over the table, and having been watching her try to save Bridgette, I follow her gaze.

Everyone's looking at her.

She clears her throat. "Yeah, well . . . I think we did a lot of good work here tonight. Got a lot of what's been weighing us down out into the open, which is always uncomfortable. But remember, uncomfortable is where growth happens, so this was progress."

Samantha's dropped into her professional therapist voice as if this whole dinner debacle was nothing more than a therapy session.

I should be mortified. Or embarrassed? Or something? I'm certain I'm expected to feel some sort of shame for this whole thing, given the angry glare my father's sending my way. But when I search my gut, all I find is satisfaction. She's right, this was a long time coming.

Okay, and a little humor because did Dad really not see the nearly literal steam coming out of Aunt Vivian's ears? That's fucking hilarious. But if I laugh, I'm going to be in so much trouble.

Not that I care, but I don't have time for it. Not now when I want to twirl Samantha around and whoop in delight, because I was right. This was our best family dinner ever.

"I think we should go," I say straight-faced. My jaw's tight as I fight to stay stoic.

"That might be best," Mom says, but then, ever the polite hostess, she adds, "Lovely to see you again, Samantha."

# CHAPTER 23
# SAMANTHA

CHANCE HASN'T SAID a word since we left. After silently helping me in the car, we drove away from the estate, and I deduced about twenty minutes ago that he's heading to my apartment.

All in complete silence.

I understand why he's mad. That was a pretty dramatic and traumatic family dinner, with me at the center for so much of it. I didn't go in with the intention of psychoanalyzing his aunt and cousin, but it was so over-the-top and obvious. I mean, how did someone not intervene before tonight?

As for how I talked to Chuck, and mentioned only being in it for the dick? It was a knee-jerk reaction to their very loud assumption that any female who shows up with one of their boys must be out for the Benjamins. I should've been more polite and polished, but I am who I am, and bowing up to that sort of mentality is my gut response.

Chance had seemed fine after that . . . and when I said it to Kyle . . . and when I said it to Vivian, but now? I glance over at him to find his eyes locked on the road, jaw set like stone, and hands gripping the steering wheel so tight they're turning white.

Yeah, somewhere between there and now, he's put together that I'm not the girl you take home.

*Well. It was good while it lasted.*

*Real fucking good.*

This is why I don't do relationships, family meet and greets, and promises of forever. I fuck them up. But I'm going to miss Chance, and not only the mind-blowing sex.

I'm going to miss snuggling up on the couch while we both stare at our laptops, him working and me studying, simply existing together. I'm going to miss the way his whole face lights up and his shoulders relax when he sees me, like I make him happy. I'm going to miss the way he acts shocked when I say something scandalous but then grins and compliments the way my brain works. I'm going to miss . . .

Chance Harrington.

I cut my eyes the other way, staring out the window. On the way here, the stars twinkling had seemed like little sparklers cheering us on for a great night. Now, they feel like the last tiny flame of burned-out sparklers—pretty and flashy, but only for a short time, and then you're left holding ashes and hot, pointy sticks.

When Chance pulls up to the curb in front of my building, I say, "I'm sorry."

He holds up a hand, nearly putting his palm in my face. "Don't say a fucking word."

Well, I tried.

I knew this thing had an expiration date. I'm not Chance's type, and to be honest, he's not mine. But for a minute, I thought maybe there was a chance.

When he opens my door and helps me out, I expect him to ditch me there on the sidewalk and peel away to leave me faster. But Chance is more of a gentleman than that, so he walks stiffly to the building, holds the door open for me, and follows me inside.

I fumble with my door key, and he takes it from me, probably thinking I'm dragging this on in desperation because he unlocks the door easily. "I understand—" I start to say, again thinking this is goodbye.

He shoves me inside and slams the door behind us. He doesn't even look at me when he growls, "Get that damn dress off or I'm gonna rip it off." He makes a fist a few times, his knuckles creaking with the repeated movement.

"What?" I blurt in utter confusion.

Chance moves closer, getting right in my face, nose-to-nose. For the first time since we left, I can see how clear and bright his eyes are, the little streaks of pale blue stark against the deeper blue. "Dress. Off. You. Table. Right fucking now, Samantha."

Okaaay. I understand caveman talk, but even knowing what he wants me to do . . . why?

As I shimmy my dress down, I ask, "Are we having mad sex? I know you're mad at me. I'm sorry."

He stops me from climbing on the table—I'm nothing if not obedient despite every evidence to the contrary—by grabbing my ankle. I look back at him in surprise.

"I'm fucking furious. At my *family*. Not at you. You don't have anything to apologize for. I'm the one apologizing for making you go through that. Now lie down so I can write my 'I'm sorrys' on your tits, your pussy, and maybe that ass."

My head is spinning with everything he said, trying to process. Not mad at me—that's the important one. And so . . . "Yes, sir!" I declare, ripping off my bra and lying back on my teeny-tiny dining table.

As Chance yanks my panties down my legs, I wish I had the space and money for a bigger table, one we could both climb up on to fuck wildly on its vast surface. As it is, this cheap-ass breakfast table that barely seats two is all I have room for.

Chance leans over me, cupping my jaw firmly, but his kiss is gentle. I keep my eyes open for a second after his close, watching him, waiting for the trick.

But one doesn't come.

As we kiss, his shirt brushes over my nipples, causing them to pearl up. Wanting more, I arch my chest into his and reach down to grab at his waist, but he pulls back, taking my hands and placing them to the tabletop. "Don't move. Let me."

Palms pressing to the surface, I try my best to be a receiving partner, but it's hard. I want to run my fingers through his hair, I want to guide him to my nipples and lower, I want . . . whatever he's doing right now.

He's pressing soft, fluttery kisses down my neck, and every once in a while, he takes a little nip of the skin that surprises me each time. At my collarbone, he drags his tongue into the hollow and places a kiss at my shoulder before repeating the move on the other side. More kisses down my sternum and to my belly button, and my hips buck, begging him to keep going until he reaches my clit. But he doesn't.

His hands cup my breasts, weighing their fullness, and I moan as they ache for his touch. Slipping his thumbs over my already stiff nipples, he watches how they react for him, going diamond hard. Only then does he take one into his mouth. His teeth are sharp as they bite down, but fuck, does it feel good. I arch again, not able to stop it, and thankfully, he doesn't punish me for it. No, he keeps going—sucking, nibbling, and licking both nipples until I think I might come from that alone. That'd definitely be a first. But every time he draws deeply, a thread to my core pulls tighter and tighter.

Moaning, I splay my hands on the table, the cool surface keeping me grounded because I'm in real danger of simply shooting away like a rocket.

"Good girl," he murmurs against my skin as if he knows how hard I'm working to obey.

I'd already figured out that dirty talk does it for me, but apparently, I've got a new praise kink going on too because his words make me so wet that I can feel the juices running down from my pussy to my ass. I'm probably leaving a puddle on the table, but rather than grossing me out to dirty my eating space that way, it's sexy as hell, like we're marking everything, everywhere, with our arousal.

He kisses lower, across my belly and hips, and finally, he splays my legs open. I'm ready for him to lick me there, but when I lift my head, he's simply looking at my center, his eyes worshipful. "Beautiful," he says, right before kissing my inner thigh. I groan in disappointment even though his touch there still feels good, and he chuckles. "Patience."

"Running out," I gasp as his fingers dance right above my clit. I'm sweating with how hard it is to stop myself from lifting my hips to get his fingers where I want them.

"Here?" he hisses as his thumb barely grazes the top of my clit.

I surge mindlessly, my hips bucking before I can even control it, and Chance open-palm swats my pussy with his fingers, right over my clit. It's not hard, but not soft either, and the shocking jolt of it nearly makes me come. "*Fuck*," I cry out.

"Be a good girl. Let me love you."

There's a deeper meaning to his order, but I can't think about it now. Not when every fiber in my body is fighting it. My hands are clenched into tight fists, my toes are curled, my back is arched, and my heart is pounding. I breathe in little pants, trying to relax to receive this pleasure he wants to give me.

*This love?*

*Don't go there, Samantha*, I warn myself. *One thing at a time*.

When my back touches the table again, he purrs, "There you go. Good girl." The grit in his voice tells me he wants this as much as I do, and that's enough to give me another burst of strength.

I can do this. I can lie here and let him torture me with pleasure, enjoying every moment of it. I can accept this. I deserve this.

The mantra forms in my mind unconsciously, but I roll with it.

"I deserve this." Speaking it aloud makes it more real, and Chance responds with a growl.

"Fuck yes, you do."

His tongue lashes over my clit, speedy, quick flicks focused right on top of it that drive me insane, while the rest of my pussy begs for attention of its own. I feel empty and want him to fill me, not caring if it's with his fingers or cock, and I can feel my muscles clamping down, looking for something to squeeze. But he doesn't . . . not yet. He's just getting started with me, and he eats me out like a starving man given a luscious dessert. Licking me like ice cream, sucking me like candy, even nibbling my clit like chocolate.

As my cries get louder, Chance zeroes in, finding a pattern over my clit that I can't withstand for long. "Come for me. Scream my name and tell me you accept my apology, Samantha. Please," he grunts, keeping me going with his thumb on my clit while he begs. As he dives back for more, I explode into shards of glass, light reflecting everywhere inside my soul.

"Chance! No need . . . to . . . apologize," I manage to stutter out amid my release. *"Yes!"*

I mean it, there's nothing he needs to apologize for. His family's behaviors aren't his own. And for the most part, his family was great. I knew what I was walking into and handled the rest.

So if I don't need to apologize . . . and he doesn't need to apologize . . . what are we doing?

Falling back to reality, I reach for him but he pulls away.

"Not done. By a longshot." It's all the warning I get before his fingers fill me, pumping into my pussy hard and fast and wiping any logical thought from my mind.

*Is that two fingers? Three? His whole damn hand?*

I don't know, but with my being so close to the edge, the onslaught is a lot. "Oh, shit. I don't know if I can."

"Give me another one," he demands.

The stretching feeling relaxes, and Chance lays his arm over my hips, holding me down as he slams his fingers into me staccato, brushing them over my front wall with every stroke. "This is what I felt like, held down by the seatbelt while you made me come for you."

I lift my head to look at him, finding him grinning darkly as he watches his fingers disappearing inside me, enjoying my messy pleasure. "You gonna make me come again?" I ask, knowing the answer and wanting the orgasm. "Hold me down and take what you want from my pussy?"

I'm turning the tables a bit. He told me to be still, not to be quiet, and he's as turned on as I am. He almost made me come sucking on my nipples, and I wonder if I can make him come with only my words.

His strokes get sloppy, his hand curling a bit, and when his palm bumps into my clit, I'm done. I fall apart again, or come together, I'm not sure which. All I know is that waves keep coming and coming, taking me deeper and deeper until I'm drowning.

Suddenly, I gasp, the air rushing into my lungs after unconsciously holding my breath.

"Fuck me, please, Chance," I beg. I'm a ragdoll, but I want him to come too. I want to give him pleasure.

And bluntly, I want his cock.

He pushes off from the table, looming over me. It feels obscene somehow that I'm a naked mess and he's still wearing his clothes from dinner, his shirt even tucked in. But I can see the humongous bulge behind his zipper straining to be set free, wanting to be unleashed on me.

He doesn't take his shirt off, though, or undo his pants. He walks away after a gruff, "Stay there."

He disappears into my bedroom, and I hear him opening and closing my nightstand drawer. He knows where my toys are, and I'm both excited to see what he comes back with and disappointed because I want his real-life dick, not a silicone one.

He comes back with a new toy, though. At my questioning look, he explains, "Got it from your work stash, already washed and ready. I'll buy it for us."

For us. Not for me. For us.

For some reason, that makes a fresh rush of wetness pour from me and my heart race.

There's just one problem. "I don't think I can take that monster."

It's one of our bigger products, both in girth and length, plus it has vibrating rabbit ears. The silicone is purple glitter, and it's called the Mad Hatter because this thing will wear your pussy like a hat. It uses you, not the other way around. Plus, you might actually go a bit mad from repeated use.

"You can," Chance reassures me, sounding certain.

He swipes the head of it through my juices and adds a bit more lubrication from a bottle he also brought from my room. "Breathe," he tells me as he works the huge dick into my pussy. He lazily strokes over my clit, keeping me aroused as he gets it fully inserted.

In and out he moves it, slowly getting me used to the ridiculous stretch and deep fullness. As my body relaxes, making it easier and easier, he praises me. I cry out, climbing the peak for another orgasm, and Chance asks, "You ready?"

I think he means to come, and I nod woodenly.

That is *not* what he meant.

Suddenly, he turns the Mad Hatter on, and my entire body vibrates as he holds it fully inside me, stretching me almost to the point of pain as the rabbit ears destroy my clit, buzzing not just on the surface, but through the nerves well into my body's core. He gives me tiny strokes, staying deep and making the ears bounce against my clit in a punishing rhythm.

I die.

Maybe literally. I'm not sure.

All I know is the entire world goes black, and distantly, I feel my body spasming. I think I scream. I know I squirt everywhere, but only because when I come back from the other side and force my eyes open, I can see the wetness all over Chance's shirt.

"Ohmagawd . . . ohmagawd . . ." I gasp over and over, trying to get oxygen to my brain.

Chance pulls the Mad Hatter from me with care, sets it down with decidedly less, and yanks his tie off. He only gets three or four buttons undone on his shirt before he gives up and rips it over his head. Belt and slacks drop to the floor, and I guess he kicked his shoes off at some point. When he shoves his underwear down, freeing his cock, it's huge and hard, the tip nearly purple from holding back his orgasm.

He takes himself in hand, stroking roughly. "Told myself this was for you. It's my apology." I want to say we've already figured this out and that there are no apologies needed, but he's rambling so fast. "I need to come, Samantha. I don't deserve it, and I'm sorry . . . I have to."

He starts jacking himself, and I sit up, sending sparkles through my vision. Blinking, I put a hand on his, stopping him. He grunts in desperation, and I wonder if my Boy Scout is going to push me down and take me. The idea with Chance is exciting. I love when he goes beyond his own boundaries.

"You don't have anything to apologize for," I tell him again. "Don't punish yourself."

He grits his teeth, panting jaggedly as he presses our foreheads together so that he can look deep into my eyes. Of everything else we've done, this feels the most intimate, and the most important, and though it's only a moment, it feels like forever. He starts to say something, but I feel him physically swallow the words and change course.

"Roll over and put that ass right here for me."

He releases me and steps back, tapping the table.

I do as I'm told—standing up, but bending over to press my cheek to the table, with my ass right in front of Chance. I wiggle enticingly, knowing what we're about to do and wanting it.

Wanting Chance.

His hands grip my cheeks, squeezing the handfuls of flesh delightfully tight, and I remember warning him about fingerprints on my thigh earlier. Here? On my ass where no one can see them but us, I welcome them and arch for more.

He spanks me twice, hard, and I cry out. "You like that?" he asks. His voice is demanding, daring me to say no, but he's truly checking on me too.

I nod mindlessly, twitching my hips for another. He spreads my cheeks apart, and I feel vulnerable in an entirely different way. I feel him but lube on my asshole, and then his thumb slides through it, teasing at my entrance to test whether I'm ready.

His thumb pops in easily, and he chuckles, quiet and dark.

I'm so far gone, a complete and utter slut for this man and what he does to my body.

I hear him slathering lube on his cock, the wet smacks getting me ready too. "I'm not gonna last long, Samantha.

Getting in this sweet hole after watching you take that big dick for me. Can you help me?"

"Yes, anything," I promise.

"Good girl. Slide your hands underneath you. I want you to rub that clit while I fuck your ass hard. I want to feel you come again, feel your ass convulsing around me. Can you make me come, Samantha?"

His words are already doing half the work for us both.

"Uh-huh." I'm doing as he said, sliding my hands under my hips and cupping my pussy. "I'm ready, just do it."

I don't need him to go slow. If there's any pain, I welcome it because I want him inside me—here, there, anywhere, as long as it's him.

*Only him.*

He groans at my invitation, and I feel the tip of his cock at my back entrance. Despite my words, he presses in slowly, but given his jagged breathing, I think it's for his pleasure and control, not my comfort. I feel a sharp pain for a split second, and then I sigh as my body relaxes to take him.

Deep inside me, he holds my hips in his punishing grip and then unleashes himself on me. He pounds hard and fast, my ass cheeks recoiling with every slam of our hips. It should hurt, all logic says it should, but it doesn't. With my fingers blurring over my clit and Chance fucking my ass like a beast, I'm close in seconds.

He's grunting behind me, and I can feel his sweat dripping onto my spine. He's holding back for me, letting me get there too so he can feel me come around him. I know what we both need.

"Fuck my ass. Take it, it's yours." I forcefully inhale because he's pounding harder with my words. "I'm your slut, Chance. Yours only. Fill my ass with your cum . . . *please!*" The last part is another scream because I spasm as he thunders, pouring himself into me as he fucks me into the table.

This time, I focus on Chance through my own orgasm, intentionally milking every drop from him. "Yes, give it to me." And he does, pulse after hot pulse filling me.

When he's done, he takes a big breath, recovering, and I sigh, "Good boy."

He laughs, the sudden movement unfortunately pulling him from my body. Leaning forward, he gets right in my ear as I look back at him. "That sounds like you're talking to a dog." His grin is good-natured, and it's obvious he's much happier now that I told him he didn't have anything to apologize for and he came like a monster in my ass.

I grin back, arguing, "Well, you called me good girl."

"Difference is . . . you liked it," he says cockily.

He's not wrong, I did like that, so I shrug flirtily and start to get up from the table. Chance helps me, and as soon as I stand, I realize what an absolute mess of cum, lube, and juices I am.

"Shower?" he offers, and when I nod, he disappears to the bathroom to start it for us.

I'm wide-legged stepping around trying to gather our clothes when there's a knock at the door.

Nope, not answering that.

Which is my plan until I hear, "Samantha, it's Wanda. The landlord."

Oh, shit! There's only one reason she'd be coming to see me right now, and it's not because my rent's late. Because it's not. I already paid this month's and have next month's in savings, which is an exciting mark of my success with Bedroom Heaven sales.

I grab a blanket from the couch and wrap it around me, making sure everything is covered. Still, as I crack the door, I stay behind it just in case. "Hey, Wanda, sorry about the uh . . . noise."

Her smile is nearly ear-to-ear. "Not here about that . . . well, not exactly, although you might want to remember that the walls of this old building are thin. Like 'who's Chance?' level thin." She leans to the side, trying to peer into the apartment.

She heard me calling his name? That means she heard a hell of a lot more, too.

"Oh, my God, I'm sorry. I'll remember that, for sure," I vow, trying to close the door before I burst into flames of embarrassment.

"Wait!" she cries, holding up her hand. "I heard you're selling uhm, *stuff* now? Can I get a catalog or something? For your products?"

She makes it sound like I'm a drug dealer with a catalog of merchandise. Page three, cocaine. Page twelve, ecstasy. Page twenty-seven, meth.

But I know what she means.

"Yeah, hang on." I push the door closed and reach for my purse, pulling out a business card for Bedroom Heaven. Opening the door again, I hand her the card. "The QR code is on the back. Scan that with your phone, and you'll be in the catalog under my name. Buy what you want, and I'll deliver it within a few days at most, maybe sooner if I have it in stock. And if you have any questions, let me know. I'm happy to help."

I'm making sales at my front door, while I'm naked beneath a blanket with who-knows-what wetly running down my legs. Kara was right—sex sells. Wait'll Jaxx hears this story. She'll probably turn it into a new sales strategy—Demos with a Purpose.

As I close the door, Chance reappears, and his brows jump up his forehead. "Making a run for it?" he teases, though there's a thread of worry in his voice.

"Making a sale," I explain with a laugh. "That's two in one day, counting the one you just bought." I pick up the Mad Hatter, surprised at its weight and suddenly a little ashamed that I took all that.

*Does that make me a slut? Like not in a sexy-talk way, but in an actual way?*

I know the science behind it. Vaginal openings are meant to stretch and can easily handle penises of every size, considering an entire baby head comes out it. But there's an expectation that women be 'tight' and virginal in our society, and if they're not, there's a stigma. And I haven't been a virgin in a long time. I never gave it a second thought, long ago dismissing the idea of a body count until I'm looking at actual proof that you could drive a Mack truck in my vagina without touching the walls.

"Hey, where'd you go?" Chance asks, coming over and taking me in his arms.

I shake my head, trying to rattle those thoughts loose. I know they're not true, but I'm as much a victim of society as everyone else. I just have to keep reminding myself that it's all bullshit.

"Wondering how in the hell this fit," I admit.

Chance chuckles. "With a little bit of work and a whole lotta lube." He drops his hand between us, using the lube that's still there to slide two fingers into me and pumping them slowly. I can feel the delicious stretch around him again now that I'm not as aroused. "You want it again? I'll get you there."

There's no jealousy in the question, no concern that he thinks I want a toy over him, especially a particularly large one. With Chance, there's only a willingness to enjoy each other.

But I don't need another round. I'm blissfully orgasmed out, mentally satisfied, and physically exhausted.

I press a kiss to Chance's lips, so quick he doesn't even pucker to kiss me back. "Let's take a shower."

After washing off, we curl up together in my bed. Naked beneath the sheets, I carefully ask, "Are you disappointed in tonight? It's okay, I probably shouldn't have gone."

I gave him so many chances to say no before we went, but maybe I should've made the no-go call myself and not risked things going so badly. But I'd wanted to support Chance, and he'd kept saying he wanted me there.

*He was probably being polite. That's how he is.*

He hums thoughtfully, and I can appreciate that he's replaying the evening out, analyzing it in that way he does. "No, I'm not disappointed. I think I'm . . . pleased? That's the best way I can describe it. It's not happy, because I know people got their feelings hurt, but there were things that should've been said a long time ago that finally came out. Acknowledging it is the first step to fixing it, and now, hopefully, we can. Because of you."

He says it like it's a compliment, not an accusation.

"Really?"

Against my lips, he repeats, "Really."

And then he kisses me, his lips simply moving against mine sweetly. It's emotional, and despite all my internal protests, I can feel warmth of a totally different kind bloom in my chest. *Maybe it wasn't so bad*, I think.

I won't be writing a paper about it for my psychology class because I definitely didn't behave the way I should've, with Vivian especially. But maybe it was okay?

If Chance isn't mad at me, that's enough for me. I'm going to enjoy it, enjoy him, while I can.

# CHAPTER 24
# CHANCE

"KNOCK, KNOCK," Jim says while simultaneously rapping on my office door. When I look up, he's got a curious look on his face. "Ya busy? There's some visitors here for ya."

"Visitors?" I echo dumbly. A quick mental check of my calendar reaffirms that I don't have any appointments today.

"Thanks, man," Kyle tells Jim, pushing past him and into my office. Jim steps out of the way as the rest of my siblings all file in too.

Cameron, Carter, Luna, Cole, Kayla, and Kyle are all standing in the small space that's not designed for more than me. Ah, so it's one of those visits. "Uh, hey guys, what's up?"

I'm scanning faces, but none of them give me a clue. This is a first, though. About the only thing that gets all of us in one room is Mom requiring it, or maybe Gracie's annual graduation at school.

Nope, I remember, Cole skipped that last year. Said he was 'busy'.

"What's up?" Cameron snarls. "Are you serious?"

Ever the peacemaker, Kayla steps forward. "Nope, not yet. Hold that piss and vinegar in for a minute longer. Where else can we talk so that all of you aren't in danger of running ramrod over Luna and me?"

She spins, leading everyone out of my office like she knows

where to go. Following her, I call ahead, "Last door on the right. It's our biggest meeting room."

Inside the room, Kayla closes the door behind us, directing everyone to grab a chair and have a seat. Despite this being my club, apparently, she's in charge.

Once we're seated in a circle, Cole notes in a wry tone, "This feels like an intervention."

Pulling his big brother act, Cameron demands, "How would you know?"

Which makes Cole clam right back up, as per usual.

"Okay, we need to talk about last night," Kayla starts.

"Doing Mom's bidding again?" I deadpan. "Cut the crap, say what she wants you to say, and we can all get on with our days. I know we all have shit to do." I point around the circle, still awed that they're all here on the fly like this. "Cameron probably has some big shot deal to close, Carter has a stock market to obsess over, Cole has whatever the fuck he has, and Kyle probably has someone tied to his bed naked at home, waiting on him."

It's not exactly what I think of my siblings. Or at least not *all* I think of them. But it's not too far off.

Kyle smirks. Is he telling me I'm right or telling me I'm wrong? Who knows.

Kayla points a sharp nail at me. "This isn't Mom. It's me, and I'm not gonna have my family implode because you can't keep it in your pants. You're the one I don't worry about usually, but here we are."

A grumble works its way through my brothers, the general consensus being 'you don't need to worry about me', but Kayla's not having it.

"I feel like this is my fault. I was so surprised to see Samantha at your place that I was curious. I could see the way you were looking at her, feel the sparks between you, and I guess I thought if I invited her, it would push you. I had no idea you were even seeing Samantha, or anyone else, for that matter, before then, but you were obviously much more than casual. Nobody likes to be hidden away like a dirty little secret, Chance, but that's what you were doing to her."

It sounds like my sister's talking from experience, and I wonder what I don't know about her too. Of all the siblings, we're the closest, but she's right. I didn't tell her about Samantha, so it'd be logical that she has stuff she holds close to her chest and stays silent about.

I don't like it. She's my baby sister, and if anyone's treating her poorly, I want to know about it. Between us five brothers, we could take him down—financially, mentally, and physically.

Kayla's staring at me, waiting for a response.

"I'm sorry. I should've told you, but Samantha and I aren't some big *thing*. We're casual, just hooking up." Even as I say the lie, I cringe, knowing that hasn't been the truth for a long time.

Kyle laughs first, but then everyone's laughing—at me.

Carter speaks up, though. "If you believe that, I've got some shit to sell you, brother. I'm an admitted and well-documented dumbass, and even I can see that you love her."

I look around the room, not at my siblings, but like Samantha might jump out and yell 'gotcha!' from a corner or from behind a stack of chairs.

"Shh! Keep it down," I tell him, a finger to my lips. At their confused looks, I explain, "I know I'm in love with her, but she . . ." I get up, pacing around the room and pulling at the strands of my hair, not caring about how it looks later.

And then I see Luna. Samantha's best friend.

She's so quiet, I think I forgot that she was here. Looming over her, I order, "You can't tell her. She'll panic and run." When Carter glares at me for speaking to his wife that way, I say it again, slightly softer, "Please, don't tell her."

I'll beg her to stay silent if I have to, but Samantha can't know she has my heart. If she thinks for one second that this is more than serial, repeat hook-ups, she'll be gone in a flash.

"What's going on?" Cameron asks. "Is she anti-love or something? After last night, I wouldn't be surprised."

Normally, I'd be all over him, but as it is, I fall back to my chair.

"Listen, here's what happened . . ."

I tell them everything, from what the 'conference' really

entailed, our first night when we didn't know who we were, Carter and Luna's ice-skating invitation, dates, dinners, talking all night, and more.

"And lots of sex," I finish. "Hence, the hook-up mentality. But it's so much more than that."

Luna jumps in, carefully explaining, "Samantha's dad blindsided them, leaving them in a bad situation, and if that wasn't enough, he was pretty awful about it. She doesn't trust guys, at all. She dates and stuff . . ." Luna looks at me. "Or she did. But she keeps everyone at arm's length so that when they leave, it doesn't hurt as much, because it's not *if* they do, it's *when* they do."

I add on, "You ever see one of those movies where they're trying to knock down a fortress wall with a battering ram?" When they nod, I go on, "Samantha's like that. Her walls are fortified with steel, and I've got a teeny, tiny stick trying to get through to her heart. It's gonna take time for her to trust me."

Cole and Kyle are snickering, and Kyle holds up his pinkie finger. "You said you've got a little stick."

"Really, assholes?" Kayla scolds them, and they shrug. I can't fault them, it was a pretty easy pitch on my part.

Carter leans forward, his elbows on his knees as he pins me with eyes that are scarily similar to my own. "This is real? She's one of us, not as Luna's friend but as your . . . *whatever* you're calling it so she doesn't bail?"

I nod. It feels good to admit it aloud, to tell someone because I can't tell Samantha. Not yet.

"Okay, we've got your back, then," he declares, as if she's now part of the family, not just a de facto member of our gang of misfits.

As I look around the circle, everyone nods my way, on board with Carter's words. This is the first time in a long time that we've all been on the same side of something. It feels good.

Maybe Samantha fixed my family more than she realized.

"On that note, you need to know what happened after you two left last night . . ." Kayla says.

"Shitshow circus," Kyle blurts. He flashes a boyish grin, throwing me a thumbs-up. "Kinda awesome."

Judging by everyone's faces, he's not wrong. At least about the shitshow part.

"Grandpa Chuck and Dad basically hate Samantha, said she was, and I quote because I don't want you to think this is from me, 'mouthy and outspoken'. Mom and Grandma Beth love her, for the same reason, basically," Cameron explains. "Mom called her a breath of fresh air when Grandpa grumbled about a big family blow-up being bad for his heart at his age."

I laugh, knowing Samantha would appreciate all of those descriptors, taking them as compliments regardless of how they were intended. And Grandpa Chuck's heart is completely fine. The man brags about still doing five miles a day on his recumbent exercise bike. And now that he's retired, he and Grandma Beth ride horses nearly every day and take care of them too. They have help, of course, because they can afford it, but he always says he likes getting his hands dirty now because he didn't for so many years when he was sitting at a boardroom table.

But I can see that the brutal conversation with Aunt Vivian probably wasn't something he was looking forward to.

"Okay, but I don't care what Dad thinks. I haven't in a long time," I argue.

Kyle snorts. "Of course you care. We all care. He's a shit father way too damn often, but he's ours. It's human nature to want his approval."

*Whoa*. That's the deepest admission Kyle's ever expressed about our father. At least that I've heard. Usually, I think he gets a kick out of trying to drive Dad into the ground, but maybe there's more to it.

Carter nods, agreeing with Kyle. He's worked miracles, extracting himself from Dad's clutches at Blue Lake to start his own firm, doing the work Dad taught him to do. They're not competitors since Carter works for a singular client, but getting to the point where they can have business discussions about the market and joke about projections took a while. "I damn near killed myself, working twenty-five, eight, three-sixty-six, so he'd see me through that one's bright-ass shine." He points at Cameron, who is the first-born, and therefore, the automatic golden child. "But even now, deep down, I want to show him that I'm not just good, I'm *great* at what I do."

Luna places her hand over Carter's, smiling at him sweetly. "You are great."

"Is nobody gonna tell him the best part?" Cole asks, drawing my attention.

There's a ripple of laughter and, confused, I ask, "What?"

"Vivian came back," Cole tells me.

My eyes widen as I scan his face, looking for any hint of a lie. "She did not."

He holds his hand up like he's testifying, "I swear. It was fucking hilarious." He mimes her stomping out, whirling around, and wagging her finger. "And another thing! Blah-blah-blah." Laughing hard, he says, "I swear she did it like three times, just ranting her ass off each time, making less and less sense. There was even something about her cat when she was a kid."

"No way!" A little part of me wishes I'd seen that.

Cole holds his hands out, shrugging. "I guess Grandpa Chuck told her Muffalina died—legit, the cat's name—but it actually ran away and he didn't want to search the whole damn town to find the beast because it was a mean thing, always biting and scratching people. Vivian included. He thought it was a blessing in disguise then and still does now. She did not agree and was sobbing that he never cared about Muffalina or anyone else, and that maybe she should've gotten a tomcat so he would've looked for it. He apologized, but she said it was too little, too late, and stomped off again."

I close my eyes, picturing Aunt Vivian wailing about a cat from forty-plus years ago. Not that it died, but that some other family probably took it in and it wasn't hers anymore. Hell, it probably ran away on purpose to get away from *her*.

"But guess who didn't go back with her?" Kyle hints. "Not the cat. Aunt Vivian."

"Devin?"

"*Ehnt*! He was following Mommy around like a puppy on a leash, back and forth with her each time, glaring at us when we laughed at her outbursts and telling her that she's *sooo right* to be upset. But Bridgette? She got progressively annoyed with the whole thing, and the last time Devin tried to shoo her after Vivian, she waved him off. Told him to 'sort his mother out' and that she'd take an Uber.

Apparently, I missed a lot when we left.

"What happened?"

"I took her home," Cole answers. When all eyes shoot to him, he adds, "Dropped her at the curb, told her to listen to Samantha, and pulled away as soon as she walked in the front door. I don't know if she's gonna take the good advice, though. She was pretty quiet the whole way." I get the feeling he's already told them this at least once before.

"After that, the party broke up pretty quickly," Kayla says. "So that was our night. How was yours?"

She's fishing, big time.

"I apologized to Samantha for our family, she apologized for upsetting everyone, and we shook on it, deciding to leave it in the past." Technically, I'm not lying. We definitely did some apologizing and shaking, just not in the way I'm making it sound.

"Good," Carter declares, not calling me out on the lie.

"Maybe we can double date sometime?" Luna asks hopefully.

"As long as you don't call it a date, maybe so," I answer, more of a realist than she is.

"If we're done here, I really gotta go," Cole says, looking at his watch. I'm surprised he's sat here this long with us, to be honest.

When he gets up, everyone starts to leave, but Cameron hangs back. I'm not surprised. He probably wants to do a big brother speech, better known as Dad 2.0.

"What's up?" I ask.

He swallows hard and looks up at the ceiling, gathering his words. "Be careful, that's it. I can tell you have real feelings for Samantha, but if she's not . . ." He trails off, and after a heavy sigh, tries again. "I've been in love—real, deep, forever love. I've held it in my hand until it didn't even seem special anymore, and I took it for granted. And when I lost it . . . it fucked me up, man." He grips at his chest over his heart, showing more emotion about the loss of his wife than I've seen from him since her funeral.

My instinct is to throw my arm over my brother's shoulder, but he purposefully steps away from me, not wanting any comfort.

"Cameron, what happened to you was—"

He cuts me off. "Just . . . I do hope it turns into something more. For you, for her. Because I'd go through ten more decades of the hell I feel every morning for the good years I had. But be careful. Because if this is one-sided or Samantha can't give you what you need, it'll burn out just as fast as it started, leaving you alone to realize you burned your whole world to the ground for someone you can't have a future with."

He leaves, not giving me an opportunity to respond in any way. Perplexed, I walk back toward my office.

"Hey, Chance!" Stephen calls out, stopping me.

Distracted, I nod. "Yeah, what's up?"

He furrows his brows, looking at me curiously. "You good, man?"

"Yeah, yeah," I repeat, filing away the heavy thoughts Cameron laid at my feet.

"You know where Samantha is? We have an appointment today, but she's not in the counseling room."

"She has a test today," I answer without thinking. "You shouldn't have a session scheduled. Maybe you got the day wrong?" I suggest.

"No, it was today," he answers tightly. "Guess she forgot."

That's not like Samantha, but she maintains her own schedule of classes and mentoring, so I can't be sure. The test I know about because she's been studying for weeks and I helped her with flashcards over breakfast. "Is there something I can help with? I have a minute," I offer.

But Stephen shakes his head and starts walking away. "Nah, that's okay. I wanted to talk to her."

I'm not too worried about him. Stephen has been showing huge strides in his confidence, and that's the main thing he was lacking. He's even been acting as a mentor for some of the newer members, and I can understand why, if he's got something going on, he might prefer to talk to Samantha about it. Especially if it's info from class or girl-related.

Still, I call after him. "Hey, Stephen!" When he looks back, I smile. "You meant *Miss Redding*, right?"

He blinks a couple of times before he gets it, then nods, "Yeah, Miss Redding."

But his voice has gone hollow and when he walks away, his head is down, and I remind myself to ask Samantha about her schedule later.

## CHAPTER 25
# SAMANTHA

I'M KICKING ass and taking names! The last week has been amazing.

Chance told me his siblings came by and said dinner after we left was even more of a showdown than before, so in a lot of ways, I've been wiped from their memories as the instigator of Family Nuclear Meltdown '23. Plus, he reassured me again that he's not mad at me for any of it.

Jaxx and I are still selling. In addition to the four—four!—products Wanda bought, I had three other tenants in the building come by to purchase things. Thankfully, they hadn't heard my loud recommendation of the Mad Hatter, but they did get a glowing referral from Wanda.

I aced my test at school, which was more of a presentation followed by a mock counseling session with my professor. And on the flip side of the student becoming the teacher, my classes at the club have been going well.

The last one, 'Make Your Own Meet-Cute', was a big hit. I'd worked with the guys on genuine approaches that don't feel creepy, ways to be an actual nice guy, not a pseudo-nice guy, and small talk that helps you both decide whether you're compatible. My favorite part of that class was when I had the guys practice some typical pick-up lines . . . on each other . . . while I videoed it. They'd quickly seen how gross it feels when a guy leers at you and tells you that 'you'd be a lot prettier if you smiled' and been horrified that their 'sexy eyes' were more 'I'm going to wear your skin like a coat'.

Lucas had nearly jumped Enzo during the latter's demo, and not in a sexy way. Jim had to come in to stop their arguing, but in the end, every single guy learned a lot and several came up to me afterward to thank me. *Swoon!*

I've also been working with Evan on the podcast they asked me to guest on. Rather than a typical chat session, we've decided to do it up big with a *He Said, She Said* discussion. I've invited several girls from school, and we've hand-selected a few guys from the club, all with the intention of putting them in a room, throwing out a topic or question, and seeing what sparks fly.

It has the potential to be fantastic or a complete failure, which is ridiculously exciting. And sitting down in the meeting room we've turned into a temporary studio, I can feel the excitement in the air.

"Thank you for agreeing to be part of our discussion today," Evan says as everyone shifts in their chairs. "I'm Evan White, and before we begin, I'd like to go over a few rules. First, please stay in your chairs. The mics we've got aren't exactly ready for a lot of movement, and I'm not good enough with the tech to do reworks on the fly for ten-plus people."

Evan continues with the rules, covering language, respect, staying on topic, and more, and though everyone's listening, they're mostly eyeing each other, sizing up the verbal competition.

"Okay, since Samantha is the only one who knows all of you, I'm gonna let her do the intros," he says, turning it over to me.

"Thanks, Evan. We tried to get a mix of young adults, but you're all between the ages of nineteen and twenty-five and attending classes at the university, so we're not exactly a varied demographic, but hopefully, that'll help us find some common ground because we only have an hour here. Quick basics on everyone—from the club, we have . . ."

"Lucas—he's majoring in sports marketing and speaks his mind all the time, whether you want to hear it or not." I grin at Lucas so he knows I mean it mostly as a compliment, and he nods his head, agreeing with me.

"Stephen. You ever hear the Mr. Rogers saying 'look for the helpers'? That's Stephen, so if you need anything at the club today, ladies, he can probably help you, whether it's the vending machines or the restrooms."

Stephen nods at the women across the table with a warm smile and tells them, "Jim, our security guard, will be near the restrooms today so you feel safe to use them."

My heart grows at how they're listening and learning because having Jim stationed in that area for the guests' comfort was Anthony's idea.

"Anthony—he's our goofball with a good heart."

Anthony interrupts me, mock-scolding, "Don't tell 'em that, Miss R. You're already messing with my game!"

In response, I tap my forehead and tease, "What game is that, Toro?" He blushes at the reminder of the suction cup circle that lasted for ages, but he's not really embarrassed. He's pretty proud of the nickname his antics earned him, and he and I are totally good now. He's apologized, is thinking in an entirely new way, and he gave me and Jaxx money for the merchandise he and his friends took.

Lucas nudges Anthony's shoulder with his own. "Man, you ain't got no game. You just 'spray and pray' that charm around, hoping to get some ass. You need to narrow that scope, bruh."

Anthony laughs at the dig, popping back, "Like you're out there sniping 'em one at a time." They devolve into laughter with fist bumps and copious 'bros'.

"Guys." Chance says the single word, and the two of them straighten up, though they're still grinning and pleased with themselves.

Continuing on, I say, "Enzo—he's our man with a plan. Valedictorian, *summa cum laude*, law school with an emphasis on business. Never met a distraction he couldn't ignore with his laser focus."

"And last but not least, Tyler. He's new to the club, so I don't know him as well, but it felt important to include someone less familiar with the teachings of the Gentlemen's Club."

"'Sup?" Tyler says, waving two fingers at the women across from him.

"And over here, I didn't think it would be fair to include more psychology students, so I tried to expand my pool so we'd get some variety in experiences." I check my notes to make sure I get everyone correct and point as I go down the table. "First, Jaxx—she's a music major and goes to concerts of every genre as often as possible. Meli—she's a badass soccer player who hopes to play pro but is also getting a business degree. Apple—she's a lead reporter for the *Campus Community Bulletin*, the school newspaper, and plans to go into political journalism. Trixleigh—she's the entertainment chair of Gamma Lambda Kappa and plans to be a luxury party planner. And Serena—she works at the on-campus bookstore and reads every day, everything from history to fantasy."

I leave out that I know Jaxx and Trixleigh through Bedroom Heaven because that's not part of my role here as discussion moderator and their business is, frankly, their business to share or not.

"Chance, Evan, and I will be presenting topics and asking questions mostly, only stepping in to further the conversation if needed. But the plan is for the ten of you to do most of the talking. Questions?"

All ten of them stay silent or shake their heads, and I have a moment of abject terror that this is going to be an hour of us trying to pull words from their zipped lips. I shoot Evan and Chance a look, but they're doing what appears to be their usual pre-podcast checklist.

Before I know it, the intro music starts.

*Showtime.*

"Welcome, everyone, to a very special episode of *Two Men and a Mic*," Evan says, staring into his camera set up by his computer and introducing things. "I'm Evan White, and tonight we have a special episode we're calling *He Said, She Said*. To understand more, here's my main man, Chance Harrington. Chance?"

"Thanks, Evan, and welcome, everyone. Recently, we added a staff member to our roster at the Gentlemen's Club. This was an unusual one for us because . . . she's female. But that's actually *why* we hired her, to bring a fresh perspective to our members. And I have to tell you, she's made amazing progress, bringing insight to things from the other side of the coin. It's gone so well that we thought . . . let's expand the idea. And now, here we are. May I introduce Samantha Redding?"

There's no fake applause clip or anything like that, but it feels like someone just directed a 1000-watt spotlight right onto me.

"Uhm, hi, everyone," I say, a little too close to the microphone. It squeals with loud feedback in response. Jerking back, I hiss, "Ooh! Sorry!"

"Gotcha, Samantha. My bad," Evan says, taking the blame for what was surely my fault.

From a reasonable distance, I try again. "Hi. I'm Samantha. I'm a psychology student focusing on the mental wellness and physical satisfaction inside our most intimate relationships." I reuse the language from explaining it to Grandma Beth because it seems the most approachable.

"Alright then, let's get started," Evan says.

He roots around in a fishbowl full of slips of paper with topics written on them and pulls one out. "Okay, the topic is . . . ooh, this should be interesting. Beauty standards—male versus female."

It's a pretty open-ended topic, so I'm curious to see how this goes.

Meli raises her hand. "Can I take this one first?" When no one objects, she cannonballs into the conversation. "Total BS. Girls are expected to be fembots—no hair, no odor, no farting or burping or bodily functions. Gotta be 'ladylike' and do full face and hair just to go in public. But guys walk around with beer guts out, dirty hats shoved on dirtier hair, and feet that haven't seen a nail clipper since their mommies did it, and that's supposed to be fine." She leans in close to the microphone, eyeing the guys and daring them to disagree. "Again, total BS."

Lucas is first to argue, of course. "Dude, you're literally sitting here with no makeup on! And I know enough to know that under those sweatpants . . . you haven't shaved your legs or your snatch. I've got sisters. I know what sweats mean." He looks to Evan quickly. "Can I say snatch?"

Evan waves him on, like *we're live, what're we gonna do about it now?* And what else is he gonna call it because even scientific words can get a podcast flagged, so we might as well carry on.

Trixleigh laughs, looking at Meli closely. "I mean, don't get me wrong, I wear makeup because I like it, but do you seriously think she's barefaced right now?" She leans in, putting her contoured, blushed, and highlighted cheek next to Meli's, which, though subtly made up, is definitely not naked.

"Which proves my point," Meli continues. "Guys say they like a 'natural makeup' and then will point to a woman with fifteen products on her face, most of which just happen to be some shade of brown. This *is* my make-up look, because I usually wear it on the field, which is ridiculous but expected so that we look good in any still frames. I've got waterproof, sweatproof, bulletproof makeup on lock down. When was the last time you had a coach tell you put on mascara before a game, Lucas?"

He blinks, not having an answer. "Seriously?" he finally asks. When Meli nods, he frowns. "That's messed up. I usually get reminded to triple-knot my shoes, but that's a superstition, not for a photo op."

I nearly have a heart attack at the moment of clarity he's having. *Growth in progress, live in action!*

Tyler pipes up. "It's not only women who have expectations, though. I mean, what about *Magic Mike*? It made millions. And girls always want some muscled-up jock, right?" He looks to Lucas for agreement, and I'm admittedly nervous about Lucas's reaction. I hope Evan can bleep out some curse words because Lucas might let them fly at Tyler's reminder.

Lucas has made some progress, both in class and in a couple

of counseling sessions with me, but he's still hung up on a girl he liked choosing a 'muscled-up jock' over him, exactly how Tyler's suggesting. Lucas sniffs, gnashing his teeth so hard that I wonder if Evan will be able to hear that on the mics. But he doesn't say a word and stares straight ahead, though I don't think he's actually seeing anything other than his own anger.

Serena tells Tyler, "I saw the same meme, man. But *Shrek* made four times as much. Women like dad bods too. Hell, if he treats me right, I'd take no-bod, like a sentient brain in a jar that can make me laugh, tells me I'm pretty when I feel down, and offers intelligent conversation." It sounds like the plot from a fantasy novel . . . *Love At The Lab*.

"So I'm being replaced by AI now?" Enzo deadpans.

I lean in to the microphone, "On this topic, I'm hearing that societal standards create a sense of pressure. That women feel a need to be 'perfect', and for men, the 'protector' mindset still holds true, where you believe that you have to be the strongest to be attractive. Not falling into those stereotypes leaves the vast majority of us feeling outside the beauty standard."

When everyone agrees or at least seems to not want to speak on that topic any more, Evan pulls another slip of paper from the fish bowl.

We do it over and over, the topics sometimes getting a cursory answer from both groups, but more often, the conversation getting heated and personal.

"It's hard to work up the courage to approach someone," Stephen says on the topic of getting to know people.

Jaxx sneers. "Yeah, but you walking *all* . . . *the* . . . *way* over to me," she drags it out like the distance between point A and point B might as well be miles and not simply across the room, "to pop off with some stupid opener about my eyes doesn't warrant me falling at your feet. I know my worth, and not everyone's worth my time. Just because they spew trash doesn't mean I have to dig through the garbage to find the treasure."

"I'm not garbage," Stephen says tightly.

"Not you-you, I mean the general-you," Jaxx explains, gesturing at the world at large.

Anthony jumps in at Stephen's back, telling Jaxx, "The list of things wrong with that is longer than a CVS receipt."

"What's wrong is that you pretend to care until you get off, then you're all 'hey bros, bagged another one, huh-huh-huh', while she's left feeling like crap because she thought you actually gave a shhhhi—" Apple stops herself abruptly, looking around and realizing that she's revealed too much.

Lucas grins devilishly. "Ah, did your poor wittle heart get broken because you spread 'em too soon? Didn't your momma tell you he won't buy the cow if he gets the milk for free?"

"I'm not a cow," Apple snaps.

Stephen leans forward. "And I'm still not trash."

"Mooooo," Lucas bellows.

"Lucas!" Chance growls. "Enough."

Unfortunately, we seem to have crossed a line, and things devolve from there.

"*Men* have needs?" Trixleigh sputters. "Women have needs too! But did you do anything to meet them? Cuz if not, she can get better than you with $49.99 and a USB charger."

And . . .

"That's *different*? You mean like your right and left tit?" Tyler tells Apple, who looks on the verge of tears.

And . . .

"Helicoptering your dick *isn't* foreplay!" Meli declares.

And . . .

"My grandma always said, hoolies'll hooligan if you give them a second chance. Try walking away the first time he cheats," Enzo says.

We finish off the show, which is louder and more argumentative than I ever expected it would be. Honestly, I don't think we've built a bridge. If anything, both sides spend the last half of the show tossing verbal hand grenades back and forth.

Finally, our time's up, and Evan leans forward again.

"Wow, I'd like to say thank you to our guests today. I know this was hard, and there's a ton of hurt feelings right now on all sides of the room," he states needlessly, considering the glares going across the table.

"Yeah, thank you, each of you, for having the courage to participate. Might not have been the results we were hoping for. Nobody sang a single verse of *Kumbaya*," Chance jokes, trying to lighten the mood because there's more steam in this room than in a maxed-out sauna. "But a battle that's been going on for generations certainly isn't going to be settled in one hour. I do hope though that we're walking away with a greater understanding of what others might see and think, and maybe that's the first seed in this whole thing."

Evan says, "I'd like to especially thank Samantha Redding for working on this special podcast with me. I think we might need a drink after this one."

"You're buying," I quip, knowing that at most, he'll buy me a soda from the vending machine and write it off on the club's taxes.

Being a good sport, he laughs.

"I'm Evan White —"

"And I'm Chance Harrington, and this has been . . ."

"*Two Men and A Mic*," they say simultaneously.

Evan hits a few buttons before declaring, "And we're out." In response, we all sag, whooshes of exhales releasing around the table.

After a moment, Anthony laughs. "That was fun! Can we do it again next week?"

"Fun?" Jaxx echoes incredulously, and when Anthony grins wider, she adds, "You've got a strange idea of fun."

"Not enough human sacrifice and bloodletting for you, Princess Goths-A-Lot?" he teases. "We could find you some if you need a hit." The offer is accompanied by a slap to his inner elbow like he's prepping to have a blood draw for her entertainment.

Jaxx bares her teeth and hisses like a literal cat. "Don't invite what you're not prepared to handle, Toro."

Are they . . . *flirting*? After all that horrifying, dramatic craziness, are they actually flirting with one another?

People are so weird, and I *love* it. If I could sneakily tell Evan to start filming again, I would so that I can analyze their interaction later.

But they're not serious, and people start to leave, Stephen offering to show the ladies to the front door while Evan, Chance, and I reset the studio space.

I pick up a box of microphones, taking them to the walk-in closet next door for storage. I find the space where Evan has clearly-labeled the shelf 'microphones' and set the box down. When I turn around . . .

"Aah!" I scream, throwing my hands up. If the choices are fight, flight, or freeze, I'm a fighter every time.

Lucas is standing in the doorway, his eyes wide and hands held out in surprise. "What the hell?"

Evan and Chance rush up, looking panicked. "What's going on?" Chance demands, ping-ponging steely eyes from me to Lucas.

Panting to catch my breath, I wave Chance off, seeing how worked up he is at my fright. "It's fine. I didn't hear Lucas behind me, and when I turned around, I was startled."

"*Shiiit*, Miss R!" Lucas says, holding a hand to his chest like I scared him. "I just wanted to ask you about, uh . . . class this week. Same day, same time as usual?" Lucas asks.

"Wha—? Uh, yeah, same as always," I answer automatically, not sure why he'd be asking me that. He knows when class is scheduled.

"Bet. See ya then," he says, dipping out quickly.

Jim is hustling down the hall, and I swear Lucas shoulder bumps him on purpose even though he apologizes to the old man.

"Whatha hell'r'ya hollerin' about?" Jim asks, looking us over.

"Sorry. Everything's fine," I tell him, reassuring all three men with a laugh. "I didn't hear him and freaked when I turned around. Just an old-fashioned jump scare. It's all good."

"You're sure?" Jim asks, not looking certain.

I nod, smiling at my own overreaction. Mostly convinced, Evan and Jim walk back toward the front of the building, leaving me and Chance in the storage closet.

"That was a clusterfuck," I tell him, shifting subjects. "The show, I mean."

He steps in closer to me, scant inches between us and our breath mingling. "I don't want to talk about that."

In an instant, the worry and disappointment over the important podcast dissipates, replaced with the heat I see in Chance's blue eyes. "What do you want to talk about, then?" I ask, flirting hard.

"I have plans for you," he answers, his voice going husky and deep.

The possibilities run through my brain like a ticker tape of filthy fun, and I want to try every single one. "Anything."

He moves so fast I don't see it, his hand going to my throat and squeezing slightly. My breath hitches and my core goes molten. If he wants to have a quickie right here, I don't think I'll be able to say no, for either of our sakes. "Chance," I whisper hotly.

"You're going to be my slut tonight," he informs me. He's keeping his voice down because of where we are, and the quiet roughness of his words makes them that much sexier. "I'm going to take my time, fucking you in every way I can think of and every way your body can handle. You're going to be covered in my cum when I'm done with you and you're going to love it."

We're always so careful at the club when there are people here. Half of the fun is the tease of 'Mr. Harrington' and 'Miss Redding' and the stolen glances and touches we share, but now, there's no teasing, no build-up. This is caveman Chance, raw and powerful, and the danger of it being where and when we shouldn't behave this way is intoxicating.

"Please," I beg quietly. "Fuck my mouth, my pussy, my ass . . . you can have anything you want."

"I will," he says with a sex-filled smile. "I just wanted you to think about it all day like I am."

With that, he steps back and adjusts his cock in his slacks. After one last heated look my way, he resets his entire being, hiding the beast he is with me beneath layers of rules and becoming his usual proper self. "It wasn't a clusterfuck. Those topics incite a lot of feelings, and the people talking about them showed that. You helped them speak their truth and hear the other side. You were *amazing*. Good girl."

He disappears into the hallway, and I think I melt to the floor in a puddle of gooey lust.

# CHAPTER 26
# SAMANTHA

BY SATURDAY, the podcast is all but forgotten. Or at least, I'm trying to push it out of my mind. Hopefully, lunch with Mom will help with that.

"Have a good day," I tell Chance as he presses a kiss to my forehead. Although his place is definitely more comfortable, we make it a point to stay at my place occasionally. I tease him that sleeping on cheap polyester sheets keeps him humble and he threatens to get me accustomed to his rain-head shower. "You have appointments all day?"

"Yeah," he says, his eyes seeming far away for a moment, and I know he's checking his mental calendar. "Wish I could go to lunch with you, though."

"It's okay. I think Olivia would go nuclear if I showed up with a date too, so it's probably for the best," I reply with a shrug.

Today's lunch is a milestone for Mom and Marvin. They're introducing the kids to each other, so it'll be Mom, Marvin, Olivia, me, and Marvin's son, Noah.

"And I have a couple of counseling sessions this evening, so it'll be late. Maybe I should . . ." I prompt, not wanting to outright ask if Chance wants to see me tonight but obviously wanting to see him.

"Come to my place for dinner? Yeah, you should," he answers firmly. "I'll have something ready around eight?"

I lift up to press a kiss to his lips. "I'm having steak and potatoes for lunch, so if you want to do rabbit food for dinner, I'd be game for that."

"Uh, be still my heart." He presses a dramatic hand to his chest and rolls his eyes like he's fainting. "I am wearing off on you! Maybe I'll even get a green vegetable in you tonight."

"I don't need a cucumber. I've got plenty of better options like a nice, big eggplant," I tease saucily, knowing that's not at all what he meant. When he mock glares at me with a raised brow, I laugh, "Okay, fine. But not asparagus. Anything but that."

Chance once made bacon-wrapped asparagus for us, promising I was going to love it. I did *not*. It was so bitter even the bacon couldn't save it, so I unwrapped it and only ate the bacon. Meanwhile, he scarfed down his own plus my naked asparagus.

"I'm thinking roasted brussels sprouts," he says. I fight to keep a straight face, I swear I do, but he shakes his head at me, feigning annoyance. "I'll sprinkle some parmesan cheese and olive oil on them."

I nod happily then. "Oh, that sounds good."

He laughs at me, swats my ass, and says, "Have fun at lunch. Stick to 'therapist', not 'sister', with Olivia."

He's quoting back my own words to me, my plan for today being to treat Olivia with calm, kindness, and patience, not snarky sibling fighting. Because while today is big for Mom and Marvin, it's a big deal for Olivia too.

"I will," I vow, mostly to myself.

———

The young man who opens the door is ridiculously tall, rail thin, and laughing at something someone must've said before he turned the knob. "Hey, you must be Samantha. C'mon in," he says, standing back.

"That must make you Noah?" I answer with a smile.

"All day, every day," he quips back. Looking over his shoulder, he calls out, "Samantha's here!"

"Hey! We're in here," a male voice says from deeper in the house.

I follow Noah through the living room, which is simple and warm with a deep gray couch, a few red throw pillows, and white curtains, and into the kitchen.

I know instantly that the man at the island is Marvin, not because it's his house but because of what Mom has said about him. He's wearing an apron that proclaims *Mr. Good Lookin' Is Cookin'*, has warm, dark eyes, and is doing some sort of arm-waving dance move as he sprinkles seasoning on a tray of meat. He's the epitome of fun, happy, and welcoming, saying, "Hey, Samantha! I'd give you a hello hug, but I'm giving these steaks what-for." With that, he dramatically smacks one of the steaks, rubbing the spices in. "Ungh, ungh, take that, and that."

I laugh at his 'fight' as Mom leaves her station at the stove to come over and give me a side-hug. "Hey, honey. Glad you could make it. Lunch'll be ready in about twenty minutes if Marvin'd put those things on the grill."

"Can't rush perfection, baby. Takes time to get it *just right*," he answers, tossing a wink her way. As Mom goes back to the stove, Marvin holds his cheek out, and she places a quick kiss to it. "Ooh! Yes ma'am, put a little sugar-sweet on it!"

Mom blushes—actually *blushes*—as she stirs the pot of whatever she's cooking. She tries to hide it, but I could see her pleased smile from outer space.

Mom is happy. And I couldn't be happier for her.

"I'll grab the potatoes from the grill to make room for the steaks, Dad," Noah says, going out the back door.

"Thanks, Son!"

I see Olivia sitting at the kitchen table, staring at her phone, and wonder if she's bitching about the annoying old people to her friends. *They're all happy and helping each other. Ugh.*

"Hey, whatcha doing?"

She cuts her eyes away from the screen to me, and I can see

the flatness there. "Missing a pool party at Axel's house," she says forlornly.

"That guy is a frog's hair away from prison, Olivia," Mom warns. "I told you to stay away from him."

My sister rolls her eyes hard and goes back to her phone.

Grabbing the stack of plates from the counter, I move to set the table. It's the least I can do since the cooking's well in hand. Placing a plate beside Olivia, I can see that she's flipping through Instagram pictures of a bunch of teenagers at a pool. "Who's Axel?" I ask quietly.

"A delinquent, apparently," she answers dryly. When she sees that I'm glancing at the pictures, she shuts the phone off and sets it face-down on the table. "Ever heard of invasion of privacy?"

She shoots me a look of disdain, and if looks could kill, I'd be six feet under already.

"Sorry," I apologize, though I'm not really sorry considering what I just saw. "Is he as bad as Mom says? Surely, he's not even old enough to go to prison. Juvie, maybe." I'm trying to make it a light thing, but I'm curious because the guy I saw in the pictures was shotgunning a beer and had tattoos on his neck and chest. I don't care about the tattoos other than knowing you have to be over eighteen to get one, but I definitely care about the beer because my sister is sixteen.

"He's nineteen," she sneers as if that's a good thing.

I'm on Mom's side, one thousand percent. There's only one reason nineteen-year-old men flirt with sixteen-year-old girls . . . and my sister deserves better.

"Olivia! Are you for real?" I stare in open-mouthed shock at her, but she glares back like she's being completely reasonable and I'm the overreactor. "Let me guess, he says you're '*mature*', 'not like *other* girls', and you shouldn't listen to Mom because she doesn't *understand* you like he does? It's like a damn script with these guys."

I didn't realize how loud I'd gotten, but Mom and Marvin have gone silent, just watching us. "I'm gonna throw these on the grill," Marvin says, giving us some privacy. "Be out back."

When it's the three of us, Mom says, "I tried to tell her, but nobody wants to hear negative stuff about someone they like."

I don't think we're only talking about Axel anymore.

Mom is constantly having to adjust Olivia's expectations—about Dad, and now, about Axel.

"It doesn't matter anymore," Olivia says, lashing out. "Roni posted that they're dating now. Thanks, Mom, bombing relationships left and right, aren't ya? You and Dad, me and Axel. It's only a matter of time for you and Marvin."

I see the sharp pain in Mom's eyes. She usually shutters it behind maternal care, but I think my sister's pushed too far this time.

"That's enough, Olivia," Mom snaps. "I'm done apologizing for the divorce. I did everything I could for as long as I could, damn near killing myself in a misguided attempt to be what your father wanted. But I was never gonna be younger, blonde, and look up to him like he's some sort of god when I'd spent the last twenty years making his dinner, picking up his dirty towels off the bathroom floor, and nagging him to do the bare minimum for you girls. Let's be real, he hadn't so much as bought his own underwear or poured a bowl of cereal since he was in college. And he sure as hell didn't remember your birthdays or plan a single family vacation. All those childhood memories you want to replay like *he* did something?"

Tears are flowing down Mom's cheeks steadily as she says, "*I did it* . . . for him, for you, for Samantha. And if you can't see that, I'm sorry. But I deserve to be happy, and now, I am."

Mom points at the back door, where Marvin stepped out to the porch. "With a man who's *nothing* like your father. Marvin wants to be my partner, wants to take care of me when I need it and appreciates it when I take care of him. He makes me laugh, cares if I had a good day, and understands that I'm a little messed up after everything I've been through and gives me space to have a freak-out in the middle of a *nice family lunch!*"

The last bit borders on hysterical, but mostly, I'm so fucking proud of Mom. She's been stuffing down her feelings every time Olivia said ugly things and blamed her for the divorce, letting them fester, and it's time to dredge them up and time for Olivia to stop acting like a petulant child.

I hand Mom a napkin, and she wipes at her bloodshot eyes. When Olivia doesn't say anything in response, Mom sighs and says, "I'm going to go apologize to Marvin and Noah, and we can go home. I guess it's too soon for this."

She pushes back from the table, gives me an apologetic look, and steps out back. Through the window, I can see her fall into Marvin's waiting arms. He rocks back and forth, comforting her.

"Do you think she's right?" Olivia's eyes are downcast to her lap where she's picking at her cuticles. I think if I asked her if she said something, she'd probably tell me no and that I was imagining it.

Exasperated, I sigh. "About Dad? Of course. Mom did literally everything for our family. PTA, homework, shopping, cooking, cleaning, paying the bills, making sure we weren't feral, taking care of us, and I don't even know what else. But yeah, she's right."

"No, I mean . . . about Marvin?" Olivia's eyes lift, and she looks at me through the curtain of her hair. "Is he . . . I dunno, *different* than Dad?"

That brings me up short. Mom and I talked about the possibility that Olivia was trying to be protective in a twisted way, but honestly, I'd kinda written that off considering how bitchy and accusatory she's been, especially about Mom. But maybe . . .

"I don't really know him," I admit. "I've only met him for a few minutes like you, but it sounds like he is. I know that he's been a single parent for a while, and Noah seems happy, so that's a good sign. He can cook and clean," I say, pointing at the house around us, "and Mom was smiling and dancing with him, so he makes her happy too. And now . . ." I look out the window again. "He's taking care of her."

I take Olivia's hand, stopping her from making her cuticle bleed. "So yeah, I think he's different. All guys aren't the same. All guys aren't Dad."

I'm talking about Marvin, but I think about Chance too. He's nothing like my dad either. Chance is kind, generous, and cares so much for others that he's dedicated his life to the guys in the club. He's fun, smart, and makes me feel special. Every day is better with him in it.

I love him.

The thought is heavy, not with fear but with excitement, and for the first time, I think I might be able to let someone inside my walls.

He's already there, I realize. He snuck in, little by little, and has been there for a while. I just hadn't admitted it, even to myself.

"Okay," Olivia says, nodding to herself. "If you and Mom say so, I'm okay with Marvin. But I reserve the right to say *I told you so* if he's an asshole too."

She smiles, the sadness starting to fade, and for a moment, I can see the sweet, innocent girl she once was. The one still hiding deep in a dark well of distrust and fear. The one that looks a lot like . . . me.

"Deal," I say, speaking on behalf of both Mom and me. "You think we can stay for lunch, then?"

"Yeah, I guess." Olivia looks out the window, and I can see the moment she gets embarrassed about this whole scene. "Oh, my God," she gasps, her jaw dropping open in horror.

"It's okay," I reassure her. "You fix the drinks. The lemonade's right there. And I'll get everyone to the table. Hopefully, our steaks aren't hockey pucks because I'm having brussel sprouts for dinner." At Olivia's questioning look, I laugh. "Just do the lemonade."

Out back, I tell Mom, "I think we're good. As long as Marvin isn't secretly looking for a sugar momma so he can sit around and do nothing."

Marvin laughs loudly. "Hell no, I'm too busy for that."

"What's a sugar momma?" Mom looks from me to Marvin blankly.

But I'm not explaining that to her because that conversation will segue into sugar daddies and sugar babies, so no, thank you very much. "Ask Google later. For now, Olivia's pouring the lemonade so we can have lunch."

"Really?" Mom asks with hearts practically in her eyes.

"Really."

―――

"Hey, Jim, here's your cinnamon roll," I tell him as I enter the club. "It's not exactly the dinner of champions, but I didn't think you'd mind."

He takes the bag from me happily. "Well, it's gonna be the dinner of this champion, that's for sure. Thanks, Samantha."

"You're welcome. I'm here with counseling sessions 'till close tonight, so don't forget about me."

"Nevah," he mumbles around a mouthful of ooey, gooey cinnamon goodness. "Lemme know if you need me to knock around one of these knuckleheads."

I grin as I head back to the meeting room. Jim plays the gruff, 'get offa my lawn' part well, but you can tell he really cares about the guys here. Chance asked him again about doing a car maintenance class, and though he still said no, it was a lot less 'hell no' and little more 'we'll see'. Not a slam dunk, but I think Chance'll wear him down eventually and the club will be better for it.

My first session is with Tyler. I'm excited to get to know him better because other than the podcast, I haven't spent much time with him. He hasn't even come to one of my classes yet.

"Hi, Tyler, you ready?" I ask when I find him already in the room.

"I guess. Lucas says you're pretty cool or whatever," he answers.

The compliment, flippant as it may be, from Lucas is unexpected. Half the time, I think he's the antagonist to my protagonist at the club and Chance's adversary in action.

"Are you two friends?"

"Yeah, we've been bros for a bit. We play ball together sometimes. That's how he got me down here to the club—the court out back."

"Oh, it's a pretty cool space. There's the court, a turf area, some heavy weights, and one of those big tractor tires to flip. Do you work out a lot?"

It's a baby step into conversation, giving him time to get comfortable talking with me about whatever's brought him in for a counseling session, and it works. The time passes quickly because Tyler's an open book, telling me about his classes and hopes for post-college as easily as telling me about his homelife, which wasn't the happy family it appeared to be.

"I don't know if I'll ever find a girl," he confesses. "My head's all messed up with 'be this, do this, that's not allowed' on one side and what I want on the other, ya know? Or what I *think* I want."

"There's no rush. Take your time to examine everything you think a romantic relationship should be—what your parents told you, society tells you, your heart tells you. Some of it, you'll trash instantly. Some of it will take some deeper reflection. And some of it will feel right." I place my hand over my heart. "Give yourself time."

We wrap up, and Tyler thanks me for listening. "That's what I'm here for," I say with a smile. "I'm happy to talk again, and I'd love to see you in class."

He leaves, I make a few quick notes in my files so that I can track Tyler's sessions. I'm mid-type when a throat clears.

I look up to find Stephen. He's my next appointment. "Hey, Stephen! Come on in. I'm just finishing this up."

As he sits, I click save on my phone and set it on the table beside me. "How're you doing?"

"Not so great," he confesses sullenly.

"I'm sorry to hear that. What's happening?"

"I thought I met someone great, but turns out, she's a whore like the rest of them."

*Whoa.* That is not like Stephen at all.

He's usually smiling, helpful, and friendly, occasionally more of the quiet type, but he's been making huge strides in his confidence. But right now? He sounds angry, sad, and resentful.

Keeping my face blank, I say, "Okay, can you tell me more about that?"

# CHAPTER 27
# CHANCE

FINISHING UP DINNER, I check the clock. My timing's perfect. Samantha should be here any minute. I can't wait to hear about lunch with her Mom and Olivia. I hope it went well.

I put the sheet pan in the warming oven, giving the mix of turkey sausage, carrots, and brussels sprouts a shake. It's a new recipe and it smells delicious. To me, at least. For Samantha, I balanced out the questionable brussels sprouts with sausage and carrots since I know she likes those.

Dinner is going to be great. And then after is going to be even better. It always is with Samantha because she keeps it so fresh and exciting, whether it's a quickie, a long lovemaking, or a rough fuck. Toys or no toys, filthy language or quiet moans, it's somehow different every time, and I can't get enough of her sexy body, creative mind, and beautiful spirit.

Sitting on the couch, I pull out my phone to check the news while I wait for her.

Eight o'clock comes and goes, but I'm not worried. Her sessions probably ran long or she got caught up talking to Jim about something or other. He's incredibly chatty for a guy who claims to not like people.

At eight thirty, I send her a text.

*Hey! Dinner's ready when you are.*

At nine o'clock, I call her and it rings and rings, eventually going to voicemail.

"Hey, uh . . . just checking in. We said eight o'clock for dinner, right? Are you still with one of the guys? Call me."

By nine thirty, I've decided that lunch with her Mom went awful and she's home dealing with the fallout. Or that, for some reason, she's ghosting me. Or that her phone died and she'll be here any minute.

Or that she's done with me.

That's the thought that keeps coming back, over and over. I know she's skittish. Maybe something happened today that made her realize how deep we've gotten and she's running scared like I knew she would.

But I deserve a phone call at least.

I know I'm going to look like an idiot, but I can't help it. I need to know, so I get in my car and drive to her apartment. And now, I'm here, knocking on Samantha's door, trying not to look like a psychopath. "Samantha? Samantha, if you're in there, we need to talk."

No answer. Hunting around, I find the loose tile in the façade above her door, pulling it out to reveal her spare key. Skipping any internal thoughts about the fact that I'm technically breaking into her apartment, I unlock the door and slip inside.

Nobody's home. There's a light on by her old sofa and what looks like a pair of pajama pants kicked off in the middle of the floor, but that's it.

There are no dirty dishes in the kitchen and nothing to tell me where she might be. Confused, I pull out my phone and dial her number again. "Hey, Samantha, I'm at your apartment, looking for you. Call me, please."

I hang up and look around like she might jump out of hiding and say, "Get the fuck out of here!" But there's nowhere to hide in her tiny place.

If I had her mother's number, I'd call there—not to be creepy and stalker-y, but to make sure she's okay. And while I don't have Susan's number, I do have Luna's.

Too far gone to worry about how desperate it looks, I call Luna.

*"Hello?"*

"Hey, Luna . . . it's Chance. Have you talked to Samantha today?" I ask as one run-on sentence.

*"What? Uhhh, no?"* she answers slowly. Luna's not a very good liar despite the way she and my brother got together.

"I'm at her place, and she's not here. She won't answer my calls—"

*"Did you break into her apartment?"* Luna squawks.

Angrily, I spill my guts, "She's running, I get it, but I need to know she's okay. I love her. You know that. Don't . . . don't make me beg. I just need to know where she is." I swallow thickly and shout, "Luna! Tell me!"

*"What the fuck, man? Why're you yelling at my wife?"* Carter demands in the background.

Snarling at the delay, I tell him harshly, "No time to explain. I need to know if she's talked to Samantha today."

*"Today? Luna's been head-down in Alphena-land all day. She didn't even talk to me, much less Samantha,"* Carter says, coming into the foreground of the phone call. *"Why?"*

"Seriously? She hasn't talked to her?" I repeat.

Concern is starting to niggle at the edges of my mind. If Samantha is panicking, she'd go to Luna first.

*"No, she hasn't. When did you talk to her last?"* Carter asks.

"This morning," I answer, my thoughts racing. "She was having lunch with her mom and sister and then going to the club for a few appointments. We were supposed to have dinner together hours ago."

An idea strikes me.

"Hang on, let me check the alarm system. I can see what time Jim set it. Samantha would've left around then too."

I click into the app for the alarm. In the background, I can hear Luna telling Carter, *"What if she's in a ditch somewhere along the way? We need to go check."*

I'm about to agree with Luna when I see something weird.

"Huh, that's strange. Jim hasn't set the alarm yet, and he never forgets. Let me call the club."

*"Okay, but call us right back either way,"* Carter instructs. *"Luna's panicking now too."*

I dial the club mainline and get the automated messaging system we use. I press zero to get the front desk where Jim sits and wait.

*Ring. Ring. Ring. Ring. Ring.*

Every unanswered ring makes the hairs on the back of my neck stand higher. Something's wrong, I can feel it in my bones.

I call Carter and Luna back quickly. "Hey, there's no answer. I'm going over there now."

*"We'll meet you there,"* Carter answers, not waiting to be asked.

I mean to say thanks, or maybe I do say it. All I know is that I'm in my car, driving as fast as I can to the club. Speed limits be damned. Rules, don't give a shit. Laws, fuck off.

I need to get to Samantha.

I pull up to the club in minutes and am surprised to see two cars still in the lot. One is Jim's, one is Samantha's.

A horrifying thought pops into my mind unbidden.

Could Jim have done something to Samantha? She always talks about how guys are two-faced, acting friendly and non-threatening, and then turning. Jim has certainly befriended Samantha. It's always seemed paternal, but maybe I missed something? Is he a wolf in sheep's clothing?

There's a cold pit in my stomach as I throw the car in park and run for the front door. It opens easily, which it shouldn't do. It should be locked, just like the alarm should be armed, but neither have been done.

"Samantha! Jim!" I yell, and my voice echoes back to me in the empty space.

"Unnnngh . . ." A groan sounds out from the far side of the desk.

Running that direction, I see Jim on the floor. "Oh, my God, Jim! What happened?"

He's trying to move, but his face is contorted in pain and his jaw is locked tight. "Sa . . . man . . . tha . . ." he stutters out.

I realize he's trying to point down the hall and sprint that way.

"No, no, no, no . . ." I say over and over. I don't know what I'm saying no about, but nothing can have happened to her. I need her to be okay. "Samantha!"

In the room she holds her sessions in, I spy her phone and bag on the table. But it's otherwise empty. No Samantha.

Running back to Jim, I find Carter and Luna standing next to him and my other brothers and Kayla coming in.

"What're you doing here?" I say, but I don't wait for an answer. "Jim! What happened?"

"I've already called 9-1-1," Kayla says. "He keeps saying Samantha and I think Stephen? Or maybe it's *SamStephen*? I don't know, he's slurring pretty badly."

"That's how he always talks," I tell her as I drop closer to him, turning my ear toward his mouth so I can listen carefully. "Say it again, Jim. Who was here?"

"Sa-me-than," he mumbles.

"See? Does that make sense to you?" Kayla asks.

Confused, I say, "Stephen? They might've had a counseling appointment? I don't know her schedule."

Jim makes a noise, and Cameron kneels down, placing a hand on his shoulder. "Try to be quiet. Help's on the way. I think you're having a heart attack."

But Jim's not having it. He takes a big breath, the pain causing his left shoulder to lift up almost to his ear. "Stun. Gun. Took. Her."

There's a beat where we all hear what he said without processing it, and then . . .

I get right in Jim's face. Nose to nose, I look in his eyes. "Stephen took Samantha? He stun gunned you? Is that what you're saying?" I demand urgently.

Despite the pain, he's clear-eyed and fights to nod. "Tried to stop him."

"Oh, my God," Luna gasps.

The reality of the situation has become so much worse. Samantha isn't missing. She's been kidnapped.

"I'm calling 9-1-1 back to let them know we need the police," Kayla says.

"I'll call her mom," Luna says.

This is my fault. I brought her here to help these guys, told her she'd be safe when she warned me that there's no such thing, and exposed her to a threat none of us saw coming. And now?

I don't know where she is. I don't know how to save her.

"Samantha," I whisper, the heavy weight of guilt and fear shattering my heart in my chest.

Cole slaps the shit out of me, his palm sending my face flying sideways as the smack echoes in the hallway. "No time for that right now. Pull it together, man. Tell us about Stephen. Why would he do this? Where would he go? Think."

I fucking needed that.

Refocused, my brain starts spinning. "He's a nice guy, one of the actual nice guys . . . I thought . . ."

---

### Samantha

"Wakey-wakey," a voice says from far away.

My head throbs, and I wonder how long I've been asleep. It's kinda like one of those naps where you mean to sleep for twenty minutes but wake up the next day not knowing what year it is.

But this feels worse than that, and my bed feels hard as a rock, making my whole body sore as I try to sit up a bit.

I blink, trying to force my eyes open, but it's like they won't respond.

*SMACK!*

Something slaps across my face hard, popping me in the cheek right below my left eye. "Ungh!" I groan at the sharp flash of pain. That cut me, I'm certain. But it does help me get my eyes to flutter open a bit.

"There you are," a blurry figure says.

The voice is familiar, but somehow not.

"What . . . what's going on?" I mumble.

Now that I've pried my eyes open, I can see around me if I concentrate hard enough, but it hurts my head. Still, I force my gaze to zero in on things one at a time.

I'm in a room that looks . . . unfinished? Around me is raw drywall, beneath me is concrete subfloor, and there are tools and dust everywhere. There's a work light shining creepily at the ceiling, throwing shadows everywhere. The place doesn't look familiar at all.

But the face of the man kneeling in front of me does.

"Stephen?" I say in confusion. "Something's wrong. My head—"

"Yeah, you hit it pretty hard when you fell."

His voice is flat and emotionless, but for a split second, I think he's here to help me. I don't remember what happened or how I got here, but Stephen will help.

And then it comes back to me . . .

*He was talking about a girl he likes being blind to what's right in front of her, choosing to go after the asshole who treats her like shit instead of the good guy she could have. It was an all-too-familiar story, and I'd been sympathetic at first. But he kept calling her names, his language beyond the pale for anyone, but especially out of character for him.*

*I called him on it, saying that her not seeing him doesn't make her a bitch.*

*Stephen had stood up, pacing the room angrily and saying I still didn't understand. He'd said an acronym I hadn't known . . .*

What was it?

*AWALT. I asked him what it meant.* All women are like that, *he said with a heavy sigh.*

*And then . . . darkness.*

I don't know what he did, but I realize that he did this to me. The throbbing headache, the dirty location, the bruise I can feel blooming on my cheek.

The terrifying reality slaps me in the face almost as hard he did. I look around with new eyes, everything a threat now.

There's a bunch of my Bedroom Heaven toys on the floor next to Stephen, and I realize that's what he hit me with. He smacked me with one of the products that's supposed to make people happy and satisfied. But hitting me with one seems like the least hurtful thing he could do with those now, and pure, hot fear dumps into my bloodstream, coursing through my veins and clearing my head.

When I look at him again, the cold darkness in his eyes is shocking. "Now, you're getting it. You're just another bitch, leading good guys around by the dick because you've got all the power between your legs in that cunt. Not anymore, Samantha. Now, you're mine."

I kick out hard, making contact with his chest, but though he stutter-steps back, he doesn't fall over. He catches my ankle, and grinning evilly, he says, "Feisty. I like it. And I know you do too."

He's up in a flash, dragging me a few inches until I'm flat on the floor as I scream. "HELP! HEEEELP!"

I'm still fighting, kicking with my free leg and flailing, trying to grab anything I can use as a weapon. But Stephen's bigger and stronger than me, and when he climbs over me, sitting on my hips with his feet locked over my thighs and his hand wrapped around my throat, I freeze.

"Fucking slut, you want my hand necklace, don't you?" His hand tightens, and it's *nothing* like what Chance and I do and is definitely not a necklace. Stephen is choking me, hurting me, wanting to punish me. I grab at his arm, scratching him as hard as I can as I try to pry his hand off. "Don't try to deny it," he hisses. "I saw him push you up against the wall like this. You nearly fucked him right there."

I have no idea what he's talking about and then . . .

After the podcast, in the storage closet, Chance put his hand on my neck, sandwiching me between the wall and him. Stephen must see the memory coming back to me because he nods. "Yeah, this mouth, pussy, and ass are mine too. You're giving it away anyway. It's all you're good for."

He drops down, trying to kiss me, and I manage to turn my

head the barest bit so his lips land, wet and sloppy, at the edge of my lips on my cheek. "No! Stephen, STOP!"

"Scream all you want, Samantha. I know it's a false flag. I'm a Red Pill man now. I'll give you what you *really* want," he vows.

The only reason any of that made a lick of sense is because I've heard Chance and Evan talking to the guys at the club. Every word Stephen is spewing is Jake McGibbons propaganda.

False flag? McGibbons says it's when women say one thing but mean another. Red Pill? It's the belief that women want a strong Alpha male for fucking but a Beta to mate with. It's some throwback to the red-pill/blue-pill thing from the Matrix, like the red pill is supposed to be some hard truth to accept but once you do, you're free from the illusions created by society.

I squirm, trying to bump his weight off center with a jerky lift of my hips. It doesn't work exactly as intended, but it does get me enough space to scramble away.

"This is not what I want, Stephen," I shout, and I see his brows knot together like he's confused.

"It's not?" he says quietly.

I'm looking for an exit, anywhere I can go to get away, and scanning for a weapon. But my best defense is my mind. I know Stephen, or I did before he went head-first into Incel territory.

"No, I love Chance," I tell him. "Remember, in class, we talked about communicating with your partner? Chance and I did that. We still do, all the time."

He's slowly stepping toward me, unconvinced, and I'm just as slowly moving back to keep the distance between us. "He called you names, was rough . . . you liked it."

I nod, holding my hands out to keep him at bay. "Because I told him to, and I say things to him too. But other times, we're gentle and sweet and slow. We make love."

Tears slip down my face. "I love him, Stephen. I love Chance, and I think . . . I think he loves me too."

Stephen's confusion is growing, his eyes jerking left and right as he tries to make sense of what he's heard and what I'm telling him.

I take advantage of his distraction . . . and run for my life.

## CHAPTER 28
## CHANCE

THIRTY MINUTES AGO

"Sir, tell me again. Who do you think took Miss Redding?" the police officer asks for probably the fifth time.

Thankfully, the ambulance hasn't left with Jim yet. He pulls the oxygen mask down and rasps, "Stephen Simpson . . . six-two, one-ninety . . . brown hair and eyes." He stops to take a hit from the mask, obviously out of breath. "Drives a '14 Toyota Corolla, silver, damage on tha front right corner. Piece'a shit, couldn't've gone far."

I blink, completely unaware that Jim had that type of description at the ready for any of us.

The officer nods. "I'll put out the info. Thanks, Delaney."

Having done his part, Jim puts the mask back on and sags. He's doing everything he can to help, but at what cost? He's obviously unwell. "Thanks, Jim. Go to the hospital. We'll keep you updated," I say, praying he'll listen, but he's tough as old leather, and I worry he'll stay until his heart completely gives out.

Thankfully, the paramedic doesn't give him a choice. "Loading," she calls a second before she shoves the gurney into the ambulance, not giving a shit whether Jim is ready to go or not.

"Incoming with cardiac arrhythmia post-stun gun shock," she says over a radio, probably calling ahead to the hospital.

Evan arrived a few minutes after the police, and he offers, "I'll check Stephen's file for his address."

"Already got it," another officer says, holding up his phone where I can see Stephen's driver's license.

"Do you have any idea where he might've taken her? Other than his house, any place special? Or even readily available?"

I'm racking my mind, my family at my back and Samantha's mom staring at me hopefully as if I hold the entirety of her world in my hands.

Samantha's my world too, and I'd gladly take her place in this situation if I only knew where she was.

I look around, seeing the people along the curb who've come out to watch the drama unfold like this is some sort of television show, not my life ripping apart at the seams.

People.

There's not a lot of them because so many of the buildings around here have been redone for businesses that are open during the day, and it's late. But there's one . . .

"What about Zack's place?" I ask Carter. "It's close, empty, private."

"Where?" the officer demands. "Let's check it."

Carter frowns, thinking hard. "The address is . . . 11359 Jordan, I think."

The officer nods, pushing a button at his shoulder and talking to the police at the other end of the channel. "Roll a unit to this address—"

But I can't stand here and wait. I need to do something. It's too far to run, and my car is blocked in by emergency vehicles. I hold my hand out to Kyle. "Key."

His eyebrows jump up, but he digs in his pocket and puts them in my outstretched palm. "I will kill you if you so much as cuss at Lucille. She's sensitive."

I haven't ridden a motorcycle in a long time, and only a few times at that, but it comes back to me literally like 'riding a bike' as I sling my leg over the machine and start it. The loud rumble draws everyone's attention, and I rev it a couple of times before I speed out of the lot.

It's not even a minute later that a patrol car cuts me off, rolling to Zack's place with sirens and lights wailing, so I follow them.

*She's got to be there.*

*Please let her be there and be okay.*

The building looks deserted at first, and my heart sinks. But I see the police officer waving me off, so I park the motorcycle, keeping a close watch. His partner moves toward the side of building, and it's then that I see it.

A silver sedan.

He's here. That means Samantha's here.

I run toward the door, only to have an officer stop me, physically shoving me back a split second before the door pops open.

"HELP! HELP!" Samantha shouts so loudly that her voice breaks as she runs free of the building.

Her steps stutter when she sees the lit-up police cars and officers with their guns drawn. I yell, running toward her, "Samantha!"

"Chance!"

In a heartbeat, she's in my arms. Safe, alive, and hugging me as tightly as I'm squeezing her.

Stephen runs out too, following Samantha, but when he sees the police, he tries to reverse, his legs going *Scooby-Doo* wild. But an officer grabs him, roughly shoving him to the ground face-down and locking handcuffs to his wrists. "Stephen Simpson, you're under arrest . . ."

"Samantha! Tell them you wanted it. You want ME! You're mine!" His eyes are wild, his grin maniacal, and his shouts are hysterical and bordering on nonsense, but Samantha's shaking her head, clearly understanding every word.

"He hit me, kidnapped me," she declares loudly to the police.

"Did he . . ." I ask softly, noting her disheveled clothes.

She shakes her head. "He threatened to, was going to, but I got him talking so I could get away."

An officer whose nameplate says *Beverly* is listening to every word Samantha says, and she adds, "Sounds like you were lucky. That's usually not the case." She offers a pressed-lip, tight smile before asking Samantha to sit down with the paramedics to get checked over. "Your eye looks pretty bad, and you probably have a concussion."

It's all I can do to let her go so that the paramedic can do her assessment, but I'm watching Samantha closely. I might never take my eyes off her again.

"Thank God!" Ms. Redding says, running up. She must have arrived in all the ruckus. My family is running behind her, looking at Samantha and me with relief.

"She's okay?" Luna asks me, giving the mother and daughter a private moment.

I nod woodenly. "Yeah, concussion, they said."

My brothers and Kayla lay heavy hands on my shoulders, supporting me because now that Samantha's safe, I feel like collapsing myself. "We gotchu, Chance," Cole tells me. "And Samantha too. She's one of us."

There's a murmur of agreement among my siblings, and we circle around Samantha and her mom protectively.

Samantha might be one of us, but she's also . . . *mine*. And I almost lost her before telling her how much I love her.

I squat down beside her, needing to say it right now. "Samantha, this might not be the time, but . . ."

"I love you," she blurts out as her tears finally fall.

I gather her into my arms but stop short before she puts her head on my shoulder, wanting her to see the truth in my eyes. "I love you too."

When she nods and buries her face into my shoulder, the relief in my soul is instant. She not only loves me, but she's accepting my love. Those are two very different things, and that she trusts me enough to let me inside her heart is a gift I will never take for granted.

Suddenly, there's a chorus of shouting, and chaos breaks out as Stephen wrenches free from the officer trying to put him into an SUV. Running straight at us, he screams, "Samantha!"

I move in front of her protectively, ready to do whatever it takes for her. I've never killed before, but I will do it now for Samantha.

But before Stephen gets within three feet of Samantha, Kyle steps in his path and punches him square in the nose. Stephen goes down sloppily, crumbling unconsciously to the ground with blood spurting all over his face.

It's oddly anticlimactic, especially when Kyle holds his hands out and says, "Self-defense and defense of others. Totally legit, yeah?"

When none of the officers move to cuff him, he turns around with an 'aw, shucks', sideways smile. "Figured if there was gonna be a fall to take, it'd be better if it was me than you, Chance. You got a reputation and shit. I don't. Besides, a punch like that might mess up your manicure."

Dark and twisted as it may be, his logic makes sense in a sweet sort of way. Not that I have a manicure, but if the police did press charges for assaulting a restrained man, I'd be done for. I don't think Kyle'd give a single fuck.

"Thanks, man," I tell him with a nod of appreciation.

"Okay, are we good for me to ask a few more questions now?" Officer Beverly asks the paramedic.

———

"I received an update from the district attorney," the lawyer says as Samantha and I sit down in his office. On his desk is a name plate, *Thaddeus Howe*.

Thankfully, he's a man with a good sense of humor, and if you ask him about Dewey and Screw 'em, he'll go along with the joke and answer, 'And Howe.'

But we're not here for jokes, and as Samantha settles into her seat, I reach for her hand, relishing her fingers in mine. Doing that, something that once seemed inconsequential, now feels huge.

*She's okay*, I remind myself.

"What did the DA say?" Samantha asks. She likes Thaddeus, and I can understand why. He's a straight-forward, no kid gloves, rock-solid attorney who's done a good job of representing Samantha's interests in the case with Stephen.

I give her hand a squeeze, and she forces a brave smile.

Samantha has been handling everything remarkably well, better than me, if I'm honest. She says she wants to face it all head-on and has had several sessions with Sara, her friend from school who's specializing in trauma therapy. That's not to say she hasn't had some moments of tears, nightmares, and jump startles from benign noises, but she acknowledges them, does her grounding exercises, and moves on as best as she can.

I'm still stuck somewhere between murder and confusion.

I feel guilty that Stephen was thinking that way–so darkly radicalized–and I didn't recognize it. Hell, I thought he was a damn poster child for the Gentlemen's Club, and I wonder if in thinking of him that way, I failed him. At the same time, I want to destroy him for what he's done. Slowly, painfully, and with more malice than I've ever felt.

Which is why I'm following Samantha's example and going to a therapist too. Big boy's don't cry? What bullshit. Real men can, and do, cry . . . and get help when they need it.

"Stephen's made a full confession and is pleading guilty," Thaddeus says. "The DA tells me they're taking a plea deal that'll give Stephen around fifteen years."

Ironically, of all the charges, the one with the longest possible sentence is the attempted murder of Jim. Stephen saw that the shock of the stun gun had messed with Jim's heart, sending him into a cardiac arrest, and instead of rendering aid, he'd stepped right over him, hauling an unconscious Samantha from the club.

That image is the stuff of my nightmares.

"That's it?" I ask hotly. "With good behavior, he'll be out even sooner than that."

But Samantha speaks over me. "That's fine. It'll be done, right? No trial, no testifying, no waiting. Just *done*."

"You can do a victim impact statement if you'd like, but yes, it'd be finalized within the week unless you want me to tell the DA no on the plea deal." Thaddeus looks at Samantha blankly, not pressuring her either way. I do my best to do the same.

This is her choice. I'll support her, always and forever, but she has to decide what will be the most healing for her.

"Do it," she says with an affirmative nod. "I want it to be over. I want to focus on me, not a trial or Stephen. He's already taken so much from me–my time, my trust, my mind. I won't give him another minute. I'm doing what's best for me, and he can go fuck himself in prison," she says bluntly.

That's my badass, fierce, strong girl. Later, I know this will be hard on her, but for the moment, she's solidly in control.

Thaddeus nods. "Okay, then, I'll pass that along to the DA," he says, looking at the paperwork on his desk. "I think that clears things up."

Samantha and I stand to leave but stop when Thaddeus calls her name.

"Miss Redding," Thaddeus says, "the scars of what you went through can last a lifetime. But those scars do not have to stop you from having a happy and fulfilling life. You're training to be a counselor, yes?"

"Yes," Samantha answers, smiling a little. "Sex therapy still means a lot to me."

"Then may I suggest, although I'm just a lawyer," Thaddeus says, "that you use what happened and become the best sex therapist you can? Maybe even work with victims if you're able to do so without jeopardizing your own mental well-being."

"Thanks, I've already been thinking about that," she tells him.

That's something she's discussed at length with Sara because though Samantha wasn't raped, there's been some pretty significant triggers she's had to work through from the things Stephen said to her. For now, we're taking things really slow, discovering new ways to be physical that don't cause her to have any flashbacks, and letting her be in charge of it every step of the way.

"On the other hand, from what I've heard, your work with the remaining members of The Gentlemen's Club has yielded amazing results. Help those guys, and as many others as possible, to prevent future Stephens from occurring," Thaddeus recommends. "Best of luck to you on every front."

We leave Thaddeus's office, and outside, the sun feels cleansing, warming away the cold sterility of the legal business. Gathering Samantha into my arms, I hold her, letting her know that I'm here. "I love you."

"I love you too," she says, relaxing into me. "I just . . . wow. I didn't think it'd all be over so suddenly."

"Me either," I reply, stroking her hair. "What do you want to do now?"

I mean literally right now—like going home or getting lunch. But Samantha has bigger plans.

As we walk across the parking lot, she tells me, "I've been thinking about that. I want to write a book. About the consequences of radicalizing young men, and how ultimately, we all lose if there isn't equality, respect, and communication between men and women."

She pauses as I open the door for her. I wait for her to sit and then close the door, striding around to the driver's side.

"It's a work-in-progress," she says as I get in the car. "But what do you think? It'll be a long road, because I'll need professional experience, letters after my name, and I don't even know what else to be taken seriously, but yeah, that's what I want to do."

I smile at her as I start the car, in awe of the brilliance of her mind. "That sounds amazing."

"Good, because I'm going to ask the guys at the club to be my initial interviews. They have a unique perspective on what listening to people like Jake McGibbons can do. They lost a friend to it."

She's extraordinary, thinking of the loss the guys at the club feel at a time when she nearly lost herself. But I understand her point. The whole incident has been messy, painful, and sent shockwaves through our entire membership.

I've largely said 'fuck it' to all that and put my entire focus onto Samantha. She might be ready to care for others and put some good into the world, but I'm pretty locked onto making sure she's safe, has what she needs, and is supported at all times.

I'll go back to the club eventually. Plans for an official reopening are already in the works, but for now, we've chosen to provide a space for the current members to get together without any gossip-hungry newbies, and Evan has been running everything while I take some time with Samantha.

"I think they'd appreciate talking to you," I reply, heading down the highway.

After a few miles, Samantha looks around. "Where are we going?"

"Carter and Luna's," I answer. "They're vying for the Best Uncle and Aunt award, and I thought we could have a little fun usurping them. I'm thinking ice cream for Grace, a pup cup for Nutbuster—peanut butter, of course, and a game of tag in the yard. Once they're totally wound up and think we're the best, you and I will sneak out, leaving Carter and Luna to be the bad guys who require things like baths and bedtimes." I look her way with a mischievous grin, hoping my plan for distraction and fun sounds good.

Samantha laughs. "Love it. As long as I can get strawberry cheesecake ice cream."

# CHAPTER 29
## SAMANTHA

TODAY HAS BEEN a long time coming, and I'm ready. But I stop outside the front door of the club and Chance stops at my side.

"We don't have to go in. I'll call Evan and tell him to reschedule," he says, his brow wrinkled and worry in his blue eyes.

"That's not it," I reassure him. "This is the first step of something new. I want to savor it."

The new thing is the next evolution of the Gentlemen's Club.

Chance and Evan have done so much good work and changed so many lives for the better, and now, the hope is to expand their outreach. And I'm going to be a part of it.

I wish it hadn't taken something traumatic to get to this point, but I'm excited to move forward.

I smooth invisible wrinkles from my gray skirt, straighten Chance's pink tie, and take a deep breath. Chance waits for me to nod and then opens the door. I step into the coolness of the club and see a friendly face.

"Well, issa'bout damn time ya got here. And where the hell's my cinnamon roll, young lady?" Seeing Jim at his desk with a smile on his face patches up a wound that was still bleeding. I knew he was okay, and I've talked to him on the phone, apologizing that Stephen used my stun gun on him, which he promptly told me was 'a pile of cow manure', but that's not the same as seeing him in person, vibrant and giving me shit.

"Knew I was forgetting something," I say with a matching smile.

He comes around from the desk with his arms out, and I hug him, squeezing him tight. "Thank you so much," I mumble into his shoulder. "I'm so glad you're okay."

"Girl, it'd take a whole lot more'n a lil zippy-zap to keep Ol' Jim down. How're you doin', though? To hear Evan tell it, you fought your way free like a bear scrabbling to get outta fishin' net."

I have no idea what that means, but given the proud look in his eyes, I take it as a compliment. "I'm okay," I answer. "Just want to get this thing started."

I look past him, all the way out to the basketball court area, at the gathered people—family, friends, club members—who are watching through the windows as Chance and I come in.

"Yeah, guess I'd best let'cha git out there before the wolves come."

I flinch at the wolf comment, thinking of Stephen, but Jim is having none of that. "You've got ghosts whisperin' in your ear," he recognizes, wiggling his fingers with the woo-woo comment. "I get that. Got 'em myself from years on the job. Know what's best for 'em?" He doesn't wait for me to guess, just continues with his advice. "Pardon my language, but you tell 'em to shut the fuck up." He laughs hard, the sound rusty and rough.

"That work?" I ask with a smile. "If so, it's gonna put my friend out of a job."

"Well enough, I s'pose. But the wolf thing? You're their queen, Samantha. They're all out there waiting on you, not this pissant." He jerks his head toward Chance with a spark in his eyes.

"I'm not even offended," Chance says good-naturedly. "You're my queen too."

I warm at the compliment from both of them.

Chance leads me out to the court, where there's a bunch of

plastic chairs in the middle and folding bleachers on the side, and every seat is filled with people here to see Chance. And me.

Suddenly, applause breaks out as they stand, watching Chance escort me to the front, where Evan is standing beneath the basketball hoop.

"Thank goodness you're here. I was about to start reciting *pi* as far as I can," Evan says. "Problem is I only remember three point one four."

"Glad we could save you, then," I tell Evan.

"More like save them," Chance murmurs, amused as Evan heads up front. "He's totally lying. He can probably go to twenty or thirty past the decimal point."

Evan holds out his hands, and the crowd quiets. "I won't pretend you're here for me, so without further ado, my best friend and partner, Chance Harrington."

Chance meets my eyes before stepping away, checking on me, but I'm okay. I want to watch him take back the helm of the ship he created. I smile encouragingly, and he takes the handful of steps away.

"Thanks, Evan. For everything, including most recently, keeping the lights on here at the Gentlemen's Club." Evan nods, acknowledging the thank you, and Chance turns to the audience.

"We've created a community here, a family of sorts, with the mission of improving men. And we've done a good job. Each and every one of you is an example of that. But it's an imperfect journey, with distractions and disappointments along the way. *Because that's life.*"

People shift in their seats, expecting Chance to give more of a rah-rah speech.

"That's the truth. It's never easy, but being your best self is still a worthy goal. Recent incidents have taught us something—becoming gentlemen isn't something that happens inside a vacuum. Men *cannot* develop without an understanding of, and being in the presence of, women."

A murmur of agreement goes through the crowd, and then there's one voice over the others.

"We like Miss R better than you, anyway!"

There's laughter as everyone looks for the speaker, and I see Lucas standing up, grinning widely.

He's already emailed me to set up a counseling appointment, though I suspect it's more for him to check on me than because he needs any urgent advice. Evan says Lucas is doing really well and has stepped into the vacant leadership role Stephen left. Lucas is rougher around the edges for sure, but his raw approach works.

"That's okay, Lucas. I like her better than you too," Chance jokes back. Everyone really laughs then. "To that end . . . Samantha, can you join me, please?"

I step forward, smiling at Chance and then looking at the crowd as they get loud and rowdy, whooping and cheering.

He lets it go on for a moment and then waves his hand to quiet everyone. "We will continue to be a community and organization that focuses on personal development and on building healthy relationships among *all* people. Sex is an important part of a healthy relationship, and it's built upon a strong foundation of trust, communication, and honesty. That's hard. So I'm proud to announce that Samantha Redding will continue to join us as our relationship and sexual health counselor. She will also be a regular contributor on the podcast . . . on that, Evan, we might need to rename it, too."

"Already got ideas," Evan says in a clearly rehearsed bit. *"The Evan White Show, with some other people."*

There's a few chuckles, and Chance joins in. "Not happening. But Samantha is going to be an essential part of the new club, and our new community. And before I ask her to say a few words, there's one word I'd like to hear first."

Before I can ask what the hell he's talking about, Chance gets down on a knee and my jaw drops open.

"Samantha Redding, you are the lady of my life. You are the woman I love. You are, and forever will be, all I want . . . and *more*." He lifts a brow teasingly. "Would you do me the honor of letting me be your husband? Will you marry me?"

"Hell no!" Lucas teases. "He ain't good enough for you!"

There's laughter, but my eyes never leave Chance. I love him, of that I have no doubt. And I believe that he loves me, but is that enough? It wasn't for my parents, who once loved each other deeply but eventually grew apart to the point where Dad broke Mom's heart.

*Chance wouldn't do that.*

So many times before, the voice in my head has whispered 'don't trust him' and 'it's only for now, so don't get attached', but now, that inner monologue has changed. I've done my own growing, healing the old scars and learning to trust again. Chance shows up for me, time after time, letting me see and feel his love and presence in my life every day, even when he's not by my side.

Out of the corner of my eye, I see Mom and Olivia holding hands right below their chins as they stand together, shoulder to shoulder like they're two peas in a pod with eyes glittery from unshed tears. We've done a lot of talking since the incident too, mostly about what's important and how we can depend on each other as a family, even if Dad isn't dependable.

Beside Mom is Marvin. He's got his arm around her and he's smiling happily. Mom's learned to trust again too, and Marvin is proving himself worthy of her heart. He's cooked dinner for all of us for more nights than not, even serving up grilled vegetables for Chance as he made sure 'his girls', as he's taken to calling us, have what they need to talk, cry, or rage about the hand we've been dealt. Noah has learned from his father's example and has been a good friend for Olivia too, especially as Mom and Marvin get more comfortable around us. They usually groan in harmony when Marvin pats Mom on the butt or she kisses him because 'the gravy's too good not to'.

The truth is, there are good men out there. Sometimes, they're not the ones you expect. They don't check any of the boxes, come at the right time, or say what you want to hear. They're the ones you dismiss as too this or not enough that, and sometimes, the truth is, you're the one who needs to adjust. Fix your own damage, heal your own heart, be happy in yourself and take the time—however long it may be—to do it right so that you can be receptive when it goes awry and a hook-up becomes the man in front of you, waiting with bated breath for you to speak.

I know my answer and proudly say, "Yes. Of course! Yes!"

Cheers break out, and from his pocket Chance produces a ring that almost defies description. It's beautiful, gold inlaid with thin tendrils of silver or maybe platinum surrounding a stunningly cut diamond. It's fantasy and reality come to life, and of course, it fits perfectly.

The applause rises, the crowd cheering as Chance stands and we embrace. The kiss is another first, deep and passionate as usual, but our first as an engaged couple.

But eventually, we step apart and I move forward, clearing my throat. "Well . . . how do you follow up on *that?*" I ask, earning laughs. "Uhm . . . gimmie a second because I've totally forgotten what I was going to say."

Wiping away tears, I decide to wing it and smile out at the crowd. "I love you guys, all of you. And I'm looking forward to creating something special together. I don't know what the future is going to look like. I don't know all of the details. But I'm looking forward to finding out. Together, all of us, men and women working to be our best selves."

"As part of this bright new world, can you do a toy demo class? I got my eye on one of those diamond-studded numbers," Anthony calls out, his voice unmistakable. "Oof!"

I follow the sound and see Jaxx at his side, an evil grin on her face, and Anthony rubbing his chest, where it seems she backhanded him. "Looks like that might already be covered, but we'll see," I answer.

"Are they . . .?" I wonder quietly.

Evan leans over. "Yeah. Apparently, after the podcast, Anthony apologized and apologized and apologized, and eventually, Jaxx told him if he was going to keep getting on his knees, he could make himself useful." I look at him in shock, and he shrugs. "Like your meet-cute was any better," he jokes.

"Hey!" I balk, and he laughs.

"They're . . . different," Evan admits. "Anthony said something to me the other day, something about Makima and chainsaws? I had to Google it and I'm still not sure I get it beyond Jaxx is suuuper-bossy and Anthony's enjoying the hell out of following her around like a dog."

I can totally see Jaxx with a dominatrix vibe, but I have no idea what Makima is. "Are you sure he wasn't talking about Bedroom Heaven's Father's Day line? We have a chainsaw dildo, called Timb-her, and a combo cockring-prostate stimulator called the Mow Me Down."

Evan blinks, still computing what I said, but he shakes his head. "Nope, let's say I learned a few things, and saw some things I can't unsee too."

I chuckle at the haunted look in his eyes. "Just because it's for them, doesn't mean it has to be for you," I say gently.

"Good. I'm going to find Reagan, and remind myself that plain, old vanilla is a delicious classic for a reason. You should mingle, but don't overdo it. The guys are really glad you're back, but don't let them bombard you. I told them to give you space to breathe and not to circle around you."

"Thanks, *Dr.* White," I tease, truly thankful that he's being so thoughtful about things that might bother me.

Everyone gets up, shuffling around the room to talk and people take turns making their way up to me and Chance for congratulations.

Luna and Kayla nearly tackle me, demanding to see the ring and proclaiming that they're going to be bridesmaids, along with Olivia. "And any of your friends from school too, of course," Luna allows.

"Yeah," Kayla adds. "The good thing about Chance having a ridiculous number of brothers is that you can have a big bridal party too. Just don't put Olivia with Kyle."

My brows jump, and Kayla rushes to clarify. "He'd let her down easy, of course, but let's be real, any woman who walks down an aisle on Kyle's arm is going to be fantasizing it's their wedding. It could be the frozen food aisle at the Piggly Wiggly and she'd still be singing *dun-dun-dun-dun* while picturing babies with steel blue eyes."

Luna laughs. "Really? I think they'd be trying to run away.

Cole, on the other hand? He's got that mysterious angle working for him." She pulls a face reminiscent of *Zoolander*'s Blue Steel, something I can't picture Cole doing at all.

"Are you two trying to marry off more of my sons?" Miranda Harrington says, obviously overhearing Luna and Kayla as she approached and mock-scolding them.

"Leave them alone," Charles says warningly about his boys, "or we'll start trying to marry you off too, Kayla." He raises his brow at the uncomfortable double-standard. She responds with a glare, her raised brow a near-mirror image of her father's.

"Congratulations, Samantha," Miranda tells me, taking the conversation back and hugging me gently. "You too, Chance," she says as he comes back to my side after escaping a conversation with Jaxx. If I heard correctly, I think she was suggesting a toy vending machine in the lobby called 'Dicks on Demand' and Chance was saying that the guys probably wouldn't buy enough dildos and vibrators to warrant that, but a QR code on the bulletin board might be okay.

"Thank you," I say, cutting my eyes to Chance. "I wasn't expecting it." He grins, quite pleased with himself for surprising me.

"Really? We all knew. I've known for like ever, but Uncle Chance promised me a new Nintendo Switch if I kept my mouth shut for a change and didn't spill the secret," Gracie says, having come up with Cameron.

"Grace!" Chance shouts as she coldly throws him under the bus.

Cameron chokes out, "He said what?"

Gracie pats her dad's arm sadly. "I know. I tried to negotiate for the *Animal Crossing* game, but I couldn't get the deal to stick. I've got some ideas for that, though, don't worry. And" —she holds a finger up proudly— "none of them involve bribery or blackmail or what's that word . . ." She taps her chin, thinking. "Oh, yeah, *misbezlement*."

"Embezzlement? That's not—" Cameron starts to argue, but who in the hell is gonna convince Grace that there's anything wrong with being paid for her silence? And she did say her

*Animal Crossing* acquisition plans *don't* include those things, so that's good. Mostly.

"Grandpa Chuck and Grandma Beth are about to climb out of their skin. We'd better get over there," Chance says, pointing at the family members still sitting in the front row. As we head over, he whispers, "They could not only walk to us, but probably skip, but it's a respect thing. We need to come to them to show off the ring and accept congratulations."

"Like they're royalty?" I surmise.

"Something like that." I frown, seeing the conniving look in Grandma's eyes. "Or maybe condolences in your case because Grandma Beth is probably gonna tell you all the bad things I've ever done and why I'm not worthy of you."

Grandpa Chuck grunts as I hold out the ring, but Grandma Beth grabs my hand and squeals. "Ooh, it's a good one. You did a fine job, Chance." And then she winks at me. "And I'm not talking about the ring. I like you."

"Thanks. I like you too," I answer.

I'm pretty sure her statement is the equivalent of her laying down the law for the family, and her ruling is 'I'm in'.

Grandpa Chuck doesn't give in easily, though, and huffs, "Still gonna need you to sign a pre-nup."

"Grandpa!" Chance hisses.

"Okay. If Chance wants me to, I will," I reply casually, truly not giving a fuck. "He's built something to be proud of here, and while I'm happy to be a part of it, it's his baby. Plus, I don't have any plans to need a pre-nup later."

"That so?" he says, his eyes narrowed as he takes my measure.

"Yeah. I gave Chance my heart and took his in return. No take-backsies."

Chance's laugh is bright and deep. "Definitely no take-backsies. I'm yours, and you're finally mine, Samantha."

I wouldn't have it any other way.

# EPILOGUE

SAMANTHA

The painting isn't huge, only about the size of my computer screen, but it's not the size that has me in near tears as I look at it. It's the content, me and Luna, sitting side by side in the park, arms around each other as soul sisters. Of course, it's a Luna original, so the grass is turquoise, the sky is purple, and there's a neon yellow glow to the edges. It's a vibrantly alive representation of us.

It means a lot, and as I clear the sob from my throat, I hug her. "You didn't need to, but thank you."

"I absolutely did," Luna says, hugging me back. "I *had* to. I mean, sisters-in-law? Seems appropriate, right? And this place could use a little pop of color."

I look at it on the wall of Chance's . . . excuse me, *our* home. I can't help but smile. "This still doesn't seem real," I confess.

"Preaching to the choir, girl. I sometimes pinch Carter in his sleep to see if I dreamed him up like one of my characters," she confides. "He wakes up spitting mad, too, and then has to prove that he's real."

She doesn't sound sorry at all, not even a tiny bit. In fact, she's grinning about it.

"Maybe I'll try that," I say thoughtfully. "After graduation."

It's almost here, the day I didn't think would ever come. But

I've finished all my classes, have my cap and gown ready to walk the stage and receive my Masters of Psychology, and secured a position at a local women's shelter, where I'll be working under another psychologist until I complete my needed hours to get my own license.

Best of all, I can do that job while still working at the club and selling for Bedroom Heaven.

"You excited for what comes next?"

I have to think about that before I answer. School has become such a comfort zone for me, where I know my professors, spend time with friends, and am mentally challenged every day. Moving on from it, even with how excited for the future as I am, is going to be a change.

But that's where growth happens. Living life on repeat, listening to an echo of your own voice from the void, and never considering any other possibilities, while easy, isn't truly living. It's existing. And I want more than that.

So much more.

"Yeah, I'm ready," I answer. "Bring it on, life!"

―――――

**Chance**

"Chance."

I flip on the bedside lamp and turn over, propping up on an elbow. Samantha's snuggled up in our bed with the blankets pulled to her chin.

I stop, looking into her eyes. Did she have a nightmare? Or hear a noise? Or need a midnight cheese stick and not want to go to the kitchen by herself?

But the look in her eyes is different. It's one I know well, but I haven't seen it in a while.

"You have to say it. Tell me what you want and I'll give it to you. You know that, Samantha," I say, letting heat trickle into my voice slowly even though my cock is already rock-hard beneath the blanket.

I want her. I always want her. However she wants it.

For a bit after the incident, she couldn't let me touch her and we would watch each other masturbate. Slowly, as she's been comfortable, we've worked our way back up to using toys, alone and together, gentle lovemaking, and even rough fucking a time or two. The only real difference there is that if I'm taking her from behind, she needs it to be in front of a mirror so that she can see my face, and if I call her 'slut', it needs to be face-to-face so she can look into my eyes. But she still enjoys that, saying it's different between us and it's just the pathways in her mind that get a little mixed up sometimes.

We also always have sex with the lights on. I don't mind, enjoying the beauty of her body and also watching her every expression to make sure she's with me.

"Watch me," she says, kicking the blanket off both of us.

I swallow thickly, licking my lips but staying stock still as she pulls her nightgown over her head. Her hair falls to the pillow behind her, the dark curls framing her body, and her bare nipples stiffen in the cold. Or maybe it's to Samantha's touch as she dances delicate fingers over both tits. When she pinches herself, plucking at the peaks, I groan, "Feel good?"

"Mm-hmm." Her lashes flutter as her eyes try to close, but she forces them open. Moving her hands down her body, she says, "I had a dream about you."

"What was I doing?"

She spreads her legs wide, throwing one over my hip. She doesn't answer my question, asking one of her own instead. "Want a taste?"

"Always."

She dips a finger inside herself, gathering her juices, and then holds it out to me. I lick around the tip of her finger before taking the whole thing into my mouth and sucking. "Fucking delicious," I moan.

She grins, pleased at my rough description. She touches herself again, spreading the slickness up to her clit and circling lazily. "You were watching me like this and then you got a vibrator from the nightstand."

I understand the instruction and quickly reach behind me

into the top drawer where Samantha's favorites are kept at the ready. I lie back on my side, and she puts her leg back over me. I hold out the toy, not making a move on her yet, even though I want to slide the thick dick inside her and fuck her with it until she's screaming in pleasure and all thoughts are wiped from her mind for a moment of blissful blankness.

Instead, she takes the toy—I think this one's called Pretty In The Pink—and slips it into her mouth, coating it with spit. Then she notches it at the entrance of her pussy. "What do you want me to do with it?" she asks coyly, knowing exactly what I want.

"Fuck yourself with it, Samantha. Fill your pussy with that dick while I watch you and try not to come from how sexy you are." My voice is gravel, the words gritted out. My hips twitch as my cock looks for any contact—her leg, the bed, my hand.

Her cunt.

She presses the vibrator in steadily until it's fully seated and then slowly starts to move it in and out in a wave motion. I can hear the wet sounds of her pussy as it tries to suck the vibrator in, and I'm so fucking jealous. Smiling lustfully, she whispers, "Turn it on."

I do as she says and press the button at the base, holding it down until it comes on in a pulsing pattern. She cries out almost instantly, holding it deep inside, and I can feel a gush of fluid on my fingers. "Good girl," I praise her.

"I want . . ." She pants, blinking heavily. "Fuck me with the vibrator while I do my clit. Jack yourself too, but don't come."

She doesn't have to tell me twice. I got every word, every instruction, every detail. I shove my boxers down as I flip over, getting on my knees between her spread thighs and taking control of the vibrator.

I give myself a single tight stroke and grunt at how good it feels. It's nowhere near as good as Samantha feels wrapped around me, but I can wait for her. I'll wait forever if necessary.

We find a rhythm—her fingers blurring across her clit, me fucking her hard and fast with the vibrator, and my hand nearly ripping my cock off with how hard I'm gripping myself. I have to stop every few strokes because I get too close to the edge, but I do it for her.

"Yes, yes, yes!" she screams. This time, her eyes do slam shut, her head rolls back, her body arches, and her legs try to close around me, keeping me right where I am, as if I'd go anywhere. Still spasming, she pants, "You. I want you. Fuck me, Chance. Please."

I search her face to make sure she knows what she's saying, and as I pull the vibrator from her and drop it to the bed, I lean over her to press a hard kiss to her lips. "I love you so fucking much."

Without waiting for her reply, I slam into her just like she told me to. "I . . . love . . . you . . . too," she says, the words coming with every deep thrust.

She wraps her legs around my waist, locking her feet behind me, and I run a hand down her thigh to grab a handful of her ass, never pausing my strokes. Her pussy grips me like a velvet vise, and I fight to stave off the orgasm again and again so that I can stay inside her.

"Say it," she begs.

I know what she wants. It's one of the desensitization tricks Sara taught her, and it's become a way for her to hear the sexy, dirty things that send her flying while still keeping control and staying safe.

"Whose slut are you?" I demand, gripping her jaw and forcing her eyes to mine. That's the deal—full eye contact or the dirty talk stops.

"Chance's."

"Whose whore?"

"Chance's."

"Whose beautiful goddess?"

"Chance's."

"Whose pussy is this?"

"Chance's."

I decide to add one to our list, thinking it's going to be one she really likes. "Whose wife are you going to be?"

"Chance's!"

She shatters, screaming my name over and over until it's a jumble of sounds, not a word. I keep pumping into her but have to wrap my hand around the base of my cock and squeeze hard so I don't come. My name on her lips is the sweetest and sexiest music in existence, but I want her to tell me it's okay before I fill her with my thick cream.

Grunting and sweating, I watch her until her eyes open and focus. She must see my desperation because her eyes go needy. "Come in me," she begs. "I want it all, make me your cum slut."

"*Fuck*," I grit out, coming so hard that I see stars behind my closed lids. She makes little noises, telling me how good I feel inside her and that she loves my cock.

I keep thrusting long after I've drained every last drop, not wanting it to be over, but eventually, I sag, holding my weight off her as we both catch our breath.

"Wow," she whispers.

"Is that how your dream ended up?" I ask with a smirk.

"Huh?" she says, her brow dropping. "Oh! No, in my dream, you got the vibrator and then went to make eggs, using my new Pretty In The Pink as a whisk."

I stare at her in shock. You could've asked me to list out a hundred different possible dreams with Samantha, me, and a vibrator. Making eggs? Never would've been one of them.

"I love you," I say, pressing a kiss to her smiling lips.

"Lub you goo," she says against my lips, because I'm going to kiss her all night.

No, forever.

Because Samantha Redding is going to be my wife.

The End

If you haven't read Carter and Luna's story, read Never Marry Your Brother's Best Friend.

**Don't say goodbye to these characters! Never Say Never Book 3 is on preorder… Never Fall For the Fake Boyfriend!**

# ABOUT THE AUTHOR

*Big Fat Fake Series*:
My Big Fat Fake Wedding || My Big Fat Fake Engagement || My Big Fat Fake Honeymoon

Standalones:
The French Kiss || One Day Fiance || Drop Dead Gorgeous || The Blind Date || Risky Business

*Truth Or Dare:*
The Dare || The Truth

*Bennett Boys Ranch:*
Buck Wild || Riding Hard || Racing Hearts

The Tannen Boys:
Rough Love || Rough Edge || Rough Country

*Dirty Fairy Tales:*
Beauty and the Billionaire || Not So Prince Charming || Happily Never After

*Pushing Boundaries*:
Dirty Talk || Dirty Laundry || Dirty Deeds || Dirty Secrets

Printed in Great Britain
by Amazon